THE DIZYGOTIC TWINS

BY

TONI PARKS

PUBLISHED BY

DOUBLE
elephant

ASSOCIATES

Published by
Double Elephant Associates Limited
Orchard Cottage, Lanton, Jedburgh
Roxburghshire TD8 6SX

The Dizygotic Twins
First published 2014

ISBN 978 0 9926261 2 9

A CIP catalogue record for this book is available from the
British Library

TONI PARKS is the pseudonym of Tony Parkinson. This is now my second book, having started the first at the ripe age of 61. As no doubt with other authors my characters have now taken on a life of their own and so this becomes the second book in 'The Gemini Borders Trilogy'.

A move to the Scottish Borders after retirement enabled me to put behind me the time consuming period of my life with running a business and to focus more on assisting in the upbringing of my grandson, Tyler, gardening and the thought that perhaps I can write after all. Therefore once again, I have become possessed by the main characters from the first novel and taken them on the next stage in their quest.

My background is in Advertising, although not in the creative field itself. However, having been surrounded by copywriters and creative designers I hope that I have learnt at least some of their craft by osmosis and so written a thriller, which could, dare I say it stand alongside the Scandinavian authors for whom I have the highest admiration.

I hope you enjoy reading this novel as much as I did when writing.

The Gemini Borders Trilogy

BOOK ONE

BLOOD IS THICKER (2013)

Love to Jean and Tyler

For still allowing me to sneak off and write when
I should be doing other things

In Memory of Mary Cochran

My cousin Brendan's partner, who tragically passed away at
the young age of 58

Congratulations to Kerry and James

My niece, Kerry Parkinson and her fiancé, James Ferguson
on their wedding 17th May 2014

Practical Thanks to:

My brother Bryan for copy checking and editorial comments;
Jean for plot queries and copy checking; my son Thomas for
his formatting skills in again getting the book to completion;
Sarah Thompson for MAC artwork of the cover;
Shutterstock for the cover photography

PROLOGUE

May 2013

"Dissygotik twins? What are you on about? Are they Martians or something?" asked Emma with her usual confused look on her face, when faced with anything out of the ordinary.

"That's what it says here on the Internet. And no, not that they're from another planet, but D-I-Z-Y-G-O-T-I-C twins are fraternal rather than identical: they come from two separate eggs as opposed to one egg splitting in two. I reckon that must be what we are." Jessica spelt out the word as if it would help Emma understand better but her frown said otherwise. "You'll have to dig out some old photographs to see if we looked alike when we were younger. I've got plenty from Grannie's, have you got many? And even if we did look the same, we wouldn't be able to know for definite if we're identical or fraternal without a DNA Zygosity test; well that's what it says anyway. Perhaps that's why the police only had that close match on the DNA lipstick smudge from the first murder victim, rather than an exact match," she mused.

"I'm not having a Zyg-whatsit test, sounds too painful and talking about the first victim, what was his name, John was it? When are you going to tell me what's going on in that head of yours? And why you killed those people in the first place?" asked Emma continuing to cultivate her worry frown, which had now both corrugated her forehead and flattened her normally arched eyebrows.

"Oh I see what you're doing. I'm getting too technical, so you're changing the subject," said Jessica closing her iPad as she met Emma's questioning eyes. "You know the time is not yet right to go into all that. I'm still fighting off my demons just as you are fighting yours. Leave it alone and let's just enjoy the break whilst it lasts." That statement became a signal for the two sisters to move out of the kitchen and abandon the washing up for a while and embark on a far more interesting activity. They put on their windproof jackets, jumped on their bicycles and rode off in the direction of the cliff tops; neither seeming to have a care in the world even though both were, in reality, unconvicted murderers, with Jessica outnumbering her sister by a ratio of five to one.

They were spending a few days in Creetown on the west coast of Dumfries and Galloway. Jessica in particular, felt it would serve as a bolthole from the media's prying eyes and anyone else who knew her; anyone asking questions she had been thankfully ordered not to answer anyway. 'It couldn't have worked out better' she thought. 'Being sworn to secrecy over murders which Emma and I have committed. I couldn't have planned it better.' The reality was that Police Scotland had become concerned for the safety of the remaining inquiry team, as the only two officers with any detective rank on the cases, had vanished without trace and so subsequently it was presumed 'under suspicious circumstances'.

And even though they had been in each other's company non-stop for a couple of days now, Emma was still struggling to come to terms with being part of a family. "Jess, I do like it here and being with you. It seems as if my life's now more complete; well, apart from you know who not being around," shouted Emma, nudging Jessica out of her daydream as she strained to catch the words being buffeted and stolen by the strong breeze coming off the sea. Jessica unscrambled in her mind what had been said and nodded in acknowledgment as they turned their bikes on to a rough track, leading to a snack bar overlooking the sea and the small cove below. "But what

I'm still struggling to understand, particularly after nearly thirty-three years of being a single child, is what makes you so sure that we're twins?" They stopped at the side of the glorified hut under the guise of a snack bar.

Jessica jumped off her bike, propped it against the wall side, reached across to her sister and whilst giving her a big hug said, "I'm happy too, M, and surely you can see the resemblance between us, for a start. Then our heights are the same; we're probably even similar in weight. Well you're a little on the plump side if I'm being honest, but that's probably all your boozing with no proper exercise and don't you think having the same birthday is a bit of a giveaway? And we're not going down the DNA route, it could open up a whole can of worms and put information out there, in the public domain, which is best kept to ourselves. It's just a shame we've had to spend so much time apart but now we're together that's certainly not going to happen again. Race you to the beach!"

"Oh come on. I've no chance, what with carrying this extra weight! Like you said you've lived far more healthily than I have, not to mention all that running that you do. And anyway my legs are all wobbly already from just riding up here," moaned Emma disconsolately as she saw the back of Jessica running down the cliff path and zigzagging around the hairpin bends. 'Even if I threw myself off she'd still probably beat me,' she thought meeting defeat with equanimity.

A gentle lapping of surf breaking on coarse sand greeted Emma's senses as she breathlessly descended to the bottom of the cliff path and reached the sheltered cove. Jessica had already moved on to the base of the cliffs where she was investigating the small rock pools for any trapped fish or tiny crabs, which would be expectantly waiting and hoping for the returning tide, before their small underwater surroundings shrank away to nothingness from the power of an unexpected warmth generated by the sun beaming down, mimicking a ticking time bomb. Emma caught up with her and linked arms as they spent the next thirty minutes doing nothing of importance, knowing that afterwards they would climb back up the winding path, which Emma would moan about but then would receive a well earned coffee for her troubles.

And so the two spent their first few days together as sisters, hand in hand or arm in arm, after meeting for the first and almost the last time five weeks ago. Their first few days together, getting to know each other, after spending 30 years apart. 30 years of such diverse lifestyles where opportunities were given and choices were made, which now inevitably brought them together in the most unexpected of circumstances. And both, at this moment, in limbo and waiting for the right time to release their demons on themselves. But the demons could wait. Jessica in particular had kept them both busy exploring the small town with its big history. Boasting, its legacy of the tons upon tons of granite that had been excavated nearby; over innumerable years, and transported to Liverpool for use as the mainstay, to its own vast seafaring dock area.

Its huge silver granite sphere sculpted by Hideo Furuta, positioned in the main square with the granite clock tower and granite houses close by; all complementing each other in their hues of grey and all requiring the two young women's attention so that their minds remained active and didn't dwell on other more serious matters. Jessica even located the bar in the Eltangowan Hotel, which had been one of the settings for The Wicker Man film set and still sported photographs of Willow MacGregor, famously pulling her pints. Information readily available around the town then led them to find external film locations in the surrounding area, thus prompting Emma's desire to lose herself in the film itself.

The countryside was no less impressive either, with snap shots of hidden gems at every turn. The old stone bridge over the burn leading to a cascading waterfall; Balloch Woods with the oak roundhouse perfectly reflected in still water and so encouraging passers-by to stop and ponder a wee while;

Kirmabreck church with its blaze of daffodils and crocuses epitomising life after death; and the haunting salmon nets on the river Cree, whether captured eerily in the misty morning or romantically at dusk with the backdrop of the sun sinking into the Atlantic. All unexpected pleasures, which enabled the young women to relax and return to the chalet of an evening, tired and ready for a refreshing shower, a hearty meal and a few welcome drinks.

A chalet that was both rustic and basic but that offered and catered for the necessary needs of tranquillity, privacy and peace. Tucked away on the hillside with expansive views overlooking the River Cree estuary; the view that became a prerequisite each evening for both girls' anticipated delight in seeing and admiring the ever-changing sunsets that greeted them.

One of the most difficult aspects of their time together was Jessica's adjustment to the fact that her sister was a drug addict. In her line of work, she encountered many addicts dependent on various drugs but had never personally been subjected to its close proximity before, and now faced with it she was not happy about it either. The whole day seemed to revolve around this constant need and worry about when and where, to administer the drug and that was once it had been located and bartered over.

Obviously, if Emma had not brought the required amount with her then she would have had little chance of searching out a pusher in such a rural area but that was not the worst of it; as each evening the heroin, by virtue of its selfishness, would devoid Jessica of her sister's company possibly when she most needed it. The sight of the syringe puncturing her sister's skin as it sought its swollen vein target, etched itself on Jessica's eyeballs, repulsing her even more, yet at the same time making her more determined. More determined that this need and interruption were not going to be tolerated indefinitely.

*

Just over two weeks earlier, Jessica had still been utilised as an intrinsic member of the inquiry team, using her profiling skills to try and track down the serial killer who at the time had murdered four, allegedly, innocent people in and around the Scottish Borders. No one apart from Jessica and Emma knew who the actual killer was and Emma had consciously held the perpetrator's confidence. Jessica knew this, and was thankful, but she being the actual killer still could not understand Emma's reticence at that time, in identifying her. And Emma knew too as, with shock, she had recognised the eyes of a face, a face that greeted her everyday as she looked in a mirror. Even though she had just seen those eyes for a split second and through a ski mask, the resemblance to her own was uncanny and for that reason alone she still withheld the information from the investigation team. It had proved almost fatal for Emma and she still contested that brush with death as one of a series of issues to be rationalised and put to bed with her newfound twin sister.

The investigation had been broken up subsequent to the disappearances of both DI Terry Barnham and T/DC Claire Murray. The former had been in charge of the cases up until his vanishing act and the latter had been taking a week's holiday in Yorkshire, but had never returned to duty. And to further muddy the water, a flatscreen TV and matching DVD player belonging to Joe Foster, the fourth murdered victim, had been found in T/DC Murray's home. Speculation had been rife as to whether the two disappearances were linked and whether or not there was a more sinister motive or some form of collusion at work. Now Police Scotland were not only investigating the original three murders, plus the death of an amateur private detective, Joe, but had the disappearances of two detectives actively involved in the original cases, to contend with as well. The Chief Constable, Bernard Stone, had no alternative other than to hold a complete review of the situation and transfer over authority on the cases from Chief Inspector Brogan and his colleagues.

This entailed a complete debrief by the remaining members of the original inquiry team with a hand over of all possible leads to date. Even though Jessica had been seconded to that team, she too received the same treatment and was cleared to return to her original job at The Borders Agency, as a counsellor of physical and/or sexual abuse for both men and women. Emma's details were still held on police files as the killer had attempted to murder her too, but it was now accepted that she did not play a role in the murders and, even though she was romantically linked to the DI, none of the remaining officers had a desire to slur his character with this fact becoming public; the fact that he had been cavorting with a prostitute.

Both women had spoken sparingly to each other at the time and had agreed to lie low for a few weeks to allow the new investigation to take a different course. Jessica would return to her full time job whilst Emma would fleetingly continue in her form of work, even though as she admitted her heart wasn't in it, but she still had a habit to feed and the pay was good.

Jessica had indeed returned to work as soon as she had been released from the investigation. The office she returned to was still in a state of shock resulting from her colleague, Joe Foster's, death. Tess Danvers, her case line manager, welcomed her back even though it was under extremely distressing circumstances, particularly as she felt personally responsible for taking the decision to second Jessica to the murder inquiry team in the first place. The atmosphere was sombre and everyone skirted around the subject of Joe's murder rather than meeting it head on. Jessica had been asked various questions with regards to her work with the police but was under strict instructions that no active line of inquiry could be discussed or information imparted, other than that which was already in the public domain.

She found it difficult to re-adapt to her previous job and requested compassionate leave due to her close proximity to the murders and the ensuing investigations and the effect it was now having on her wellbeing. In truth this was a lie but Jessica did want to spend time with Emma and so fabricated a way of taking leave. Tess felt it better that she took time out now rather than getting back into the swing and having to then drop new cases in the upcoming weeks. So within two days of starting back, she had taken compassionate leave and without anyone suspecting her of any complicity in the murders themselves.

Now Jessica found herself facing a dilemma. The dichotomy of on the one hand, returning to the permanency of a job that would bring her normality, when she could never be normal again; or on the other striking out on a new and different path, and so embracing the unknown. Either choice must inevitably include Emma, if only to save her from herself. During their last evening at the chalet, as Emma lay comatose following her final heroin injection of the holiday, and therefore oblivious as to what decisions needed to be made for her ongoing life, Jessica began making a 'to do' list to cover both, their short- and long-term futures. And as the clouds finally allowed the shining orb of the full moon to break through, mirroring its own rippling reflection in the river below, she reflected on the possibility of a fun packed life ahead. She promised herself that before leaving the chalet she would soak up the atmosphere one last time as a treasured memory to unlock and experience in times of need. And so she did.

But in the morning both young women had to meet reality head on and undertake the menial task of tidying round, vacuuming, washing up and leaving their little haven hideaway for the next lucky inhabitants; and to head back to the real world, although Jessica had some concerns about that. As at present, Emma was somewhat, of a loose cannon, with drugs and to a lesser degree alcohol, both perceived by Jessica as being her twin's worst enemies, and if they did not have a comatose effect they could certainly make her character somewhat vociferous and leave her in constant need of supervision. This, added to her newly acquired knowledge of the Borders' murders' subject matter, was a recipe for disaster; so a clean break was called for and quickly too. To that end, Jessica had invited Emma to stay in her flat, which meant that her office cum bedroom would now be converted into a bedroom cum office.

The logistics of Emma's working life still needed clarifying, and rules drawn up, as did the continuing purchase of her 'friend' heroin, albeit in decreasing quantities as dictated by her hopefully, reducing dependency. And, not to mention Emma's circle of actual friends, who would need to be made aware of her new circumstances and the fact that she may be living away from her own flat, either short- or long-term.

Then there were her continual highs and lows to contend with over the fate of DI Barnham and the part she had played; her sibling survival instinct had prompted her impulsive action in the Kirkyard and Jessica's glib summary of Barnham's worth had neither alleviated her guilt nor enabled her to forget the part she played. Either the moment she had struck him with the syringe or the man himself. Jessica more objective by nature, had seen him basically as a womaniser but her forthright comments had fallen on deaf ears when she had said, "M, he called himself a 'roving DI'; forget the 'D', it seemed to me more like he had just a roving eye, one which was constantly focussing from one girl to the next; and just as Grannie said, 'Never run after men or buses: you'll always get left behind'! You can never tame a man like that, no matter what you think. And if that's not enough for you he was unravelling the serial killer's myth and I wasn't ready for incarceration."

Emma feeling somewhat sorry for herself, had replied, "Well, it's easy for you to say that, but your hand didn't do the deed, did it? You're not carrying the 'what if?' scenarios that constantly attack my brain, are you? And it was different with him and me, we had something special."

"M, we've been over this before, what's done can not be undone; you'll have to change your mindset and re-channel your energies more positively. Perhaps, we've done wrong but it is important, very important, to keep it to ourselves, and that way we'll get away with it. Look back on our holiday as a springboard for a new start where we are both still at liberty to live our lives and where we can really get to know one another and be comfortable around each other."

CHAPTER ONE

Being at liberty, comfortable and together was not quite the modus operandi or panacea that they had anticipated or expected, and soon everyday normal living started to get the better of them both. Jessica had returned to her work a second time and was still no happier, whilst Emma had not returned to her work and was not happy either. They had discussed plans for their future together based on the lists Jessica had made but found that they were both equally as strong willed and set in their own ways and unfortunately their ways didn't point in the same direction. Jessica had cajoled Emma into continuing the health kick they had started on holiday but it was proving a struggle, whilst Emma tried to coach Jessica in the streetwise ways of her lifestyle, but to no avail. In the end a compromise was reached, albeit one that had already reached breaking point. Thankfully Jeremy Longthorne came to their rescue.

Jeremy a solicitor for over forty years had been hopeful of making their acquaintance for a considerable time. Although it was to be a professional charge of work for him to undertake, he had nevertheless undertaken the task at a personal request from longstanding but departed friends, too. The only downside was that he had not realised it would take over 30 years for that personal request to come to fruition. He made contact via Emma's mobile, the number having been given begrudgingly by Jonnie Raey, a former beau of hers; Jonnie himself being forever the optimist was hopeful that by divulging the number his chances of changing 'former' to 'present' might prove fruitful.

Mr Longthorne had cultivated a time-honoured financial relationship with a pliable member of staff at Scotland Yard, whom he knew worked in the 'Cold Cases' Unit. This contact was responsible along with his colleagues for searching through data, originally hard copy material but latterly web based and social media that could link into any of the dozens of names held on a 'wanted' list. Jonnie had inadvertently triggered a software match between search engines and the Yard, due to his use of Luigi Agosti's name. Once the solicitor had been put on the right track as to where the connection led, it had not taken him too long to trace the culprit. Particularly, as the surfer had become famous overnight at work for his loose connection to the serial murder inquiries, especially when you took into consideration his romantic involvement with the only surviving victim.

Little did Mr Longthorne know but one bent copper does not have to stop at one bent deed; the informant in question had also been feathering his bed on the other side and so had sold the same information to another acquaintance too, thinking that 100% extra cash was a worthwhile bonus for just taking the one risk.

Upon receiving Mr Longthorne's call, Emma was worried and concerned as to what a solicitor could want with her. Her immediate thought was that the police had pieced together the evidence that would connect her to Terry Barnham's death. But he soon put her mind at rest, if her almost permanent confused state could be called rest. "Hello. Could you please confirm that I am talking to Miss Emma Flynn?"

"You are. I am. But who are you to be calling me?" asked Emma somewhat clumsily.

"My name is Jeremy Longthorne. I am a solicitor based in Aberdeen. Before I proceed further I have two additional questions, sort of like security questions. One, could you confirm your date of birth and two, could you confirm your father's name?"

"Are you some sort of detective or fraudster? You're not going to hack in to my bank account mate and even if you did you'd be disappointed as there's nothing in it. So you better be quick with the reason for the call or I'm pressing the red button."

"No, no please don't do that. I promise you I have information to your advantage and in no way am I trying to compromise your financial situation, but please just answer my two questions. Do you need me to repeat them?" He asked warmly.

Emma felt soothed by his gentle fatherly type voice and said, "No need to repeat. My date of birth is 31st May 1980 and my father's name was.." at this point she needed a few seconds to recollect the name she had found in the newspaper cuttings, a name she had only read a couple of times. "..Luigi Agosti. Or was it Agnosti? No, I'm sure it's Agosti."

"You're correct it is Agosti and I am pleased to say for both our sakes that you are the person I've been looking for; for quite some time I might add. I have an urgent need to meet up and hand over a package but first off I have to locate your twin sister. You are aware that you have a twin sister?"

"Yes, well aware. Well, aware for the last five weeks anyway." 'If you count from the time she tried to murder me,' she thought cynically.

"Are you still there?"

"Yes, sorry, Mr Longthorne, wasn't it? I was just reminiscing. Why do you need to find her? Us?"

"The information I have to impart is for both twins at the same time unless one of the party is deceased, which I'm pleased to hear from the sound of it is not the case. How can I make contact with her?" Again, Emma held up the conversation thinking, 'If you only knew how close to the truth, you are?'

"Well, if you come and see me, you'll see her at the same time as I'm living in her flat at the moment. But are you sure you can't give me a clue as to what you want to see us about?

My sister quite a private person and doesn't take kindly to strangers."

"Sorry, no. I never discuss sensitive information over the phone; you never know who is listening in. And you can pacify your sister with the fact that as well as being a solicitor, I'm a longstanding family friend. Can you give me the address and a time of when you'll both be available?"

"The address is 33 Main Street, St Boswells." And then Emma thought aloud of Jessica's movements after work. "Well she gets home about six, then usually goes for a run, so that makes…. oh no, she's at the gym tonight, then picks up an Indian takeaway and is home for 7.30. So we should be free from 8pm onwards, if that's OK?"

"Well as it's the weekend tomorrow, could I be rather presumptuous and make it Saturday instead and afterwards take you both out to lunch?"

"I don't see why not," said Emma who had not been wined and dined by a man since that fateful night in Edinburgh. "That sounds great."

"OK. I'll see you at noon."

Before Emma forgot about the appointment, she texted Jessica to put her in the picture. This gave Jessica the rest of the day to mull it over, both before and after her weekly meeting with Tess, her case line manager, where she would off-load the fewer than usual cases on which she was working. As predicted by Emma and being a creature of habit, she then visited the gym and then collected the Indian takeaway too.

She was desperate to lambaste Emma for being so cavalier with their privacy, especially so soon after sliding unnoticed from under the shadow of the murders and the subsequent investigations. Emma casually defended herself by saying that she didn't think they had anything to lose or worry about and that the man on the other end of the phone sounded too posh to be the police. And there she rested her case, by concluding that they would find out more on Saturday, so why spoil a good

Indian or indeed the rest of the evening arguing or worrying about what was now inevitably to come.

True to his word Jeremy Longthorne LLB pulled up outside the flat in his BMW 5 series with two minutes to spare, adding fuel to the sensitive debate that every second counts in the land of the law. He stood on their doorstep, all 6ft 1in, dressed in a well-cut sombre suit and clutching a battered briefcase. He was invited in and on being quizzed about his punctuality he admitted that it was more good luck than good management but seemed quite proud of the fact that he was less than two minutes out on a journey, which started in Aberdeen.

Showing him into the lounge and offering him a drink enabled Jessica to keep her powder dry, whilst at the same time allowing the solicitor at least a chance to make his proposition.

She had to admit to herself that she too was equally as pleasantly surprised as Emma by his demeanour and immediately warmed to him as, furnished with a well-needed cup of coffee, he began his speil, "Hello, as I've said, my name's Jeremy Longthorne and I'm very pleased to meet you ladies at long last. Now, who's who?"

Emma took up the offer to reply and said, "I'm Emma. I spoke to you on the mobile and this is my twin, Jessica."

Mr Longthorne paused, swept his fingers through his full head of flecked grey hair, fixed his eyes on one and then the other of the two young faces and commented, "Yes, I can see the resemblance, more so in you, Emma, that's right, isn't it?

They looked bemused at each other; both thinking that they knew they had a close resemblance but could not understand why he found it that difficult to spot it; until the shock hit home when he continued, "Yes, you do remind me so much of your dear mother, Laura. I had the pleasure of being a good friend of both your parents, although your father seemed to be away quite a lot as I recall, so it tended to be left to my discretion to look out for Laura, and I recollect that she'd have been about your ago too when they so tragically died. And you, Jessica, you even have your father's colouring, too."

Neither Emma nor Jessica had ever heard anyone whether inside or outside the immediate family talk about their parents before, let alone someone with so much fondness and sadness. It was almost as if the grief was being released for the first time. They thanked the solicitor for his solicitude and Jessica asked, "Perhaps you, or this or whatever you've brought with you, can fill in some of the gaps for us as my Grannie and Emma's aunt had never been particularly forthcoming with information about the past? But maybe after all this time, whatever you say will only seem like a token gesture anyway?'

"Jessica, I hope you'll find my visit and the gift I bear from your parents more helpful than you ever imagine. But one of the stipulations of me handing it over is that I am not to remain present whilst you view the contents. I think that's to ensure that you two and only you two have possession of the knowledge it imparts. But as I've already safeguarded it for over thirty years with the past twelve being spent actively searching for you, I too feel that the information may be useless, especially if it turns out to be time sensitive. Although looking at it selfishly, at long last I have had the opportunity of meeting you and I will now be able to hang up my briefcase for probably the very last time; as this was always going to be one of my final assignments."

As he said this he extracted from his case, and handed over, a flattish rectangular shape, similar in size to a ream of A4 copy paper but neatly wrapped in kraft paper and bound with twine. Emma took hold of it and held it at arms' length as if handling a bomb or worse, a newborn baby. Jessica was more pragmatic and prised it out of her hands, placing it under the TV unit behind the DVD player.

"I don't know why I think it's safe there, but out of sight, out of mind,' she said.

Emma replied 'Yes, a burglar's not going to see that when he's got the DVD tucked in his swag bag, is he?"

"Ladies, now I've carried out part of my duty, I'd be delighted to fulfil the other part, the part I'll take most enjoyment from. What about that lunch? I'm sure you've got an hour or so to spare before your thief turns up unless you've actually booked one for a specific time!" Both women looked at each other and burst out laughing and then all three left the flat, leaving it as a clear run for the would-be burglar, if he so wished to take the opportunity.

As this was Jessica's neck of the woods she navigated the BMW to a small bistro in Melrose with Jeremy in the driving seat looking impressively professorial sporting his half moon glasses; and Emma luxuriating in the back as she sank even further into the soft brown Nappa leather. At the bistro both ladies chose the salad nicoise with a glass of Chardonnay but their constant eye contact betrayed the fact that their curiosity had got the better of them and that they would rather be ripping open the brown paper package to unearth whatever mystery lay within. However, with patience being a virtue, they both made small talk and flirted gently with Jeremy, as he was now known, and waited for him to finish his chicken with cassiatore sauce.

Try as they might, even allowing for Jessica using all her intellectual skills and Emma endeavouring to use her more base sexual allure; neither succeeded, to any avail, in persuading Jeremy to divulge any searching information about their parents' pasts, nor any clues either about the present package. So to speed things along they turned down the chance of a dessert but felt it rude not to take up the offer of a coffee. They both chose cappuccino, whilst Jeremy showed his manliness by ordering a 'double shot' expresso. Then, the solicitor in him urged Jeremy to check his Baume & Mercier watch, exclaim, 'Is that the time?' and immediately ask for the bill; knowing in reality that the two ladies were desperate anyway, as if on Christmas Day, to dash home and see what

Santa had left them. He dropped them at the door and by way of goodbye said, "Well, thank you for a most pleasant lunch. I hope your parents' gift is all that you could desire and I can honestly say that they would be immensely proud if they were here now to see you both. Arrivederci."

He, in turn received their thanks for his effort in locating them, lunch, his wishes and kind words; and as he waved goodbye and headed north in the direction of Edinburgh Emma said both sarcastically and wishfully, "I don't know how proud I'd be of knowing my two daughters are murderers! But it's a shame he lives such a long way away, I'm sure I could spend a little time getting to know our Jeremy on a different professional, and more intimate, basis."

"Mm, already it seems like I've known you all my life. How predictable you are. Always ready to link money and sex in the same sentence. Well sugar daddy's on his way back to Aberdeen, so you'll have to learn to drive first before you can get your claws in to him. And anyway, you're still in mourning, aren't you?"

"All I said is he seems like a nice man. I wasn't suggesting a threesome, was I? And don't be mentioning you know who or I'll end up getting all meloncally, melonally, what was that word again? Anyway, never mind that, where's that parcel gone?"

*

Paydays were not always as lucrative as expected. Certainly not in the case of Detective Sergeant Dennis Stanning, now former DS as he retired from active service due to injuries suffered in the line of duty and transferred to a desk job with the 'Cold Cases' Unit. The DS was not all he seemed as, unbeknownst to the Met hierarchy, he had been groomed for a number of years by a fellow informant to take over that role when the situation arose. It did so some 5 years ago when the incumbent officer retired on full pension with a clean record of achievement. Who said 'crime doesn't pay'? DS Stanning now had a payday of his own in his sights with the data resting in his intray relating to a cyber tracking request for an Italian male 'Luigi Agosti'.

Unfortunately for him he had been on an Easter holiday break when the information originally arrived and was placed there, so he just hoped that his contacts would not notice that it was already nearly two weeks old. Shrugging off this slight time lag he had been in touch with his solicitor contact, who was shocked to hear from Scotland Yard anyway after so many years of silence; so he felt vindicated that another couple of weeks seemed to have made little difference in the scheme of things.

The DS enlightened Mr Longthorne of the intelligence he had been party to and offered the information for a fixed price. A price that was extra to the retainer he and his previous colleague had received regularly over the years. The fixed price was agreed upon and the information imparted and so the game began to play out. DS Stanning did not enlighten the solicitor to the fact that he was also going to sell the same intelligence to another interested party. This he felt was his right and he justified it by giving Mr Longthorne, 24 hours grace before he made contact with the other beneficiary. His intention was to pool both payments together and place a bet on the Oxford Blues in the Boat Race, as he felt confident that he could at least double his already double money and so be ensured of a significant boost to his retirement fund.

His expectation of the second transaction running as smoothly as the first, had not banked on him being subjected to a double-cross. As DS Stanning naively thought that he was the only crooked copper in the department and so never watched his back for others of a like mind. When he made contact with the second party it was arranged for a face-to-face meet at The Gun in the Docklands area, a 250 years old pub with a face-lift considerably more recent. Dennis felt comfortable with this arrangement, as being police trained he always made certain meetings were very public and accessible from all directions, more recently in case of a speedy getaway.

He never had a fear of the docklands in either his present or his previous life and knew the area well, an area where questions were always asked after the event rather than before it. He turned up at the rendezvous on time, carrying his copy of the Daily Telegraph displaying part of the horse racing section and made eye contact with his prospective benefactor, who had reciprocated in like manner and immediately nodded to the door even before a drink could be ordered, let alone drunk. This threw the DS but he understood the protocol of neither person wishing to be seen together in public, and especially with each other. However, once outside and with that very public being nowhere on the scene, fear did rear its head if just for a second. They walked over to a black Rolls Royce and were ushered into the back by the chauffeur who closed the door behind them and then stood nonchalantly yet protectively outside whilst a deal was struck.

Dennis' cockiness had already left him and he could tell by the look in the hardened eyes of the Roller owner sitting opposite that this was not going to be a friendly business meeting. Several minutes elapsed before the hardened eyes curtailed a mobile conversation, turned fully to face Dennis and said, "I thought we had a deal? You were paid a retainer and then an additional sum by way of a bonus based on results. Is that not correct?"

Dennis looked to the side of the man opposite and replied to his profile, "Yes, Sir. That was the deal, passed down by my former colleague, and the one I've been adhering to."

"Well, according to the call I've just finished, I think you haven't adhered to it thoroughly enough! You see Dennis, in this game it's always better to have someone watching someone else so that nobody knows which shoulder to look over. That way you never know which one has got your chip on it, if you get my drift? And this someone has let it be known that you've already imparted our bought and paid for information to another interested party. So, what's to do, I ask myself? Is your chip already fried?"

Nervously and with sweat beginning to prick up the hairs at the back of his neck the DS answered, "No I'd never get involved in any kind of double dealing. I'm as straight as a copper."

"Ah, but there's the rub, don't you see. You're as straight as a bent copper, ergo you can't be straight. And do you know what's worse than a bent copper? A two-timing bent copper!"

The DS rushed in with, "I've only done it the once. I wanted to make a break with all this as CID are closing in and asking questions about operatives who disappeared in Scotland, so I panicked a little, that's all. I just needed to make a bit more for my pension like and then call it a day."

"Oh my heart bleeds. You have been busy thinking and who's to say that thinking might have already turned to talking. And then you're busy worrying about your old age. About having enough to live on. Perhaps a few little luxuries. A holiday maybe? Well, let's see how this pans out first. So for starters, you're going to tell us the name of this other party to whom you've sold the information. And then we'll think about your pension rights and whether we'll even let you pass go and collect £200."

This concluded the conversation and the hardened eyes nodded acknowledgment of that fact to his silent colleague, who then opened the door and accompanied the DS to a Ford Mondeo, parked behind the Rolls. The chauffeur returned to his seat and led the cars away, convoy style, from the area. The Rolls drove in the direction of the West End where the man with the hardened eyes had, no doubt, a somewhat more pleasant prospective engagement at a restaurant in Greek Street. The Mondeo, less conspicuously, drove to a run down area of Poplar, East London, where a safe house of sorts awaited the occupants.

Dennis had a nervous suspicion that he was going to become more acquainted with his contact; the man who had the Daily Telegraph opened at the horse racing section. He turned out to be one of a team of two and answered to the title,

'Assailant', being the operative who committed the deed. Whilst his colleague, positioned at two-ability level grades lower within their recognised structure, was referred to as the 'Accomplice', who could step up to the mark too, if so commanded. Both descriptive nouns, and along with employee code references, used solely for the purpose of protecting their true identities, that is at least until the work was done and when their visitor would be no longer capable of hearing, let alone remembering their actual names. And so, the safe house proved anything but safe, let alone hospitable, to Dennis Stanning. He was ushered upstairs, buffeted from wall to wall as he ascended, by two much younger and more powerful men, which did not inspire him with self-assurance as to his prospects for future wellbeing. Stanning was shown to his seat, well thrown into it actually and straps were stretched around his wrists and neck so that movement was nigh on impossible. The questioning did not stretch the imagination as he was asked once, "Who else have you given the information to, about Luigi Agosti?"

Stanning didn't answer and was rocked back in an instant by a blow to the face, a blow, which came out of nowhere. He had seen plenty of rough and tumble whilst on active service in the force and felt that this sort of thing was his stock in trade but after another frenzy of blows the Assailant became bored and moved on to phase two. He brought out a rusty chisel and hammer and nodded for his Accomplice to hold Stanning's head still. The chisel was placed against the man's two nicotine-stained front teeth and just before the blow was struck, the DS mumbled something. The Assailant looked annoyed at the fact that he had not been able to carry out his phase two but his Boss had already briefed him on the etiquette of torture and the rules by which he should abide. At this point the DS spilled out as much detail as he could remember in the form of a last will and testament. The Accomplice recorded the information on his mobile and then, with the Assailant's authority, rang the Boss and played it back.

The Boss listened and replied, "Good work. Destroy this recording and tell Babyface," which was the pseudonym the Assailant went by, "to conclude the interview." Brute strength was always a good advertisement for strong leadership and no one in the gangland fraternity was going to be under any misapprehension that the Boss was nothing if not thorough as well as, perhaps a little ruthless too.

"OK Boss understood."

Babyface was elated. The Boss had only taught him how to show kindness to victims up to the point of them making a confession, as a way of encouraging them to reveal the necessary information, but never afterwards. The afterwards, belonged to Babyface. He abided by the Omerta of the Camorra and because the DS had broken that code of silence, admittedly with a little needed inducement, he would not now die just from a bullet to the head. And so it was to Babyface's advantage that he had the privilege to reposition his hammer and chisel, much to Stanning's shock and horror and proceed to knock his two front teeth out. Ollie, the Accomplice had to use all his strength to hold Stanning's head still as he writhed and screamed in pain and it was not until the latter fainted that both colleagues could take a rest.

A pail of stale water, which had accumulated from a leak in the roof, was thrown into the victim's bleeding face and even through the shock of the cold Stanning still managed to raise a roar of pain as it hit his mutilated mouth. Babyface and Ollie both became concerned about the noise, so one gagged the victim, whilst leaving the other to hammer energetically at his kneecaps. The DS passed out yet again as the two still standing, who hadn't fainted, were becoming bored with this mediocre entertainment. They had expected more sport by way of a spirited fight from the crooked DS and now realised that neither will nor time were on their side and definitely not on Stanning's either.

Babyface looked around for any heavy object and was

satisfied on spying a pile of cobweb covered concrete breeze blocks, that must have been lying around for years. Ollie went off and checked in the boot of the car for rope that he was sure he had placed there several weeks before. Finding it as expected he returned to the attic and securely bound the victim, who was more than unconscious now, as Babyface had given him the telltale gangster death: a bullet between the eyes and his tongue cut out as a sign of his dishonour to the Omerta; making the necessity of a gag doubly superfluous, apart from to staunch the blood. The DS was then manhandled back down the two flights of stairs with less care than would have been afforded to an old upright piano. He was bundled in to the boot of the car for the commencement of his last ever journey.

Babyface perceived that they would be too early for Stanning's final departure deadline and so suggested a break for a snack, a cup of tea, a comfort stop and a clean up at a 24 hour transport café, which both knew had no CCTV, nor any interest in upholding the law; none of the above courtesies were afforded to the now deceased ex DS. On leaving, this nonchalant lack of security enabled Ollie to obliterate both front and back registration number plates on the vehicle by way of black masking tape. And as the night light had faded to black, and was equally assisted by an insipid crescent moon hidden away behind low heavy cloud covering, the Mondeo departed and later pulled up on the Hammersmith Bridge where the bonnet was raised as if to indicate a breakdown.

Once the light level of traffic became used to the obstruction both men searched for their opportunity and with an elaborate drama of looking for tools in the boot, they lifted Stanning with one hand each whilst the other strained to heave the accompanying breeze blocks over the parapet and lowered both down the side of the bridge; making sure that the ropes did not snag on any visible protruding objects. The attached bent copper then went to meet his maker without fully understanding the irony of his death. It being that in less than a week's time this 'man in blue' would be overshadowed by the Oxford men in blue as they would approach the Surrey Bend of the Thames, having rowed over his watery grave on their way to victory. A victory that would have given him a payday he would never now collect. How poignant.

CHAPTER TWO

The Camorra

Organised bands of criminals first appeared in Southern Italy in the mid 1800's; the first being Camorra, meaning 'gang', a shortened derivative of 'prison gang'. With growth, they merged into clans with the Sicilian Cosa Nostra Mafia clan, becoming the most infamous through its initial organised crime of extortion, cattle theft and political election rigging leading on to protection, pressurised renegotiations of building contracts, counterfeiting and black market dealings.

In the latter day, exploits of prostitution, arms dealing, money laundering, and murder were also added to the list - in fact anything illegal that could turn misery in to money and vice versa. The truth was that with wealth being the key and enrichment their sole goal, they became just as much capitalists as today's businesses and traders in the FTSE, Dow, Dax and Nasdaq stock exchanges. However, unlike today's entrepreneurs their operations' results tended to be derived from exploiting the antithesis of bona fide organisations.

A serious rift opened with the introduction of drug trafficking by the Sicilian Mafia; the Camorra itself, was split over the venture and the breach between them could never be repaired nor the damage healed.

At the beginning of the 1950's, in the old farming suburb of Secondigliano, to the north of Naples, there was about as much chance of finding a child being born with a hypothetical silver spoon in his or her mouth as there was of finding a plump ripe olive with sharp edges. The reason being that the said spoon, should it exist, would have been stolen and melted down before that child had even uttered its first cry.

Secondigliano boasted one of the dozen or so clans, which made up the Camorra, a mafia type body responsible for running and controlling the organised crime in and around Naples. All Neapolitans accepted the Camorra rule, to the extent that it became known as the system, a mini state within the country of Italy. In the main it was to the public's advantage as it worked reciprocally; offering security to enable the inhabitants to earn a living and prosper in order to make repayments by whatever means possible in return; and so receive automatic protection from their own and other clans against roaming, opportunistic predators.

Luigi Agosti was born into this world in August 1951 and from an early age quickly learnt where the hypothetical silver spoons were buried. He was one of five boys and by 10 years of age he had acquired a street knowledge of someone twice that. Luigi blended in to the landscape both externally and at home and for his patience and stealth he was rewarded with invaluable information, which he stored and compartmentalised for future use.

Even to his farmer parents it soon became obvious that Luigi was not born for his present peasant life. His memory for statistics and voracity for reading made him a favourite amongst his siblings and their friends, generally as a consultant, with any problems that they faced, being easily solved and erased. And so, having reached 10 years of age and whilst performing the role of altar boy at his eldest brother's funeral, a brother who had suffered an untimely death at the hands of a runaway tractor, he came across Franco Di Larno a fellow altar boy who would become instrumental in transforming Luigi's future. Franco, then only 8 years old, knew all about poverty, having been orphaned at an early age, and he did not care for it. Subsequently adopted into an already large family, he aspired to make a name for himself by joining the clan at the earliest age possible, and naively thought that he would then change everyone's lives for the better. He had a particular penchant for maths, as did Luigi, and this led to a lifelong friendship between them and at just sixteen he instigated a life-changing introduction to Aniello La Monica, the then ruthless local clan leader.

It was at this age that Franco was allowed to not only suggest changes but implement them too, so as to enhance profits, streamline costs and, more importantly, afford himself Aniello's trust. So although both Luigi and Franco perceived themselves to be intellectually on the same level it was only Franco who had been given authority to pull any strings, He operated in the exact opposite way to his leader and both soon found that all their areas of business: extortion, protection, counterfeit goods, black market cigarettes and latterly election rigging, gravitated towards his personal orbit. This inevitably led to friction within the clan itself, and brought about open warfare onto the streets.

As time moved on, Luigi's grieving mother pleaded with him to leave Naples and study abroad for his safety and her peace of mind if nothing else, as having already lost three sons to gang warfare and with the youngest boy, born two years after Luigi, running off to Sicily with Franco's nephew to try his luck with the true Mafia; she was in serious danger of out living all of her children. She had approached the clan head and arrangements had been made for Luigi to complete his studies as a law student in Aberdeen. Geography not being his strongest subject, Luigi consulted an atlas to see which country and indeed continent Aberdeen was situated in and on, and with the distance and the latitude he was not happy on either count. However, despite these statistics Luigi's fortunes flourished both in his academic and personal life.

He met and serenaded the young Laura Flynn, a student of accountancy one year his junior. For the following four years neither student had eyes for anyone else and Laura became immersed in the alternative Italian world of silent nods and hidden dealings. Luigi quickly realised why Aberdeen had been chosen as his university base and was not long in waiting before being embraced by the small but fanatical community that awaited and welcomed his arrival. Franco's name had preceded him and became Luigi's passport to gaining his access rights in this newly formed, tightly knit clan offshoot. He proved a very useful sounding board on all issues concerning the legality of ownership, both of property and business and it was not long before his name was shortened to L.A., pronounced 'EL-LAY AH' and soon the whole of the Italian contingent knew to whom it was being referred. By the time he had taken and successfully passed his law degree, arrangements had been made for his return to Italy with the girl whom he hoped would be his future wife.

Both now professionals, as Laura had now qualified too with an MA in accountancy, they were received back in Secondigliano as if royalty. Luigi's mother was a stream of tears as Franco accompanied her to the arrivals lounge at Naples International Airport where she greeted her son and possibly future daughter-in-law. Laura received innumerable kisses from the extended family; leaving Luigi and Franco to just punch each other on the shoulder by way of greeting.

Their bonding had strengthened and blossomed as they had continued to meet on the occasions when Franco had visited Aberdeen, and they had also been in written communication on a regular basis. Initially Laura had little knowledge of their business relationship but once the white gold wedding ring signified her betrothal and commitment to Luigi, for better or for worse, she was drafted in and her accountancy skills were put to good use in furthering that elusive alchemy of making dirty money clean, as if by magic. The whole business was one huge risk, as transferring different currencies between countries was legally limited to small amounts and lira notes weren't exactly conspicuous with their low value and hence huge volume ratio. And since the advent of oil in the North Sea, Aberdeen had become a lucrative place to operate and with the protection racket and restaurant trade, the prospects were looking positive for Franco and his fellow clan members to further expand their empire. Around the UK other infant cells of the Camorra clans had been secretly forming and branching out surreptitiously like gossamer spiders' webs, invisible to the naked eye unless touched by the morning dew. By their success, Aberdeen became recognised as the UK nerve centre for their money laundering activities; overseen and controlled by Mr and Mrs Agosti, two upright citizens of the city with professional qualifications and an outwardly clean-living lifestyle.

Their lives together flourished and whilst Laura would visit her mother in Seahouses, Luigi took the opportunity to become a more frequent traveller to Naples. Franco, by now having ousted the previous clan leader in a bloodless coup, needed a second in command to watch his back and who better than his lifelong friend. Luigi spent time convincing Laura that the Bay of Naples was the place to be in the summer time and that it could easily overshadow the pull of Seahouses, and once Laura was back there on the sun-kissed Amalfi coast she didn't need any further convincing. Her previous short visits had only encompassed the trip from and to the airport plus the localised area of Luigi's birthplace, neither being a good enough advertisement for returning regularly.

But that first occasion had been purely a business trip with an introduction to his Mama thrown in on the second visit. The third trip had been the wedding itself, which once proposed and accepted: had taken some time preparing for, some time undertaking the actual vow and some time celebrating; all in true Italian style. The only thing Laura remained ever grateful for was that the finale to the actual vow itself had been consummated, in private. So none of the visits to date offered an opportunity for sightseeing or being a lazy sun-worshipping tourist.

Laura had, indeed, returned on occasion over the next couple of years, but only for flying visits and mainly to see Mama and help Luigi with the business end of things. But on her first vacation of any length she was determined to relax and indulge herself, not least with pandering to her reading list and crosswords even though she knew that they would only keep her entertained for so long. So this was to be complemented by copious sightseeing trips, taking in the recognised sites. Luigi, being used to having so much history on his doorstep, spent most of his time adjudicating over petty quarrels between clan members and other clans within the neighbourhood. His negotiating skills and legalese proved invaluable to Franco and between them, any emerging cracks were smoothed over.

But Laura was not prepared to sit on her hands and so went in search of her own history by way of a visit to Pompeii and Herculaneum and even a scramble up Mount Vesuvius. Gabriella, a cousin of Luigi's, had been chosen to accompany her in the capacity of guide, translator and chaperone, but if the truth be known both girls were enjoying their freedom and became firm friends before they had even reached the outskirts of Pompeii. They both marvelled at the frozen capsule of time with the preserved remains of streets, buildings and frescos still visible after nearly 2000 years and were amazed at how they could physically walk where Romans had walked all those years ago. And then, in the energy sapping, early afternoon heat of the day they sauntered slowly up the meandering dusty track to the top of Vesuvius, where the crater rim becomes its own amphitheatre and contains the tons upon tons of magma, pumice and ash that's just waiting for the next explosive eruption, of unbelievable force.

Gabriella and Laura sat there, on a bench, each with a well-earned bottle of water from the equally well-positioned shack. "Can you take it all in?" asked Gabriella. "There was a huge explosion just where we are sat now. An explosion much bigger than the atom bomb, with lava spewing and rocks, pumice stones and ash all being hurled up into the sky and carried westwards to those unsuspecting Romans. They reckon over 16000 people died from the fall out but as well as destroying, it's amazing to think what it preserved as well. Without the eruption and the ensuing catastrophe both Pompeii and Herculaneum would have probably been total ruins now or even non existent."

"I'm impressed at your knowledge, Gabriella. Is it compulsory to study this at school? And, aren't you all worried about the constant threat that it could do the same again?"

"Well yes, it could erupt again but you just live with it and presume that there will be enough warning for everyone to be transported to safety. And yes, I have been here before and read up on the volcano's history, but it has been more of a personal interest to me than school subject matter. In fact, I've sat on this very bench, that's why my father thought it would be a good idea to accompany you today."

"Well thank you on both counts; for being so informative and for accompanying me. I hope you're enjoying yourself as much as I am?"

She acknowledged Gabriella's nod as shyness, not comprehending that it was Gabriella who thought Laura should be thanked. She idolised her for being tall, slim and auburn haired with milky white skin, a beautiful face as well as for being both fashionably yet elegantly dressed; in fact to Gabriella, Laura epitomised everything she herself wasn't. So being able to spend the day with her had been 'a dream come true'. Once refreshed, they then took the same route back down to the awaiting bus which returned them to Anfiteatro Square in Pompeii and from there they jumped on the train for the return trip back to Naples.

Laura had spent the time, as she walked off the volcano, daydreaming about the best way of optimizing the monies that were now flowing in to the clan's coffers. She rationalized that just like Vesuvius, their livelihoods and those of the people of Secondigliano could be wiped out at any moment. But in this instance through an eruption of violence created by a power struggle. She surmised that it would be easy for both Luigi and her to start up businesses or merge with already established ones and then transfer start up or expansion funds between them. This would create opportunities to launder a volume of their incoming cash through these vehicles; but Laura was concerned that inflation and the weak lira on the International currency market were not ideals or a healthy combination, so she formulated a proposal that she hoped she could sell to Franco and Luigi, who to all intents and purposes were now numbers one and two in the clan.

That evening Laura had a chance to test the water with her theory. She approached it professionally by treating Luigi as a prospective client rather than her husband. At first Luigi had been too playful to concentrate with his mind being on more recreational activities before dinner. She, in return, playfully slapped his hand as he tried to cup her breast and was forced to whisper 'later' in his ear as she nibbled it suggestively, with the intention of hopefully encouraging his brain to re-divert to more business-like matters. Luigi knew time was limited anyway and decided to behave and to take his wife's somewhat serious demeanour, seriously. Once, she had his undivided attention and convinced him that 'yes' the promise still held, she delivered her proposal and backed it up with sound financial logic.

Luigi looked in to her eyes as if a mist had suddenly dissipated to reveal a crystal clear vision and said, "Cara mia, that's fantastic. We're all going round with blinkers over our eyes thinking that we need to keep our clan's fortunes all in cash and in businesses but as you've pointed out the logistics of doing that are getting harder and harder with the amount of lira notes we've to hide and the crack downs from the fraud squads. Gold would be so much more ...," here he searched for the word, ".... tangible. Definitely less bulky, but heavier. Perhaps even diamonds too. But where could we store them? Something like: a safe deposit box, in a bank. Somewhere safe like: a bank in Switzerland, for instance."

"Well you're getting a little ahead of yourself but you're going in the right direction. First, you're going to have to convince Franco that it's a sound idea, and above board too, if you know what I mean."

"No. You're going to have to convince him and if you argue it as you've just done with me, with maybe leaving out the promise of sex, I think he'll still be all for it. He's already concerned that there is too much cash floating about and too many greedy hands grabbing at it, that he may decide to kiss you anyway."

Laura had a once only opportunity to convince Franco that the bulk of the clan's fortunes, after wages and day-to-day living allowances were distributed, needed converting into harder currency. She made her play successfully at dinner that evening. Luigi looked on with pride in his eyes as he saw his wife lay out the arguments one by one, not dissimilar to a Turkish belly dancer relinquishing her veils and just as artistic; and all to ensure that the clan's and their own future finances were secured.

After desserts, but before coffee was served, it had already been agreed that the concept would be explored thoroughly and quickly and that steps would be taken to hive off a given percentage of cash to undertake an initial trial run. The clan itself was beginning to splinter and concerns were high that loyalties to Franco and his new ideas were on the wane. Later that night in the privacy of their own bedroom Luigi received his second dessert, for his role in supporting Laura's theory as well as the fact that he was the most gorgeous husband in the world and she could not get enough of him.

They were now entering their third year of a true Agosti, Catholic marriage and the only disappointment was the fact that Laura had not yet borne any children to continue the line, a line tragically shortened already with the deaths of three of the four of Luigi's siblings. Alone at last in bed, but before the couple reached the point of no return, although with their breathing becoming that little bit faster and so betraying its imminence, Laura whispered in a husky voice, "Cara mio, are you free tomorrow? It's going to be our last day; can we spend it together? You always seem so busy with meetings? I never get chance to do any pleasurable things with you. Well apart from this," she giggled as she squeezed his manhood. Luigi grunted, which could have been taken as either a yes or a no, but whether or not he would be available tomorrow he was certainly going to make them both happy tonight, and it would be guaranteed to be pleasurable too.

*

True to his grunt of the night before, Luigi reorganised his day and accompanied Laura on her anticipated trip along the Amalfi coast. They stopped off at the colourful cliff side village of Positano and roamed the narrow steep streets and alleys before choosing to stop for lunch at a small restaurant with breathtaking views. Once replete, they took the opportunity to retain the moment for posterity as Luigi asked the waiter to take a snap of them with his trustworthy Polaroid Swinger. Happy with the result but not yet satiated with the beauty of the coastline, Laura was desperate to take a boat trip and get the opposing view from out at sea. This gently conveyed them eastwards, passing Praiano and dropping them off in Amalfi itself where Laura joined the thousands of people before her who have suspiciously kissed for good luck, St Andrew's icon on the doors of the Duomo di Amalfi.

Afterwards she remained standing on the top of the steps that had led to the huge brass doors and looked in awe and admiration at the majesty of the builders' craftsmanship which dated back to at least the 13th Century; and then glanced around to take in the panoramic vista of the town and surrounding hillsides. Still one more sight remained on her itinerary, that of Ravello and its even more stunning views. She wanted to visit Villa Rufolo and its Gardens to experience the magical atmosphere created by those Wagnerian operas played out each year in the Festival to commemorate the German composer. But even Laura's energy had to flag sometime and relief spread across Luigi's face when he heard the words, "I'm done. This heat is unbearable. Take me home for both a cool drink and a cool bath."

"Cara mia, I can do half of that now," as he took her affectionately by the elbow and led her through a open door entrance in to a darkened bar with an overhead fan whirring effortlessly, but still only managing to displace the warm air with other warm air. Luigi ordered two spritzers plus a side dish of olives. Laura caught her breath and cooled her forehead as she carefully rolled the side of her glass along it before sipping her drink and nibbling on the olives.

"Thank you, darling. You certainly know how to fulfil a girl's needs. Now I feel fortified enough to cook in the car on the journey back. Shall we set off? There might be time for a rest before dinner," she hinted with a mischievous grin. Luigi knocked back his drink, threw an olive in the air which he caught in his mouth with aplomb and scooped his keys off the table as if to say 'I'm ready'! A taxi proved far quicker than waiting for the service bus back to Positano and from there Luigi made good time by getting back to Naples in just over an hour.

In their absence, Franco had not been resting on his laurels as a full meeting of the clan had been called for 10am the following morning, just before Luigi and Laura's flight back to Aberdeen. The three of them had spent the evening before formulating plans as to how the liquid cash could be siphoned off and transported to a safe haven. Matters were made easier by the fact that Franco, the now leader, had been the previous treasurer and Laura was the present one, albeit in an honorary capacity. This had put a stop to Laura's intimations and indeed interrupted Luigi's plans in the bedroom department but he was able to put that to one side in the knowledge that they were discussing money and in huge amounts. Decisions were made between the three but nothing was written down as a pact of love bound them and was safer for their own wellbeing and securities. Both Franco and Luigi understood that as well as the other clan members benefitting, so too would their surviving next of kin be beneficiaries in the event of their untimely deaths. And both parties agreed that if either one was killed, then the other would automatically instigate a plan to safeguard the secrecy of the stash and decide what to do with it and when; on the clan's behalf.

The meeting was held, and even though the majority of the clan were in favour of converting the bulk of their cash in to gold bullion and precious diamonds, particularly pink and blue ones, agreement had to be reached on its methodology in order to prevent a coup at the worst or friction at the least. Franco and Luigi manipulated the decision in their favour with it being agreed that a minimum of two officials within the clan should be party to the crediting and any subsequent debiting of the gold or gems in to, or out of, the safe deposit box. Thereby jointly safeguarding the security of all their futures.

As the Agostis flew back to Scotland via Heathrow, a concerted effort began in Naples to build the clan's fortunes even further in order to maximise the amount of cash available for conversion to bullion. Luigi and Laura arrived home to begin work on the logistics of finding a bank location, opening a deposit box and planning a method for the physical transfer of a large and bulky volume of notes. Once in place, it was established that Franco would hold the safe deposit key and Luigi the safe deposit code. The result being that they now both held 50% each of the methodology required to open the box. But what even Franco had not been accorded was the fact that the code holder could obtain a duplicate key on site, in case of emergencies.

Two years quickly passed by and having smoothed out the glitches, highlighted by the first and subsequent runs, a large volume of cash was being transferred by land or rail across the border to Switzerland every three months. Franco and Luigi were becoming familiar characters in Zurich and made good use of their time there, as sounding boards for each other's problems and so, converting them into solutions. On several occasions, Luigi had to take a volume of cash from the UK with the Aberdeen contingency wanting to get in on the act too. For this additional work and risk Luigi received a percentage of that deposited money and always insisted that Laura accompany him so as to enable them to blend in as just another holiday couple, which to all intents and purposes was the illusion they portrayed. An enigma depicting them as retiring, sombre, successful and conservative, when in truth informality coursed through their veins.

To add to the charade they had bought an attractive, although slightly modest house in Osborne Place in the city, close to Victoria Park and both ran professional practices from business premises overlooking Marischal College on Broad Street. And to ensure continued privacy their close friends still did not extend to two hands' worth and thus their history remained history unknown.

Life remained at a status quo in both the North Sea and Mediterranean cities until joy and catastrophe struck, and both during October 1979. Joy for the Agostis in that Laura found herself unexpectedly pregnant and catastrophe in the shape of an attempt on Franco's life. He escaped with a bullet in the shoulder and found the interrogation by the police more troublesome than the surgery. He knew it was an inside job but had to keep true to the Omerta. The gunman, a younger member of the clan who thought he was up and coming, knew that he had just the one chance and he had failed, the next bullet would be heading in the opposite direction. Surprisingly, it didn't as Franco agreed to meet with the rebel instead. A neutral location was arranged with both men having significant support covering their backs. Franco broke the ice with, "Alberto, I presume by the shooting that you are no longer happy with how I run our operation? But surely you know that trying to kill your own, breaks the code by which we're bound together? What is your justification, for disputing my leadership in such a ruthless manner? If this is to be a bona fide democratic challenge you must indicate your objectives and strategy and specify how much support you have from the other clan members."

Alberto Pugliese certainly felt out of his depth with the number of questions thrown at him as, being younger, he could neither answer nor argue with any articulation; brute force being his usual answer for everything. But looking over the expectant faces of his supporters he replied, "Our concerns are that the hard earned cash is being siphoned out of the clan without authority and that you, yourself, are being blinded by your new friends who think they know better than our forefathers and all the good people here!" He stopped and looked across the sea of faces, surprised that the words had come out in the right order and with meaning; then with a sweep of his hand he indicated that the generations of different families stood witnessing the argument could not be wrong?

He even embraced his own family in his gesticulation: his wife and children, plus the neglected one, who was his bastard from a relationship with a Norwegian beauty. The child, both had created but neither had wanted, and Alberto had reluctantly brought back to his wife and in to the family home and still at three years of age she was neither accepted nor loved. An orphan in all but name, whose only real and true friends and family were now being ripped apart by the greed of her own father. An orphan, who's only present from her uncaring mother, was her name, Pernille. Again, Alberto reiterated his point, "We deserve better than just listening to, and being guided by these new friends, these pseudo Italians!"

"Pseudo Italians! Luigi was born right here amongst you all and became a good friend of your brother, from when they were both only six years old. He's as much right to be called Italian as you. Remember it was the Don who agreed to finance his studies in Scotland and we know what a benefit that has been to all our families, including yours. As for the money, let me just give you a lesson in monetary affairs. The lira is constantly losing value against other European currencies. Its downward spiral is as regular as the change of seasons. In order to preserve our hard earned capital we need to diversify and look for more secure commodities. And at the moment there are no safer purchases than gold and precious gems. Now you all must know as well as I do that Italy is not renowned for its banking security and word would travel fast once our little nest egg began to grow. So steps have already been taken to protect it and if anyone is not happy with the cut they are already receiving on a weekly basis, then perhaps it's time to move on. Our neighbouring clans are always on the look out for disgruntled Camorristi!"

"I hear what you're saying and I need to speak privately to my supporters. If we do go, it is our entitlement to take a percentage of what has already been banked. We helped build it, so we own it by right."

Franco held Alberto's stare as he angrily replied, "What's already been moved, stays where it is. The clan created the businesses as a long-term investment to bring in that money over many years and even though it is now converted into gold and gems it belongs to the collective neighbourhood, not just to a few individuals. If there's to be a dispute over that decision then blood will flow over these dusty streets and yours may be the first."

The usurpers looked at their spokesman and showed him their hands, palms down. They wanted no more shootings without discussion and agreement to that possibility, and even Alberto was fearful for, not only his status but his life too, and was obviously taking the threat very seriously. In the end common sense reined and a partial truce held for the next two years with eventually a small compromise from Franco, being required. Because of increased aggression from other Camorra clans muscling in on their activities he agreed, with the majority of the clan's blessing, to increase Alberto and his supporters' cut by an additional 10% in order to prevent an all-out power struggle and divisive split, of their much needed manpower.

As Luigi had returned to Italy to play an active part in these negotiations he nearly missed the birth of his twin girls. The two most precious items that either, Laura or he had ever acquired. Their own personal gems became a life changer for the professional couple who had nearly always placed business before pleasure but who now really appreciated the true meaning of family. Laura's jet-setting days were behind her as she marvelled at how two tiny babies could flourish and grow in such a short space of time. Even Luigi cut down the number of times he visited Naples and Zurich, but not to the detriment of the financial deposits continuing growth.

On the girls second birthday Luigi had returned from a particularly difficult trip where Alberto had rekindled his aggression and once more begun spreading rumours that the deposits in Zurich would never be returned to its homeland. This had prompted Franco to again challenge him democratically, for outright leadership of the clan, with the loser being banished along with his supporters. Although Alberto had peer support from other clans he did not yet have the strength of support from his own nor the balls to accept the challenge and so a peace of sorts was restored. On the flight home Luigi, in recognition of the fragility of the truce, formulated a plan in his head, which he was eager to pass by Laura. She, understanding the enormity of the plan's sacrifice but at the same time appreciating the love and safety it would bestow upon their children, agreed in principle along with the proviso that Franco was made fully aware of its existence. Her fervent hope and prayers were that it would never come to pass but she always acknowledged that she might have to get her boots dirty when walking in shit.

As Franco was in the front line of the action and therefore more vulnerable, he appreciated their pact and had the forethought to establish a chain of command nearer to home, should he become incapacitated or killed. He had no dependants living locally at the present time as his mother had passed away and his immediate family were scarce. His only surviving younger relative ran off with Luigi's brother, to hone his skills with the Sicilian Mafia. So Franco's primary devotion for his people further strengthened his driving conviction that they should become the sole beneficiaries of his endeavours. This was to prove his downfall, having confided in several of his closest compatriots as to where the clan's hard earned cash was being stashed. He didn't actually mention a bank by name, but gave too much of a hint as to its location by stating that it was being held securely just north of Lake Zurich.

And to compound his fate, forethought became hindsight when on the twins third birthday he was gunned down in a cowardly act as he sat eating Sunday lunch at an outdoor restaurant, on Corso Umberto in the centre of Naples. A prearranged lunch that he could not cancel and where three good friends also died too. Had he taken up the Agostis' invitation to visit them for their daughters' third birthdays he would be alive and well, but for how long?

And not just satisfied with his death, his body had then been taken from the crime scene by the perpetrators. His clan cell subsequently became ostracised, subsequent to Pugliese's Camorristi merging their Secondigliano faction in with the other cells of Napoli's Camorra in order to form a more substantial power base. Like all businesses: growth was paramount and keeping abreast of technology became the new driving force; Pugliese's union acted as the final force necessary to add both strength and impetus to the Camorra and lead it, in later years, to become a member of the fledging 'all seeing' *SpiyWeB*. Whilst at the same time Di Larno's wilting supporters were left to their own devices and soon became reliant on the charity of the State and other less scrupulous benefactors. And with large unemployment in the 1980's severely affecting Italy's balance of payments and its public debt increasing significantly through the additional social security spending, their own standard of living had only one way to go and that was downwards. But not everyone could accept this spiral into oblivion. And so, the secret location of the possible bank in Zurich with the alleged hidden treasure was wrestled from the clutches of a Di Larno supporter, and very cheaply too.

The struggle for power had finally turned and Luigi knew that they would be next in the firing line. They had spent considerable time planning and converting their cash into inflation proof securities and placing their house on the market. Laura had been communicating with her sister, who was instrumental in ensuring that a major part of the plan was successful. And during that period Laura also paid her mother one last visit to discuss the safest options for their two most treasured possessions. Luigi put their final letters and package in to the safekeeping of his long time close friend and business associate, Jeremy Longthorne, and then the die was caste.

And it proved to be the estate agents who made the final play and set their final downfall in motion. They informed the Aberdeen clan that the Agostis had placed their house up for sale and so were inevitably on the move. This information soon found its way to Alberto Pugliese, now the new leader of the Camorra in Secondigliano, after an otherwise bloodless coup, and the chase was on. Even though the Agostis had taken all precautions to change their surnames in order to disappear from the Tax and National Insurance records, as well as invalidating their doctor and dental records, it was all in vain as the Camorra's ever widening links through

SpiyWeB, even whilst in its infancy, had already trapped them via its ever-lengthening, almost imperceptible, gossamer threads of information.

As the ultimate insult, the clan had ransacked Franco's house, having already despoiled his dead body in their eager quest to obtain the key to the untold fortune that they were certainly now prepared to continue killing for. And they knew that the only other person standing in their way was Franco's childhood friend, Luigi.

CHAPTER THREE

The rectangular package lay on the carpet equidistant between the two young women. Jessica had the strength of willpower to firstly make a coffee for them both whilst Emma's instinct and urge was to rip it open and at least see what lay within, even if she might not be able to understand its significance. As they now crouched over the unexpected and mysterious package she did just that. In her haste several items spilled out on to the floor narrowly avoiding a quick dunk in one of the coffee mugs. With hindsight, these were then moved out of harm's way whilst the contents of the package were studied more closely.

"M sit back. Let's see what we've got," said Jessica. "An envelope addressed to us. A thin oblong box with Dad's name inscribed on the front; this will most probably contain a watch or men's bracelet or some such jewellery. Doesn't it seem strange saying Dad after all these years? A family Polaroid, bless, and some kind of homemade crossword with clues to boot."

"Well, that doesn't seem much, after waiting over twelve years for its delivery!" said Emma disappointedly.

"Maybe, maybe not. But until we've seen what's in the envelope and worked out this crossword we just haven't a clue what we've got here or why we've got it? You heard what Jeremy said. Remember, he's held on to this for thirty years so he must think it's important," replied Jessica as she scrutinized the Polaroid closely. "Hey, M we did look pretty much alike as tiny tots. And look at Mum, wow what a stunner."

Emma grabbed for the Polaroid, which was the only photograph they had seen showing them with their birth parents and indeed one of only a few of the two girls together. Tears sprang in to her eyes, "Yes, she was and she had a bit more weight just like me," she said imagining what life could have been like with Mum and Dad.

Jessica reached out and gave her a hug, and further interpreting her stream of consciousness, she said, "M, after reading the old newspaper editorials we knew that they had chosen an unusual path. We grew up without them and may never know the full implications of why but we owe it to them and ourselves to open this envelope and perhaps understand what history this whole package contains. If it's an encapsulation of their lives then all of it must have some relevance and so must be significant." She glanced across at her sister who gave a little sigh and silent nod for the envelope to be opened. Several pages of differing size and colour spilled out. Jessica picked up the folded letter first, opened it to its full foolscap size and studied the tightly knit, turquoise, script.

She began to read aloud:

'My Dearest Darling Girls

There is nothing imaginable in this world that can compare to what you two bundles of joy have meant to your mother and me, so not being with you now will probably be all the harder to understand. In the three years since your births our lives have been changed out of all proportion and for the better I might add; but things that happened in the past, prior to your arrival, cannot be wiped clean and so you are only reading this rather than us telling you in person.

Do not ever think in your wildest imaginations that the steps we took were in any way your fault; what we did, we did out of love to protect you and keep you away from harm. It was a joint agreement and we always hoped that as in life your Mama and I would be together in death. Sorry to sound morbid or even melodramatic but we told Jeremy not to let you see this until you were at least 21, so if you are reading it I hope that you now have the strength to continue reading and to understand and respect our decision.

Just like your Mum's crossword I have written this letter and left tokens, both in cryptic fashion so that, heaven forbid, should they fall into the wrong hands then nothing would be lost to our extended family or gained by our enemies. And yes, unfortunately there are enemies. Made, over a number of years, in my native homeland, Italy, and our present home city of Aberdeen too. Plans were made and carried out to ensure that you two innocents were not harmed in any way and that with hope you will both now have the desire and the brains to do the right thing; and so conclude what we were unable to do, all those years ago.

Always search for the truth and be charitable to others. Do not criticise or chastise other people for faults they cannot control and always be gentle in your actions just like your Mama has always been.

I love you in this world with my whole heart and will do so in the next.

Lots of Love, Papa xxxx

Neither girl could contain herself and both cried openly, for parents that they never really knew and for this first and probably last communication, fleetingly showering love and security, which neither parent could ever give them physically. Jessica was the first one to return to her senses as she picked up another smaller letter and a black-framed card, which had fallen from the envelope on to the carpet. "Well, it's a good job he's not around today to see what a mess we've made of our lives or he'd be spanking us over his knee. Looks like the charity and gentle bits passed us by; can't have inherited them from Mum, as Dad so wanted. There can't be many families that have a skeleton hidden in their cupboard, let alone six! That would probably take up the whole of the kitchen storage space as well as the bedrooms! Do you think Dad was a killer, in his line of work?"

"I don't really want to think about that, Jess. He sounds as if he was a really nice man and I can't imagine that I'd have turned out like I did if he'd been around. And I certainly wouldn't have got involved in your messy murders. Anyway, we said we weren't going to think about those things yet. What else is there that dropped on the floor?"

Jessica picked up the two items off the carpet and looked at the card first. "Looks like some kind of religious thing," she said as she studied it and turned it over in her hands. "I think the Catholics call them mass cards; when someone close dies and then people that knew them offer up a mass in their memory, that sort of thing. 'Franco Di Larno. 1952 – 1983 Francescane Missionarie Del Cuore Immacolato Di Maria'. So presumably he was one of Dad's friends? I don't read Italian but it looks like he lived in Secondigliano, wherever that is?"

"Yeh, OK. What's the other item, Mother Teresa?" asked Emma impatiently. Jessica unfolded the coloured paper and looked fondly at the clear dainty script in front of her as she glanced down to the end of it to see if her guess was correct. And it was; probably the only communication she would ever hold of the woman who gave them birth and then for reasons as yet unknown abandoned both her and her sister. She read:

'My most cherished babies

You will never know how much happiness you have both brought into my life and now too how much sadness, as your father begins preparations for the arrangements we planned some time ago. It is a truly horrific prospect, but one that I know in my heart is right, as it will protect you both. After being married to a Catholic for over 3 years I thought that we would never be blessed with children, but by a miracle your Papa and I were able to enjoy three wonderful years of family life with you both, which I will always treasure until the Day of Judgment arrives. And now almost because it was too precious, it had to be taken away. If and when you get this you will be grown women and hopefully the best of friends. Be good to each other and, above all else, be happy.

All my love and kisses always, Mum xxx

PS I've always been fanatical about cryptic crosswords - hope I've passed it on!

PPS If you read this whilst Jeremy is still around - say Hi from me and thank him for being a watchful godparent, to you Emma, and for fulfilling our demands on him.'

Again tears welled up in the eyes of both women. Emma broke the spell first with "I can't take much more of this. With the life I've already led, I don't know if I'd have rather that they had taken me in the car with them."

"What and be burnt to a crisp! Aren't you a teeny, weeny bit excited about where this is leading?"

"Well, anything's got to be better than you having tried to kill me. And anyway, how can we still be here, if two small children were found in the back of the car?"

"Yes, I must admit it does seem a little bewildering as to who the two children were? And we agreed that we'd talk about that 'killing' thing later when we could rationalise it more clearly. Anyway, why aren't you looking on the positive side? We've had letters from our parents! Perhaps, we'll get some answers there," said Jessica with equal parts of confusion and optimism on her face as she swept her hands over the slightly bewildering objects that had come out of the equally slightly bewildering package.

"Yes, I suppose we know they're probably going to be the only letters we'll ever receive, as even I know that you can't really communicate with the dead."

"You possibly could if you believed in Ouija boards."

"Well, there's as much chance of that happening as there is of me making a move on sugar daddy Jeremy."

"Yes, a bit of a Catch 22 there, M. Finding out he's your Godfather and all. Anyway, I'm going for a run to clear my head. We'll leave the rest until I get back and don't you be thinking that you'll have an opportunity to run to your medicine chest for help, whilst I'm gone. You're cutting down on all that, remember."

Emma did remember but it was hard all the same. That monkey, sitting on her shoulder, was constantly reminding her of how much she liked the feeling that her friend 'heroin' gave her and how it missed being as big a part of her daily routine. The truth was that it would have to continue missing playing that part, as Emma had nowhere to buy it at the moment and even she accepted that there would be no opportunity to go back to her old stomping ground in Edinburgh anytime soon. To take her mind off the urge she busied herself with tidying up the kitchen and then set about making ham and salad sandwiches with lashings of mayo. She knew Jessica wouldn't be concerned about the calories but she wasn't too convinced about herself? To underline the point, Jessica returned and seeing what Emma had prepared exclaimed, "Hey super, I hope you've put plenty of mayo on mine. Just off for a quick shower and then we can get back to solving this mystery."

They both sat silently as they ate and Emma turned on the TV news so that the quietness didn't freak her out. She was really more of a radio person but knew that Jessica was not a big fan of music constantly blaring out of the speakers nor did she like the fact that the DJs always seemed to be talking endlessly to the detriment of the music being played. But fortunately nothing untoward had been reported on the regional news channel to suggest that there were any positive leads on the serial killer's identity, let alone the person's imminent capture. Jessica contemplated on the fact that the new team seemed to be floundering equally as much as the old one, but even so she was not prepared to rectify that for obvious reasons. Emma registering Jessica's faraway look took the initiative and cleared away the plates and came back in with another pot of filter coffee, which became the indicator that part two of the exploration of the package was to begin. Jessica looked at her as if to say, 'Do you want to do it?' and Emma's shake of the head whilst pointing her chin in Jessica's direction was a strong enough suggestion that she didn't.

"Right then. Let's have a look at this jewellery box." It was beautiful in its own right; covered in leather effect Skivertex in a rich burgundy colour with 'LUIGI AGOSTI 31-05-1980', gold foil embossed across the centre of the top and complemented with a gold foil geometric pattern along the outer edges. Jessica opened it and found a gold watch resting on a black velvety type material. "Dad must have bought this to celebrate our birth," she said affectionately as she took out the watch and held it gingerly. "It's beautiful. It's got a name on the face. It says 'Paul Gerber'. I've never heard of him, have you?"

She then turned it over and engraved on the back it read 'TO EMICA LAMBLYNN WITH LOVE, PAPA'. "Right, I'm totally confused now. Was Dad two timing or what? I mean I'm called 'Lambert' which is Grannie's maiden name and you're called 'Flynn' which is Grannie's married surname, so who is called 'Lamblynn'? Could it be our surnames mixed up together? And, presuming he has joined them together, then why? I can't make sense of it, can you, M?"

"If you can't get to grips with it, then what chance have I got? Although I reckon your thinking is on the right lines, because 'Emica' is part of 'Emma' and 'Jessica', a mix just like the surnames. And that's me just about done."

"Well a right pair of clueless detectives we make. No wonder the serial killer was never caught! Where's a detective when you need one?" Jessica asked flippantly. "Perhaps we ought to make a stab at this crossword and see whether that's as cryptic as Mum made out?"

"Hey Jess, wouldn't it be great if we could go back in time in Doctor Who's thingy. You know that police box. The Tardis! That's it. Then we could meet up with Mum and Dad and ask them in person without having to strain our brains. And I reckon I could be more than a companion to the Doctor. I bet I've got more experience than those other girls, too. Talk about the mile high club. How high is the universe, anyway?"

"Come on back down to Earth, please. With or without the Doctor, nobody's going to help us solve this but ourselves," continued Jessica, preparing for the challenge as she picked up the makeshift crossword, grabbed a pen and looked at all of the clues and then with a sigh went back to the beginning and read out the first one.

Across:

2. This is 'of the Irish' (4)
5. 'Suivez' – musical direction (6)
7. Not the same as 'belonging to them' (5)
8. What are we? (5)
12. Not for mooring boats (3)
13. One of the five w's used in journalism (4)
15. Number minus w (2)
16. Informal greeting (2)
17. Is this what you live by? (4)
19. As fifteen across (2)
20. Swiss swiss word (6)

Down:

1. Not the opposite of 'yes' (4)
3. Seb Coe's 1500m 3:32.03 world record (6)
4. Plural demonstrative pronoun (5)
6. Testament (4)
9. Hire purchase (6)
10. Macbeth extols one of these themes (4)
11. And I could be vertical or horizontal (1)
14. Definite article (3)
18. 'solfège' syllable (2)

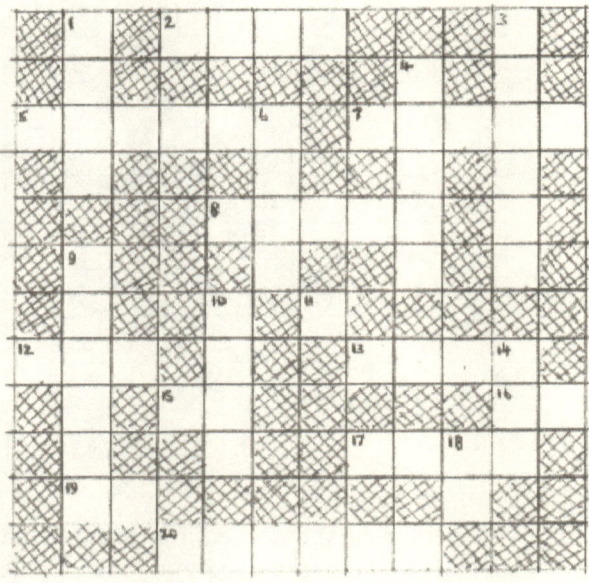

"2. Across: This is 'of the Irish'. What is of the Irish? Guinness? The Craic? Constant rain? Blarney? Could be anything. We're going to be lucky to crack these clues," said Jessica despondently and already ready to throw in the towel.

"Well done Jess. That's it, 'lucky' you said. The luck of the Irish," replied Emma triumphantly. "Can't be as thick as I thought, can I?"

"Yes it certainly fits," said Jessica moving on to the second clue. Within an hour and with a lot of help from Emma's newfound friend 'Google', they only had eight across, twenty across and one down to complete.

1		²L	U	C	K				³Z	
							⁴T		U	
⁵F	O	L	L	O	⁶W	⁷T	H	E	R	E
			⁸L		I		E		I	
	⁹C				L		S		C	
	R		¹⁰G		¹¹£		E		H	
	¹²K	E	Y		O		¹³W	H	A	T¹⁴
	D		¹⁵T		O				¹⁶H	I
	I				D		¹⁷C	O	¹⁸D	E
	¹⁹T	O							O	
			²⁰							

Jessica's brain was frazzled and needed a break, so both girls put all the items back in the package but only after Emma had sneaked another peek at the Polaroid, which she quickly popped back and then moved the package to its generally more accepted secure position of behind the DVD player.

"I just had another peek at Mum to see if I could glean any answers," she said a little embarrassed.

"What's this? Divine intervention? I think we'll be needing a bit of that Irish magic to rub off if anything," said Jessica mimicking the Irish accent. She then scooped up her car keys and said in her usual voice, "Let's forget about it for a while and get some food in."

As they meandered through the aisles on autopilot, weaving in and out of other shoppers and picking up, inspecting and either putting back or dropping items in to the trolley, Jessica had a eureka moment. "M look. Lindt Swiss chocolate."

"Yes, Lindt. Do you like it? Are you going to buy some; chocoholic, are we now? It's not the cheapest, you know?"

"No, Lindt. Swiss chocolate. What's the Swiss word for Swiss? Suisse."

"Well that's the same as the first word," Emma said confusingly.

"Yes, it might sound the same due to my bad pronunciation but it's spelt differently. And I am going to buy some for good luck. I know it's not the cheapest but perhaps that Irish magic might just help with the other two clues!"

The girls continued with their shopping and were eventually corralled into a queue for one of the only three open tills. After a mind-numbing wait, their trolley was empty and their carrier bags full. The task now complete until the next time. Rather than returning home in a refreshed frame of mind, both returned exhausted and in need of refreshment, itself. A cup of green tea later or in Emma's case, a Diet Coke, brought karma and a renewed vigour to solve the final clues. Even though Jessica was impatient to try out the Swiss clue she was also concerned as to what the crossword was intended to reveal, but she thought it not necessary to dwell on that until all the clues were in place.

"Right. Let's try 'SUISSE'. 20 across. 'S-U-I-S-S' and the 'E', is already there. Mm, it doesn't help with anything else.

What's left? 8 across. 'What are we?' Second letter's 'L' and the last letter's 'S'. So it's not 'HUMAN'; 'GLASS'; 'CLASS'. Could be 'CLASS', as we all make up different sociological classes. 'FLOSS'; 'BLUES'; 'CLUES'. Yes, what are we? We are 'CLUES'. Let's put that in. Come on Emma just one to go and then you'll be able to read a message from the past. Hopefully. 1 down. 'Not the opposite of 'yes'. Well we know the opposite would be 'no' and if 'FOLLOW' is correct, we've got the third letter as 'O'."

"The only word I can think of that sounds like 'no' is 'know' and that's got a 'W' at the end," said Emma enthusiastically.

"Emma, I think you've cracked it. 'K-N-O-'. That does it, now what does it all mean? We had better write the words on paper and try to unscramble them?"

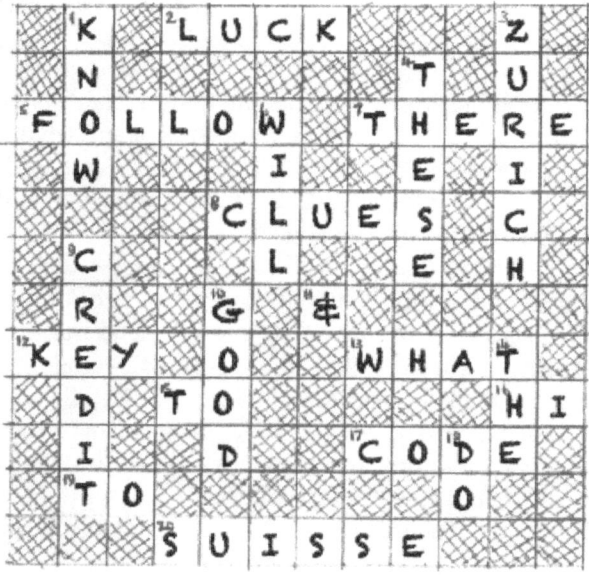

Emma found the paper and scissors, wrote out the words and cut each one in to a neat rectangle just as she'd seen on Blue Peter. "That's that. Now Jess, can you make anything of it?" The words were placed in the order they had been written, across and then down.

LUCK; FOLLOW; THERE; CLUES; KEY; WHAT;
TO; HI; CODE; TO; SUISSE; KNOW; ZURICH;
THESE; WILL; CREDIT; GOOD; &; THE; DO

"OK. Another cup of tea is out of the question; this calls for something stronger. I'm going to get a glass of wine to relax my brain. Do you want one M?"

Emma looked at the clock on her mobile and then at Jessica with a pleading shrug. "Hey, come on M. It's a bit early to be taking your diamorphine. I need you to be thinking too, not crashing out on me."

Emma took that as a 'No' and said begrudgingly, "OK then, I'll have a glass, too."

Both took turns to move the words around and soon sense emerged from the nonsense. A few final tweaks and they were content that they had the correct message, even allowing for the odd word being slightly out of order.

It read:

HI
FOLLOW THESE CLUES TO CREDIT SUISSE
ZURICH
THE KEY & CODE WILL KNOW WHAT TO DO
THERE
GOOD LUCK

"Well," said Emma finishing her wine I'm none the wiser, are you Jess?"

"No, I'm not really, but we've got to crack this and whilst it's still fresh in our minds. What else came in the package?

The mass card thing. Dad's watch, made by Paul Gerber, if you remember. Look him up on the Net, M. What else? A family snap shot showing all four of us. And the two letters: one with Mum hoping that we like crosswords and cryptic ones at that. That must be a clue in itself," she mused curling the ends of her hair around her fingers as she stared into space and chanted, "Cryptic, cryptic, cryptic."

"Cryptic's right. That watchmaker's still about and he comes from Zurich. We presume from the inscription and date that Dad bought the watch there to celebrate our birth. So, perhaps he had one of those fancy safe accounts there, that nobody knew about."

"You mean a safe deposit box, don't you? Maybe. Bloody hell; imagine if they had a deposit box stashed with loads of money and other stuff. Like you see in gangster movies. But what am I talking about? We've no key. And it specifically mentions both a key and a code in the clues. We haven't got either. We'd better read the letters again and take a closer inspection of the items. Each one is there for a reason, but it's got to be obscure so that no one else could easily work it out." The girls were almost in a panic as they scanned over the letters and looked at the watch and its box. Jessica studied the Polaroid snap so much that she was convinced the emulsion would melt. She began having a conversation with herself, starting in a low whisper and becoming louder as the pennies dropped.

"Why the photo? Why the photo? What photos have I got of them? Well none actually. But Grannie always insisted that I kept hold of the photo album showing the pictures of when I was really young. What were her words now?" She racked her brain and heard the words as if coming from her Grannie's mouth. "'It's part of your heritage. It's where you came from and maybe where you're going too.' Or something along those lines. But she was always referring to the album that had the key ring attached to the spine. The key ring, that I used to kiss because it said on it, 'Love from Papa'. The key ring that had one solitary key on it! Could that be the key? M, I think I know where the key is?" Jessica blurted excitedly as she reached a crescendo.

"What. The actual key, to a safe deposit box, in Switzerland!" exclaimed Emma equally excited, having firstly been confused by hearing the mumbo jumbo thoughts, her interpretation of her Grannie's voice and then shocked by Jessica's final outburst, which she quickly followed up with her rendition of, "We're in the money. We're gonna be rich."

"Well, I won't know if it's the actual key until we get to Zurich and try it. But then there's still the code?" Jessica said dejectedly as elation turning to despondency when the words left her lips.

"Yes, the code," said Emma as she turned her Dad's watch over and over in her hands as if trying to wring it dry. "I've been thinking about that and you're probably going to say it's silly and that it can't be as simple as that ...". Emma trailed off into silence, adding extra weight to the melancholy pall that was now hanging over their heads.

"M. You can't leave it like that, say what you mean. I'm not going to bite your head off if you say something silly. It's just that we've got so far and seem to have come up against a brick wall."

"OK. Well, it's this 'EMICA LAMBLYNN' made up name. That's a nonsense inscription to put on such an expensive looking watch and especially when it's meant to be a celebration of our births. Dad would have known that the engraver had got it wrong and made him rectify it. I'm thinking that it's there for a reason and as the code's the only thing left to crack it must surely have something to do with that?"

"Yes, but we could be at the bank for hours trying all those letter permutations and I think these safe deposit boxes will have some sort of timer or a three times and you're out limiter, just like the hole in the wall cash points."

"If it's too long for letters, what about numbers? On the first name it could be two of my letters to three of yours," pondered Emma with stupid written across her forehead.

"And our surnames would be four each!" exclaimed Jessica as she rushed over and gave her sister a huge hug, which knocked them both off balance and caused them to land in a giggling heap. "M, you have cracked it. You're a genius. If this is what taking drugs does for you, then I'll be the next in line." She realised what she had said and her euphoria wore off in an instant. "I'm sorry, M. I didn't mean to make fun and I know you're trying really hard to kick it but you are the tops. If you're right we've now got the key and the code. What was it again? 2-3-4-4." And she finished quite matter of fact with, "Well we can always take the watch if we think we'll forget."

"Oh, Jessica. How can we forget! It's a chance of a lifetime that's just waiting to happen. And it's landed in our laps and after all that we've been through too. I don't know what to do next?"

"I do," said Jessica forcefully as she wriggled free of her sister's grasp. "I'm going to get another sheet of paper and an Atlas. We're planning on taking a trip. Would you be a sweetie and pour us both another glass of wine?"

Emma collected up the glasses and gingerly poured more Chardonnay in to both, holding her hand steady and breathing slowly so that through her excitement she didn't spill it all over the coffee table. 'Sweetie' she thought. 'Where have I heard that recently and in what context was it said?'

On Jessica's return, Emma's mode had changed to the secretary that never was. She had replenished the wine glasses and sat back proudly on the sofa with the laptop screen displaying a map of Europe and showing a straight red line from St Boswells to Zurich. Jessica's response to this was "M, you never cease to amaze me. Talk about proactive and here's me thinking I'd have to support you. This murdering lark must certainly agree with you. All you need is your hair in a bun and glasses and you'd make a great personal secretary!"

"Yeh, yeh, yeh. It's not rocket science and what have we said about talking openly about the 'murders'?" She whispered the last word and held her hands up, showing her fingers mimicking the inverted commas sign. "You're always telling me that walls have ears what with being so paper-thin as they are, but still you seem to mention the word at the drop of a hat. Don't you like it on the outside?"

"I like it just swell, sis. And maybe I'll like it even more so, when we set off on our travels. And I promise from now that I won't mention the 'm' word; even though I'll still call you 'M', if you know what I mean. Now you have got a passport, haven't you, M?"

"Mm. Well yes I do but it's still in the flat, back in Edinburgh along with my hidden money."

"What you've left money hidden in the flat! Why didn't you tell me? Is it safe, there?"

"As safe as anywhere else, I suppose," replied Emma looking a bit concerned. "Don't you think it will be? I'm sure my friends will be looking out for me."

"With friends like yours, the first thing they'll be doing is looking out for themselves. Weren't you telling me about that guy BJ? The one who thought he could get into your knickers just because you happened to be in his girlfriend's bed. Now just remind me what you were doing in her bed in the first place? Yes, that BJ was certainly looking out for you!"

"OK, OK. So not all my friends, then. Anyway, yes I have got money there. At a rough guess I'd say about £1200. And haven't you ever had to console a friend in need before?"

"£1200. Why's it not in the bank or a building society? You do know how flimsy those doors are, don't you? Probably, worse than the paper-thin walls, I'd say. And is your passport there too; and your other identity documentation?"

"Yes, everything. And you must know I can't put money in the bank when I'm claiming benefits. Even I know that," Emma said triumphantly.

"Right. Forget all that I've said about you being a good secretary et cetera. I think we'll be starting from scratch again on that one. First thing tomorrow we're going to Edinburgh to collect the lot, unless someone else has collected it already, then I'll show you how consoling a friend I can be. Just as a matter of interest, where do you hide it?"

"Well my druggie stuff which I always feel is replaceable, I usually hide that in the Manolo Blahnik shoe box; but for stuff that's important and cash, well they go in the Gap carrier bag, hung up in the wardrobe."

"Jeez. If I hadn't had these two glasses of wine I'd be taking you there, tonight. You better change that map starting point to Edinburgh now," harangued Jessica as she felt pangs jabbing at her stomach. She placed her hand over it as a soothing act and mentally calculated how long ago it was since she'd eaten, picturing her metabolism's enzymes searching unsuccessfully for any available carbohydrates to boost her depleted energy supply. As the gripes became stronger she knew that with what little body fat her petite frame held, they would not recede unless satiated.

So on her way to the bedroom she grabbed a couple of biscuits to nibble whilst looking for the key. She shouted through the doorway, "M, can you be a love and look in the fridge and freezer. See what we can have for tea, so that I can tell my stomach to stop giving me such grief." She chided herself as she pulled items from the back of the wardrobe, in her search for the key attached to the photo album. 'Better not admit that I keep important items in my wardrobe too!'

Coming back into the kitchen, clutching a numbered key on the key ring that said 'Love from Papa', Jessica found Emma juggling with four or five dishes, all at various stages of going in and coming out of the microwave. She looked on at Emma's culinary skills and surmised what was happening. "Right. When we've eaten the chilli con carne we'll get washed up and spend the evening planning and packing so we can get off bright and early tomorrow. That means no more wine for me and you'll have to limit your methadone intake tonight too; and make sure you've got, or can get hold of, enough supplies tomorrow as we won't be back for a while. And I'm not going out of my way looking for any on the black market, do you hear?"

Once in their beds, Jessica as usual found it hard to sleep, not least because of her conscience churning over the murders she had committed and the lives of those remaining she had ruined but also because of the constant need to add to her list of 'things to do' on the bedside table. Emma had no such trouble; in fact she went straight off, until nearly 4.00am. Jessica woke with a start at the movement she imagined she was making in the bed. She thought she had awoken needing the loo but as she rose to get out of bed she collided with another body, which was moving in the opposite direction. "Whoops, sorry Jess," said Emma. "Did I wake you? I've got to tell you about this awful dream I've just had."

"Well, can't you wait until the morning?" asked Jessica as she lay there undecided as to whether to relieve herself or not.

"No. I don't think I can. It's about Jonnie. You remember Jonnie. He helped me when I was really ill from that overdose. Well, of course you'll remember the overdose, you know the one you were involved in ….?" She trailed off embarrassed at bringing it up and in the middle of the night at that. "Anyway. Jonnie. I dreamt that some people had got him and were hurting him because they wanted information about me."

"Aren't you getting confused with Jeremy? He'd never hurt a fly. He's the perfect gent."

"No, it wasn't Jeremy. It was bad people. They were after us, as well. But like Jeremy they were going to get our number off Jonnie. Only this time they weren't even the nice guys, let alone perfect gents"

"It's just a dream but it's not to say that we should dismiss it. You never know it may contain some underlying truth. Supposing that contact of Jeremy's did tell somebody else.

Just like the people who were after Dad all those years ago. They could be still searching for what we imagine is a safe deposit box, if that's what it turns out to be."

Emma, now unburdened of her nightmare, snuggled up to Jessica's warmth and quickly drifted off with only her light telltale snoring giving her presence away. Her sister was not as fortunate and lay there, thinking: of what confronted them and now also of the added dimension of possibly someone else being on their case too. As sleep refused to compete with her active mind she made the best use of her wakeful state and padded off to the bathroom.

CHAPTER FOUR

The trip North proved long, slow and boring. Babyface and his accomplice had a toss up between the A1 and the M1. Both roads were going to be laborious, although the A1 looked to be more straightforward. So they plumped for that and regretted the decision every ten or so miles thereafter. Roadworks, roundabouts and turnoffs were far too regular and their target of Edinburgh never seemed to get any closer even though the hours ticked off like clockwork! Also, there had been a whole half hour spent discussing whether to drive, take the East Coast train or fly. Flying had been discarded as it left behind too much identity information and then there would be the need to hire a car, which would just further compound the trail. The train would not be as intrusive but still there would be the need to hire a car. So they had chosen to travel by car over the 400 miles of metalled roads, which at least allowed them plenty of room for private equipment; equipment which could prove useful in extracting information from any unwilling interviewees.

"Who said Sunday driving was more relaxing than the working week. This is a bloody nightmare," said Babyface sporting a puce baby face in support of his anger. They needed to reach Edinburgh before offices opened on Monday as they had an un-prearranged visit to make at the National Records of Scotland offices at Ladywell House on Ladywell Road EH12. This was the location from which Scotland Yard's 'Cold Cases' Unit had pinpointed the activation software on the name, Luigi Agosti. Once there, Babyface was in no doubt that he would be given the opportunity to wheedle his way into the employees' confidence. To start with he was Italian and then his baby face could really melt the iciest of demeanours. His only undoing would be whether his temper would improve enough by then to carry it off. When he realised they were only at Peterborough, he thought not.

Sleeping rough in the car overnight for a maximum of three hours did not enhance Babyface's chances, either. After the subsequent short drive into Edinburgh City Centre on early Monday morning, he commanded Ollie to stop outside the front of The Balmoral Hotel on Princes Street. Here he scooped up his Hans Kniebes travel wash bag, alighted and strode confidently through reception heading in the direction of what he presumed to be the gents' washroom. Twenty minutes later he strode back through reception, in the opposite direction, feeling and looking a new man. He now lived up to his eponymous baby face name, having rid himself of the ravages of yesterday's journey and the rough few hours' sleep.

Next stop, he anticipated an unhealthy 'greasy spoon' type breakfast with plenty of black pudding and a large mug of black coffee to match. On coming down the steps, Babyface stopped momentarily and checked his TAG Heuer, to ensure that they would still arrive at Ladywell House at its earliest official opening time, continued descending and only narrowly avoided a collision with a couple of attractive pedestrians; a quick sidestep, à la Gene Kelly, proved most effective.

Even allowing for the time taken in consuming the fat fuelled breakfast, Ollie could still not have timed it better as he pulled into the Ladywell House staff car park along with ten other vehicles, from which all of the occupants spilled out and headed for the door marked 'Staff Entrance'. Babyface slid out of his car and entered through the building's main front doors, hopeful that when he came back through, he would have at least one additional set of important details. Details: which would lead him one step nearer to achieving the Boss' objective.

*

Unless you care for young children or have an early morning start time at work, there are not too many other reasons as to why you would perceive 4.30am as being a good enough excuse for leaving a warm bed, but Jessica had been forced to do just that. Clarity had crept in along with Emma and now with the silence too, she sat patiently awaiting that final tinkle; she shuddered imperceptibly and remained pensive on the throne for a further five minutes whilst putting the world to rights. Washing her hands, her understanding of the situation realised itself and then her resolve began to take hold as an imaginary sequence of events played out in her head.

On returning to her bed, she struggled to drift back off due to Emma's self-invitation to spend the reminder of the night there. Jessica remained restless, not primarily because of her sister's light snoring, nor the reduction in space available to her, but more due to what Emma had actually said. Jessica's initial thoughts that they could plan the trip at leisure and travel in a relaxed manner, maybe even taking in some sites en route, were now completely out of the question. And she could already envisage the possibility of danger and the veiled threat that someone else may have also waited for over 30 years to get their hands on the alleged safe deposit box, too. A safe deposit box, which she knew might not even exist.

The prospect that Emma and her could become the hunted energised her in to leaping out of bed and showering straight away so as to leave the bathroom free for her unsuspecting twin, who Jessica had no intention of letting sleep much longer. Particularly now, as she knew that they would have to travel north before they could go south; and the fact of 'time being of the essence', never rang more true. She made coffee, by way of a bribe, to get Emma moving and to boost her own adrenalin. She then grabbed her laptop, started Googling various sites, and wrote down snippets of information as she landed on the relevant ones. By the time Emma was dressed and made up, Jessica had packed the last of the basic essentials in her wheelie case; laptop, mobile, passport and money; and double-checked that she had her credit and bank debit cards.

At 6.22am, after having given her sister ten minutes to pack her own case, they left the apartment and set off for Edinburgh. As Emma yawned her way through the first half hour of the journey and muttered incessantly about the fact that she was hungry, Jessica assessed their progress and pondered whether they were still in front of the rush hour.

"We'll have to grab something to eat in Edinburgh. But before I forget, you did bring your mobile, didn't you?" Emma nodded and yawned at one and the same time. "Good, can you get it out and text Jonnie?"

"What, you want me to tell Jonnie that we're going to Switzerland?"

"No! I want you to tell Jonnie that you are concerned for his safety. You know, your dream."

"Oh that. I'll feel silly telling him I dreamt about him."

"Emma. We're not talking about erotica here! Just text and say that it might not be safe for him to go into work this week and suggest that it might be a good idea to ring in sick. Tell him that Jeremy thinks that someone else might want to get in touch with him and he strongly advises against it. It might even be dangerous."

"He doesn't do 'dangerous'. We nearly went there before with the police thing. I can't frighten him like that? Anyway, we're only guessing, aren't we?"

"Well maybe we are. But wouldn't you rather have at least one boyfriend who's alive? Input the text and then read it back to me before you send it," she commanded as she checked the road signs. "Dalkeith turn off coming up, if we going to hit traffic it'll be as we turn on to the A720. We're heading for Burnwood, aren't we?"

Emma nodded vigorously as she concentrated on getting her full text message across. "Yes and done," she exclaimed triumphantly.

"OK. Read it back," commanded Jessica. Emma did and was given approval to press send. "That should buy us some time at least. Do you think we need to let Jeremy know about this too, M?"

Emma thought and said logically, "Well, if as we presume the baddies, in quotes, are on our trail; they would have to find out where the computer input was made from about Dad and we know that was Jonnie at the NRS offices. But alternatively they may want to know who initially instigated the search and what that person intends to do with the information. That being the case then both Jonnie and Jeremy could be in danger. That's supposing there is anyone there at all and it's not just a figment of my dream and your imagination?"

"Very good Emma. I'm impressed. You're trying to reason the problem though to a logical conclusion. Only problem is, even if you wanted to action it, do you have Jeremy's phone number?"

"Course I do," said Emma triumphantly. "I'm not going to drop a would-be sugar daddy without good reason."

"Forever the optimist. And, by the way, I would be impressed if you pulled it off; especially as we now know he's your godfather. You can't exactly have a sugar godfather, can you? Anyway we're wasting time. Send him a warning text too, that we think there maybe someone snooping about. And then when we get to Edinburgh, you're going to have to change phones. We don't want anyone tracking us, presuming that they do find out your number." Jessica could sense that Emma had pulled a sad face at this statement, thinking of the considerable amount of time she had taken to build up her list of clientele on the phone, but Jessica continued, anyway; "Don't worry. It'll just be the SIM card. I'll have to do the same too. If all goes well I won't make you swallow it. You may get to keep it for use later on. But, by then, you might not need to go back to your either your old life or your old friends. You know if we find a pot of gold or something at the end of this rainbow."

"Mm. Pipedreams. Now who's wasting time? Right, that's a text sent to Jeremy too. I hope he understands text speak?"

Jessica approached a roundabout showing the A71 signposted for Burnwood. She turned off left and headed right and then right again in to the estate. From there, Emma directed her towards The Towers and as Jessica took in some of the sights of her sister's upbringing she could appreciate her foibles a little better. Surveying the surrounding landscape brought tears to Jessica's eyes as she remembered her own comparatively happy childhood and carefree safety in Seahouses. A town: where she was allowed to grow up leisurely and securely without gang warfare; or the alcohol, sex and drugs peer pressures being an everyday occurrence. But that was at a price as she recalled her own abuse and then the tears could no longer be held back and ran freely.

They pulled up outside The Towers, and Emma, misunderstanding, looked across and gasped, "Don't cry, Jess, it wasn't all bad. There were good times too." Jessica just gave a shrug, which made her sister none the wiser as she feverishly searched for the key to the main entrance. Memories flooded back as Emma bounced through the open front door and took the steps two at a time.

She had been away for two or three weeks but in a strange way still she felt the affinity of home, such as it was. She reached her flat door and heaved a sigh of relief as she punched in the code 1320, whilst reminiscing where that had come from; a music track title by Megadeth as she recalled, a group her fella at the time, had a penchant for. 'The door being still locked is a good sign, let's hope the wardrobe doors are still intact too?' she thought with a mild panic running through her. She struggled to open the door wide as an accumulation of post, junk mail and freesheets were jamming its movement. Quickly sifting through, she held on to what looked to her important, although if truth be known, she could never tell the difference between actual post and junk mail and so left the majority in a neat pile, stacked behind the door with a view to throwing it away later.

She entered the bedroom to: clothes discarded and struggling to reach the wash basket; a towel thrown over the edge of the bed and dirty underwear still in the specific spot from where they had been stepped out of. Her panic had proved in vain as with relief she realised that the bedroom was in exactly the same state as she had left it; 'Well I did leave in a bit of a hurry,' she thought in her own defence as she tidied around to a limited degree before opening the wardrobe and grabbing her passport and cash. She toyed with the idea of taking her drug paraphernalia, now residing back in its regular spot after having been retrieved from Jonnie's flat, but thought better of it. 'She might be happy with my hard earned, ill gotten cash but Jessica's definitely not going to let me get away with taking this lot on the trip!' she thought resignedly.

Coming back out through the tower block's entrance door, Emma, imitating a lottery winner, cheerily waved both items in the air in disbelief, by way of acknowledgment that her precious items had still been there. Jessica immediately ordered her back into the car so as not to draw any more attention to herself, and to put a stop to her freely advertising a large bundle of cash by waving it around above her head.

Once on the move again Jessica said, "Right, stage two. In to Edinburgh for a quick breakfast, then I need cash and we need mobiles," as they retraced their steps to the A71 with a view to heading north-east into the city centre. Whilst driving along she pulled out a list for Emma to study. On it there were six mobile phone shops all within a half-mile radius of Princes Street and Jessica knew that finding ATM's for cash withdrawals would not be too difficult in that vicinity, either.

She contemplated whether or not the use of debit and credit cards would leave her pursuers with an identity trail but believed that she had no option as their liquid cash would dry up all too soon, even allowing for Emma's windfall. With it still being early in the day they were able to find a street-parking bay quite easily and then walked along Princes Street, passing The Balmoral on their way to breakfast. There, they narrowly avoided a collision with a well built, youngish looking man as he descended the steps from the hotel and heard his, "Mi scusi signorina," apology as he abruptly swerved to avoid them. The two girls glanced back with a slight nervous giggle by way of acknowledging his apology.

11.30am, money drawn out and purchases bought. The girls left the City and were skirting around Holyrood Park on the A1 heading south, unaware that less than twelve hours earlier their would-be hunters had past the exact same point going in the opposite direction. Jessica now wearing her business head began to relay her plan of action to Emma and to check that they had carried out all the necessary purchases and transactions in Edinburgh. Transactions, which had proved very time consuming and so taken longer than anticipated due to the requirement of the annoyingly lengthy paperwork. Emma had a different head on. She knew that she was in for a long journey and so intended to keep the atmosphere light for as long as possible. She started with the near accident outside The Balmoral. " 'Scusi Signorina,' wasa he a youra kinda fella? He a certainly hada youra colouring, signorina."

"I a don't a ..... You've got me doing it now. I admit he did have a Mediterranean look about him but I was concentrating more on not being rugby tackled than on how attractive he was. And I make it a rule not to tangle on first dates," she chortled. "Anyway, stop changing the subject; we need to firm up a plan of action by the time we get to Dover. Did you get any texts back from Jonnie or Jeremy?"

"No, and I don't expect any. You told me to change the SIM card."

"You did still keep it though, didn't you? So just switch it back over so that we know what we've left behind us." Emma did as she was bid and sat quietly, feeling a bit stupid for jumping the gun, but she was adamant that Jessica had given her the impression that she should switch the card, straightaway. Jessica decided that she would have to undertake all the forward planning on her own and basically direct Emma as to what she had to do. Perhaps there had been a misunderstanding on the SIM card changeover and Jessica had certainly wanted it done before they reached the A59 turnoff for York, as after that point she hoped anyone tracking them would be then in a quandary as to whether or not they were headed east for Hull or south for Dover.

*

Excitement had turned to confusion, despondency and panic when Jonnie received the early morning text from Emma. He had not had any communication with her for over two weeks and had almost given up on any chance of their fledgling romance being rekindled. The text read 'Hi J Don't tink it iz sAf 2 go n 2 wrk DIS week, rng n 7k. Jeremy thinks dat SOME1 bad mite wnt 2 git n tuch w us & he strongly advises agAnst U CN dem. It mite evN b dangerous. Lol Em.' Jonnie being text literate, read it as 'Hi J Don't think it is safe to go in to work this week, ring in sick. Jeremy thinks that someone bad might want to get in touch with us and he strongly advises against you seeing them. It might even be dangerous. Lol Em.' He began to text back but thought better of it as there was no hint in Emma's text whatsoever of any light still burning for him. Instead he decided to take the message seriously and contact work to say he would be late and then ring again later in the morning to check how the land lay.

*

He walked through the front doors of Ladywell House, in between Jonnie's two phone calls. He purported to be a Metropolitan police officer from Scotland Yard 'Cold Cases' Unit and was following up on the search engine incident of a 'Luigi Agosti', which had occurred some three weeks previously. The receptionist knew all about the case as it had turned Jonnie into a minor celebrity within the office, especially when it became linked to the attempted murder of his recent girlfriend by the Scottish Borders' serial killer. The fraudulent officer asked to see the gentleman concerned and was told within moments that he had not yet arrived, in fact he had rung in to say he would be late. Babyface, aka the fraudulent officer then asked, "Could you give me confirmation of the gentleman's name so that I can ensure that it agrees with my records?"

"Yes sure thing, Sir. His name's Jonnie Raey."

"Have you got his mobile number handy? I'll bet it's a number you know personally? What, a pretty girl like you, Felicity, you probably have all the eligible gents' numbers, don't you?" said the fraudulent officer glancing at her identity tag and inferring that Jonnie and her might be a little more than work colleagues.

Felicity the receptionist blushed slightly at both the fact that she'd been found out for having both Jonnie's and other colleagues' personal numbers and at being flattered too, so she promptly searched for his number and handed it over without any police pressure being applied, whatsoever.

"I think that's about all I'll be needing at the moment. There's nothing else you'd like to add?" Babyface was on a roll and thought he might be able to flirt Jonnie's address out of Felicity too, but she unexpectedly gave him an even more valuable nugget of information.

"Well, there was a very smart gentleman in on Friday who met up with Jonnie. He said he was a solicitor but looked too posh for that, very upper class, to me anyway. He left me his card though, for if I ever needed any help in that department, you know. Is he on the wrong side? I thought he might be too good to be true. Shall I give you his card and be done with it?"

"You are a bright girl, Felicity. I think you're wasted here. Yes, hand over the card and we'll get this chap checked out. Might turn out to be a rogue, you never know with those toff types? Anyway, you've been a great help and I'll make sure that you get a mention in Scotland Yard's files when the case is concluded." With that, Babyface pocketed the card, shook Felicity warmly by the hand, gave her a mischievous wink and left Ladywell House with the first beam he'd had on his face for two days. Ollie was shocked on seeing him approach the car in such a jovial mood and with not a laughter line to be seen anywhere, so true was he to his name.

"Like taking candy from a baby. She was literally putty in my hands and if I went in for that sort of girl then she was there for the taking. I don't know if it was my natural good looks or whether it was that police power thing. But, and this is the honest truth, I didn't show her any identity at all and she just opened up, like a daffodil turning towards the sun. Let's hope it carries on being this easy?" Now however, his joviality turned to puzzlement. He had the dilemma of: staying around Edinburgh on the off chance that Jonnie would appear from wherever he had hidden; or travelling north to Aberdeen, on the hunt for a solicitor.

*

Emma had sent a very similar message to Jeremy as the one to Jonnie and that one got no response either. Jeremy knew how to open text messages but he had refused on principle to learn how to answer them. His text speak was non-existent, so that usually counted as to the reason for his non-reply. The one from Emma had read 'Hi J We tink dat SOME1 c%d b trackN our movements. We've told Jonnie 2 b careful & advise U d sAm. dey mite evN b dangerous. Lol Em xx.' Jeremy opened the message whilst waiting at a set of traffic lights, saw it was from Emma but as the lights changed he accidentally pressed delete instead of the accelerator and this before even trying to read it. But in all fairness he would have needed it translating into English in order to understand the meaning, anyway. So Jeremy travelled on, oblivious to the fact that anything was amiss, other than the fact that it was Monday morning, which tends to be the usual stumbling block for the vast majority of the British workforce.

He spent the morning in prearranged meetings with one existing and one new client and with the intention of finishing around 3pm. That was until Rachel his secretary informed him that she had booked in an appointment with a prospective client for 2.30pm to which his glum expression led her to say cheerily, "A Mr Nelson, who wishes to discuss the ramifications of making a will. I hope that's OK. You have asked me on more than one occasion to use my own initiative. And your diary is clear."

Mr Longthorne replied, "No, Rachel you are quite correct. Good job. Any business is welcome in this day and age. It's just that with the drive on Saturday there were a few things I needed to sort over the weekend and consequently I was hoping to finish early today. In fact, I was going to let you go before time, too. So after you've shown in, Mr Nelson, was it? After you've shown Mr Nelson into my office you are then excused for the rest of the day. If I decide we're having a drink, I'll sort it. OK?" Rachel had been delighted with that and began ruminating on what she could do with an extra two to two and half hours of free time. Jeremy was calculating how quick he could get through the preliminaries of advising someone on making a will without appearing rude or doing the law profession a disservice.

All parties concerned were happy with how the afternoon began to pan out. The client had turned up at 2.30pm prompt at Jeremy's Union Street offices, so he himself did not now feel that the whole afternoon would be a write off. Rachel had organised to be picked up by a friend, with the intention of visiting a shopping centre, and so once Mr Nelson was ensconced in Mr Longthorne's office she was free to go. The only person not happy was Babyface's accomplice as he remained outside and watched a female leave, via the same door through which Babyface had entered, and get in to a black Fiat Bravo, which had just pulled up. He was confused, as he had been ordered not to let anyone leave or enter the offices once he had been given the signal. But he hadn't been given the signal as yet, not until two double rings on his mobile with a five second gap between; in fact, just like he was listening to now. Babyface had explained quite clearly what he intended to do on entering and it mainly consisted of checking out, who else was on the premises. He would ask to be directed to the bathroom so that he could reccy the layout of the offices and once he knew the body count he could quickly calculate the chances of overpowering them. When he realised it was only Jeremy and the receptionist he made the signal call. Ollie knew it was too late, as the bird had flown, but Babyface didn't. He calmly returned to Jeremy's office on the presumption that the building was now secured.

As he sat back down the solicitor smiled, took out his note pad and Mont Blanc pen and said by way of introduction, "Right Sir, I'm correct in assuming you wish to make a will. Could I have the full name?"

Babyface looked Jeremy straight in the eyes and coolly replied, "Mr Jeremy Longthorne," as more of a question than a statement.

Jeremy looked back, totally confused, with that name being the last one that he expected to hear. Flabbergasted, he searched for the right question to ask but Babyface beat him to it. "Yes, Mr Longthorne, you might well be confused. If you haven't already made a will of your own now is the time to think about it." He said as he held his captive forcibly to the chair and rang for his accomplice to help with the next stage in the proceedings.

Ollie came in looking a little sheepish, glanced at Babyface and said worriedly, "There was a woman. She went out before I got your signal, Baby.... Eh, boss." Babyface glowered and used the same time to formulate a new plan, seeing that it would not now be possible to torture and/or kill Jeremy and any of his colleagues in situ. And the receptionist was one witness too many, so it would have to appear that the meeting ran smoothly and that Mr Longthorne suffered some kind of mishap once he had left the premises for the day.

Babyface took advantage of the half hour originally designated for the will advice to explain their reason for the visit, which Jeremy had already surmised, and now wholeheartedly regretted not reading Emma's text.

Having checked that the coast was clear Ollie bundled a hand-bound Jeremy in to the back of his own BMW with Babyface sliding behind the wheel. Babyface turned to Jeremy and asked, "Do you live alone?" Jeremy nodded in the affirmative. "Good, I'll set off and you can give directions." The drive took less than 15 minutes, taking them west on the A9013, branching off on to the B9077, Great Southern Road and stopping just before Duthie Park, with Ollie following behind in their own car. He drove past the house and parked up discreetly 100 metres further along the road. By the time he had returned to the BMW carrying a satchel, Babyface had untied Jeremy's hands and was helping out of the back as if the latter had had too much to drink. Both men came together and approached the impressive looking granite terraced house, nursing Jeremy firstly along the path and then up the steps leading to his own front door and then assisted with its opening.

Once inside the niceties stopped. Jeremy was bound securely to a carver chair in the dining room situated at the back of the house, with views overlooking the well-tended garden; stocked with fruit trees, shrubs, bushes and an immaculate lawn. Babyface presumed that the greenery would absorb some of the noise from this location and at least it would give them a pleasant aspect from which to operate; but just to make doubly sure he flicked on the TV in the lounge, ensuring that the volume would work to his advantage. He returned, switched on the closest available floor lamp and directed it into Jeremy's eyes by way of intimidation. Then sat opposite his proposed victim and began explaining how the interview would proceed, whilst Ollie opened up the satchel and took out two sterile polythene bags.

"Jeremy, we need to extract some information from you and we are considering doing it in one of two ways; sadly for you in either case the end result will be the same. But, and it is a big but, if you cooperate you don't have to suffer. My accomplice here..." at this he nodded to his left by way of introduction... "He's the bad cop and I'm the good one. So we'll show you how it works as we go along, you'll pick it up soon enough. And if we don't get what we want we'll both have to end up being bad cops." By this point Ollie had covered the dining table with a polythene sheet and begun to place on it various threatening looking pieces of hardware.

Both visitors then climbed into forensic type overalls and overshoes as confirmation that they meant business. Jeremy, a former public school boy, rugby player (albeit not through enjoyment) and TA Sergeant retired, understood the seriousness of the situation but also knew where his loyalties lay; these being principally in withholding clients' confidences and ensuring a dear friend's final wish was carried out to the letter. Both of his best friends had died to preserve the identity of their two children, so Jeremy knew that he would suffer pain and that his end and the game end were tantamount to be one and the same thing. "First question. You received a tip off from Scotland Yard that a search had been instigated for a 'Luigi Agosti', on the Internet. Correct?" Jeremy nodded.

"Good, good. Second, on whose behalf are you working?"

Jeremy thought for a few moments and could not see any reason why he should not answer this question either. "It is on behalf of Luigi Agosti."

Babyface looked annoyed at this answer but thought that there might be some truth in it and so replied calmly, "Don't be witty, Jeremy. The guy's been dead for over thirty years. We want to know who's interested in him now. Preferably someone that is still living?" Jeremy shook his head to indicate that he would not answer. He then clenched his teeth together as Ollie hit him about the head with a leather truncheon. "Enough," commanded Babyface. "I don't think we'll have time to be constantly bringing him round. OK Jeremy, now you know we mean business. I'm still waiting for an answer to the last question? Again the victim gave a shake of the head and so Babyface looked at Ollie and advised, "I think the same as we gave the bent copper."

He dutifully complied by picking up the chisel and hammer and handing them to Babyface, and then proceeded to firmly hold Jeremy's mouth open. As the chisel approached, Jeremy pulled his head back and grimaced against the expectant pain but the accomplice held him more tightly as his front teeth, firstly felt a cold chisel and secondly a blow, that instantly made him scream out. A surgical gloved hand muffled the majority of the noise and came away with blood mixed with mucus and fragments of the two front teeth. Ollie went into the kitchen to rinse his hands and brought back a bowl of water to throw over the now unconscious victim in the hope of reviving him more quickly.

Babyface shook his head at his accomplice, lifted one of Jeremy's eyelids and said authoratively, "Smelling salts will do the trick." Unfortunately for Jeremy they did, as once they were placed under his nose he became aware of his surroundings with a start. At first, he was unsure what was happening but then the pain shot though him and he heard a voice say, "You are a brave chap, Jeremy. But we won't stop until we have some answers, so you understand what that means? I'll ask you again, as your brain might be a little bit scrambled after that shock. Who do you know that is interested in Luigi Agosti?"

As Jeremy searched his mind for a suitable reply, he thought he heard Roy Orbison singing 'Only the Lonely'; and realised it was his mobile. This reinforced his determination not to answer, being that the ring tone had not been chosen at random. The lyrics 'There goes my baby, there goes my heart' had been his hidden mantra, his way of dealing with his best friend, Luigi marrying his other best friend, Laura; the girl he had secretly loved. A mantra, that no one else ever knew about, and which was now about to die with him. He remained lucid enough to appreciate the irony that even with having no next of kin, the recent circumstances had prompted him to make a will himself. And now he was going to die at the hands of someone else, who duplicitously requested that self-same service. His mind acknowledged that it had been just one element of the work he had undertaken in the furtherance of justice for his clients; although generally with himself never knowingly being placed in danger. But now with this Pandora's box having been opened, there was only ever going to be one outcome.

So it was likely to transpire that the close friends of years ago who helped Jeremy to set up and prosper so successfully in his solicitor's practice were now to be instrumental in bringing it all crashing down. With the double irony that the very girls, to whom he had delivered the package, would now become the sole beneficiaries of his very own will, too. A will he had put off making until he was sure that they were alive and well, but a will now in place; being that he had no other next of kin and thus his only tie with extended family was his tie of godparent to Emma through his all too brief personal and business relationship of 12 years with their parents: his dear departed friends. He had always known they had swum in murky waters but the depth of the murkiness was only now hitting home; and his only remaining wish was that he could metaphorically drown without swimming at all, and so hasten the inevitable.

Babyface took his silence to mean belligerence and frankly, bloody-mindedness. "Jeremy, old chap. I'm losing patience and now you're turning both of us into bad cops. Why can't you just give us a name?" he asked as he waved two longish flat-headed nails and a hammer in front of the victim. As he twisted one of the nails between finger and thumb, he threatened, "I've got one of these for each hand. They are four inches long, so to be fair to you I'll give you four seconds for each hand, a second per inch; before I hammer them all the way in and down through to the chair arms." Jeremy struggled helplessly to move his bound arms and hands away from the danger zone but then slumped forward and just sat resigned to his fate, making a constant whistling through his damaged teeth. He tried to blank out the pain in his mind of the cold air jangling at his nerve ends as he greedily sucked in the air; but still no words of betrayal escaped from his damaged lips. He heard a scream and realised his first four seconds had expired and the nail had passed straight through his right hand and splintered the chair arm with its force. Again, he passed out and was brought round with either the smelling salts or 'Only the Lonely', or both. He was delirious with the throbbing pain in his hand yet lucid enough to know he had four seconds before the next strike.

But it never came; instead Babyface looked at him with a concerned expression and wiped away the blood that was still dribbling from Jeremy's swollen mouth as his ashen face grimaced in defiance at the next expectant blow. Babyface said in a controlled voice, "Jeremy, you don't have to take anymore. You've been brave, far braver than some we've dealt with. But I've got to say that we've never yet had one who didn't talk in the end. Are you sure you want to continue with this pain?" He knew this to be a white lie, which was presented somewhat tongue-in-cheek, as there had been a few of his own kind who had been true to their Omerta code.

Jeremy did not say a word in response, or even shrug to acknowledge his understanding of what had been said, as both were too painful to undertake. He just remained slumped in his dining chair silently praying for the end and for the strength needed to get there. And as if to give Jeremy a respite, Babyface handed the other nail and hammer to Ollie and said, "Do the honours." The accomplice duly did by driving the nail in to the victim's other hand and breaking Jeremy's knuckles in the process with the force of the blow. He did not scream this time, or thought he had not as nausea and then blackness clouded his brain. Whilst he was unconscious, Babyface uncovered his watch and commented, "Only time for one more try and then we'll have to finish him. He's a stubborn bastard."

"Yeh, Boss. Harder men have cracked by now. All credit to him," replied Ollie.

"Mm. I'd class him as one of the hardest. You wouldn't think so to look at him, but he can sure take his share of pain. Seems a shame to finish him off after all he's been through."

*

"I hope he's alright, too? But you've made two calls without success and now we're approaching the A59, so you're going to have to change your SIM again. Call me paranoid, but I don't want us to be leaving any kind of trail, whether real or imaginary, be it cyber space or physical, and talking about physical my gut feeling definitely tells me that all is not well," said Jessica massaging her stomach.

"What; you really think that Jeremy might be in danger? I hope it's not because of us?" replied Emma innocently.

"Of course, it's because of us. You heard what he said; he's been looking after that stuff from Mum and Dad for over thirty years, and spent the last twelve years of those looking for us. So this wild goose chase has got to have some value to someone even if it turns out not to be us. Right A59 coming up, SIM card out."

*

The nauseous smell brought Jeremy round with a jerk of his head as both his heart rate increased and his breathing became faster. He was in so much pain in so many places that his brain could not compute which was the worst. And when he decided on a particular spot, the other pains mercifully seemed to reduce in severity to a lesser degree. Babyface tapped him almost gently on the face and studied him closely as if he was his protégé going into the final round of a boxing match.

"Jeremy, Jeremy. Glad you're still with us. You've taken quite a beating and we don't want to see you in any more pain. This can all be over if you'll just give us the name. You do understand that this is purely business, nothing personal like. But as my colleague here reports to me I've got to report to my boss, and so on. They're not going to be happy further up the line if I can't even get a squeak out of you. What sort of an interrogator does it make me out to be? So do us all a favour. Your bacon's already cooked but perhaps you can yet save mine. Just give us a name?"

By the end of this pep talk Babyface was almost pleading for some answer. But it was not the one he wanted. Jeremy just about managed to hold his head straight, look into the assailant's eyes, the one who had said he was the good cop but who in reality had caused him far more pain than the other one, and then shook his head. His eyes remained in a steady stare and his crooked mouth faintly smiled, knowing that the pain would soon be over, even though it was at present rampaging through his head and body.

Babyface was the first to break off and look away; he turned to the dining cum instrument table looking for his next 'lever' but picked up the revolver with the silencer instead. Turning round slowly with the gun hidden behind his back he approached Jeremy and calmly drew the point of the silencer up to his forehead and pulled the trigger. It only took a split second for the puff of the bullet, followed by the jolt of Jeremy's head and spurt of blood and bone to bring an end to his misery, an end that he had been praying for as he feared he might have broken down and revealed the names of those two innocent girls. Two girls, whom he knew as tiny babies and who belonged to his first, and most trustworthy, best friends. Two girls, who unbeknownst to him had between them killed six people: six more than Jeremy. But as far as he was concerned their parents' wishes had been carried out to the letter and their secret was now safe, it would die with him.

Ollie beginning to collect up their armoury made so bold as to say, "What do we do now Boss? We're not going to get any name now, are we?"

Babyface turned and replied, "He didn't deserve any less. People need a bit of dignity in death, especially if they've put up a respectable fight. And you can't say this guy didn't do that?" He then shrugged himself out of his morose demeanour and finished with, "Right, back to Edinburgh. We're going to have to track down this Jonnie guy now. We'll see what he wanted in the first place with this infamous Luigi Agosti."

Carefully, the two remaining men disrobed from their 'forensics' outer clothing and placed it securely in the sterile bags from which it had originated. Babyface switched on the wall lights so as to have a good look around the room to ensure that they had left nothing incriminating behind and glanced at the only other witness to the proceedings. A large gilt framed print of The Laughing Cavalier, hanging pride of place on the end wall; he had overseen their handiwork and not smiled one jot, let alone laughed at the end result. Babyface still could not get a tune out of his head and asked of Ollie, "Where was that Elvis song coming from?"

"That wasn't Elvis, Boss. It was Roy Orbison. It sounded to come from over there by the dresser." Both men hunted around for the source, which turned out to be a mobile that Ollie pulled out of Jeremy's overcoat. There you go Boss."

"You hang on to it; you're good with technology and that social media stuff and all that. Check out who has been trying to get in touch with him recently."

And just as they had arrived at his door looking like two friends helping another slightly inebriated friend; they left as no more than two salesmen canvassing door-to-door. The sort of sombre suited unwelcome visitors most neighbours go out of their way to avoid and so invariably pretend to be not at home. Jeremy remained nailed to his chair waiting patiently for a concerned associate or one of his very few extended friends or any of those non-intrusive neighbours to suddenly question his whereabouts.

CHAPTER FIVE

SpiyWeB

SpiyWeB: a double, double entendre: in one respect, paying homage to the humble industrious spider, symbolised by its endless determination to entrap prey through continually enlarging and expanding its webbed home territory; and in another, epitomising man's constant need and desire to spy on fellow man, and now even more dramatically too, through possibly the greatest achievement of the 20th Century, the World Wide Web, the ultimate tool.

SpiyWeB, fronted by Prometheus Conglomerates is basically an intelligence-gathering network. Its strapline 'You know, We know' succinctly indicates what importance is placed on specific knowledge and information. Although not necessarily as all-encompassing as the World Wide Web it can be certainly as revealing, once the right buttons have been pressed; particularly where otherwise secure private data is concerned.

Its creation had taken a number of years to finesse but now SpiyWeB mapped and encompassed the globe. Its cumbersome manual systems having been converted over to cyber technology enables it to spread laterally across all utilities' companies as well as large organisations, specifically those that embrace the power to influence and affect individual countries' policies through lobbying at the highest government levels. This influence then extends vertically in order to facilitate its attachment to all levels of management, as high as chief executive officers and even non-executive directors.

A fountain of knowledge: **SpiyWeB**'s *growth has been exponential since the inception of the World Wide Web itself. It stands as the antithesis of all governments' secret information gathering bodies: CIA, Mossad, SVR – the former KGB, MI. Is apolitical to and totally independent of: the Mafia, Camorra or any other like-minded organisations' influences.*

Each cell or clan member body pays an annual usage fee plus a percentage of profits per annum. The fee structure dictates the level of data that can be accessed and is calculated based on three base prerequisites. One: size of the cell/clan in relation to its penetration within its country of occupation. Two: country's GDP equated to proportion of the overall global economy. Three: the necessity or otherwise to tap into cross-border information. The result of any or all of the above calculations is known as the 'operating ratio'. Being a member on any of the three levels allows for approved right of use to all past data and present intel search facilities across the designated parameters, even without live input from **SpiyWeB** *employees.*

Prometheus Conglomerates came in to being in the early 1980's and slowly built its knowledge and powerbase by gathering and storing hard copy records and information, manually collected by its own dedicated staff. This all changed in 1989, when Tim Berners-Lee, whilst on his second sojourn at CERN, the largest Internet node in Europe, saw an opportunity to join hypertext with the Internet: by what he stated as a simple task of 'taking the hypertext idea and connecting it to the Transmission Control Protocol and domain name system'. A procedure never previously considered or attempted. The rest became history and **SpiyWeB** *flourished as a result of this innovation, as if what had gone before was just in preparation for the unstoppable technological revolution.*

So the true concept of **SpiyWeB** *came in to its own with* *the dawning of cyberspace itself; its position within a specific genre quickly enabled it to achieve top spot in that field, and profit beyond its wildest dreams along with the millions of other beneficiaries that the Internet explosion spawned; thus producing hard cash in quantities of billions upon billions, and in whatever currency you'd care to mention.*

But this Web is different, too. To explain this, its creators use the analogy of: 'The Universe being the Web with each star in every constellation representing a satellite. A satellite, that gathers and stores all available information, for the planets to access at a pre-agreed cost. The planets, representing countries, and moons symbolising organisations within countries who buy information, on a needs must basis, information which is relevant to their status, growth and continued success and power'. The end result can be internecine warfare, fought by two sides, which basically represent the two faces of the same coin warring amongst themselves; it may be that they are just tossing up a cent, rather than a euro, or a euro rather than a krugerrand, dependent on where on the planet they call home. However, it is more generally the case that the obverse of the coin is opposition in the guise of: the CIA; Mossad; SIS (MI6); SVR or any of the other native secret intelligence organisations operating in those respective countries.

And as with all businesses, in its desire to sustain ever increasing infrastructure growth and thus ensure its own continued expansion, commercial sense dictates that SpiyWeB must gather in this information at a cheaper rate than it sells it on. Hence, each member body pays their fixed fee plus 2% of nett profit annually, guaranteeing that the cost is always pro rata to their ability to pay. In return for this agreement, SpiyWeB remains totally unbiased, independent and honour-bound to take no part in the adjudication on, and furtherance or prevention of, conflicts of interest between member parties. To this end, SpiyWeB retains total secrecy over the services it offers and therefore never addresses

90

individuals of any cell or clan member by name, but rather by their ID number. And in order to remain true to its ethos all employees' of **SpiyWeB** have their actions and conversations constantly recorded and monitored, both digitally and personally with each member of staff being scrutinised and rotated to a different strand of the **SpiyWeB** network every four weeks.

We have already ascertained that an 'accomplice' is two ability level grades below that of an 'assailant', even though the primary prerequisite qualities of both positions are to be particularly ruthless and be prepared to kill. For every assignment, the operatives are paired up randomly, one from each grade, with the understanding that for continuity they follow through each mission to its conclusion or until such a time as one or both are put out of action by either capture or finitely by death. In order to be easily identified by **SpiyWeB**, the respective member clan issues all employees with a member/country/employee coding: the one for Babyface being C/IT/703: the 'C' referencing Camorra and 'IT', Italy. This reference is then used at all times by the retrievers and their superiors; should the employee wish to use a pseudonym too, then that is entered against their coding at the time of recruitment. C/IT/703 had chosen Babyface Nelson, whilst his present accomplice had simply wished to be known as Ollie with a code of C/UK/1668.

*

In the psychometric tests, 'Decision making skills' had always come out at above average for Jonnie. Although this had not necessarily improved his chances of advancement within his working environment it had proved of good value in his personal life. However, this skill at present had failed him. He had already rung in to the office to take a 'duvet' morning and was uncertain of what to do next. Ever since receiving the text from Emma, indecision coursed through his brain. He had hoped the text would be reconciliation but it turned out to be the exact opposite, and added to that was the double whammy of a little concern and a soupçon of fear for his safety.

He knew Emma revolved around a sphere of drugs and nocturnal activity, which generally invited violence of sorts but when he weighed up his desire for her against his common sense to stay clear, his decision-making met a brick wall. It was the same with the text. He could not stay away from work forever and if someone was allegedly trying to find him, then how long would that someone look, before losing patience and drifting off to hassle somebody else? The whole scenario was making him jittery and that too contributed to his inability to think clearly and lucidly.

Since receiving the text he had tried a couple of times to get hold of Jeremy Longthorne, as he felt that with him being a solicitor he would have experience of what to do in these situations, but each time he had just been patched through to voice mail. He had even contemplated ringing Emma but then thought that she would see it as a sign of weakness and he did not want that, nor to appear desperate in trying to win her back either. So indecision it remained, and as he resigned himself to that idiosyncrasy, until that is the decision itself was made for him. His phone rang, making him jump and nervously look behind him even though he knew he was the only person in the flat.

"Hi, Jonnie. Are you OK? I keep getting asked if you're coming in later, what with you suddenly taking this morning off? Are you sick? People are concerned? Have you been on the booze? I had a few too many the other..."

"Felicity. Hi. I'm OK but I can't decide what to do for the best. I've had some worrying news, which I'm trying to get my head around. I just needed to talk to someone about it but they're not there," replied Jonnie cutting Felicity off before she could get too strong a grip on the conversation.

"Is it something the police said to you?"

"What police? Why would they want to talk to me?"

Felicity responded with a little guilt-edge to her voice, "Well, a policeman from Scotland Yard was looking for you about that 'Acosta, no that's the coffee shop. ... Agosta... Agosti bloke; the one you'd been looking up on the Internet. I thought he might end up ringing you, especially with me giving him your phone number, and all."

"What do you mean 'and all'? What else have you given him?"

"Well, just your name. Have I done something wrong? It was the police. Scotland Yard, no less. That big police station in London, the one with the revolving sign, I think!"

"No Felicity, you've haven't done anything wrong. As long as you didn't give him my address? But you could have rung me a bit sooner to let me know about him."

"No, I didn't give him your address and it was only with you suddenly taking the morning off and people here asking me what was going on that I remembered about that police chap. Anyway, are you coming in or shall I just say that you'll be in touch with your supervisor when you know what you're doing?"

Jonnie did not hear that last couple of sentences as his brain was whirring with the new information it had just begun to process. He just stared out of the window expecting cars with flashing lights to surround his flat and escort him off to who knows where. He began to fantasise that he would be held for questioning, and would remain strong and stubborn under interrogation and not give up any of the secrets he knew. What secrets? And whilst he was considering this the other half of his brain was formulating the reality of the situation. Both versions mirrored each other but in one of the options it was not the police doing the interrogating but someone posing as the police. Someone to be worried about and who, inevitably, might want to track down Emma. Someone who could be dangerous, just as Emma's text had said; and then the interrogation scenario and the withholding of his secrets did not seem quite so gung ho. It was all beginning to fit into place and Jonnie was not in the least bit happy about it. The only saving grace was that his decision-making skill had returned and it said quite categorically, 'don't go into work'. It also said, 'lie low for a while'; but he chose to interpret that as meaning stay at home for a few days as opposed to the extreme of disappearing. After all, he thought, 'Felicity didn't give them my address.'

*

Pulling off at Ferrybridge Services brought immeasurable relief. Jessica had been driving for over 220 miles and both her and the car needed a rest. Emma was all for eating in the restaurant but time was against them as Jessica had an inert need to keep moving so that the distance between her and Edinburgh continued to grow and quickly. Just a short stop then for the toilet; sandwiches, snacks and drinks; refuel plus a stretch of the legs and then they would continue south. The weather reflected her mood, both in its darkness from the heavy cloudburst and its gloomy ambience with the spray being thrown up by the huge articulated lorries, all-adding to the stress and strain of driving. And now that their previous contacts were disconnected, they could only resort to the radio and Jessica's selection of CDs, for news updates and personal entertainment. Once back on the road, Jessica tried to brighten up by saying, "At least half way to London now. If this rain eased we would make better time, although this section of the A1 tends to be fairly congested anyway."

She tailed off realising that she had not made either of them feel any better, least of all herself, so felt that she must continue with, "M, sorry I didn't let you have a proper meal back there but we've got to keep moving, you do understand that, don't you? I want to be in Dover by early tomorrow, so that we can catch the first ferry across to Calais. We'll be able to slow down a bit then. Promise."

Emma just continued nodding and chewing on her Haribos whilst plugged in to her iPod world, leaving Jessica unsure as to whether her pep talk had hit the spot or not. The rain eased and the sky brightened so she began to relax more and increase her speed back up to 70mph, but even then there were considerably more vehicles doing the overtaking than being overtaken. Her boredom level increased with every mile they covered, but she knew that the further south they travelled the more necessary it became for her to formulate a sound plan. And if nothing else the long drawn out miles gave her considerable time to contemplate just that.

*

"OK boss, it's sorted. Do you want to know what I've found?"

"Of course I do, you moron. I wouldn't have given it to you otherwise!" replied Babyface almost coming to grief under the back of a slow moving lorry as he momentarily took his eyes off the road to berate his accomplice.

"Right. Text wise, there are two or three in the 'inbox' but they all look to be from the same number, so could be the office? Nothing in the 'outbox'," commentated Ollie as he pressed various buttons. "Incoming calls. There are a few numbers here. And I think one is the same number as the one you've been given for that Jonnie guy. In fact he's rung a couple of times, both am and pm. Then there's another number that rang twice, too, which I don't recognise. No messages left from either number. Outgoing, he rang a number on Friday. Interestingly, that's the same number as the one who has rung him back twice today, but apart from that, nothing else. This guy was either very tidy or he was a bit of a 'Billy no mates'."

"So our Jeremy and Jonnie have already been communicating, have they? Has *SpiyWeB* got anywhere with Jonnie Raey's mobile records? Chase them up and see if there's anything we can be doing whilst we're looking for him in person."

With this resource behind them it was no surprise to Babyface that a specific mobile number would unearth not only the owner's address but that person's recent usage history could be easily retrieved as well. The analyst doing the retrieving even went so far as to highlight the most likely 'in box' text messages/calls that Babyface might be interested in and identified the senders plus supplied their addresses too.

Ollie selected the print mode on his iPhone and pressed 'print'. Information was transferred via the portable eprinter on to several sheets of A4 paper, which represented, to all intents and purposes, a family tree. Jonnie Raey's phone number had been the prime search, and so was subsequently split in to various sub headings for both incoming and outgoing texts/calls. The important numbers from these were highlighted in bold and these again were split off into further sub headings.

Eventually Ollie would be in a position to analyse what communication Jonnie had been undertaking and with whom. Babyface could not contain his excitement and pulled into a lay-by. He sent his colleague off to the parked-up snack kiosk so that they could then both sit in comfort as they digested the information in tandem with their square sausage sandwiches, and formulated the next stage of their plan. Fortunately for both men, brute force was not their only skill. Babyface was good at management as well as assimilating and adapting to ever changing situations, whilst his accomplice had a sound knowledge and keen interest in technology. So both looked at the information greedily, identifying and following the significant key links and ignoring the ones they perceived as red herrings or dead ends.

"Looking at this Boss, I'd say we've got another night in the car; unless you want me to search for a discreet B&B?"

Babyface replied, "As much as I'd love a soft bed and a good sleep, I have to agree with you that it'll come down to the car. We don't want to leave too many clues around indicating our presence, especially as we've already got one murder to our names in this neck of the woods, and there could be more, before we're done. So a low profile it is." With that they went back to studying the text messages and rows of numerals, which were now and again interspersed with a name and an address. "What do you think so far?" Babyface enquired.

"Well, we've got this warning text message from someone signing off as Em. According to the number, our retriever tells us that her name is Emma Flynn. So thinking backwards we can presume that she's probably the one who for some reason was interested in finding out information about Luigi Agosti and so co-opts this Jonnie in to helping her to find it. He, innocently, triggers off the contact at Scotland Yard, whom we now know was playing it both ways. He tells Jeremy about Jonnie or at least about the location from where Jonnie initiated the Luigi request, and they end up communicating. Jeremy now has the identity of the person who really wants to know about Agosti, that being the girl, Emma. So he rings her on Friday and whatever he told her must have been important enough and secretive enough for him to die over it. And that's as far as I've got. Funnily enough though, according to *SpiyWeB*, our Jeremy had deleted a similar warning text message as that which Jonnie received, again from the Emma number. And with the available technology, *SpiyWeB* has been able to retrieve this with it being obviously still on the provider's hard drive. Can't really understand why he deleted it, rather than acting on it?"

"Yes, good logic. I can follow your reasoning all the way. But I don't see what spooked this Emma or why she thought someone was tracking her in the first place? And like you say, Jeremy will rue the day he didn't act on the text, that would be presuming he wasn't dead already, poor chap! But to be fair he did hold fast on his fatal confidence which, in turn, has made it more urgent that we find this elusive Jonnie. However, on the bright side, we've now got two trails to follow: one, to this address in Burnwood, where Emma lives and two, a visit to Jonnie's abode. Shall we take them in that order?"

"I would say yes, Boss. And if we get her at Burnwood we probably won't need to go to the other address, anyway."

"I'm inclined to agree with you there as the time codes on that Emma Flynn number make it most likely to be the one that rang out the 'Only the Lonely' ring tone, when Jeremy was being otherwise entertained." They neatly binned their coffee cups and napkins, more out of the habit in protecting their DNA but also partly due to their tidy nature too.

Ollie jumped behind the wheel whilst Babyface input Emma's address details in the Sat Nav. As they had just skirted around Dundee on the A90 they estimated that they should reach Burnwood, Edinburgh within the hour dependent on other traffic. And sure enough an hour later they were driving slowly around the ramshackle landscape searching for The Towers. It stuck out like a sore thumb, the proverbial 'carbuncle', one of the few remaining tower blocks awaiting the same fate as that which its fellow eyesores had received. Surveying their options, they parked up circumspectly and secured the car with its in-built alarm and a steering wheel clamp for good measure to give that extra-added protection.

Babyface knew that he could have left Ollie to protect its vulnerability; it being very much 'a prince amongst thieves', but decided he might be put to better use accompanying him on the visit. They arrived on the third floor and found Flat 61 with a mechanical code block attached to the door, instead of a keyhole, barring their entrance. Ollie used his own initiative and instantly brought out a lump hammer from the satchel as he said sarcastically, "This will be a first. Using it for a job it was made for instead of busting kneecaps."

Babyface's laugh was smothered by the sounds of a metallic clang and splintering wood. He then replied, "I can't believe that noise will raise any concerns about the suggestion of burglary around here, chances are that it's the same goods that get nicked all the time and they just go round and round from flat to flat like some kind of perpetual motion theft. Let's get in and see what she's got." Even though the door was now unsecured it still would not open fully, as there was so much post, freesheets and junk mail flyers stacked up behind it.

Babyface was first in and picked up what he presumed were the serious pieces of correspondence, but on further inspection realised it was still just payment request reminders. "Looks like any important, personal post has been taken," he said as he betrayed his middle class leaning by turning his nose up at the smell and untidiness of the place. It took thirty seconds to verify that Emma Flynn was not in residence, but they had surmised that already with the 'postal door stop'.

"You do the lounge area and kitchen, I'll do the bedroom and bathroom," said Babyface. The bathroom being smaller, he did that first. Grime was the order of the day, and night, both around the basin and the bath and even the shower tray. He checked in the toilet cistern but that was empty, then lifted the seat and lid and again that was clear of any extraneous hidden items but certainly not of germs. Babyface presumed that the whole suite was meant to be white but could not be 100% sure. He opened the bathroom unit and was not in the least surprised as one of the doors came away in his hand. Feminine items spilled out, along with a few bottles of pills but nothing that caught his interest. Now there were only two other possibilities, but these locations needed some hardware assistance. Babyface picked out the hammer and chisel from the satchel and set about first taking off the bath panel and then removing the old linoleum, in order to reveal any possible secret apertures that could be concealing useful information, cash or contraband.

Neither proved successful. So he moved into the bedroom, looked around and thought, 'here we go again'. The wardrobe proved the most obvious and most lucrative. Apart from the designer clothes hanging from the rail, with each item sporting a brand logo hanger talker and a hole where the security alarm tag had been cut out of the fabric, he found a Manolo Blahnik shoebox. This contained various drug paraphernalia but no drugs. Now he understood why she lived like this and why each piece of damaged fabric clothing had a telltale hole, because to those in the know and in need, it acted as collateral, their very own bit-coins. They either gave her a source of income or certainly more buying power, out on the streets.

He continued looking but only half-heartedly as nothing he found was of a remotely interesting nature and did not reveal anything as to whom she was, where she was or her relationship to Agosti. He had initially thought that she could be some kind of investigative journalist, but a journalist of any description, even one with true anti-capitalist intentions, would not live this way, in this hovel. In the end he disbanded the search and cleared a space on the sofa, for a quick résumé with his colleague.

"I've found absolutely bugger all apart from some druggie gear and a load of clothes that she looks to have nicked from various stores up and down the high street, presumably to fuel her habit. Have you done any better?"

"No, Boss. Nada. Well except for this photo of her with some guy," at this he took the photo out of his pocket. "I thought it might be that Jonnie guy but that's only a fifty, fifty guess."

"Yes, it could be. But there's only one way to find out. Have you got his address handy? Oh, by the way did you find any cash and documentation about this woman or even a passport?"

"No, nothing like that. Seems like all her personal stuff's gone."

"Yes, I thought that too. One of her drawers in the bedroom was almost empty apart form a few sex toys and teddies."

"What's she doing keeping sex toys and teddies in the same drawer? Is she a bit kinky, do you think?"

"No you dork. Not the cuddly sort of teddies. These are the ones that women wear to make themselves more alluring and sexy looking. Anyway, it was empty apart from those items, so I'm thinking that all her underwear things have probably gone because she's either moved out or gone on a trip." Babyface put forward this conjecture as they headed out in to the hall.

"Make sure you pull the door to on your way out. We don't want any opportunist burglars sniffing round, do we?" he smirked.

Relief and joy spread across the two men's faces as they returned to the car. Relief: that it was still there and in one piece and joy: that *SpiyWeB* had further stretched its gossamer threads and come up with some revealing information. Emma Flynn had been the victim of an attempted murder by the so called 'breakfast serial killer' and was supposedly the only person still alive who had come in contact with the perpetrator. The retriever of the information had forwarded a newspaper clipping which showed a photograph of Emma coming out of a police station where she had been interviewed and then held for her own safety. Subsequent to that she had been placed in a safe house.

But the retriever's research had not rested on its laurels there, as additional information had been supplied by fast-forwarding through all the serial murders and then the subsequent disappearance of two of the officers involved, one being the leading detective inspector. As the strands of the net widened and cogs within cogs turned, the retriever had found the names of the full inquiry team involved in the cases. One of those, who had been seconded to the team rather than being an actual active officer, had mobile links to Emma Flynn's phone records and both had been in communication with each other within the past seven days. In order to confirm the validity of these new facts a fast track router request was instigated to redirect the data towards the very centre of *SpiyWeB*. Once verification was received and clearance given it could then be passed outwards to those relevant interested parties only. Both Babyface and Ollie were employees of such a party.

"This makes our job so much easier," said Babyface. "I don't know how they get all this info but I sure am glad we're batting on the right team. I bet this lot can find out everything about everything!"

Even though the accomplice was subordinate to the assailant, he still took this to mean that he could pass comment, so he said, "Yes, it would make one think twice about going off message. That is, if one ever contemplated doing so in the first place."

"Two words of advice," barked Babyface. "One, don't ever think about going against the Boss, not in your wildest dreams. What the Camorra does to rogue operators is not worth knowing, he would have run rings around you before you've had chance to shit your pants. And two, you're not the Queen you know, so we don't use the royal 'one'. OK? Closest you'll get to any Queen is, 'Another one bites the Dust', enough said! But I must admit, this intelligence is pure gold. Does it give the name and address of the one who was seconded to work on the murder inquiries?"

"Not only that, it's gives the mobile number and a newspaper cutting with a photograph, too. Here it is: the caption says 'Jessica Lambert, seconded to the inquiry team as a 'profiler', will give the detectives working on the case the added advantage of speculating on, and understanding, the killer's expected next move.' It's just a shame the photographer didn't think to shoot it in focus!" Ollie then passed the A4 sheets over to Babyface so that he could study the intel more closely.

"Ah, and here it says that the photo was taken after a press conference, 'where the profiler, Jessica Lambert, was very forthcoming by giving 'no comment' answers to all questions.' Talk about being sarcastic. And I agree, it would be hard to recognise your own mother in a picture like that!"

"She can't have found out too much though, can she? Or was she keeping her powder dry?"

"Well, we'll never know the answer to that one as she was taken off the case when the DI went walkabouts. In fact, according to this the whole inquiry team was disbanded," said

Babyface as he was studying the last page of the print out. "So what's the link between them? Why do they still communicate when one was nearly killed and the other was involved in the case? A case that is no longer in her remit. I mean it's not legit to fraternise with witnesses and anyway you can't become bosom buddies that quick, can you? Still, we've got the address, right; of this Jessica Lambert?"

"Yes, Boss. It's here," said Ollie as he scanned through the various printed sheets. "Just a second. Yes, this is it. 33 Main Street, St Boswells."

"OK. Punch it in to the Sat Nav. Looks like our Jonnie boy may have got himself a reprieve. No pain for him, if only for the present." The accomplice drove and the assailant thought. He enjoyed his thinking time on the shorter journeys but could never cope with the tedium of the longer ones. Those were the occasions when he wanted to fly or take the train, anything but be stuck in a car for hour upon hour. So this time he was thinking and his mind was piecing together all the jigsaw pieces to make sure he understood how everything had happened and thus ensure that nothing was out of place or hidden away from view.

"Stop the car. Stop the car. We need to find out who put this Emma in the safe house and then who signed her back out? Can we ask for priority on that?" enthused Babyface. "If it's whom I think it is then it could clear up another part of the puzzle."

By the time they arrived at St Boswells, Babyface was eager to get inside the flat. He knew in his mind what to expect and if it were the case, then at least both men would not be sleeping in the car this night. As they approached the house the windows were in darkness; a good sign, which was further complemented from the outside with the absence of a moon, so there would be no fear of twitching curtains spotting two strangers snooping around. Just in case, they still parked the car a hundred yards away, innocuously, by the side of a long high garden hedge, to smother any unnecessary noise from banging doors and boot.

Once at the correct building, Ollie had just opened the door with a modicum of both dexterity and brute force when his phone chirped and gave hope to the answer that Babyface expected. It had been DI Terry Barnham who had both signed Emma in, and signed Emma out of the safe house. "Good," whispered Babyface on entering Jessica's flat, "It's either pure coincidence or it confirms my thinking that they could have run off together. Only thing is we'll have to find out where he lives now. Although, why would she still be in touch with this Jessica? First things first, let's get her place checked over and if it seems secure enough we'll kip down there for the night as well."

What a contrast. Two flats could not have looked and felt more different. As he walked through it, drawing curtains behind him, the permeating fragrance reminded him of fresh Scandinavian forests and the décor from room to room was in muted tasteful shades and patterns, with furniture to match. Ikea no doubt, and it certainly blended in and gave a very pleasant restful ambience. 'This girl has taste. She's definitely the one I've got to meet,' he thought, hoping that her involvement would lead to the crossing of their paths. He ordered his accomplice to do a quick search in the kitchen and to get some coffee on the go at the same time, whilst he undertook the more personal search of the main bedroom. He breathed in the slightly musky scent that still hung in the air and let his brain drift as he scanned the dressing table, opening make-up pots and small lidded trinket boxes, all the while respectfully leaving everything as he found it. Again, the tidiness hit him; not a thing out of place but on opening drawers and wardrobes he found that there was not much in place either. 'Looks like you've gone off on a little holiday,' he surmised. 'So, where to and what for? Anything to do with Mr Agosti, I wonder?'

Moving back into the hall he caught the aroma of coffee, which activated a Pavlov's dog response via his rumbling stomach with salivation to match. "Nice place," he commented as he sat and sipped at his mug. "I've checked the main bedroom, you have a look in the other one and the bathroom and I'll give this lounge area a going over. No damage though. Our Jessica has spent a lot of time and money creating this atmosphere, so it's not right that we trample all over it. She might not be coming back to it, who's to say, but that doesn't mean we should act like vandals. OK?"

Ollie nodded as he continued drinking and biting on one of the muesli bars he'd found in a cupboard. Babyface looked at the overly healthy bar and went in search of bread so that he could at least have something more filling. A muesli bar was not going to satisfy his hunger pang for long. As he was spreading marmalade over his toast he asked, "What's your assessment of this place, so far?"

"Well, there's no one here. So like the other one, Emma Flynn, this one's either sleeping out or gone travelling too. Looking at first glance, I think we can presume that this profiling business and whatever her other job is, must be pretty well paid. She's very particular and neat but may have a flat-mate who is not so. I had a quick peek in the other rooms for any sign of life and that second bedroom is a bit like a bombsite. What with clothes strewn across the floor, and a towel thrown over a chair. Not dissimilar to the other flat, I hasten to add. In fact, a lot like the other flat. A closer inspection will hopefully reveal more facts as to who we're dealing with."

"Yes, we'll finish up here and start having a closer look," answered Babyface thoughtfully as he took his last mouthful of toast.

Both men did their professional sweep of the remaining rooms and reconvened in the kitchen for another coffee break. Neither had found anything of note, except that the second bedroom had a printer and broadband link but no computer;

and also in there, Ollie had found an interesting photograph. Babyface studied it; a framed digital print out featuring a close up of two young ladies standing astride bikes. It had been shot from above as if one of the two subjects had held the camera at arm's length, an up and coming 'selfie' fad. "Bingo. I think you've just found the link," he said. Ollie looked back at him, a little nonplussed.

"What, can't you see it? The likeness, between these two girls? The one on the left is obviously Emma, so we can presume that the one on the right is Jessica, and don't they look a pair of lovelies. And more than that, even allowing for different hairstyles and, pardon me for saying it, one having bigger boobs I'd say they're close enough to be sisters of a similar age. Can you get back in touch with *SpiyWeB* and check whether we're meant to be looking for one or two women? I'll get this kitchen stuff washed up and see where we can sleep."

Just like the Worldwide Web their own web network never slept either. With information gathering now stretching across both hemispheres, the strands were constantly spreading wider and capturing, analysing and storing more and more data. Therefore, it was no surprise that one of their three designated retrievers would receive requests at any time day or night and be able to undertake and process them. This particular request was easily resolved as it only involved the reanalysis of existing data, and in this case data dating back 30 years. The retriever forwarded several newspaper cuttings, which indicated that Mr and Mrs Agosti had been sucked into a retribution murder and subsequently had been found in their burned out car along with their two young children. In order to complete the circle the retriever had also checked hospital records, even though data protected, and ascertained that Mrs Agosti had only ever given birth to two children, a set of twins in late May 1980.

Ollie passed his iPhone across and Babyface studied the data in more detail. "That's a shame. Both the children died," he said half to himself. His accomplice thought that he was going soft until he continued, "but just imagine, if they hadn't died they would be young women now. If they were born in 1980, was it? That would make them thirty-three now. Looking at these two, they could be around thirty or so. Even thirty-three. Even thirty-three! You'll have to humour me here. What if this Mr Agosti somehow planned it so that his kids were saved instead of being killed in the car? And the burnt children's bodies were decoys? That would leave these two, Emma and Jessica to grow up not having knowledge of their real parents. That is until one of them, Emma, triggered off this chain of events when searching for information about her birth father, Agosti."

"Shall I send back up to *SpiyWeB* and get it checked out, Boss?"

"No, we'll pass this information over when we get back to UK Headquarters. And look we've another link here. It shows where the satellite pinpointed Emma's last mobile phone call at 15.56am; I bet you that transmission was to our ex-friend, Jeremy. It was detected on the A1, north of the York turn off and no doubt they thought they were being clever with leaving us guessing as to which direction they then planned to take. But what they didn't realise was that the phone's last signal transmission to the satellite was received nearly half an hour later at 16.22pm and again that pinpointed them as still being on the A1, just north of the M62 link. If I'm right, then we won't have to go to that copper's house either. I'd been thinking about that anyway. If he vanished a couple of weeks ago, presumably or allegedly with Emma, as I thought then it begs the question as to why at her flat wasn't the post all higgledy-piggledy behind the door, if it had been accumulating for that length of time? Those 'reminders' had dates from just last week on them and I can't believe she has a cleaner in, especially with the rest of the place resembling a tip. I suggest we try and get some sleep, it's been a long couple of days and I've a feeling we'll be heading south tomorrow, so that could mean another equally long day, too. We'll hopefully get some answers back from *SpiyWeB* on their movements by the morning and then know for definite which way to jump."

But little did Jessica know that for all her deviant planning to disguise the route they were taking, *SpiyWeB* was not deceived. The retrievers knew that the girls had indeed headed south, passed Newcastle airport and continued on into Yorkshire. They were not fooled by the phones being deactivated either just before the turning for York. Nor Jessica's presumption that they might think she was heading for a boat in Hull or even Leeds Bradford Airport, with both proving equally fruitless foils. They continued tracking her south on the A1 as she slowly but surely moved closer to her first goal, London. *SpiyWeB* secretly accompanied the two girls on their journey with the DVLA having been considerate enough to furnish them with her car registration, whilst the Highways Agency had enabled them to track the car's progress as the girls drove passed each southbound roadside camera.

CHAPTER SIX

By the time they reached the M25 junction, Jessica's tiredness had really begun to kick in. She had not slept well the previous night, what with visitations and her mind subsequently racing: primarliy with the possibility of being pursued but then with the nightmares that she thought had been locked away and compartmentalised, at least for the present anyway. At first light, she had then driven north to Edinburgh in order to drive all the way back down, almost passed her door. Instinct now told her to keep going but after such a long day her willpower was not at its strongest. So, changing her plan, she drove past the M25 turn off and continued on the A1 heading for the centre of London, pulling off with the intention of looking for an Internet café in the vicinity of Brent Cross Shopping Centre.

This proved a relatively stress free exercise and once there, she garnered as much information as possible, to enable them both to remain hopefully that all important one-step ahead of their pursuers. Whether real or imaginary she was still as yet uncertain, but as her Grannie had always said: 'A danger foreseen is half avoided'. And even with the knowledge of the added danger that any online purchases would eventually pinpoint their present location and so leave her open to online fraud by buying with a credit card in an unsecured Internet environment, still the risk had to be taken. Emma, feeling a little left out on the academic activity went off and bought various sandwiches and two coffees so that at least Jessica's hunger for food was satisfied at the same time as her search for, and gathering of, information. Clicking on to the Eurostar website she was able to book the final two seats on the 7.01am train departing the following morning. She then checked on late availability at various hotels around St Pancras and decided on the Crestfield, situated just off Euston Road behind Kings Cross Station. She did not book this one online, as in order to safeguard their anonymity, even if only for the night, she was prepared to pay cash. The last problem was the car; she called up the 'parkatmyhouse' site and found an available spot on a driveway just off Pentonville Road, which would then only make it a short taxi journey to their hotel. She confirmed this by email and paid for a minimum of two weeks through PayPal, stating that she also wished to reserve the option of extending it at short notice, a service for which she was prepared to pay extra.

Everything was now in place to take them as anonymously as possible out of the country and begin their quest proper; but for what? They were both devoting a lot of time, energy and now money into something as yet intangible, but neither wanted it any other way. They had not had the benefit of their parents' love, cherishment and guidance for the last 30 years, so both felt a little indulgence would not be out of place now. 'And who knows at the end of it, our parents might even be still alive,' thought Jessica hopefully as she climbed back into the driver's seat for the final stage of this part of the adventure.

If you had asked her three weeks before about going on adventures she would have scoffed as she was not that type and anyway she always needed considerable time to plan rather than just taking off on the spur of the moment. But that was then, when she didn't even have a sister, let alone a twin sister! Her daydreaming, or evening dreaming as it now was, almost made her miss the turnoff for the A501, Pentonville Road, but Emma was riding shotgun and on the ball. Their directions to the driveway parking were explicit and within five minutes they had found their destination and parked up and all thanks to 'Emma Nav' skills. A silver haired pensioner, being the proud owner of a lovely large semi detached house, with an equally large drive, greeted them. Here, two expensive looking cars were already in situ, that put Jessica's own car to shame; but the lady had no qualms as everybody's money was worth the same value and she was doing good business from being fortunate enough to live in one of the richest capitals in the world. After the paperwork had been completed and she had organised a taxi, her parting shot had been, "And the added benefit of parking here is that you don't have to pay that filthy congestion charge, with us being just outside the zone." The girls thanked her as they grabbed their bags and waited for the arriving taxi to pull to a stop.

It deposited them outside the front of the Crestfield Hotel just as Jessica was beginning to enjoy the sensation of being chauffeured rather than being the chauffeur. At reception, she took out her purse and handed over £85.00 cash and before Emma could interrupt she gave their names as Louise Sawyer and Thelma Dickinson, secretly in homage to the film characters and hopefully to bless them with the better elements of fortune that they would be hoping to receive on their travels. On leaving the reception area Jessica asked for an early morning call at 5.30am and once in the room informed Emma of the rules, "I'm sticky and tired and I've been driving all day; so I bags a shower first. And I don't want you knocking back your tablets and zonking out, so put the TV on for a few minutes and I'll be in and out before you know it."

True to her words she re-entered the bedroom wearing a hotel bathrobe and to the familiar sound of voices from NCIS on the television. She thought that she might just about stay awake until the end of the programme, without her brain being taxed too severely but at the same time commanded, "Your turn!" Then seeing the lack of response that generated she used a stronger lever, by way of inducement, to cajole Emma in to taking her shower now. She recognised from her recent holiday experience that should Emma deliberate and wait until the morning then it would never happen, especially when they had to leave at about 6.15am. "I'll take your tablets away unless you get in that shower now!" She knew how to treat a girl and this treatment worked a treat. Emma could not afford to be without her Methadone or Diazepam, no matter what.

*

Although Jonnie Raey's day had not been as hectic as the two girls, it had nevertheless been no less stressful. The more he dwelt on his predicament the more frightened he became. Were the police really looking for him or was it someone more sinister? Already there were villains with sawn off shotguns braying at his door and thugs, the size of houses, menacingly swinging clubs, or so he imagined. After speaking to the receptionist at work he had stayed at home, door locked, secure behind his twitching curtain and trying to believe it was not happening. But, in reality, what had happened anyway; 'a cop had come to work asking for confirmation of existing information and at least he didn't know my address. Then, Emma sent me that spooky text telling me to watch my back, fat chance I have of doing that. And Jeremy's not replied to any of my calls; some new friend he's turned out to be. That's what's happened. But Jonnie boy you know what they say about too many coincidences,' he concluded worriedly. He made a pact with himself that he would sleep on it, as best he could, and make a decision in the morning. Perhaps ring in first to check that there had been no more official looking people asking for him and if 'not,' then he would have to presume that the coast was clear.

Had Babyface been a little more considerate in his nature he could have rung Jonnie, posing as either the police or a villain, and told him that he was off the hook for the moment, but life doesn't work that way, so Jonnie has to continue fretting alone.

*

The 5.30am early morning call came far too early. It was in fact exactly 5.30am but Jessica thought she had only just

112

dropped off to sleep. However, once awake and moving her adrenalin kicked in, as she felt exhilarated by the knowledge that further travelling was imminent, and this time on the continent. The effect of the alarm call on Emma was such that it had no effect at all. Therefore, she was given another five minutes of peaceful rest whilst Jessica finished in the bathroom but after that all pleasantries were discontinued. The duvet was removed in equal measures of playfulness and seriousness and the TV news channel turned on, albeit at a sensible volume. Emma stuck it out for several minutes by lying prone on the bed with a pillow fastened to her head, but on seeing that Jessica was now dressed and applying 5.45am make-up to her, already pretty face, she reluctantly took herself off to the bathroom.

At 6.30am they joined a parade of early morning holidaymakers, shoppers and commuters, either travelling across the UK or, as Emma and Jessica, to Continental Europe; and all contributing to the cacophony of sound as the differing suitcase wheels drove across the cracks between the stone flags and the subsequent pitched hums on the marble substrate, as everyone traversed the pavements and concourse in their robotic convergence on the St Pancras platforms. They passed through the automatic check-in, boarded the awaiting train and found their seats before 6.50am and so spent the last eleven stationary minutes drinking in the early morning atmosphere of the architecturally imposing Grade 1 listed railway station. The young women made themselves comfortable and relaxed, in anticipation of the exciting journey experience ahead as the statue of Sir John Betjamen, gazing up in wonder and offering a cheery bon voyage to all prospective travellers, acknowledged their departure.

The motion of the train was like a starting pistol for Emma to immediately jump up and go in search of the buffet car. Jessica advised her that it might not yet be open and that they should wait for the announcement. Emma adamantly disagreed and was given approval to go as long as she did agree not to speak to any strangers, particularly men. "Oh, come on Jess, I speak to men all the time, it's my job. We don't have much of a conversation, right enough, but they do have to know the menu and sometimes there's a bit of negotiating to be done. Anyway, I can't be running round Paris on an empty stomach, now can I?"

Jessica was shocked that they were having this conversation and at just after 7.00am. "Yes, but you know why I'm saying it, don't you?" Emma shrugged. "Just go," Jessica whispered, "talk to whomever you like!" Annoying as she was, triumphantly she came back with coffees and croissants accompanied by little pots of jam. She had not spoken one word to anyone of either gender except the buffet car attendant, a young French man, who spoke fluent English and whom Emma did not class as a stranger as he was on the train all the time. They both tucked in to their breakfasts and when finished Emma was able to put her head back and promptly fall asleep. Jessica sat there pondering their next move as they had under one and half hours before reaching Gare de Nord, and no clue as to how to get to Zurich from there, without being totally obvious to their phantom pursuers.

She intended staying awake so as to identify any suspicious looking characters but on glancing around saw that, apart from the heroics of the workaholics on board, wrestling with iPhones, iPads and lesser recognisable brands of mobiles and laptops, most travellers were quietly reading or snoozing; so she took that as her cue to do the latter too. She awoke to a bright sun, shining in through the window as they scythed their way across a swathe of different coloured crops, all heralding its warmth and she presumed that this must be France. 'Do their crops really look so different to the ones in England? Is it the soil, or the sun or the rain?' she pondered, only to make a decision that she didn't really care anyway. 'Let that one at least be someone else's problem,' she decided positively.

Looking at her watch, Jessica said, "M, are you awake? I don't think it will be too long before we reach Paris. And I know that you're excited about seeing all the sights, so sorry to disappoint you but I'm really anxious to move on as quickly as possible." And in a more caring lower voice, not to be overheard, she continued, "and I still keep getting this shivery, niggling feeling that we are being watched all the time, which constantly gives me the urge to be at least two steps in front, not just the one. You do understand, don't you?"

"Yes, I understand Jess. Is this what having a sister's all about? Someone who's too sensible for her own good let alone my good and so spoils all the fun? You take me to the door of the sweet shop and then make me walk away! Surely a little look around wouldn't hurt. If we have to run we can do that thing where you go in one door and out another, really quickly. It always works in films."

"Yes it does, M. It always works in films. But this is real life. And I either have imaginary or real villains chasing after us in my head and you don't; now is that the movies or real life? Don't forget it was you who had the nightmare to start with, not me. But the shopping bit might not be a bad idea, I've a few purchases in mind which could come in useful," replied Jessica. Emma took this to mean that she had won and threw her clenched fists in the air accompanied with a shout of 'Yes'. She then promptly closed her eyes and went back to sleep, leaving Jessica to continue carrying the whole burden of this adventure on her shoulders alone.

The Gare de Nord arrival did not quite match up to the St Pancras departure but both girls were now eager to disembark and take in the French ambience of its capital. And with Jessica relenting where better to let Emma have a quick sightseeing tour than by heading for the Left Bank in the 5th arrondissement. Jessica had checked the Metro map on the train and knew which station she was looking for – St Michel on the Porte d'Orleans line. Ascending the steps from the Metro, Emma caught her first glimpse of Notre Dame Cathedral majestically positioned on an island in the middle of the Seine, which divided the river in to its two banks. Along the left bank of the river there were small wooden stalls selling magazines, books, paintings, CDs and photographs et cetera, whilst to their backs was the famous 'Shakespeare & Company' bookshop dominating the roadside.

Even at this early hour both girls could almost taste the atmosphere as the busy city was waking up from its all too little sleep. The artisan entrepreneurs ready to greet passers by with eager smiles in the hope of, and expectation for, another profitable day from those thousands of impulsive-buy tourists. After Emma had ooh'd and aah'd at the stunning structure of Notre Dame Cathedral and asked Jessica if the hunchback would be working today, they caught one of the Bateaux-Mouches and travelled serenely along the river in the direction of the Eiffel Tower.

Jessica pointed out the sights en route: the Musee D'Orsay, formerly a railway station but now containing priceless Impressionist paintings; the stately looking buildings making up the Louvre with the Tuileries Gardens stretching down to the water; and finally stopping off at the Tower itself. Even though time was pressing, Jessica gave in to Emma's pleas to climb to the top, yes climb. She did not want to take the lift, although she regretted that decision before even achieving the halfway mark. Jessica coaxed her to continue and said jokingly, "Well you chose your lifestyle. Being fit and healthy is not something you can turn on and off like a tap. You've got to continually work at it."

"I promise that if you give me a hand up the last few flights I'll change my ways when we get back home," said Emma crossing her heart with her equally crossed fingers.

"Yes, it's always 'mañana' with you or should I say 'demain' as we're in France, but here give me your arm." After they had reached the top and admired the 360-degree views of the city, Emma was exhausted as was her desire for sightseeing too. They slowly descended and made their way to the Avenue des Champs Elysees, via Quai Branly and Pont de l'Alma. Now it was Jessica's turn. She almost carried Emma through various stores, still holding her arm and not allowing her to alight at any one counter; Jessica knew what she was looking for. Once located, they spent a good ten minutes of fun and laughter trying on various wigs, Emma to make her look 40 years older and Jessica the same, as well as making her look even more Mediterranean, too. The sales assistant was totally nonplussed as to why two English ladies should behave in such a manner but a sale was a sale and that's what she was there for.

Next, the girls tried on variety of clothing to complement their new aged personas. And by 12.30pm they had exhausted Paris and due to Emma's lack of stamina were down in the bowels of the Metro working their way back under the river to Cluny La Sorbonne, in the Latin Quarter. Here they went in search of an Internet café and a light lunch. Once found they ordered and ate their ham baguettes, as they mingled with the students of varying ages coming and going from the university, whilst at the same time waiting for an opportunity to grab a terminal. Jessica's only need was to surf for a local branch to make her last Paris purchase, which was just a rental really and she found it at Eurocar, just a few streets away on Avenue d'Italie. Here, she hired a comfortable car with air conditioning for a minimum period of two weeks with the knowledge that it could be left at any of the designated Eurocar compounds across Europe.

As they both familiarised themselves with the car, Jessica turned to Emma and said, "Right, M. How's your map reading skills? I'm going to have to rely on you to get us heading in the right direction whilst I play dodgem cars by making sure I avoid colliding with these crazy French drivers."

Emma looked across with horror and replied, "I could get you around Edinburgh with my eyes shut but you must know that navigation's not my forte, hasn't it got a Sat Nav thingy? But I suppose that would be in French too?"

"Come on M. Where's your sense of adventure. Look, hold the map. This way round! We're going to be heading in that direction, looking for the A5 or E54 towards Troyes. Once we're on the move all the signposts should say, 'Toutes Directions' until the city we want is mentioned. That's the theory anyway. Are you ready?" Jessica set off without giving Emma a chance to argue and apart from it being slow progress, the direction they were heading and the road they were looking for proved less problematic than they had expected. It took them two and half hours of steady driving and Jessica's confidence increased with every one of those miles covered.

By the time they turned off the E54 and headed towards Troyes city centre, the sky had become cloudless with the sun making light work of burning off the recent downpour and both girls sat open jawed as the car slowed to an almost pedestrian speed. An ensemble of medieval half-timbered houses came into view, whisking them back to the 16th century. They parked up and continued their journey on foot, so as not to miss any more of the hidden delights.

Multi coloured three and four storey, narrow, colombage houses surrounded the Cathedral, presumably in the historical owners' eagerness to be that bit closer to God, whilst the gargoyles crouched and mocked them from above for their foolishness. Ruelle des Chats, one of the narrowest streets bordering along one edge of the Cathedral, sat incongruous with the almost open-plan sidewalk cafes and restaurants that surrounded the remaining sides. The tall buildings leaning inwards on each side, allowed for their protruding balconies to almost touch each other on the upper storeys, thus robbing the area below of any natural light and hence the sun's warmth. In the adjacent square the regimented tables and chairs, complemented by the uniform parasols, had no problem as they invited passers-by to shelter awhile from the now fierce heat of the sun and rest in the shade of their embracing protection.

"All we need now is to walk round the corner and see the barricades from Les Misérables," said Emma stepping along the narrow street and soaking up the atmosphere.

"M," exclaimed Jessica shocked by what she had just heard. "Well, you learn something everyday. I never had culture as one of your strong suits."

"What do you mean? I can read and watch films! There were some subjects I was interested in at school; in fact literature and French language were probably two of my best. And I feel that I can relate to this period, you know, when Jean Valjean and his peers struggled for their rights and survival. I mean it wasn't a picnic living where I did, and if you mixed in the brutality and stirred in a bit of nostalgia from bygone days, well you're almost replaying the same now as what happened then. That's what I think anyway."

"Wow, M. This is another side that I've not seen before. How deep do you go? Was it really that tough living with your aunt? Our aunt?"

"Jess, you don't know the half of it. But I think we'll have to put this subject on the back burner; to be discussed at a later date, along with the other stuff that we've not yet talked about."

"Yes, M. Agreed. It is a bit inappropriate discussing all that whilst stood on the pavement admiring architecture that must be over 500 years old."

*

With the two girls picking over the finer points of French history and of Emma's education, their two pursuers arrived back in London, from north of the Border. They had spent a slightly better night sleeping in Jessica's flat, even allowing for the fact that a long haul southwards was back on the cards the next morning. Their nominated retrievers at *SpiyWeB* had been feeding through information with the latest, arriving before their departure. This revealed that Jessica's car had now been spotted by cameras on the A1 as far south as Edgware and as confirmation of that, there had been a credit card transaction carried out in the Brent Cross area. But then, nothing. No information to signify that the car had entered the congestion zone and no further camera sightings to indicate that it had continued in any other direction outside of the zone either. It took until they reached North Muskham services just before Newark-on-Trent before the breakthrough came.

The online credit card purchase had been for two one-way tickets on the 7.01am Eurostar to Paris. "Ooh La La," said Babyface jokingly as he mixed a French accent with his Italian one. "Our little girls fancy some French Chic, do they? Get in touch with the Boss and let him know that we should be back in London in...," he had a quick glance at his watch and guesstimated how far they still had to travel; "... in say another three hours, allowing for heavy traffic. If there's no additional news when we get there, we're going to have to catch the first available train to Paris on Wednesday." At this, he looked at his colleague and said, "Unless you fancy driving across with the car. It would save hiring one over there and leaving a credit card trail behind us and it should make it easier to keep our hardware discreet, too."

"Makes sense to me," replied Ollie. "Do you want me to ask if we can get away tonight on the Shuttle? Or shall we leave it until first thing tomorrow?"

"As long as *SpiyWeB* continues to spread its net wider, I think we'll be still on their track tomorrow, unless our travellers resort to solely spending cash; so it shouldn't take us too long to relocate them. But that's not a worry for today, therefore yes, we'll go asap tomorrow morning. However, they'll have to let us know what time shuttle, so we can prepare for the drive down to Folkestone. But first we'll have to touch base with HQ."

*

French classics aside, the two girls left the charm of Troyes and continued on the same road, south to Dijon. Emma's frown confirmed her dismay at leaving such a beautiful city but as Jessica informed her, "The quest was never about finding the prettiest place to visit in France". The journey on French soil was now a similar distance to that of their first leg in the UK and Jessica's confidence at driving on the wrong side of the road had increased considerably. Unfortunately it could not be said the same for Emma as there had been more than one occasion when as the passenger she had given the all clear to overtake, only for Jessica to have to take drastic action at the last second, to avoid meeting an opposing vehicle head-on or ending up in a ditch. Emma's lack of driving knowledge of any description was proving far inferior to her literary prowess.

But still, two and half hours saw them entering the city of Dijon, the capital of the Cote-d'Or, and again with awe inspiring picturesque buildings featuring: tiled roofs in a multitude of colours, pretty and elaborate drinking fountains, another cathedral, a plethora of churches and its Porte Guillame, a replica of the Arc-de-Triomphe in miniature. Jessica was happy to assuage Emma's pleas to stop for the night as she was again feeling the strain of the constant driving and more so now with the strange roads and fluctuating weather, ranging from cloudbursts to brilliant sunshine within minutes. And as recompense for dragging Emma away from reliving history in Troyes, she even agreed to book in at Hotel Victor Hugo on Rue des Fleurs by way of consolation and even helped her locate a pharmacy, too.

*

André's bombshell was activated less than ten minutes after he had entered the café. In himself he looked out of place; dressed so smartly in a tailored striped shirt, charcoal grey pin-cord trousers, complemented with Crockett & Jones loafers; yet so typically French too, with his pochette bandoulière, hanging casually off his shoulder and a linen jacket tucked through the strap. Jessica intended doing nothing more than babysitting Emma and having a relaxing evening as opposed to her usual earnest Internet search for the next day's itinerary or for possible clues of their pursuers, but she had to admit that even her head had been reluctantly turned.

André approached the girls and to Emma's surprise and Jessica's consternation began speaking in fluent French, presuming that either or both could understand the language which introduced us to 'amour' and consequently his obvious intentions. Emma being Emma and therefore more interested, looked to her nearest neighbour for assistance, so that nothing would be lost in translation. The neighbour, a primary school teacher in her forties, already appeared red faced and flustered at overhearing the proposal as it was initially delivered and needed more than a little gentle coaxing before she would offer up an edited version. "In the first instance, he is inviting you both to dine with him with a view to getting to know you both better. I can't say anymore. That's as close to the translation as my sense of values will allow." And at this she pushed her glass away, stood up, grabbed her bag and left the café.

Even though Jessica was now trying to concentrate on two things at once, being that she had begun casually surfing the net, she still appeared to catch more of the insinuation of the conversation than Emma and was aghast when the shocked translator's final reaction filled in the gaps. She felt obliged to put Emma in the picture rather than leaving her somewhat innocently in the dark by saying, "This French gentleman, who isn't quite gentlemanly by the way, is offering to wine and dine us with a view to a possible threesome at the end of it!"

Emma's exclamation was, "Never."

Jessica's exclamation was, "Never."

But both with a totally different meaning. The girls were now sat bang on the middle of the fence. The proposition of a threesome by the suave Frenchman had tickled Emma's fancy to an alarming degree. She saw no harm in it and was interested in knowing more, not least because André was proving to be somewhat bold as well as gorgeous, whereas the same proposal was filling Jessica with concern and suspicion.

Not necessarily, at the sexual act, although admittedly for some time Jessica had not contemplated any form of physical relationship, but mainly due to the mental angst during and after her recent killing spree. She was not overly shocked either at the suggestion of a threesome with her twin sister and this mysterious man, but was more concerned that it could be a set up to entrap them. And entrapment, they definitely could not afford, not at this early stage of the trip, especially with having already fled down most of the length of the UK and now being in the throes of adding yet more miles across mainland Europe. So Jessica was adamant that she would not fall for a simple proposal of this nature.

The conversation thus proceeded in a stilted fashion with Emma, playing dumb and supplying the lines for Jessica to begrudgingly translate, by using her schoolgirl French with a little pigeon English thrown in. André reciprocated with simple French/pigeon English replies for Jessica to then translate back into English whilst watching Emma's eyes light up in amazement. André soon realised that the carrot of wining and dining was not strong enough for the job and so upped his game.

Again, in broken English and simple French, but now in a whisper too, he offered 1000 euros for a night of passion with both girls together. Before Jessica put Emma in the picture as to this turn of fortune she made André aware in no uncertain terms that she would be no part of any deal. André's disappointment was written large across his face, as he'd never previously been fortunate enough to bed twins, let alone ones as attractive as the proposal sat around the negotiating table. However, he accepted the knock-back and began to rein in his ambition whilst Jessica brought Emma up to speed on the state of play.

Reading Jessica's body language and seeing her determination, Emma began fantasising about having to role play the parts of both twins by dressing up in first Jessica's, and then her own, clothes. Perhaps that would still swell their bank balance, to some degree. André was convinced by Emma's positive reaction, particularly to the sound of cash and so produced a second offer of 200 euros for a solo night with Emma. Emma was now wearing her business head and briefed Jessica to continue the charade of negotiating on her behalf using her pigeon French with the would-be punter reciprocating in pigeon English. To an outsider it sounded hilarious but to the two negotiators it was deadly serious and the deadly part worried the hell out of Jessica. Eventually, an impasse was reached with 400 euros being the ceiling and no higher limit looked attainable.

Suddenly, Emma became frustrated with the 'toing' and 'froing' of the conversation and to Jessica's surprise revealed her hidden hand by blurting out, "Montrez-moi la couleur de votre argent?" Jessica looked at her with shock and pride and knew that she would never underestimate her again. André looked at her with a broad grin across his face and knew what Emma was selling and what he was buying. Emma looked at them both and still wanted to see the colour of André's money! If she wasn't going to be getting her beauty sleep tonight she at least wanted to see the reason why not. Seemingly, Emma had followed the negotiation from the beginning but felt that playing the dumb blonde could work to her advantage. André proceeded to place four crisp 100 euro notes next to each other on the tabletop, leaving Emma to delicately and nimbly retrieve them with the faintest sensual caressing movement of her supple hand.

With Emma's new talent now being in the public domain, Jessica said jokingly, "Well, at least now you'll be able to whisper sweet nothings to him in his own language, won't you."

Emma replied quite matter of fact, "The 'language of love' doesn't need any translation, it's the same the world over. No words are needed." Suffice it to say that even in Emma's long career she had never resorted to fraternising with other EU members nor had she been trained at the Folies Bergere, but she felt that she had more than enough know-how to entertain her first European client, French dictionary or no French dictionary.

Jessica took this as the hint that the two soon to be lovers would be moving on and so took the opportunity to hand over one of their clean mobiles, just in case of an emergency, whilst thinking, 'I wonder what the 'language of love' translation is for murderer?'

André being of an optimistic nature and also being French had already booked a room for the evening in advance at Hotel Du Palais, where apparently he was no stranger.

Emma's consequent distraction and departure put Jessica at a loose end. She had no intention of spending the remainder of the evening looking conspicuous and vulnerable in a strange café and so decided she'd rather take a closer look at the town, on foot, in her running shoes.

For the first 30 minutes of the planned out and back route, her pace was laboured, mainly due to the previously thought of refreshing beer she'd consumed, the late heat of the day and the effects of the constant travelling which had left her totally exhausted. But then her heart sank and speeded up in the same gasp as she approached 'un marchand de journaux'; the trigger for her unexpected mixed surprise. Not only, did it sell English newspapers, but it actually sported a billboard outside the door stating: 'Scotland practitioner and Scotland Yard Met police employee in identical gangland style killings'.

As the adrenalin kicked in, Jessica's return leg back to the hotel was achieved at a far quicker pace than the aforementioned 'pedestrian' 30 minutes. Once in her room, she showered, dried off, dressed, tousled her hair with the minimum of hairdryer and headed straight back to the Internet café, sans makeup. Several terminals were now free and for safety reasons Jessica chose a different one to that she had previously used. *Scotland Yard and Police Scotland are today examining two murders with gangland style similarities, and at a distance of over 500 miles apart. One in London itself, and one in the Scottish city of Aberdeen,'* was the message which greeted her on the BBC website.

No names were mentioned but Jessica had an inexplicable fear that one was Jeremy. Not least, as the body had been found in an up-market area of Aberdeen and the description portrayed the deceased as that of a professional man; a man whom neighbours described as quiet, very smart in appearance and always the perfect gent. These qualities alone immediately led Jessica to the conclusion of it being Jeremy and that the two sisters were responsible for the, no doubt, inconceivable pain and ultimate death, enacted upon him. And apart from the other body having been fished out of the Thames attached to flailing ropes, which most probably were used to secure anchor-weights at some point; both bodies allegedly had almost the same telltale torture trademarks and final closure about them. Jessica had no idea whatsoever as to the identity of the body found in the river and so clicked off the site, in order not to visibly display any untoward interest to either unfortunate victim.

Numb from the shock her hands absentmindedly logged on to her email account to check for any messages. This came up negatively and in reality she could not think whom she was expecting one from anyway, so again she just stared into space; allowing paranoia to muscle its way back in and bestow a desperate desire on her to be on the move, yet again. But as this journey had already brought her closer and closer to the border, and with her Swiss destination now within her grasp, she could not help but contemplate how neatly she had become wrapped up in the idiom, 'so near and yet so far away'. In fact, too near by far, if she was being honest!

In her mind, her phantom pursuers were tracking her every move and gaining by the kilometre, so making it imperative that she employ diversionary tactics. She needed to voice these concerns with Emma but knew that there would not be any answer from the mobile whilst she was otherwise engaged in her working capacity. Therefore, staring into space and trying not to look too obvious into the bargain became Jessica's challenge for the next hour, or at least the required period of time until she had formed a solid plan of action.

CHAPTER SEVEN

The debrief with the highest ranking UK Boss was held in their swanky London HQ offices at Canada Square, Canary Wharf and took a maximum of 30 minutes, in homage to the clan's philosophy being, 'time stood still is time wasted'. Babyface knew that his job was to keep on the move, leaving the strategy to the thinkers and more senior hierarchy within their ever-expanding operation. He had given his blow-by-blow account of the two dead victims and the two not so dead ones too. And aired his suspicion that they were the twins who had already escaped death once, when only three years of age. The Boss was none too pleased to hear this, nor the fact that two girls could be leading him such a merry dance and ordered Babyface to put a stop to the nonsense immediately.

"How is it that an organisation of this size, which has been involved in every single illegal activity in the Oxford Dictionary, including people trafficking and not to mention, innumerable murders; how is it that you personally, are incapable of tracking and apprehending two girls before they manage to flee the country? And let me add that it's most likely to be two girls who have probably never so much as said a cross word to their Barbie dolls, let alone having any knowledge of subterfuge or any support or help for whatever mission they have undertaken!"

"Yes, Boss, sorry Boss. I'll be on the Euro Shuttle from Folkestone at 7.20 in the morning. They won't be giving us the slip for long once we catch a sniff of their trail on the other side of the channel," was all Babyface could reply with.

"And don't be carrying a boot load of hardware. I don't want you being picked up on European soil, even before you get started."

When asked if there were any other matters he replied, "Just one more thing, Boss," and then he stopped and hesitated, before continuing, "I've a sneaky feeling that Ollie, C/UK/1668, my present accomplice, although excellent at part of his job, might be skimming off the top of the expenses and I feel I've got to report this as I don't want it to appear that I'm condoning it and benefiting from it too."

"What grounds have you for making this allegation against C/UK/1668?" questioned the Boss.

Babyface had raised his doubt and knew there was no going back. He had now successfully completed over fifty operations with a number of accomplices and prided himself on being straight, fair, articulate and numerate; in fact everything a killer and gangster shouldn't be. So, he despised any colleague, who was paid handsomely for undertaking work that he would, no doubt, enjoy but who in Babyface's eyes then persisted in trying to cream off extra from the top at the same time; so he replied to the Boss' question with, "Primarily due to my innate desire to concentrate on the job in hand and not to be side tracked by extraneous frippery plus my undisputed frugal nature. I just feel that these attributes are at odds with the expenses form that the Finance Department issued for me to sign off, and by some margin. I have no complaints about my colleague's work ethic from the physical perspective and I appreciate that accomplices are given certain responsibilities in order to assess their honesty, ability and loyalty to the cause but those figures that Ollie must have supplied just do not add up. I feel that I would not be doing my job, if I did not highlight this matter now. I might be wrong but all I'm asking is that you check our present account more thoroughly."

At this point Babyface pulled out a sheet of paper containing a list of recently purchased expenses items with approximate costs, which in total came to nearly £3000. "This is roughly what I think we've spent over the past week. That should tell you if my gut feeling is correct."

The Boss took the sheet of figures and dismissed Babyface with a handshake, an offer of good fortune and a command that he find these two girls forthwith. His parting shot being, "I'll have this looked into straight away, but it will now delay your trip by 24 hours whilst we find your present accomplice's replacement." Babyface left the office rubbing his rear as if he'd been punished by the headmaster, and equally annoyed with the imposed detention but still knowing that his talent and ability were not being questioned, at least for the present.

Leaving the building, he drove despondently to his grace and favour flat in Lewisham. On arrival he inspected the car boot as ordered so as to ensure that nothing illegal could accidentally be transferred across to the Continent, paying particular attention to the guns and tools' hardware. The hardware that had worked so well on Stanning, but not so on the solicitor, and which would be readily available, if you knew where to look, once over the Channel or in Babyface's case under it.

Hence his only prerequisite at the moment was to check and guarantee that their lifeline to *SpiyWeB,* via the eprinter and respective mobile, were to hand. This task completed and the bulky items transferred to his flat, he was left to his own devices, to while away 24 hours which he neither wanted nor needed but which were necessary in order to nominate, assess and brief a new accomplice before allowing that person to become the new part of his team.

He need not have worried about where the time would go as no sooner had he relaxed with a cup of coffee than he awoke eight hours later with a sticky patch on the arm of his chair and an upturned cup on the carpet. Tidying up the mess, showering and attending to his other toiletry requirements, then eating a late breakfast brought the time round to just after 12.30pm. His brain was contemplating a rebellion due to his unease at being without purpose, when it was rescued by his mobile chirping. HQ expected him back at 3pm to meet his new team member. He arrived without mishap and their first introduction was carried out in the departure-briefing zone where they were given basic details for the next stage of their mission.

Plans were agreed and instigated whereby the new accomplice would collect Babyface at 5am on Thursday, in order to give them both plenty of time to travel the 60 miles or so to Folkestone for the 7.20am Shuttle. At the introduction, both accepted that they now formed the nucleus of the new team and it was taken as read that they would further cement that relationship when starting their journey on the morrow. Babyface was counselled that he should put behind him the lost 24 hours, caused by the financial irregularity question mark hanging over the incumbent accomplice, and to continue taking advantage and enjoyment of what little free time he had.

Once again he found himself at home alone. He showered for the second time that day knowing that an early morning one was out of the question, packed and then dined on a 'microwave meal for one' and all before 9.00pm. This left him with the remainder of the evening to mull over whether his vindication of being honest would prove to be his former accomplice's condemnation. By instigating an investigation he knew that he had probably already seen Ollie for the last time, and was unlikely to be informed as to whether he lived or died; and he had to reconcile this probable fatal fact with his conscience. The outcome proved in his favour and the reality was that the accomplice actually died or more accurately, was executed, and by his own employers. An execution that even the accomplice himself could not understand, excepting the fact that working for such a fearsome organisation came with both, huge benefits and the same size pitfalls.

Examples had to be made and Ollie, C/UK/1668, was the latest, with not only losing his healthcare perk but losing his life too. Having been proven guilty of misappropriating allocated funds on no less than four occasions with three different assailants, the ex-accomplice suffered the same fate as that of other misaligned colleagues; and for a fraud that he neither committed nor knew of its existence. He was shot between the eyes at point blank range and, then his fingerprints were burned off with a blowtorch and his face and teeth disfigured beyond recognition; before finally being left to the elements and any passing four legged or winged scavengers, who took a fancy to a ready-meal.

And so at 5am the following morning, the new accomplice, C/IT/1423, aka Lydia Gwilt, parked outside the flat awaiting Babyface's arrival. Both now having had time to digest the realisation of their new respective partner, more so Babyface as he had never previously been allocated a female operative. And even though the 5am morning greeting was cool but civil, the journey south on the M20 to Folkestone became a sharp learning curve for the new accomplice with Babyface constantly bringing her up to speed, by filling in the gaps, on the cat and mouse hunt which had preceded her inclusion in to the operation. Whilst he, at the same time, suppressed his prejudice and his secret hope that his new assistant, being female, might just be able to out think the two young women whom they were chasing. He only had himself to blame for the present predicament and knew that time would tell if he had made the right decision several days ago. The niceties of getting to know each other personally would have to wait until much later when traversing mainland Europe, if it was to happen at all.

*

With the discoveries of one of Scotland Yard's own Metropolitan officers, Dennis Stanning, and the solicitor in Aberdeen, Jeremy Longthorne, both being found murdered with gangland style similarities, the CID and Police Scotland were immediately placed on the back foot. Metaphorical Mafia fingerprints were all over both killings, and were the most unwelcome link that either force desired or needed, but particularly in London these were magnified many times over. Especially, when taking into consideration, the added knowledge that Stanning was minus his tongue; that in itself posed the serious questions of how deep the rot burrowed into the force's very soul and what Stanning had done or not done to deserve that final brutal insult?

The questions they did not want to ask themselves but had to ask anyway, were: 'why should there be a death of one of their own kind in the first place? And what link, if any was that death to the one in Aberdeen?' One answer was as plain as the nose, still on Stanning's face: a bent employee at Scotland Yard had either reneged on, or been caught out double-dealing, and with an organisation far too powerful for his own health; as proven by his body being fished out of the Thames. So their approach was one of softly, softly, until the layers of authority had been peeled away to reveal how deep the corruption leached into the fabric of justice that was their sole remit to withhold. Police Scotland's answer was less palpable. The dead body on their patch was a respectable private citizen who ran a legal and honest business, at least on face value, anyway. The movements of Jeremy Longthorne, his associates and clients would now need to be thoroughly checked and then assumptions drawn.

*

Not only had the newly created Police Scotland undertaken this task in Aberdeen but it had also formed a new Inquiry Team in Edinburgh too, to pick over the debacle of the Scottish Borders serial killer murders. One team was re-examining the murders whilst a DC was nominated to the task of connecting a time-line between the two missing officers. Both, at worst, were purely exercises in damage limitation and, at best, any positive results being recognised as a bonus.

In reality it was just so that they could not be accused of sitting on their hands and doing nothing after the original team's efforts had ground to a halt, so spectacularly. The momentum had certainly dissipated from the cases and the scent could now not have been any colder. Therefore, their youngest DC was assigned to the task of looking inwards on the previous team's shortcomings. DC Denny Blister took up the challenge with relish and breathed new life into what was a dying corpse, if you'll pardon the pun, by dissecting the professional and personal movements of the DI in charge of the previous murders. Blister had no concerns for rank or personal status and with the added impetus, in his mind anyway, of it being a career breaking investigation, was soon delving under the thin layer of silence, which had previously been protecting both DI Barnham's and T/DC Murray's reputations and holding them in such high and lofty esteem.

His own views, not yet fit for hierarchy consumption were that: they had been very careless in their handling of the murderer or murderers; had possibly been in cahoots with the said person or persons; or that they had some form of personal relationship, which had been so far kept under wraps and that they might have both flown the coop together; and all for reasons yet to be identified and verified. If age was against him, confidence certainly was not and he was convinced that his ambition and drive would lead him on a positive path and to the correct and only conclusion. A conclusion that a more experienced detective might consider as being totally misguided.

*

As our pursued and pursuers are both on, or soon to be on, foreign soil in pursuance of their flight and chase; and the forces that be, are holding back the tide of gang warfare and trying to interpret recent happenings under their jurisdictions, our interest takes us back to the Scottish East coast. And following in the tradition of 'American quilt making', where contradictory scraps of material and threads are interwoven to portray a different story in time, so to here, the story is seamlessly expanded to allow another character to be stitched in. The character in question is a self-sufficient man of forty, born the only child of what we must presume were comedic parents, if his name is anything to go by. Having spent his early years, teens and even running into his twenties as either cub, boy scout or latterly scout leader he now lives, illegally, in a small self-build timber cabin with accompanying polythene lean-to, tucked away in a small woodland area overlooking Oxroad Bay. A coastline made up of carboniferous sedimentary rock, which gives the landscape a stark and rugged beauty, albeit one that is constantly changing due to the ravages of the North Sea and so could spell trouble for the permanency of this hermit's present home.

His schooldays were one long torment in which his peers constantly referred to him as 'tractor', being that his name was John Dear. True enough, his nickname reflected his lifestyle preference, because as a child he did favour the outdoors, although, at that time, it was not in a farming capacity; but to him, it was better than being holed up inside; even though the holing up still enabled him to acquire a solid education whilst at the same time endlessly being the butt of everyone's cruel humour. This had the effect of moulding him into becoming a loner. One, who after unsubstantiated sexual molestation accusations during his scout leader tenure, was driven to grow into an introvert too. To such an extent that he took on the mantle of recluse: but definitely not in the die of Howard Hughes - not a philanthropic recluse with cash to burn but a recluse nevertheless; excepting that he has no desire or interest in anything financial, political, or sexual for that matter.

His daily routine was made up of tending both his vegetable and herb patches, recognising and collecting medicinal plants, hunting small wildlife and sea fishing. His irregular 'financial' routine consisted of manual farm labour with 'cash in hand' naturally; a job he unnecessarily undertook as he had a sizeable amount of money already in the bank from his parents, which he could fall back on but rarely touched as he was not on speaking terms with them. Instead, he used his own hard earned cash to finance luxuries such as milk and tea plus the other groceries that were not readily available on land or sea. And having no mains electricity he used the surplus to buy paraffin for the heat required for cooking and the light to read by; plus diesel for the emergency generator, and when surplus monies allowed, the few books that he was able to purchase cheaply from the ever-increasing number of charity shops. The latter not occurring regularly as it usually turned into an all day event, in the same vein as the few occasions when he would illegally plunder Eider eggs out west at Aberlady Bay, Gullane Point and Broad Sands. These nature reserves supported an array of visiting non-breeding birds: but the Eider and to a lesser extent the Ringed Plover, were in fact, well documented for nesting and breeding there. These, and his sea fishing expeditions were undertaken in his refurbished boat with its reconditioned outboard motor; both made seaworthy and mechanically sound by his own hands from materials and manuals, either salvaged or purchased from his labouring.

It was after one such excursion that John returned to his unexpected and unanticipated guest, a guest who had now been with him for over a week and had yet to say a word. John has assessed his injuries; tended to his needs and as far as feasible kept his pain at an acceptable level. This was due to his innate ability and external desire to search out and assimilate the necessary knowledge to make a diagnosis and then dispense the required treatment, by use of his own home remedies alone. So, according to textbooks and his instinct that his guest should now be showing signs of recovery, he proceeded to rhetorically berate his patient for his present stubbornness. "Now, Joe Doe, I've spent the last seven days researching, collecting and concocting medicines which should by now have had the desired effect; and not to mention the amount of broth that I've forced down your throat. Perhaps it's that which has turned you into a vegetable! Although I know for a fact that the blow on your head had not been life threatening and that you had not broken any bones. So, give me some sign as to why you are frustrating me?"

Unbeknownst to the makeshift doctor, the guest's eyes opened and his mouth moved. "What are you saying to me? What blow on the head? Who are you? Where am I?"

John Dear's face was a picture and his cracked voice reflected the epiphany he'd just been a witness to, to the extent that he sounded more like the patient, rather than the other way round. "At long last, you've come back to the living. I've been expecting you for some time."

"What do you mean? Where have I been? I can't understand what I'm doing here. In fact, I can't remember anything at all."

"Well, yes that's probably the case, Joe. I've read that concussion after a blow to the head can leave devastating effects, but I'm sure that there was no hemorrhaging or major swelling and the fact that you're here and talking proves me right, to a certain degree. The only symptom I couldn't treat was whether or not you'd have memory loss."

As the patient looked around him at the austere basic rustic surroundings, wondering if this was how everyone lived, he said, "You called me Joe, so you must know something about me? So go on, give me a blow-by-blow account from where you found me to where I am now. It might jog what little memory I've got left?"

"Yes. I called you Joe, but I'd be surprised if that was your real name. I've actually christened you Joe Doe because I'm called John and having two Johns would have probably confused you even more than you already are. If we were going, 'John this and John that'; see what I mean, so I chose Joe instead. Now when and where did I find you?" Here he took a deep breath as he recollected his thoughts and said, "Like I say it was about a week ago. I was in the boat hugging the coast line on my way west towards the other side of North Berwick."

Here, he stopped for a moment, as he was too embarrassed to admit that he had been en-route to Aberlady Bay, but this time in search of Eider down to enhance his winter comfort. "I'd not quite skirted round the whole of Oxroad Bay when I caught a glint of light as if someone was using binoculars. I looked back at the spot through mine and realised that no sensible person would have put him or herself in such a dangerous location. My next thought was that it was a magpie or some other bird hiding its stolen contraband, so I slowed and stabilised the boat to get a clearer look. That's when I caught the glint again moving erratically, more with the sway of the boat, but I continued to follow it, right to your arm hanging over a cliff ledge. I was quite shocked at your predicament as the ledge must have been at least fifteen feet down and a good forty feet from the cliff bottom. I had not a clue how you got there or how I was going to get you down or back up for that matter, but with my scouting leadership experience I knew I had to do something. So I pulled into the cove, grabbed my rope and did a risk-assessment of the situation."

"Well, you obviously succeeded as here I am to hear the tale."

"Yes you are, but it was touch and go. I don't have any way of communicating with the outside world, and more often than not I wouldn't trust anyone even if I did. The weather was poor that morning, very wet and blustery for that time of year so there were no other people about on the beach, not even dog walkers. Lucky that there was just that hint of sun to give the alarm, in the first place. Anyway, I scrambled up the cliff side until I came to the road and from there I was able to find the spot where you had presumably lost your footing; I could also see the path your tumble had taken you, what with the vetch being crushed down in places. Climbing down to you proved difficult, especially with the concern of crumbling and loose rocks underfoot, which I didn't want to dislodge as they might have ended up landing on your head. Eventually, I got there and assessed whether or not you had broken any bones. All I could really ascertain was that you had banged your forehead, with there being an abrasion and slight swelling. That later manifested itself into a black eye, the timeline of which I've subsequently concluded that you had not lain there long; and fortunately for you it had been a lot milder night than the following morning turned out to be. Your heartbeat was somewhat irregular, on the quick side if I'm honest, and you were mumbling and making jerky movements with your arms. I had to move with speed so that you didn't jerk yourself off the ledge whilst I attempted to lower you down before the tide came in. That was a feat in itself, with the rope not being very long but I achieved it in three stages and here you are." He finished with a flourish as if pulling a string of coloured hankies out of a magician's top hat.

"Yes. Here I am. I've a lot to thank you for, which I will, when I know who I am! But at present, I'm truly grateful that you have already devoted such care of me."

"Well I'll be honest in saying that since finding you there, you've been more that a bit of an enigma to me. Out walking in all the wrong gear and with no abandoned car anywhere in sight. Not to mention, no identity of any description but loose change in your pockets along with a bunch of old keys! What's it all about?"

"Well if my fairy godmother doesn't know, then who does?" replied Joe confusingly.

John always became embarrassed at being referred to as the opposite sex and a pantomime dame was no exception, which was part of the reason for leading this hermit lifestyle. So he moved to the other end of the cabin and put a pan of water on the stove, in the hope of disguising his discomfort. From there he changed the subject and said loudly, "I've little understanding of what the prognosis is for the symptoms you were displaying but if I had to take a guess I'd say you were hallucinating and probably having some sort of trip, if you ever do that sort of thing"

A puzzled Joe, replied, "I can't really get my head around what you mean by that. Is it something you can do to yourself; or can it be brought about after a fall?"

Checking the pan John replied, "I feel we've still a long way to go, Joe." And to himself, he thought, 'How's this going to help with my need for solitude and phobia of being around other people'?

*

'Plan of action! Plan of action!' Jessica chanted to herself by way of a mantra whilst imperceptibly rocking backwards and forwards, her motion allowing her mind to flick through the variety of options available to both Emma and herself. She had already wrung all of the crucial information out of her nominated websites and transferred the intelligence, by way of copious notes, to her journal notebook. As she carefully poured the remains of her 70cl bottle of Perrier water and sipped pensively, she was uncertain whether it was the sudden voice of the waiter asking her to leave or the final process of her plans slotting in to place, which shocked her most. The waiter smiled apologetically and continued placing upturned chairs on the empty tables whilst Jessica stood, headed for the door and realised that she was probably the night's last remaining customer. Once on the doorstep, annoyance set in as it dawned that she'd missed the boat or in this instance the airplane. With the café now closing its doors, so too her opportunity of checking for and booking flights was lost at least until the morning; and still the nagging uncertainty played on her mind as to which direction to take. The most direct was the most obvious, but also possibly the most dangerous too; unless, unless, as then she recalled the maxim, 'If Mohammed won't come to the mountain', and there, lay her answer.

But first she must extricate her sister from whatever situation she had bought herself into, questioning herself as to what exactly the 400 euros might had purchased for Emma's new European client? Not yet knowing the timescale of the new plan, nor how much leeway they had before the pursuers arrived, nor indeed where Emma was actually turning her tricks, Jessica's paranoia turned to panic. She had already sent two text messages to her twin's mobile and not yet received a reply from either and with the time creeping the wrong side of midnight she became anxious and frustrated, which was in reality the exact opposite of how André was presently feeling.

In reality, André was far from frustrated having already made good use of the time available to him, so far. Emma had easily slipped in to call-girl mode and more than satisfied his lust as well as his imagination. Being a man, André had believed everything that was intimately whispered in his ear even though he had not followed or understood the majority of Emma's fantasising. During a break for refreshment and recuperation, he playfully toyed with one of Emma's nipples whilst whispering his own confession, and in their newfound version of Anglo-French pillow talk.

"Emma, mon petit amour, I have a small confession to make and I hope you will forgive my boldness?" Emma pricked her ears up in panic thinking that he perhaps had some strain of STD; something she certainly did not wish to take back through customs. He continued in a low whisper with his breath tickling her ear as he tried to grapple with the English pronunciation, "I have seen you before. Today, or was it yesterday now, when you called in at the pharmacy for medication. I was in the back sorting out prescriptions and wow, when I caught sight of you I just knew that I had to get to know you better or at least spend the night with you."

Emma's relief at one possibility and annoyance at the actual fact still brought a huge smile to her face, and a playful squeeze to his flaccid penis as she said, "Oh, André I thought it was going to be something far worse than that! You work at the pharmacy then?"

"Well, yes, I suppose I do. My wife actually owns and runs it but I'm just there part-time. I'm how you say 'dog's body'. I do the ordering, accounts and help with deliveries for the older population of the town, you know those who can't really get about."

"So how did you track me down? Did I give off some kind of musky smell, like an animal on heat?" she asked amusingly.

"No, nothing as basic as that. I just rang around a few mates and eventually that led me to the Internet café. I must say you can get better meals elsewhere in Dijon but then again, you probably weren't in there just for the food."

"No. You can say that again. It's my sister, she's a bit of a techno freak and has constantly got to be pressing buttons, whereas I like to press something with a little more meat on it," as she squeezed for the second time.

André replied in his newly acquired higher pitched voice, "Yes, your sister. I couldn't believe it when I walked in and saw that there were two of you, what an added bonus that would have been. I just had to sit down and rest, whilst I thought out how I was going to proceed."

"And now we all know what route that took, don't we. It's just that Jessica spoiled half of the party."

"No, I wouldn't say that. It was just a dream and if I had not asked I would never have known, now would I? But you alone, have exceeded my expectations and I really must compliment you on your professionalism."

"Sounds like I'm not the first lady of the night that has entertained you in bedroom exercising?"

"No, I must admit that there have been others and with good reason. I had no idea when I married my wife that she was going to turn in to a religious fanatic; I'm sure she's just a wimple short of being a nun and she seems to have taken onboard all their virtues to substantiate that fact. And you might not believe it, but there aren't many celebration holy days in the Catholic calendar where I get a look in, I can tell you. So 'when in Dijon,' you have to find it elsewhere and you looked a delightfully likely candidate and challenge."

"Well, André, you're full of surprises; so here's one for you. When I was in the pharmacy, I could really have done with purchasing something a little bit stronger than the codeine that was available over the counter, and we probably could have maybe done an EU contra deal at that. Not quite a French word but I'm sure you know its meaning. I have something you wanted and now I know you've something I want."

"What are you hinting at, Emma? Do you suffer from migraines? Are you sick?"

"Not exactly sick, no, but I do have a habit of sorts and it needs regular feeding. But don't worry I've promised Jessica that while we're on this Euro trip I'll be a good girl and only take prescribed medication and in small measure too. But I didn't necessarily promise how regular that would be. Anything would be better than the codeine I've been taking, in whatever volume."

"Mm, this does sound a bit serious. Can we discuss it in the morning?" questioned André as he showed by example what was his more immediate intention. Emma understood that a game changer had been put into play and mentally noted that the 400 euros would expire at the conclusion of the present proposed action.

Before the situation became too serious she called for time out for an urgent pee, and took her mobile with her. Sitting with relief but cursing the silent mode she read the two urgent sounding texts from Jessica and immediately called her back. The first words to greet her were, "Where are you?"

"Hotel Du Palais, I think? You knew that André had paid for the whole night, right? You didn't expect me to return to the café, did you?"

"Yes and no, but our circumstances have changed somewhat since you were, 'bought off your feet'; so I'm just making you aware that we'll be moving pretty sharply in the morning. We're not actually going to Zurich, at the moment. By the way, what room are you in?"

After a silent pause of puzzlement required by Emma, to enable her to take in the information, she replied, "Change of plan? Not going to Zurich. What room am I in? Oh, I see what room am I in? Just a second." Emma stretched her leg, opened the door further with her foot and shouted into the bedroom, "André, what room are we in?"

"André answered, "The honeymoon suite, no less?"

"I heard that Emma, the honeymoon suite, how apt. It sounds to me like he's been doing this on a fairly regular basis? He must have money to burn. Anyway, back to the plan, I'll explain it all in the morning when I get you up. I'll give you a ten-minute alarm before arriving; say at 4.50am. Enjoy the rest of your night!"

Emma glanced at the time display on her mobile and calculated that she had just over four hours left until the wake up call. Deliberating between the promise to André, her need for sleep and her confusion as to where they would be now heading, she climbed back into bed and fronted her dilemma with, "OK. Dynamo man this is definitely your last trick before the meter runs out as I'm allegedly moving on in the early hours of the morning." Before André had chance to respond, either in shock, sympathy or with questions, Emma took charge by straddling across his torso and lowering her breasts to within inches of his expectant mouth. Thus ensuring that from that moment, any sympathy or questions André thought he had, would simply disappear along with the option of any talking too.

The mobile alarm awoke Emma with a start. She took a minute to orientate herself and untangle André's arm from around her waist before being able to reluctantly slide out of bed and stagger to the bathroom. 'Really girl, you can have too much of this sex, drugs and roll and roll,' she thought as she again perched on the loo; 'wait up, though, there wasn't any rock and roll, excepting the bed, I suppose.' She then lingered in the shower, rather in hope than expectation that the searing heat beating down on her would, as if by some form of therapeutic reaction, totally refresh her mind and body. This proving in the negative she finally turned the control to cold, and exhaled a sharp gasp by way of confirmation that neither heat option had truly worked its magic, as disappointingly she still felt absolutely shattered. She patted herself dry and redressed in her previous night's clothes reminiscing, 'It was that third time that did it, what with him running on empty and me having to fake it to put an end to his marathon effort'.

Five minutes later the knock at the door shook her from her lethargy and her paramour from his sweet dreams. Obviously, it was Jessica ensuring that Emma was awake and up and she had even thought to bring a change of clothes. Emma instantly began to undress before realising that there was a man in the room. "Hang on a sec., André. We have a saying in England, that 'there's no such thing as a free lunch'!" André pulled his eyes back in as Emma covered her breasts modestly by wrapping the fresh clothes around her front and stepped in to the bathroom to continue her task.

Jessica said, "Don't look so down, André. I want a little chat with you, anyway."

Emma already exhausted from her trial of changing out of one set of clothing and in to another, stared at the mirror and asked of its reflection whether or not she truthfully looked good enough to be seen in public. The answer was truthfully in the affirmative but the unasked question was, 'Are those really wrinkles appearing around my eyes?' She already knew the answer and so was resigned to the fact that they now also complemented the dark smudges, which had mysteriously appeared beneath them. 'Perhaps, I should just stick to popping a few pills and go to bed earlier, at least then I wouldn't look as crap as I feel. Talking about pills, what was it André said last night?'

This thought bucked her up no end and she re-entered the bedroom to the sound of Jessica and André deep in a serious conversation. Emma sat on the bed next to her sister who was holding court as André held the duvet up to his chin in an unusual display of modesty. Although, he appeared to be listening intently, secretly he was fantasising over the fact that he was reclining in bed naked whilst his dream of dreams both sat piously in front of him. Emma recognising the scene too would have laughed out loud had not the tone of the conversation been so serious; whilst Jessica continued her flow as she wrinkled her nose at the musky smell permeating from the very air she breathed and brought Emma up to speed on the discussion so far.

"Your good friend, André, and now my good friend too has agreed to drive us to the airport in our hire car."

Emma interrupted with, "Oh, we're still flying to Zurich, then? I thought you said last night that we weren't going to Zurich?"

"Emma! Be quiet and listen or I'll send you back into the bathroom until we're sorted." Silence ensued. "André is going to take us to Longvic Airport, where we're going to look for a flight to Italy."

"Italy!" blurted out Emma, before acknowledging that she had agreed to keep schtum.

"Yes, Italy Emma and final warning." Emma realising that Jessica had sternly used her full name, moved her fingers across her mouth in a zipping motion, which poor André found rather erotic but knew now was not the time. "Yes, we're going to the local airport and checking on the availability of flights to Naples." Another mumble brought up a finger by way of rebuke, and a firm, "Don't interrupt! Once André has dropped us off he has agreed to continue east in the car and leave it in a car park in Basel. He'll then return by train and after a week he will notify the hire company of the car's location. That should allow us plenty of time to enter the lion's den, which hopefully will be the last place anyone will think of looking."

"Can I speak now?" A curt nod from Jessica confirmed in the affirmative. "Could it be dangerous for André? Does he want his money back for the cost of the train journey and his trouble? And here was me hoping that I might be able to do another deal with him?"

"Mm. We've discussed the first two of your questions, but I'm not entirely sure I understand the third one and: no, it shouldn't be dangerous as no one apart from the guy on reception downstairs knows of our link and no again, he doesn't want his money back." And here Jessica's composed face actually blushed as again the musky air reminded her of the energy that must have been expelled during the night. "We've discussed that too, and he is more than happy with the experience and his memories of last night that to take back the money would somehow dilute and diminish them. I think that's what you said, André. Correct?"

André, somewhat embarrassed to have one sister clarify so succinctly what pleasure had been taken from another sister, weakly replied, "As you say. Perhaps the next time we can barter for other things, Emma." Emma was delighted to know that she had not lost the knack of her trade but disappointed that she would have to continue with the weak 'over the counter' pills in order to fight off her other aches, pains and urges. André's thought of barter was more on the miniscule possibility that a threesome was not totally out of the question. At this point, the conversation ended with the two girls promising to keep their eyes closed as André leapt out of bed and headed for the bathroom. Jessica kept her word whilst Emma had a peek, in the interests of now eyeing up André's physique in a vertical position, having only seen it horizontally the night before.

By 6am all three were in the car travelling on the D996 south to Longvic Airport, a distance of approximately seven kilometres. During the short journey Jessica reminded André to let his wife know that he was going on an unexpected trip, as she did not want any police alerts searching for him and consequently finding their car too soon. As he dropped them off at the terminal and kissed both girls awkwardly on each cheek, he left them with a cheery, 'À plus tard,' and a promise that he would inform his wife, which he did. Jessica's parting shot was to hand over one of their mobiles and ask that he wait in the car park whilst they checked on available flights.

The shock of its ring brought him out of his jovial daydream but the message it brought, made him even more jovial. He started the car and edged it as close as possible to the 'Départs de l'aéroport' door, just arriving in time to hear the accompanying sound of their luggage wheels coming towards him with Emma juggling various baguettes and bottles of water. He jumped out and opened the boot, deliberately not asking what the problem was as he did not want to lose them a second time. Jessica redirected him to the driver's door and she sat in the front passenger seat leaving Emma to sprawl out in the back. Eventually Jessica opened up, "Some airport. Couldn't get a flight today going anywhere near Italy, let alone Naples. I asked their information counter about trains but they advised that we drive to Geneva, as there should be plenty of options there. So you'll be pleased to know you've not seen the back of us yet." André was pleased to know. "You'll also be pleased to know that I filled up with petrol last night, after Emma had been to the pharmacy and she's just purchased a variety of sandwiches and drinks, courtesy of your generosity!" André understood, and smiled at the thought of it as Jessica finished with, "So we should have enough fuel onboard to keep us all happy, including the car. You better get your foot down André, we've got nearly 200 kilometres to cover."

Being now in a very happy mood indeed, he headed off in an easterly direction towards the A39. He perceived this new intrigue as not only enabling him, for once, to breakout of his hometown but also it gave a purpose to his life too, if only for one day. However, his two companions proved poor company: with Jessica constantly referring to maps and being serious and Emma eating as much food as possible until the preceding night began to bring on drowsiness.

Jessica's mind was not only concentrating on maps and directions, it was also vigorously berating its owner for not thinking of flight times and destinations before the Internet café closed on the previous evening. She had worked through the scenario and knew that she couldn't have seriously asked André for use of his home Internet at such an early hour. Wasn't it enough that she was thinking of venturing into one lion's den without contemplating the possibility of entering André's convent-like dwelling too? How would he explain to his wife where he'd found two young women at such an hour of the morning, especially after being absent all night?

André's joviality had continued, even in the silence, as at the airport he'd thought he had seen the last of them but now he'd got the pleasure of their company again, and he could fantasise once more, for at least another three hours. Three hours in which to devise some form of plan of his own which could bring about a further liaison with one, or heaven forbid, both of the beauties, and so ensure that whatever the future held, he would at least die a happy man.

Emma nodded towards sleep, thinking that she had lost out. Yes, she was 400 euros richer and with the added bonus of spending her first enjoyable night, since the DI, with a macho Frenchman who really satisfied her; but she was also disappointed at the drug prospect that would now never be; she had come so close to that possibility, but now each kilometre took her further away. Her annoyance at the final outcome promptly made her fall asleep.

Part way in to the journey André was directed off the A39 and on to the N5 towards Les Rousses, where, having crossed over the French/Swiss border, it then became the D1005. Arriving in Champagnole, Jessica swapped seats and continued to drive southwards knowing that her next checkpoint was with the merger of the E25. André relaxed to the point of falling in to a slumber and snoring; Emma, as well, did her best to catch up on the remainder of her beauty sleep by staying asleep. So Jessica ended up with an uneventful, although breathtaking journey.

As she headed along the E25 towards Geneva she kept a lookout for Cointrin Genève Aéroport signs, knowing that, according to the map, these would arrive approximately four kilometres before the city centre of Geneva, itself. In the end, she passed a large part of the airport runway and perimeter before having to make the turn off into the terminal, so no help was necessary from her two unconscious navigators. Just like two small children, as soon as Jessica parked up outside the departures' doors and turned off the ignition, the two sleeping passengers awoke. Both yawned and stretched and stretched and yawned, much to Jessica's annoyance. She studied them and could not help chiding, "Well, you both should get to bed earlier!"

André knew that this was the end of the road and that this time there would be no 'third chance'. He went through the same procedure as at Dijon Airport but in this instance Jessica convinced him that they would not be coming back out.

Believing the end of the road had been reached Emma gave André a little more that two pecks on the cheeks and reminded him that it was free gratis. Jessica gave him only the obligatory customary kisses, still conscious of the knowledge that he had not yet showered, after goodness knows what, from the previous night. She finished with a handshake as she said, "Thank you for all your help and for being prepared to do it at the drop of a hat. I hope you don't get too much of a hard time from your wife. Now, you know what's to be done from here? It will be better if you drive to Lyon from here, not Basel, leave the car in the railway station car park, and travel home in style on the TGV. But straight home, mind you, no meandering. We don't want your wife panicking with you being absent longer than necessary. Who knows whom she might contact? Then in a week or so, ring the hire company and let them know from where they can collect the car. And that's it."

Emma being more of a simple girl just said, "Thanks for last night, André. Your wife doesn't know what she's missing. Look after yourself, Luv."

André held Emma's hands and choking up only managed, "Tu aussi remercier mon amour." And to Jessica, "I won't leave my wife in limbo. I'll go straight home. I promise."

CHAPTER NINE

Thirty-five minutes later, they drove off the Shuttle and were on French soil. 'Not quite the same feeling as Italy,' thought Babyface, 'but at least I'm heading in the right direction.' *SpiyWeB*'s retrievers had been hard at work and excelling themselves, particularly with the good fortune of having the extra 24 hours to gather and assimilate the most up-to-date information. Thus the assailant and his new accomplice were fully briefed as to the various stop-off points along the French leg of the girls' journey to date.

"Paris – Troyes – Dijon. What's that telling you, Lydia?" Babyface quizzed his colleague, by way of a simple test. "That's what you said your name was?" Babyface said, this time questioning more himself.

"Yes, Lydia's correct, Babyface," she replied with an imperceptible smirk. "I would say that they're heading for the Swiss border and as Switzerland is only famous for its banks and chocolate, I'd say it's one or the other."

"OK, smarty. Let's presume that it's a long way to travel for a Toblerone and concentrate our efforts on the bank idea. Where are they headed?"

"Well, if I ever had any money, my bet would be to stash it in Zurich, that's what they've done in all the films I've seen."

"Mm. We're talking about real life here but I'll give you full marks for your logic and I concur. I think they're heading for Zurich too, but that's not just based on an educated guess. Rumours have been doing the rounds for years that Zurich is the most likely resting place of our long lost inheritance. So we've two ways of playing it: one is to ask around in Dijon, that being their last signal notification we've been given or, two let's hope that they make another slip up for the retrievers to home in on, possibly further south. The task is that we intersect them and rob them of their knowledge and safety box key before they can even arrive at their final destination." Conversation concluded, Babyface relaxed into his seat, whilst Lydia, being subordinate, continued with the more strenuous task of driving the first stretch of the nearly 600 kilometres' journey, by heading south on the A26. This part of the Toll motorway network ensured that they avoided Paris totally and so remained constantly on the move. The kilometres clicked away quickly as the distance reduced until Lydia pulled off at Aire du Mont de Nizy, about 35km north of Reims. She had driven over 240km on alien roads, alien to her anyway and as she pointed out to Babyface rather sharply, she needed at least a pee. Babyface, being a considerate senior colleague, was more than happy to accommodate Lydia's request, "I'll take over the driving from here. Perhaps we'll have a bite of lunch whilst we're at it?" he suggested.

Lydia realised her snappiness was not called for and that with still having a long journey in front of them, ending up who knows where, replied, "Sorry about that. Yes, I'll nip to the loo and then meet you in the restaurant."

Babyface, now replete, filled up with fuel and drove at a steady 110 km per hour, taking him three hours in total before pulling off at Aire Langres Perrogney services. With only an hour's drive left before they would arrive in Dijon, he suggested a stop for coffee and a check in with *SpiyWeB* to ascertain whether any new data had become available, since their last notification. The retrievers had no more information to impart excepting that an emailed account belonging to Jessica Lambert had been accessed at 23.25pm on the night before last; the location pinpointed as Le Grand Café, Rue du Château.

They arrived in Dijon as tourists, very much in the same fashion as portrayed by Jessica and Emma, and admired the sights accordingly. Even though murderers by trade, there was no need for them not to be cultural murderers, too. They had just covered a little less than 600km and it was still only 5.30pm, even after allowing for refreshment, fuel stops and the fact that the continent was an hour in front. Their only mishaps on the way had been the alternating rain showers interspersed with rainbows plus a truck carrying timber, on the opposite carriageway, which had shed its load.

The Cathedral, the differing architectural styles, the coloured terracotta tiled roofs, and quaint 18th century dwellings; all caught their attention as they slowly drove through the centre in their quest to locate Rue du Château. Having located it they looked for a hotel situated conveniently close by.

And soon we found them taking an early evening meal at Hotel Ibris Styles on Place Grangier. Lydia had previously booked in at reception, shown their counterfeit passports and been designated two single rooms, initially for one night only but with the option of extending should she so wish. They had freshened up and arranged to meet in the, as yet, deserted restaurant.

Babyface, having finally put to rest his bigotry of working with women and so now being in relaxed mode, seriously studied his new accomplice for the first time as she sauntered through the dining room doors, and was pleasantly surprised with his findings. Transformed out of her travelling clothes and face, she now looked a picture of poise and sophistication. Being Italian he had not bargained on his physical attraction to a six foot tall, slender woman with short cropped blond hair, especially considering what his options were in his home country. But he could not help but be pleased with the choice of companion he had been given and for once, accepted that the female role in his workplace could, indeed, become an added bonus. However, he knew that his job did not automatically come with pleasure, unless it was of a brutal kind. The kind he enjoyed, in his line of business, to obtain information, and that pleasure he was always confident he could obtain at the drop of a hat.

Dinner completed and after their embarrassing small talk, which involved asking each other nondescript personal questions to which were given the same nondescript answers and so revealing nothing; Babyface said, "Lydia, now to business. I want you to do a sweep of the hotels that are within approximately 500 metres radius of Le Grand Café and I'll do the café itself; with my fluent French I might be able to pick up some intel discreetly. You have our story straight, yes? We are literary agents who are searching for a young woman who left us with a manuscript and we need urgently to get in touch with her. You have the photograph of the two women together?"

Lydia smiled and said, "You still don't trust me yet, do you? Babyface .. Sir, this is not my first mission and, anyway, before any of my live missions I spent the majority of my childhood and early teens being manipulated or doing the manipulating to the extent that I hardly know when I'm telling the truth or not. I understand what we're here for and I know how you want me to play it. I will deliver. And if we're trading languages, I do a very passable Norwegian and my Italian's word perfect, if you'd only asked." With that she scooped up her purse and queried, "What time and place do you want to rendezvous for a debrief?"

Caught off guard, Babyface responded, "Sorry. It's just with us being a new team, I'm used to spelling it out but I'm always happy to be proved wrong. Rendezvous, right. Here in the bar, say 11pm?"

"OK, Boss," was the only response thrown over Lydia's shoulder as she sensually walked across the dining hall in four inch heels to add even more stature to her height and with definitely more the Scandinavian than his favoured Italian look, but that was not to her detriment. Babyface, confident that Lydia would not make any waves, excepting the fact of turning every red blooded man's head, left the hotel in search of Le Grand Café, in the certainty that she would ferret out whatever information was available about the two girls.

He found it, no problem, and passing through the open doors of the glass frontage, he was pleasantly surprised to see such an appealing eating environment; one to his mind, far more interesting and certainly far busier than the restaurant he had just vacated. He chose a bar stool and ordered a glass of Chablis from one of the two attendant bartenders. Sipping it slowly whilst grazing on the nibbles provided at the bar he scanned the room inconspicuously, paying particular attention to anyone taking advantage of the WiFi facilities.

An hour in and he still had only made limited conversation with one of the bar staff and several of the other customers, and to no profitable value. The customers he spoke to had not patronized the café on the previous two or three nights and so had not had the opportunity to meet any English travellers, either male or female. And the members of staff on duty had not been working either but one knew that her colleague Amélie had, and she would be starting her shift shortly. Babyface bought another drink and waited with as much tolerance as his psychological makeup would allow; Amélie arrived and it was not long before she rewarded him for his patience. She was spun the literary agent story and upon being presented with the photograph of the two girls, she immediately recognized them and then tried to remember in what context.

She looked at the photo and asked, "Can you give me ten minutes to get back in the swing; the chef's got a rush order so I'll have to sort that and it will give me time to think too." True to her word, she returned within ten minutes and said, "If I remember rightly, it was a couple of nights ago and there was a bit of a flare up with one of our customers becoming flustered over something that had been said. She jumped up and stormed out until she realised that she'd not yet paid! Now what started that?" she mused, and then giggled. "Oh yes, I remember now, it was André, how could I have forgotten? He came in and almost caused a riot, right in front of the whole café when he asked two girls if they would be interested in sleeping with him! I don't know if he'd met them before and I'm sure at first that they didn't understand his intentions but eventually the penny dropped and I overheard them actually starting to negotiate with him."

"So André? André who? Does he live in the town?"

"Oh, yes. André lives in the town, all right. He's got a reputation for being a womaniser, but he's usually a bit more circumspect, if you know what I mean, but he excelled himself this time. Where does he live? I don't actually know but he works at one of the pharmacies on Ave de Langres, just north of here."

Well, thanks for your help. That's been really useful. I'll see if he knows where these two young women are staying?" With that Babyface paid for his drinks and left a healthy tip for the bar staff to show his gratitude. He walked back to his hotel with purpose, not least because of his success in linking a resident of the town with the two girls, but as much with the thought of seeing Lydia again, dressed in her black self-hugging sleeveless midi dress, or at least that was how he described it. He arrived back to find her deep in conversation with the hotel's bartender and facing what appeared to be an untouched glass of Drambuie, within her easy reach, on the bar counter.

"I'll have the same, please," Babyface said as he slipped off his jacket and sat on the stool closest to Lydia, forcing her to unfold her legs and place them elsewhere. The bartender dextrously conjured a coaster as if from thin air, placed the tumbler with precision in its centre, poured confidently and then moved off under the pretext of washing glasses, but in reality to leave the customers to speak more privately. "Are you thinking of drinking that by osmosis?" Babyface asked amusingly, having watched her and her stationary glass trying to out stare each other.

"No, I was just waiting for confirmation that drinking on the job was allowed."

"Well, I would say that ..,," he paused to check his watch, ".. that 10.15pm, is as good a time as any. So let's say we differentiate between 'work' and 'work-work'. 'Work' is the daytime job and 'work-work' is the nighttime job, and only carried out when necessary. Drinking is allowed during 'work-work' time as long as it does not impede the professionalism of 'work'; is that clear or do you want me to pass it by you again? And talking of 'work-work', shall we save the little nuggets of information we've gleaned until the cold light of tomorrow morning, when we start 'work'?"

Lydia looked at him blankly, raised her glass and drank the full volume in one gulp. She calmly replaced it on the counter, attracted the bartender's attention to refill and turned to Babyface saying, "Crystal clear and yes, let's. Would you care for another?" Babyface nodded his confused face, not knowing whether he had just been snubbed or not, but hoped he had been anyway, as he enjoyed the thrill of a good roller coaster ride too.

Two drinks in and 'work' took over. "That's my limit, Boss. What time are we meeting for breakfast?"

Babyface suggested 8.30am and accompanied Lydia to her room door, where he wished her, 'Goodnight' and moved along the corridor to his own room thinking that having a female accomplice might prove more interesting than a male one after all. 'Let's pray that this one's honest too,' he thought hopefully.

"Good Morning, Lydia," greeted Babyface, looking dapper in his open necked Bloomsbury Ecru Star printed shirt and already tucking in to his third croissant. "Hope you slept well?" Lydia looked equally 'arty', being that they were depicting the literary ruse, replied in the affirmative with a sweet smile, by way of a full stop.

As she sat patiently waiting for a fresh cafetiere and warm pain au chocolat, she asked, "Success in the café, last night?"

Although Babyface baulked at her forwardness, he could not help but feel that she would go far. The majority of his previous accomplices had shown nothing but respect, generally deferred to his seniority and in the main had been subservient but this one; well she had balls; she would be positively leaping up the career path ladder.

"Very good, yes. I actually ascertained that the two girls were in the café two nights ago and had a bit of a spat with a local man, André. From what I understand, he propositioned them and I think he was successful. He works in a pharmacy, north of the town. And you?"

"Well. The two women booked in at Hotel Victor Hugo, but as far as the receptionist knows only one came back to sleep, and that must have been limited as she was up and off before 5am the next morning. The receptionist remembered this as the woman who slept there made a point of settling the account before going to bed. Now the other woman, she spent the night in the Honeymoon Suite, no less, at the Hotel du Palais, with a man; you've guessed it, André. He's known in the town for being a bit of a lothario and the suite is generally reserved for furthering his cause célèbre, not to be confused with cause celibate. That is unless it's actually booked up for real honeymooners, by mistake. The only downside was that the night clerk wouldn't supply me with this André's address."

"Good work. Success all round, I think. We'll finish up here and then check out the pharmacies, I'm sure we'll be able to fish out this André character, that way?"

Lydia, being a sensible girl, surmised that to catch a womaniser would need a woman as bait and so made herself look pretty enough for the task; but wore sensible flat shoes as she was conscious of the fact that it was only 9.30am and not 9.30pm, and she did not want her height to pose a threat. With the honey trap now about to be set, the assailant and the accomplice set to work; and although casually dressed, they couldn't afford to be casual in their work ethic with their professionalism at stake.

Their ploy was that Lydia would visit each of the pharmacies and spend several minutes browsing the shelves for shampoo, deodorant, toothpaste; you name it. After parading on view for a certain period of time she would purchase a few items and ask the person behind the counter if they could suggest the best place in town for WiFi connection. It did not matter what the answer was as if André worked at those particular premises, then he would more than likely have seen and heard enough to be interested and would no doubt be spending the evening scouring the WiFi hotspots in search of this mystery lady. He could just not help himself to do otherwise.

By 10.30am the trap was baited so the two colleagues logged in and checked with *SpiyWeB* for any further updates. With no other leads being forthcoming, they then headed back to their hotel, checked out and immediately booked in at the Hotel du Palais, but not in the Honeymoon Suite. When booking in, Lydia was conspicuous by her absence, in order not to be seen by any member of front of house staff, who may then be able to link her with André, if he should fall for her charm.

With a lull in proceedings both operatives took the opportunity to spend time relaxing or in the gym. At 8.30pm Lydia, suitably dressed, made-up and accessorised with a laptop, headed for Le Grand Café. It had been decided that Babyface would keep a low profile and so remained in the hotel until he received notification from Lydia that the sting was on; and André being a creature of habit, didn't disappoint. By 10.00pm he was well and truly under Lydia's spell and all thoughts of Emma had been put to bed, so to speak, and had become nothing but a distant memory, as he thanked his maker for the gifts and talents he had been given to enable him to attract such beautiful women. 11.00pm saw them climbing the stairs of the Hotel du Palais, with André throwing a wink at the receptionist en-route to his favourite suite. By 11.15pm, André's hopes had been dashed and although he was facing not quite the Spanish Inquisition he swore that he would keep faith with the church in future, if he could but only escape from the present.

He still found this tall attractive blond alluring, even though now she was asking the wrong kind of questions, and he knew the night would not be favourable for him, when a bulky shiny-headed bouncer of a man tapped on the bedroom door and entered. This was his introduction to the assailant, whose opening gambit was, "Sorry, I'm not room service but I might be able to offer you some comfort of sorts, if you co-operate. My colleague and I understand that you may have come across two young women, probably sisters, whom we are trying to locate? Now depending on how you answer, will dictate what we let you leave here with; if you catch my drift?"

André did right to look frightened, as his assignations had proved anything but menacing in the past. His silence prompted Babyface to continue in his fluent French. "We know that you met up with them in Le Grand Café; that you propositioned one if not both; and that you were able to fulfil that proposition right here in this room. Am I right so far?" André's weak voice verified those suppositions as he trembled in his chair. "So, the question, I have for you André, is what happened next?"

With a flood of uncalled for courage André said, "I did what I always do. I left the lady wanting more." This brought a blow to his mouth, not least because it was a lie but as much for his belittling of womankind; and the shock of it was that the accomplice had been the supplier.

She glared at him through eyes that he thought were originally going to melt his heart and spoke, also in fluent French, "André, those lies and that language will do you no favours. That was a warning; take heed. My colleague has asked you politely, 'what happened next?' and you have disrespected his courtesy. Do you now understand who you are dealing with?"

Wiping the blood from his already swollen lip, André sat up straight but remained silent. Babyface made a mental note of praise: for how Lydia had stepped in unannounced, and even though he had been shocked by her actions, he knew that André would have been terrified; and to compliment her on her command of the French language, too. And so to break the interlude of silence he continued as he addressed his accomplice with, "Have a look through his shoulder bag and pockets, we still may be able to do this the easy way."

André's eyes followed her as she moved around the room with élan, in her search for any likely clues. His shoulder bag contained a 'pay as you go' mobile, a set of car keys and a wallet with credit cards and euros, at least 500 according to Lydia; her hand brushed against a selection of condoms in the bottom of the bag bringing a slight flush to her face but no quiver to her voice, "The eponymous French letter, what else? It appears that business is brisk, what with this quantity?" André sucked on his swollen lip and slumped down, at the reality that what could have been was now being ridiculed by that very same person. She reached for his jacket and started ferreting through the various pockets. "This looks a likely possibility, Boss. A one-way ticket from Lyon to Dijon, and stamped with the day before yesterday's date. Perhaps we should ask 'Madame André' if her husband has been absent without leave over the last couple of days?"

André jerked his head at this veiled threat and started talking. "No, there's no need to involve her. OK. There were two young women, much nicer than you, I might add," he made a point of glaring at Lydia, "and, yes we got talking et cetera, et cetera. Early in the morning, the one called Jessica banged on our room door. That is this room's door, and by 'our' I mean Emma's and mine. You see Emma was the other young woman."

"Yes, we understand. Two women and you were in bed with one of them and the other was at the door. Go on!" said the assailant with annoyance in his voice.

"OK, OK. We had to be up and dressed quickly as the one banging on the door…"

"Jessica!"

"Yes, Jessica. Jessica wanted to go to the airport and then wanted me to drive the car south and leave it in a car park."

"Which airport?"

Here André deliberated until he caught the swift movement of the accomplice's hand clenching into a fist. "We went to Dijon airport first but there were no flights available and so drove down to Geneva."

"And," said the clenched fist.

"And they went in and booked a flight. I drove the car on to Lyon as a decoy and was meant to ring the hire company next week to tell them it was there, ready for collection."

"You know the next question, don't you," said Babyface looking expectantly as his colleague's reflexes were tightening.

"What. What was their destination? I've no idea. Honest. They went through the departure doors and I thought, 'Great, I've been doing all this running around for nothing. Spending all this time ….'" The fist slammed in to his face unexpectedly. Blood burst from his nose and saturated his Izod Lacoste cardigan as he looked accusingly at his tormentor with the question, 'Why?' in his eyes.

"I don't need to answer to you for my actions, but I will. Do not ever again think of imagining in that tiny brain of yours, that women, any women, are your playthings. The fact that one of them condoned to sleep with you is ample reward for your services, so moan about it again at your peril. And in a round about way, I was also checking whether you were lying or not about their destination. But I think you've now got more to think about than just wasting your time; what explanation are you going to give little 'wifey' for your damaged nose, split lip and blood soaked shirt?"

Babyface interjected, "Not wanting to break up this blossoming relationship, I think we've heard enough from lover boy, here. We'll confiscate the phone, thank you very much and be heading off. Tie him up, hang the 'do not disturb' sign outside the door and let the cleaners find him sometime tomorrow." And to André he specifically said, "Oh, and don't think about informing the Gendarmerie; we frown on such sneaks and you don't want any unexpected accidents to befall your family, now do you?"

And so, what a difference a day makes. In any other situation, André may have been ecstatic with the prospect of being tied up to a bed; a bed on which he had had many conquests and memories. However, in this instance, caked in blood and struggling to breathe he was not quite at his peak nor enjoying the action to the same degree and it was certainly not hitting all the right buttons. But he did have one consolation in not revealing the girls' destination, a small victory against a crushing defeat, not least with his much-anticipated failed conquest turning out to be too feisty, by far.

The two colleagues, transformed back into their pseudonyms, returned to their rooms and grabbed a few hours' sleep, followed by an early breakfast. They then continued their journey south on the same route already travelled by the two young women when being chauffeured by their now tightly bound and bed-ridden escort. Babyface took the wheel whilst Lydia communicated with the retrievers: firstly, by handing over the girls' mobile number in order for *SpiyWeB* to check its history; secondly, by informing them of a hire car made out to one of the two and now parked in the Gare de Lyon-Part-Dieu; and thirdly, by instigating a check on the two girls' names against flights leaving Geneva within the last 36 - 48 hours. "Of course," said Lydia, "the business with the car and going into the airport could be a smokescreen; they could have still caught a flight to Zurich or just come out the other side, for all we know."

"Yes, they could. But the retrievers have not failed us yet, and if they caught a flight to anywhere we'd know about it," was the positive reply.

CHAPTER NINE

48 hours earlier

The young women arrived at the flight booking area of Geneva Cointrin International Airport at 10.30am, and after a frantic dash between different airline counters they managed to book on to a 2.00pm flight to Naples. Jessica let out a deep sigh and flopped in to one of the cafeteria chairs, which had the effect of waking her up due to its inflexibility to bend to her body-shape. "OW, that hurt. M, be a sweetie and grab two coffees; make mine black, in fact, the blacker the better." Emma knew how her sister felt as she was in accord but for very different reasons. The night had certainly taken its toll and now she had the added worry of Jessica's madcap idea to fly right 'in to the lion's den', her words not Emma's.

Whilst Emma was on the coffee run, Jessica took the opportunity to ring the silver haired entrepreneur in London. She needed to revise her plans and inform the lady that she would not now be collecting her car on the date as previously agreed, and so ensure that it was OK for it to remain in situ. The reply she received shocked her, "Oh, I'm glad you've rung, Miss Lambert. There have been all kinds of strange goings on over the last few days." The pregnant pause continued until the lady realised that Jessica was not going to comment on the statement she had just made. "Yes, very strange, dear. A man came by a couple of days ago enquiring about the purchase of your car. I said, 'Sorry luv, but it's not mine to sell.' So he went away but that's not the end of it.

Now your car's vanished. Gone. Clean off the driveway and it was parked between a BMW and a Mercedes. I don't know what to make of it? I mean I'm not being rude or anything but what's your car got that the other two haven't? Two nights ago it was there and it's not there now. Of course, I've rung the police; whether they'll get to the bottom of it or not, I don't know. I expect it happens all over London, but never on my drive before, no never. Bad for business. You are insured, aren't you?"

Jessica just let her ramble on and then thanked her for her concern and disconnected the call. She felt the noose tightening around her and what with the flight to Naples she was soon going to be squeezed from both sides; her only consolation was that she had been right to be paranoid. Emma came back bearing coffees and cookies and on seeing her sister's serious face, commented, "It can't have got any worse; I've only been gone five minutes? And I've brought some comfort food,' she said shaking the bag of cookies. "Don't tell me. The people that you think are chasing us are going to be on the same flight?"

"No, not quite M, but we're not really on a picnic either. I've just spoken to the old dear who has my car parked on her drive and she's led me to believe that there are definitely people asking after us, to the extent that they have nicked my car! Anyway, come and sit, I've still got something else to tell you, which is part of the reason why I panicked last night. I read on the Internet that a man in Aberdeen had been murdered and the police think that it was a gangland style killing. I've a terrible gut feeling that it was Jeremy."

"What our Jeremy. The one who took us to lunch the other day; who I was thinking of starting a relationship with?" she said as her eyes smarted and tears began to pool on her lashes.

"Yes, the very same, M. It's just so frightening how serious this adventure is becoming. That's why we've got to keep running, and to add insult to injury I've just realised that André drove off with one of our mobiles, so we're going to have to ditch the remaining SIM cards in order to stay off the radar. Whoever's doing the chasing must have an impressive support team, harvesting and supplying their information. Do you understand why I've chosen Naples, now? We'll be so close to Dad's enemies that they hopefully won't think to look there."

"Yes, I suppose that does have a backwards way round sense to it."

"M, that can't be the Queen's English, but I get your drift."

"Good. You didn't know I could speak 'clumsy' as well as French, did you? And if they have done that to Jeremy, is André safe or is he in danger, too?" surmised Emma still thinking affectionately of André, which would prove to be for far longer than he had had the decency to think affectionately of her.

"Well, we've got to presume that he could be in danger but I don't think we've left any trail to his door," replied Jessica suddenly placing her hand on her forehead as if to hide the shock of the brightness from the light bulb which had just switched on in her brain, "Oh no, I absentmindedly logged on to my email address last night, in the Internet café. I was daydreaming really; it was just something to do. I hope that they don't pick up on it?" she said, resigned to the possibility that they would. "It must have been the tiredness," she sighed in her defence.

"I'm beginning to think that there's some kind of curse about us. I mean how many is it you've killed in the UK? And I know I'm on one; and now everyone we meet seems to end up dead or if not, then at least threatened with death, whilst we constantly run away from people we presume want to do the same to us."

"Come on, M, don't be so melodramatic. Let's take it one day at a time and remain alert and observant. And at least we'll have warm weather on our backs, if nothing else."

"OK, Jess. But I forgot to pack my costume, I didn't think I'd be doing much sunbathing in Zurich?"

"Since when did YOU need a costume, Sweetie?"

'There goes that 'Sweetie' again. I'll have to challenge her about it, perhaps on the flight?' thought Emma not for the first time, whilst replying, "There's a time and a place to reveal all and in my line of business the only asset stripping I do is purely for cash, as André found out earlier." Not thinking of a suitable answer, Jessica fell silent as she too juggled with the question of what to wear, once in a sunnier climate.

Having boarded and taken off without mishap, the girls settled down to the almost two hours' flight; Jessica initially looking nonchalantly out of the window and then trying to snooze; leaving Emma to act like a child, it being only her second flight of any description. After the scare of the initial take off, she had been desperate for an alcoholic drink to calm her jittery nerves and neutralise her stress; so she almost gave a cheer when she heard the chinking of bottles and the chatter of requests coming from behind her and looking around saw the trolley heading in her direction. She still had the majority of the 400 euros and it was beginning to burn a hole in her pocket. She nudged her sister and said, "Jess, are you awake? I'm going to get a G & T; do you want one? That take-off has certainly put the wind up me and I need something to help me relax."

Jessica turned back from the window, out of which she had been admiring the majesty of the snow covered peaks and even tried to pick out ski resorts as the airplane navigated its way over the Alps at nearly 40000 feet. "Yes, I'll have one, M. Have you got any money? Oh. Of course you have; what André paid you."

"Yes, but I'm only sorry that I couldn't stay a little longer and do a trade at the pharmacy. That could have furthered my 'entente cordiale' with André and perhaps contributed to the trade deficit or something, at the same time. But now we'll never know." The drinks trolley arrived and the girls remained quiet apart from making their requests. When the hostess had moved on, Emma continued as she looked through her bag, "Talking of doing a trade, that's reminded me," and finding her codeine, she popped two in her mouth and took a sip of the G & T to wash them down. She then leaned in towards Jessica conspiratorially and whispered, so as not to be overheard, "And now that you're awake and I've got your attention for at least as long as it takes you to drink your drink, I think it's about time you told me a bit about this 'Sweetie' thing? Sweetie? I mean where did 'sweetie' come from?"

Jessica's pause was so long that Emma had to steal a glance at her to make sure she had not dropped off to sleep; that was until Jessica spoke to allay her fears, "What are you talking about: sweetie?" she questioned being somewhat alarmed at not seeing this coming from left field and therefore having to think quickly.

"Sweetie. You know. You've said it a few times recently and that's what you said to me when I was by that skip with Peter. Peter punter, the guy who paid and you killed …;" this word was whispered in an even quieter conspiratorial tone; "… before he could claim his purchase. Then you loaded a syringe with my heroin in the hope that I'd OD. That was £30 of quality heroin, by the way."

"Will you please stop talking about this? You can't even mention the 'H' word in such a public place, let alone the 'K' word. Yes, I've already apologised for that OD thing and I thought we were going to discuss all this when we were both in a more private environment and a better place mentally, which if I'm being honest is definitely not the case at the moment, in either instance. But in my defence, I thought you were a witness who would identify me, so I couldn't really let you live. If you can understand that?"

"Yes, I understand that, sort of. But why: sweetie?"

"Sweetie? Well, do you gamble?"

"Do I gamble? Of course I gamble, everyday of my life when a guy buys sex from me – I get in his car and who knows what might happen? But what's that got to do with it?"

"Yes, well I suppose that is a form of gambling but I mean more like poker or blackjack, you know in a casino."

"No I don't do that. I've enough vices without adding more and the money's hard enough to come by without losing it straightaway."

"Right. Well 'sweetie' is like my 'tell'. I tend to say it if I'm nervous or unsure about a situation in which I find myself. That's why I said it to you because I was unsure what to do but my gut instinct said destroy all evidence, which I was trying to do but being nice at the same time."

"You call that being nice? Anyway, I've got my answer. So instead of you having a twitch or a scratch, you say sweetie when you feel under pressure and are about to be found out. Does it work too if you're frightened?"

"Yes, I suppose it does. But what about you; don't you ever get frightened with a punter? Aren't you ever in a compromising position which you don't like?"

"Mm, most of the time actually but that goes with the territory. But I've always been optimistic that it would work out OK and so far luck has been on my side. And anyway now that I'm a big 'K' myself, I won't mention the word but it rhymes with 'Atilla', my confidence in looking out for myself is quite high!"

"So are you saying that you still have sex when you're unsure or frightened?"

"No, no. I have sex for money, period. I'd never make a penny if I backed off at every instance where I felt vulnerable. And I can't really think that I've got a tell of my own as I twitch and shuffle most of the time, particularly when I'm in need of a little something to calm my head."

"OK. We're changing the subject here. Are we done with this? Can we put it to bed for the moment? And not in the way you'd mean," asked Jessica as she looked out of the window and noticed that the Alps had vanished.

"Yes. I suppose we can but I don't really like you saying that word 'sweetie'. It brings back bad memories for me."

"Yes. I can understand that. From now on, I'll watch what I say. OK?" she replied.

"Well, it's just that I've been thinking that I might have that Stockholm syndrome thing. You know like that newspaper woman in the States. Where you've tried to kill me, but now I love you anyway? Oh, I don't know, I get so confused."

"M. I'm truly sorry for what I tried to do to you but we've already got enough baggage on this flight without adding more. Let's get Naples out of the way first before we do a full blown analysis of your mental state." And she thought to herself, 'I wish that this was the only thing that I had to worry about over the next couple of weeks'!

In the airport everyone was scrutinized and studied for their 'sweetie' telltale signs of duplicity. Everyone was treated as an enemy until they proved otherwise. And only at that point was Jessica satisfied. She had noticed neither the baggage handlers nor customs officers studying or paying any more attention to them than they did to any other travellers. Even so, once through customs, she dragged Emma into the 'signore gabinetti' or 'ladies toilets', along with their luggage trollies. Once inside, they both crammed into the disabled loo and Emma realised that Jessica, far from being paranoid at being followed, actually had a plan. She immediately followed Jessica's lead and rifled through her own case looking for the clothes, which had been purchased in Paris. Five minutes later two old ladies left the toilets and were not followed by either Emma or Jessica. Emma could not keep a straight face and needed Jessica's stern look to prevent her from giving the game away before they had even exited the airport terminal.

They requested their taxi driver to convey them to Francescane Missionarie Del Cuore Immacolato Di Maria, presumed to be in or around Secondigliano. The taxi driver headed north and dropped them off reverentially on Via Vittorio Veneto, directly outside the church. Jessica took a deep breath, walked through the green gates and up the steps in to the sanctity of the church itself. Before entering she turned to look at Emma and said, "You're not going to surprise me by speaking Italian too, are you?"

"No, I don't know a word. 'Onesto'!"

Jessica's returned look, said it all. She pushed through the solid oak studded doors thinking, 'Are these to keep parishioners in or out? And why do churches feel the need to have so much security? Is it the valuables on show or the fact that some nutter may want to defile the holiness of the place?' Before she could answer either of these questions, she came face to face with a stereotypical plump old lady, dressed head-to-toe in black with headscarf to match. Jessica was in the process of being deferential to the old dear's age when she remembered that she too looked visually like an old lady, even though nowhere near as plump.

The Italian lady had already ignited three votive candles in the hope that the offerings would aid her in her quest of stepping that little bit closer to Heaven and was now climbing into a pew in order to pray for additional steps. As the lady knelt, Emma considered lighting a few candles herself in the hope of absolving her sins, but soon realised that there were nowhere near enough to do the job. Instead she approached her and asked, "Scusi. Do - you - know - where - we - can - find - the - priest?" The latter in stilted English spoken in the same fashion as baby talk with an Italian sounding accent to assist in the translation. The acoustics of the empty church bounced the exaggerated words off the walls and threw them back at her.

The Italian lady looked dumb founded and remained just dumb, perhaps awaiting divine intervention, which did arrive by way of the priest himself, approaching the altar from a side door. Seeing that he had a 300% increase in his congregation, which was unusual at this time of day, he approached the ladies to enquire what brought them to his modest church? Emma was in the process of speaking when Jessica interrupted and brought her to silence.

"Good morning, Father, Padre, Monsignor? Do you speak English?"

A slight nod, an apologetic smile and, "A little and it is Sacerdote," indicating that things could become difficult, not to say laborious.

Jessica continued, "Could we ask you a few questions?"

The priest looked at his watch, which dispelled the belief of the Italian parishioners that he was already a saint, as he needed to use an instrument of earthly making to overcome such a basic function as 'time'. "I have to prepare for Mass but I can certainly speak to you afterwards."

Emma said, "OK," and was in the process of moving into the nearest pew, when Jessica jerked her back out and brought disappointment to the sacerdote's face, as she said, "Yes, OK. We'll grab a coffee and call back in an hour."

Three staunch Catholics became one as the two stalwart interlopers walked back through the huge oak doors, which Jessica was convinced would not now open. Once on the outside, she breathed in the air deeply to rid her lungs of the musty atmosphere she had just left and let the sun warm up her face. "I didn't realise how hot it was out here after the coolness of the church. Let's find a cafe and chill for a while. Sorry Emma, if you wanted to stay but I just couldn't face bouncing up and down for an hour, especially after the nights we've had." Emma blushed as she remembered the bouncing up and down that she and André had done and concurred wholeheartedly even though, she had been swayed by the pleasant, almost air-conditioned, temperature, which she had just vacated.

On their return they had to fight against the departure of a congregation of six; five having arrived with only seconds to spare before the service began and now piously perceived themselves that little closer to God too, for having made the effort. The two sisters sought out and found the sacerdote, who with a graceful movement of his hand invited them to sit in the nearest pew and the interview commenced with him looking slightly disappointed, that they had not stayed for Mass, but also with a certain amount of curiosity too, whilst he said, "Now then my children, how may I help you?"

Jessica opened with, "Well, Father, Padre, Sacerdote! We have a few questions that we'd like to put to you but before we start we need to know where your sympathies lie?"

"What kind of sympathies are you referring to? I am a servant of God and as such I hold sympathies across a wide spectrum and my charity is all encompassing."

"OK. Let me start with a man called 'Franco Di Larno', he died in 1983 at 31 years of age and his funeral service was held in this church. Did you know of this man and was it, in fact, you who performed the service?"

"Yes, I did know of him and no I did not perform the service; 1983 is, let me see, 30 years ago. I came to this parish in 1996, when I took over from my Uncle, but as I say I knew of the man, not personally; but his generosity, reputation and drive to help the poor of Secondigliano, preceded him. His death was a brutal shock to the whole area and has left a schism to this day."

"Is the previous Sacerdote, your Uncle, still alive?"

"Yes, he is still alive but is retired now due to poor health. As will come to all of us, age crept up on him and he has spent the last few years in a monastery, although he still remembers our townsfolk in his prayers everyday and hopes that one day the age-old rift will be healed. But why the interest?" He asked, again with a look of curiosity and puzzlement, revealing his opinion that all was not as it seemed with regards to these two elderly English ladies.

"We understand that Signor Di Larno had a close friend in Luigi Agosti," said Jessica rhetorically with a slight pained expression appearing across her face.

"Agosti? Luigi Agosti. Where have I heard that name? Ah, Agosti and Di Larno; yes, they were instrumental in setting up the famous, or some say infamous, money laundering operation by converting lira into gold bullion. It was to be the opportunity of everyone's lifetime and to preserve and increase its own monetary worth through indefinite time. Almost The Holy Grail, but not quite." Here he stumbled, became silent and his eyes drifted up to the iconic crucified Christ suspended above the altar. He made the sign of the cross, shivered imperceptibly and continued, "The only problem being that nobody ever benefited from it; but how does this come to be of importance to two elderly ladies from England?"

"Before I answer that, I must ask you again, where does your true allegiance lie?"

"I've already stated my position in relation to the catholic brethren who attend this church, but if you are asking whom I favour; either the rich or the poor, then I have no hesitation in saying the poor, as was always Christ's intention. I do not involve myself in the politics of the town but I am not blind to it either; the Camorra's infighting has split us into 'haves and have-nots', very much like your English Shakespearean play. After Di Larno was gunned down at a sidewalk restaurant in Naples, quickly followed by the vanishing act of Agosti, that partnership split spelt financial ruin for the losing supporters. The Alberto Pugliese supporters became instant Lotto winners overnight, not that the Lotto existed then, but you understand the simile; with untold fortunes bestowed upon them. This being their promised reward for would-be positive voting, even though the majority voted more out of fear than conviction. Those who stayed faithful, true to their beliefs and were not prepared to sell themselves, became second class citizens in an already poor environment, where earning a living was nigh impossible. Their lives spiralled into even worse drudgery and poverty, due to the opposition's repression, to the point of them being 'liraless' or with the advent of the euro, centless. Their only way out was to bail out and swell the numbers of the other 75% already enjoying the rich benefits of becoming one of Pugliese's supporters. To this day that struggle still continues and family loyalty comes under threat each time an older member dies and a younger member reaches adulthood, as the lifestyle they see on the other side of the fence, draws them ever closer to their perception of Nirvana. So I ask again what does it have to do with you two?"

Jessica looked across at Emma and with an indiscernible nod both girls took off their fake spectacles and grey wigs to reveal their true selves. "Sacre bleu!" cried out the sacerdote as he witnessed the transformation of elderly to youthfulness in the blink of an eye, "And you don't get many of those exclamations in my line of business. But you really had me fooled."

Jessica responded with, "We are going to have to take you at face value and hope that you will be at least compassionate when we say that, Luigi Agosti was our father." She continued despite the audible sharp intake of breath. "Our father died tragically in 1983 along with our mother, Laura, and we have recently come in contact with information which may be of benefit to the people of Secondigliano, particularly the 'have-nots,' as you so aptly have christened them. The disguises are our only way of keeping one step ahead of unknown persons, who we now know for a fact, wish to do us harm. Our immediate need is to contact any next of kin, to make sure that we are helping the right side of this long running feud. We know that there was a surviving brother, our Uncle, who left in the 70's to join the Mafia in Sicily along with a cousin of Franco Di Larno. Is there any way that either of these can be traced, that's presuming that either is still alive?"

"So reading between the lines of what you haven't said; are you putting yourself through this trouble and possible danger because you have knowledge about the missing monies? The long lost fortune?"

Jessica looked aghast at the padre, "How do you know we are talking about money? Although, I will say this, only because it is a House of God; yes, we have accurate information which we think could lead to that treasure, if that's what it is. But, and it's a big but, we have to get there before the pursuing party gets to us, and the only people we think we can trust are our extended estranged family."

"The majority of my congregation have dreamt and prayed about that money for over 30 years, and they think that only a saint could fulfil their dreams; perhaps, without blaspheming, you could be that saint, or even two saints! So, leave it with me and I'll get in touch with my contacts; we Sacerdote tend to network with all walks of life. Yes, including the Camorra and I can tell you that they have left me with plenty of bargaining tools when it comes to their Omerta and my confessional. Where are you staying? How can I get in touch?"

"I can give you a mobile number but as to where we are staying, nowhere yet. Do you know of anywhere discreet for two old English ladies?"

"Well, I would recommend Hotel Bolero Park on Via Provinciale, Santa Maria a Cubito; it's about 1500 metres west of here, so just far enough for you to be tucked away but close enough for us to reach. The owner is a childhood friend of mine and he keeps it clean and tidy. If we go through to the sacristy I'll phone for a taxi, another friend. He'll take you to the door. Then, when I have news I'll know where to find you. By the way, my name is Cristiano Abatangelo, I am obviously well known in these parts, which makes communication so much easier. In the meantime enjoy the beauty of Italy but I feel you may be too hot in your disguises, although I think they certainly do the job as you both very much look the part."

Within fifteen minutes, the young girls stepped out of the taxi again as two old ladies, and stood on the pavement admiring the pleasingly creamy yellow rendered hacienda type building, which fronted on to a tree-lined road in a quiet, low-volume traffic, residential area; just the retreat necessary when keeping a low profile. And it was here that they felt safe enough to spend the remainder of the day and night relaxing and sleeping with just the occasional snack on homemade pizza and a sip of their well-earned glass of wine.

*

An hour in to their drive and with silence filling the car to bursting, Babyface asked, "So Lydia, how did you come to choose that name?" The directive of their organisation being that pseudonyms could be divulged and used, as could their provenance be explained but only at the specific user's discretion, whereas all company staff reference numbers must be given in full when requested by any employee, no matter what rank.

Lydia sighed quietly, feeling that this could be a lead-in to a pass, but replied anyway. "Lydia Gwilt. She is possibly one of the wickedest characters in English literature, purely a fiction of Wilkie Collins' imagination in his book 'Armadale'. Every conceivable evil became her stock-in-trade, the majority being carried out on prospective husbands or acquaintances. So, hopefully that tells you something about the bearer of the name, too?" Before Lydia could reciprocate, in return, by asking the origin of the name 'Babyface', she was upstaged by the retriever's phone call.

She grabbed greedily for the handset and listened intently to the new information being imparted. Once over, Lydia relayed the new intel to her colleague, by saying, "First, the breakdown on that mobile phone which our Romeo had in his possession. No calls of note on the mobile were found; there were several texts to the inbox, sent to the one called 'Emma', stating that she and the sender would be on the move early in the morning. A call 12.40am going the other way, that is to the text sender's number and then a call at 4.50am, which the retriever presumes is a wake-up call. Then the only other call is to a number in Dijon at around 6.30am, they are still checking that one out. The car's been found in the Lyon train station and was hired out to Jessica Lambert. It's now under constant surveillance. But, by far, the most interesting is their sighting and then their act of purchasing two flight tickets to Naples, of all places, and both under their own names – Jessica Lambert and Emma Flynn. The passports indicate that both were born on 31st May 1980; so we now know for a fact that we are dealing with twins, and we've concrete evidence that they must be indeed Agosti's children."

Babyface banged the wheel and, small talk put to one side, said, "Bingo! Let's just suppose for a moment that they were headed for Switzerland, which all previous data confirms positively; then they meet this André guy and Emma, it was Emma getting the texts, wasn't it?" A nod leads him to continue, "Emma's getting the texts and a wake up call from a panicky Jessica; but what's spooked her? Why does she want to move so early in the morning? What's happened to the leisurely trip with perhaps a little sightseeing thrown in?"

"The Internet café," replied Lydia, "that's what's spooked her. She probably found some news item about the Scotland Yard murder and that other murder in Aberdeen and put two and two together. I think she had a gut feeling that you were tracking her from the start and those two deaths sealed it."

"Bollocks. I didn't expect the informant to resurface so soon, if at all, as he was well anchored when he went in but I've got to hold my hands up to the solicitor kill; I should never have finished him with a bullet to the head, but it's just that he'd been so brave, I almost saw it as a form of respect for his courage under torture. Anyway, we are where we are and by close of play today that could mean we'll be in Naples, if we get a move on."

"Yes. Forgot to say, the retriever confirmed that the Boss has booked us on the 20.45 flight from Geneva Airport, more details to follow." Lydia remained silent but thoughtful for a few moments and then said, "Do you think the organisation will now throw extra bodies in to the search? I mean, with the whole of the Camorra resource being available on the doorstep."

" I don't honestly know. I hope not, as the majority won't be trained in our line of subterfuge, and knowing them we'll just end up with an all out manhunt, and before long the whole of Naples will become aware that the search is on for two English women, who will inevitably then go to ground." This led Babyface into his own morose, downward spiral, a dichotomy of 'the best of times and the worst of times' beginning to play with his head: as he either concentrated on the future chase or dwelt on his past failings. The best time: being that the constant long distance travelling, allowed him to focus on the prospective hunt and all the brutal aspects attached; whilst the worst time: gave him too much opportunity to brood on elements of his work that had gone awry. His present mood reflected the latter and he was conscious that the consequences would surface at some later date and a price would need to be paid. Lydia picked up on the sudden shift in the atmosphere but presumed that it was all part of the bonding process between colleagues and so kept her thoughts to herself.

On reaching the Swiss Border, Babyface was triggered back to life as he shook off the lethargy hanging over him. "So, don't you want to know about the name 'Babyface'?" he asked with a little indignation.

"Well, I already know that it suits your looks and, of course, I've heard the name, Babyface Nelson, but that's about all; I don't know any of his history."

"Baby Face, spelt as two words, whereas I use one, Nelson was a pseudonym too. He was a murderer and bank robber in the 1930's; so no change there. He wasn't as tall as I am but was just as youthful looking. His only problem was to be shot dead by the FBI at the age of 26, but his reputation lived on with him having killed more FBI agents than any other gangster at that time. I'm not looking to follow in either of those footsteps as I don't see myself as a cop killer per se and I don't want to be six feet under at such a young age either, or I'd be there already."

For whatever reason, which Lydia could not quite fathom, she was happier that he was talking again and even happier that he was not dead as her future was now riding on his continued existence in his present role. She continued the conversation with, "It's amazing how fact and fiction can blur in to each other. I've chosen a literary anti-heroine with a hoard of bodies left strewn in her wake and you've chosen a real life villain with the infamous distinction of killing the most FBI agents. The only facts or fictionally 'true facts' about both of them are that they used pseudonyms and inevitably died and paid the price for their misdemeanours."

The atmosphere in the car remained jovial, even if it again returned to silence but both knew that a line had been crossed and a tiff had been overcome, even considering that there was no relationship to warrant a tiff in the first place. The final leg of the journey to Geneva International Airport was completed without a hitch with their only interruption being the clan's call to confirm their flight desk and check-in time. Even so, there was one negative aspect to the call with Lydia being informed that the girls had passed through Naples' customs and proceeded to join the long queue for the ladies toilets and although they were seen entering that was the last visual contact. The accomplice could not help but laugh as she reiterated this to Babyface, who replied, "Oldest trick in the book; they went in as young women and came out as something else. Still not a problem though; if they are Agosti's kids then we've a good idea where they will ultimately end up," he concluded confidently and with equal humour to match Lydia's.

Both operatives arrived well in advance of the designated time required and ended up spending an hour drinking coffee, whilst pretending to fool around as lovers sometimes do. In reality, they were all the while scanning the airport personnel and fellow passengers, with a view to identifying their own colleagues by any giveaway signs or mannerisms. The only problem with fooling around, as Babyface soon found, was that what started out as fun could quickly become something more serious. He was certainly at sixes and sevens with regards to Lydia, particularly with her being his first ever, female assistant and now struggled to decipher whether or not he was reading a somewhat different behavioural sign.

But their observational game was all to no avail anyway, as after having travelled another 885 kilometres in just over an hour and so entering yet another country, neither of them had caught sight of a likely candidate, colleague or otherwise, either before take-off, on touch-down or even as they sailed through customs; that was until they saw the guy holding a sign saying C/IT/703 and then they could not help but see the funny side. The irony of them scrutinising shadows and judging who was, and who wasn't of their ilk and then one of their own came along and slapped them right in the face. Babyface's smile went much deeper though; at the joy of being back on home soil, so making the occasion for him that much more special. It had its hilarious moment but also a more serious side too as Babyface now knew that he might not have quite the same control over what he had come to acknowledge as his operation; as with now being in the Camorra's heartland it could easily mean a transfer of that command to a local cell. Their only consolation being that they were not responsible for the loss of the girls, but that was nearly two days ago and *SpiyWeB* had so far still drawn a blank with subsequent zero sightings. Now a review meeting with Italian overseers would clarify the situation and confirm who was going where, from here on in.

CHAPTER TEN

Totally refreshed and having taken a taxi into Naples; then catching the local train to Sorrento at the Centrale and transferring to the public bus service for a sightseeing trip along the Amalfi Coast, all left Emma totally bemused. She could not understand for the life in her why the old ladies of yesteryear put themselves through the agony of this type of holiday. 'How could this torture have been classed as 'The European tour' when one was constantly walking from what seems like one sauna to another?' she pondered. She was sweltering under the wig and medium length prim dress, which obviously had to stay buttoned demurely, to complete both the image and the discomfort. "What size did you say this dress was, Jess? I'm trying my best here to keep everything hidden and in the right order but it's a struggle you know, what with this heat and everything."

"Stop complaining, it's your usual size, although perhaps their busts were less voluminous and probably more obedient. Anyway, just relax and enjoy the scenery. Imagine that you're gazing through Mum's eyes and taking in all the spectacular views she would have seen. It says in this guidebook: '*The ubiquitous cypress trees stand to attention as the beautiful landscape allows itself to be intersected with olive and lemon groves in regimental criss-cross formation leading to the cultivated lush terraces teaming with bougainvillea. Which in itself competes with an array of wild orchids, brooms and various species of rock roses, in a constant hustle for their own favoured sheltered spots: and all releasing their perfect blend of nature's aromatic perfume and wafting it skywards. Upwards to be enjoined with a cacophonous serenading soundscape from the overhead drift of: a merl of blackbirds, a screech of yellow-tailed gulls, and a lone kestrel preying on prey whilst in the accompaniment of great tits.'"*

Emma had turned off from just about the first word to the last as she replied, "Yes, thanks Jess. But like I say I am trying my best so that you can't see them!"

"No, stupid. I'm talking about birds. I'm reading it; can't you see? *'Positano epitomises the many multicoloured fishing villages tumbling down the cliff sides,'* and look there at Capri in the distance, surrounded by that gorgeous azure sun-stippled Tyrrhenian Sea. Doesn't that just make you want to strip off and dive straight in?"

"I am not going anywhere near that sea dressed like this and as for Mum I bet when she was here sightseeing, she wasn't trussed up like a turkey."

"Turkey or no turkey, you've only got to stay in disguise for a few days, and it's not like you'll be going dressed like this all the way until Christmas, now is it? So have another drink of water and keep your voice down, we're meant to be keeping a low profile, not advertising our presence to the whole of Italy!"

Emma took the bottle and the hint; she had a quick swig and stared blankly out of the window, managing to only fidget twice before their arrival in Amalfi town itself. The old ladies immediately headed for a bar in the shade and Jessica just about managed to prevent Emma ordering a Peroni by interrupting and requesting two lemonades instead. "I don't think elderly ladies will have a clue what Peroni is, let alone ask for it by name; so 'when in Rome,' and acting out the role of a person in her sixties or seventies, you've got to behave like one."

"OK. But talking about Rome. I really wanted to go there and look at all those old broken down buildings and see the places that Dan Brown wrote about in his book; instead we're here boiling to death and ...", struggling to think of anything else to say she finished with, "... drinking lemonade, of all things. And is anybody going to pick up on how fast this old woman is wafting her fan, so that her whole face doesn't melt away before the day is out!"

"Come on, M. I know you were disappointed at not visiting Rome but speed was of the essence and you've got to admit that it would be no fun sightseeing there if we were constantly looking over our shoulders. Perhaps you'll get the chance another time, when who knows, if all goes well you might even be rich. Then you'll be able to hire your own personal guide to show you all the buildings from Dan Brown's book and whatever else you like. And yes, OK, fan away."

Emma greedily pulled on the glass of lemonade but her thirst felt the worse for it. Only marginally refreshed, and by no way to her satisfaction, the two girls/old ladies walked across to the Piazza del Duomo with beads of sweat constantly forming out of nowhere under Emma's wig, on to her neck, and zigzagging down her back only to pool at the base of her spine whilst Jessica demurely walked on, oblivious to any such discomfort. They found themselves at the foot of the steps leading up to the bronze doors of Amalfi Cathedral, featuring its lion faced door knocker with its worn nose from over-rubbing by zealous believers. As soon as they stepped over the threshold they retraced their steps; Jessica's mobile being the culprit. A text message from Sacerdote Abatangelo requested that they return to his church, 'appena possible,' or asap to you and me.

This was easier said than executed; the journey in reverse was equally as tortuous to Emma and still without the benefit of her desired intake of Peroni. The only difference was that having exited the train station in Naples they were able to hail a taxi, for the final leg, directly to the church in Secondigliano. Once there, Emma in her haste, staggered up the steps, walked through the door in to the church's sanctimonious coolness and gasped, "Can I take my clothes off now?"

The padre and his two guests looked up from their discussion: the first in shock and the other two in bemusement at the prospect. Emma took all three in her stride and searched out the confessional, which she instantly converted into a changing cubicle, leaving Jessica alone to be introduced to the two newcomers. "Sorry to drag you back so soon from your sightseeing expedition but I know your agenda is much more than climbing Vesuvius or walking around the historical site of Pompeii, even allowing for the fact that it is nearly 2000 years old. Perhaps you can revisit, when you have more time on your hands?"

"Amalfi, actually. But now I'm being pedantic."

"Sorry anyway. Let me introduce Eduardo Martini and Pietro Agosti, both have been working away for some time but there are always ways and means to communicate. Eduardo is the nephew of Franco Di Larno and Pietro is the brother of Luigi Agosti. I think these two will prove a great help in fulfilling your task."

Jessica's tanned face physically blanched and she swayed momentarily before catching hold of the edge of the nearest pew. "Emma," she shouted, "where have you gone? I need you here now."

Emma came out of the confessional, slightly cooler, having benefitted from a short period of being underdressed but now once again rearranging her overly fussy clothing about her body. The padre, showing that a man of God could still have a cheeky sense of humour, said, "Well, that's a first, I promise you." Emma walked across to them appearing innocent and carefree but a little confused at the men's reaction to her presence.

"Private joke, M. Now let me introduce you to our Uncle. This is Dad's brother, Pietro. He's the nearest we're going to get to our father, in thirty years." Pietro was on the point of interrupting but waited, instead. "And this is Eduardo, that's right, isn't it? Eduardo, he's the nephew of the man Dad had the funeral card for. You know the one that was in the package that Jeremy gave to us." Then she addressed Pietro and Eduardo together with, "I'm Jessica and this is Emma."

Pietro was then allowed to say, "Well, actually I'm not the only relative you have in Italy. I hadn't got round to telling you two yet, but there is Mama too."

"Mama. Do you mean we still have a Grandma, and an Italian one at that?"

The sacerdote smiled as confirmation of this revelation with Pietro continuing, "That's exactly right, and she still lives right here in Secondigliano. But I'll have to arrange a private meeting, one that doesn't attract any attention. Now you've got this far we don't want Alberto Pugliese's supporters questioning the motive as to why two young English girls are dressed as two old English ladies, do we?"

Pugliese himself, had been killed accidentally at the hands of the Polizia di Stato, in what was originally staged as a PR stunt. A stunt where he should have escaped unharmed but which did not materialise that way, as one of the officers had not been briefed sufficiently and shot to kill. Just like Pugliese, the officer's career lasted just slightly less than his life as an armed officer; with an immediate transfer to traffic violations and then a head-on crash with a fully laden 26000kg brick lorry, following in quick succession. So, even though the leader of the opposing Camorra clan was dead, they continued to carry his name and were still in disarray as to choosing his successor, with no one yet having sufficient support or strength to come forward and claim it.

Pietro continued, "First, you're going to have to tell us what brings you here?"

Jessica took a deep breath and began, "Well, there is not much to tell. In a round about way, Emma found out that our Dad might be called Luigi Agosti and a chain of events was put into play which has culminated in us trying to get to ...," at this point Jessica paused and looked at the padre for support; he smiled and nodded encouragingly for her to continue. "... to Zurich. We are trying to get to Zurich. There I've said it. Now you won't need us anymore, will you?"

"Why do you say that?" asked Pietro.

"Well. You'll have all your own people to find the long lost millions; you know the Mafia type of people that you're involved with."

"You are correct in your assumption, that Eduardo and I are members of the Mafia in Sicily, but not in thinking that we would wish to take over your quest, especially as you have been so successful in getting this far, and on your own. We know that a large amount of cash was taken out of the country and converted into more inflation-proof currency. Rumour and word of mouth have always linked these transactions to one of the banks in Zurich but the final destination was lost with the ensuing feud that led to my brother's disappearance and the then Camorra leader's death. We had both left Secondigliano by that time, as the draw of the Mafia big time was too much for us to miss, and Mama wanted to keep her remaining two sons apart, so that both Luigi and I wouldn't be killed in the same gang warfare battle. She always had a fear that she might outlive her children and so far she's been proved right, as she has now outlived four of my siblings. So, we are here to help you and our diehard, but diminishing Di Larno supporters and take it as read that we have as much backing from the Sicilian Mafia brotherhood as we need."

"Wow. My sister and I do seem to be mixing in somewhat exalted company, if that's the right word for your type of organisation."

Emma interrupted with, "Yes, the only thing I know about the Mafia is that they cut off horses' heads and put them in your bed! But I can't actually remember why they do that?"

Everyone laughed as Jessica apologised and continued, "Sorry about that. But seriously, we think that we have found both the key and the code to a safe deposit box in a Zurich bank and we need your help in getting us there and your protection in keeping us safe as I feel that since we left Scotland there has been a constant shadow following our every move. And two recent dead bodies turning up in the UK seem to confirm my suspicions."

"We can do both of those for you and we'll put feelers out to check on your pursuers. Sounds like you have been tracked by *SpiyWeB* and are more than lucky to be still remaining one step in front, but now you have the support of the Mafia it will work both ways."

"In the meantime, I suggest these two young ... old ladies, return to their hotel and freshen up. I'm sure they won't want to stay feeling hot and sticky on their first meeting with their Grandma," interjected the sacerdote, who then proceeded to ring for a taxi.

"That sounds good, Padre but first, can someone tell me what this web thing is that you are talking about?" asked Emma with confusion written across her face.

"*SpiyWeB* is a huge information gathering and disseminating service that literally takes all the hard work out of tracking anyone. For you to have fooled it for as long as you have and without realising it, is quite unheard of. Although, the good thing from your point of view is that now you will have it working for you as well," answered Eduardo finishing with a flourish.

"Mm. That's makes me feel so much happier, I don't think," replied Emma and concluded with, "Boys with toys! Huh."

An hour later a senior Italian lady, unsteady on her feet and wearing the ubiquitous black of the older generation was ushered into a bar, via the side entrance; the front door being locked with a sign saying 'chiuso' or closed. Her only surviving son supported her as she walked and he assured her that she was in the bar for a very good reason. She was guided to a table that was already taken by two young ladies, but both jumped up at her arrival and proffered their chairs. She lent on the back of one as she took in the scene, which transported her back over 35 years and then, as recognition struck, she threw her arms around each girl, one after the other, smothering them both in kisses.

Not speaking English, it was left to Pietro to translate as she said, "My beautiful grandchildren, it cannot be. I've prayed for this day for so long but never expected it to arrive. You look so much like darling Laura and this one has the colouring of my Luigi too. I never thought I would see you both, my beautiful, beautiful grandchildren, although I had been told that you were not in that disastrous catastrophe with your mother and father, all those years ago."

"Mama knows all about Luigi's tragic plan but refuses to accept that it was done in the name of the cause, but rather that it was purely an accident," confirmed Pietro. "She is far stronger than her age would suggest and since that tragedy as well as the death of Eduardo's Uncle she has been taking an active part in looking after the majority of our cell's supporters' welfare. We have been able to supply a certain amount of cash and food by way of extra benefit but the thought of hitting the jackpot gives us all hope for the future. Now, knowing that Mama, quite rightly wishes to become more acquainted we can give you an hour, but then we really need to start formulating a plan, or at least the beginnings of one. "

Jessica did not know that so many tears could be shed in sixty minutes but that seemed an accurate synopsis of what had just been witnessed. The young women each held one of their Grandma's hands and through emotion, touch and an ignorance of the Italian language, all three communicated to the best of their abilities. In the end, Mama was led away clutching one of her many sodden hankerchiefs and all cried out but at least with her heart intact and bursting with love. The two girls were fairing no better, and emergency repairs were needed to restore and return tear stained faces, back to their original pristine aged illusion.

Once completed and again composed, the two sat opposite the three men. Eduardo took the lead, "We have had time to assess your predicament, although probably not enough, but suffice to say that you will need to leave here immediately. We are ninety-nine percent confident that we can rely on the majority of our own supporters but money has always been a persuasive tool and so we can not guarantee the silence of that remaining one percent."

Emma was about to interject, when Eduardo held up his hand in a preventative manner, "Don't worry. We are not going to abandon you, but you must understand we are all now in danger. Should the objective of your presence here leak out; then at least half of Secondigliano and even further afield will be hunting you down. The price on your head will be beyond imagination. To that end we have devised the following plan; it is secure and utilises the best and most reliable personnel from our Camorra cell. But, let me warn you now, don't talk of this to any other member or supporter. The five of us here are the only ones with full knowledge of the facts and, who knows, that could be four too many.

CHAPTER ELEVEN

There is always a stigma attached to investigating one's own; a stench that rubs off and clings to those charged with the remit of navel gazing and digging until the truth is unearthed. DI Johnson was allocated that responsibility and had no relish for the task, whatsoever.

Dennis Stanning had been an upstanding employee; injured, some years earlier, in the line of duty and with only several years' service remaining before retirement. The DI knew that the digging would become dirty and the bad odour of finding a rotten egg or cop at the end of it would linger and, no doubt stifle her own career prospects. She could not decide if this was the reason why the Chief Constable had briefed her on the case in the first place or whether he actually had more confidence in her investigative skills than those of her colleagues. Being positive, she presumed the latter and began formulating her methodology, but then again being negative she presumed that one bent cop could lead to more.

Her two-pronged attack meant retrieving, reviewing and following Stanning's internal paper trail and then tracking down his external investigations, which everyone knew not only flouted, but also made nonsense of, his desk job remit. However, this behaviour had been permissible and carried out under 'the turning of a blind eye' idiom. The DI isolated herself from her colleagues and as the pariah of the department, ordered cyber, digital and hard copy information to be recovered and forwarded to both her terminal and desk at the behest of the Chief Constable, no less. She surmised that DS Stanning had most probably been abducted and murdered around seven days ago: this being calculated by allowing for the four days when he had been last seen prior to his body turning up in the Thames and then a further three days until she had been given the poison chalice. As leaked to the press, his death had been at the hands of a ruthless gang and had the signature hallmark of the Mob's hand, in particular.

In no specific order DI Johnson trawled through all the Intel received on the day that the DS vanished. She ascertained that he had just returned from a fortnight's holiday in the sun, which the crueller of his fellow workers informed her in gallows-humour style, had proved not to be of benefit to his health. That period of 14 days away from the office added an extra nightmare to the proceedings, as it regurgitated 14 days worth of material that needed sifting through in order to spot the initial trigger. And as this murder was linked, in style and almost exact content, to the Scottish murder and thinking laterally, the DI kept an open mind as to any possible connection between both brutal killings, particularly when allowing for the fact that they had occurred only two days apart.

Nothing jumped out from the computer screen and the only connection to Scotland was based on recent activity, purporting to a search of a 'Luigi Agosti' instigated from a website in Edinburgh. A name, it transpired, under observation for some time by the 'Cold Cases' Unit; but that was in Edinburgh and not Aberdeen. A headache prevented the DI from continuing her incessant trawl over screen after screen of information, which bore no relevance whatsoever to the case, so she decided to inspect the site of the actual location, where Stanning's body had been found.

Fortunately, the Marine Policing Unit based in Wapping, were far more amenable and affable to the DI's request. They arranged to meet her on the Surrey side, close by Harrods Furniture Repository; a former warehouse used for storing furniture of the well-to-do, whilst they moved abroad to take up foreign government posts. But now converted to luxury flats and apartments where they stored the actual well-to-do themselves. The imposing salmon-pink terracotta clad stone building, still featured the original name in distinctive letters, writ large on the façade front elevation, as it loomed imperiously towards the river.

"This is where the body was located, and still with the ropes hanging loosely around his torso, endorsing the point that he had been sunk for good and should never have returned to the surface," said Sergeant Grimshaw.

"So was he thrown in here?"

"Good question, but no. It's likely he was tipped over, either at Hammersmith Bridge or Putney Bridge."

"Why so unsure. Isn't it a matter of the flow of the river?"

"Well, yes. You would think so; but the Thames goes both ways. You see, it also has an incoming flood tide, which is incongruous to the river's natural flow towards the sea. So it would be really dependent as to what time he was dropped. You have Hammersmith Bridge to the west and Putney Bridge to the east and with both bridges being constantly busy throughout the day and evenings, it would be a very conspicuous, not to say audacious, task to undertake. The early hours of the morning would obviously look favourite and that's the time when he could have met a flood tide; so all I can suggest is that you first check CCTV, around that period; whether for vehicles stopping on the bridges or pedestrians carrying particularly unusual loads. Based on the actual time of entering the water will dictate whether it was the natural flow of the river or the tidal flow that transported the body to this point. But I'm sorry I can't be more specific."

The DI thanked him for his time and far from being despondent with his synopsis of the events that had taken place, she was jubilant. She contacted London Road Traffic and booked a viewing of CCTV camera footage from midnight until 5am of the night after DS Stanning had returned to work.

If her, and Sergeant Grimshaw's, hunch was correct then this would hopefully be the only videotape that she would need to trawl through. Having placed it as a 'priority request at any hour'; DI Johnson found herself booked in to view in the late evening.

She took a taxi across town and felt buoyant that on her first day of investigation, already pieces were slotting into place. Her worry had been that the tapes would have been wiped but her mind was put at ease by an engineer, who informed her that they had not used video for a good number of years now and everything was archived digitally instead. On arrival, she was ushered into a booth, given a five-minute simulation of the controls and then left to her own devices. The first thirty minutes were spent on 'x8' fast forward, where she saw vehicles moving quickly, stopping and moving on again, ad infinitum. Then she became excited by a minor accident where a car had not stopped soon enough and shunted into the back of the one in front; but the culprit had turned out to be dressed in dinner jacket and bow tie which she could not imagine was her murderer's profile.

Towards the forty-five minutes mark she became very interested in a car, which stopped on the bridge. Here the occupant disembarked and raised the bonnet of the vehicle; 'Mm, broken down' she thought. The driver then moved to the rear of the car, whilst looking around discreetly at the same time. A seemingly over observant passenger also alighted from the vehicle and both proceeded to lean into the boot. Approximately three minutes later they hauled a bulky item on to the bridge side and dropped it over. The DI could not contain her excitement and went in search of her friendly engineer with the hope that he could weave some magic. He too, took on the excitement as he seized the controls and moved through frames: zooming, enhancing, contrasting and sharpening and all within what seemed like only seconds, where it would have taken the DI, hours. The end result was a clear shot of one of the culprits and a more blurred shot of the other, but the bundle they were carrying, definitely looked to be trussed in rope with some kind of weights attached; which was the reason why the two men struggled to lift it over the bridge railings.

When the DI confirmed that she had seen enough of this scene, the engineer fast framed forwards and backwards, stopping at various points and then disappointedly said, "Sorry, to say but these guys are professionals. I've been looking for their vehicle leading onto and travelling off the bridge but I can't give you any more than the make, model and colour. They have obscured the registration plates, so the whole thing had obviously been premeditated."

"Don't worry. I'm not really surprised...," here the DI left a pregnant pause, waiting for the engineer to fill in the gap.

"Roger. Roger Duffy."

"...Roger. But if you can print out any enhanced hard copies of the two culprits and their vehicle, along with frame shots of them dumping the body, it would be much appreciated."

"That will probably take some time as each frame will need a clean up and enhancement. Can I get them to you in the morning? Where are you based?"

"Yes. Sorry, it's Scotland Yard. DI Johnson, Jenny Johnson. Tomorrow morning's fine, the earlier the better."

"OK, Jenny. I'll see what I can do." With that the two professionals shook hands, both trying to ignore the spark of electricity, which tinkled through their grasp. On leaving, Jenny immediately swiped her right hand down the length of her skirt so as to negate the static feeling, but even after having done that she could not deny that the feeling had been there in the first place.

The next morning could have been her birthday; she was almost prepared to jump for joy on seeing the envelope on her desk as she arrived at work. Roger had come up trumps and the digitally enhanced photographs would stand up well in court, if she ever had anybody to charge. She sat there admiring his work when a colleague passed over a photofit copy of an APW – all points warning. She almost ignored it in her jubilation, until the realisation of recognition stopped her in her tracks. It was somewhat fortuitous that the two individual pieces of information had crossed her desk on the same day but a break was a break no matter where the 'gift-horse' came from. She sat, comparing the photofit with her slightly blurred photograph of one of the characters on Hammersmith Bridge and was almost 99% confident that there was a match. That being the case she tracked the photofit APW to its source and was even more surprised to find that it had been instigated in Aberdeen. She felt that now she had her link between the two Mob style murders and needed senior approval to take the trip north to hopefully flesh out that link.

Approval given, she found herself in a tizzy, as she dashed back to her bachelorette's flat for spare clothes, toiletries and in order to leave out enough food for the live-in cat. The flight north to Aberdeen gave her enough time to remember all the things she had not done, that she would need to ring a friend, who would help her out. She had taken the first available option on the BA CityFlyer from London City Airport, arriving at the International Airport in Aberdeen at 9.00pm, whereupon she jumped in the first taxi that presented itself and was in the centre of Aberdeen by 9.30pm. Logistics had booked her a room at the Aberdeen Northern Hotel, approximately a half-mile south of the Aberdeen City Command Centre situated on Queen Street.

Bright and early, the following morning, she arrived there; impressed by the size of the multi storey modern building and approached the reception desk with trepidation. The photofit she was chasing down had no contact name and the immediacy of her journey from London meant that introductions would have to be made now rather than meetings having been preplanned. Fortunately, the image was still fresh in the desk sergeant's mind as was the officer who initiated it.

A five-minute sit down allowed Jenny to gather herself and the sergeant to locate DS Chris Campbell, the former being happier with the rest than the latter being with the search. The DS appeared and whisked the DI in to one of the meeting rooms leading off from the main reception area. After personal introductions and an inanimate introduction to a well-needed coffee, the DS asked how he could be of help. DI Jenny Johnson reiterated her interest in the photofit image that had been sent as an APW and that she thought could have a connection with a murder in London.

"Not the DS murder? The body that was fished out of the Thames with that gangland style trademark killing?"

"Yes, the very same. I've got a very close resemblance to your photofit of a suspect along with an accomplice, throwing a suspicious bundle into the Thames and I'm here to see if we can fill in a few missing links. Would you like to go first?"

"Yes, surely. But I'll just need to nip back to my desk and gather my notes. Just give me a couple of minutes; would you like to freshen up whilst I'm gone?"

"Yes, that would be great," replied the DI, knowing that she had been windswept on her way to the station, but possibly not appreciating how noticeable the wind sweeping had been, so a look in the mirror might be opportune.

On her return, the DS said rhetorically, "Ready when you are. I've got the notes, ordered more coffee and we can have the room until noon." He looked across, acknowledged her smile and continued, "A Rachel Scott, telephoned on Tuesday morning, 22nd May, to say that she was worried about her boss who had not come into work. She felt that to be most unusual, as he would normally have left a message on her mobile or the office line or even the Dictaphone on her desk, which, she said, usually contained his correspondence, for transcribing. But this particular Tuesday, there was nothing. She mentioned that the last time she had seen him was Monday mid afternoon as she had booked in a new client for a meeting, which did seem to slightly irritate her boss at first, but then he had come around to the idea. When the chap arrived, according to her notes - a Mr. Nelson, Rachel had showed him into the now deceased's office, and was then given the rest of the day off. With hindsight, she thought that's why Mr. Longthorne, that's the deceased, had been a bit off, because he wanted time off that afternoon too."

"You'll have to slow down a little."

"No need to make notes of all this. It's in the witness statement, so I'll get you a copy before you leave."

"Well, it just helps me to log it in the brain easier, it gets there quicker and stays there longer doing it this way."

"Anyway, as I was saying. No one had seen Mr. Longthorne since that meeting with Mr. Nelson. So, because Rachel was in such a state, what with him not even answering his mobile, we arranged to call at his house. And talk about house of horrors. There was literally blood on the ceiling. The dining room had been turned into a torture chamber with Mr. Longthorne slumped in a dining chair at one end of his own dining table, dead to the world. The dining room lights were still on and the heat from them was not doing Mr. Longthorne any favours; but the agony he must have gone through is frightening to ponder. I'll get you copies of these photos; they unfortunately show all the graphic gory details. "

The DI glanced over them, trying to remain one step removed from the brutality portrayed as DS Campbell continued; "Anyway, once we had cordoned off the area, we collected Miss Scott from her office and arranged for a photofit artist to coax her through the image of this last client, initially so that we could eliminate him from our inquiries. At that time she had no idea as to what we knew but she has taken it very hard since finding out that he is dead. And since the death we've advised her to remain at home and placed the house under surveillance, as we are concerned that her life could now be at risk too."

"So, when did this photofit become your main suspect? What made you jump from eliminating him from your enquiries to an APW?"

"Oh, we showed it to Mr Longthorne's neighbours, mostly the ones we had already interviewed. Several of them had seen two men; one having a very close resemblance to the photofit, helping Mr. Longthorne into his home after what they presumed was a day of celebrating. He was assisted up his own path and steps and both men then followed him inside. The neighbour, immediately next door, had become annoyed at how loud he was playing his TV or music and much later at the fact that he'd left his lights on all night at the back. He said it frightened off the wildlife that came through the gardens apparently. He had knocked on Jeremy's front door, which he did more than once, but was just ignored. Eventually he said the noise had ended; and now we know that was presumably when the victim could no longer scream out in pain; but the lights remained on until we broke in and found his body. That clinched it. That's when we put out the APW."

"Well, at least Ms Scott will be pleased to know that the photofit she gave is an extremely good likeness to one of the suspects in another murder. That of the DS, fished out of the Thames. And if it turns out that he was involved in this brutal murder too, then she will have played a significant part in avenging Mr. Longthorne's death," concluded the DI before surmising, "so, it would appear that these two perpetrators expected broad daylight to cover their evil deed. Anything further?"

"The only other lead was again given by his secretary; she supplied us with Mr Longthorne's mobile number, which we've accessed and are trawling through but two of the numbers are proving impossible to reach: one is registered to an Emma Flynn and the other is Jonnie Raey, both with last known addresses in the Edinburgh area. And now both seem to be either disconnected or just ringing out. And that's where we are at the minute. Sorry it can't be more."

"Can't be more! You've given me more than I ever expected, Chris, eh DS Campbell."

"No, it's OK calling me Chris, Jenny.. erh, DI Johnson and best of luck. Keep me posted."

"Yes, I'll keep you posted but just one last thing before I go. Have you checked your photofit against known criminals' mugshots?"

"Yes, we have. First thing I thought of, but alas, no hits. Looks like this guy's fresh in the UK or with a baby face like that, he could be too young to have done the full circuit of court, probation, court, jail, et cetera."

"Just a thought. Anyway. I'll let you know if either Emma Flynn or Jonnie Raey crosses our radar too. I think you deserve a bit of a rest after that piece of detective work!"

"Afraid not! I've still got the victim's house securely cordoned off with forensics looking for other clues and I'm trying to locate next of kin for the deceased. To all intents and purposes a very nice man, but a bit of a loner. To keep herself busy, his secretary is checking through various pieces of paperwork at the office to see if there is a will or other documentation, which may help further identify any relatives. But unfortunately, we've already been informed that there is no address for this Mr. Nelson character, and the chances are that the name is as fake as the address would be anyway."

"Well, good luck with all that and thank you for your assistance, it is a great help."

*

Meanwhile, back in Edinburgh, DC Blister had been around the block a few times and with very little to show for his exertions. Eventually, the original inquiry team's remaining staff opened up and gave the DC various leads to explore relating to the vanishing acts of both DI Barnham and T/DC Murray. What started as a jumble, slowly resolved itself into a more logical pattern and once his new colleagues overcame their prejudice to his youthfulness and lack of know-how, their contributions increased dramatically in assisting with the DC's investigations. This to the annoyance of the new murder inquiry team, who accused him of crossing over into their territory; but due to his personal drive and lack of experience he was never daunted by their lack of patience nor charm. This led him to soon became recognised within the force as the catalyst for total confusion.

Now glancing back over his notes, he was convinced that he had enough facts to enable his DI to take up the gauntlet from here.

T/DC Murray

Friday 26th April - Returned from investigation of Joe Foster's house. Retrieved a mobile - various texts and calls from Jessica Lambert. DI spoke to T/DC and JL privately - conversation still unknown.

T/DC then commenced a week's holiday. Overheard saying she was driving to Carlisle on Sunday morning for Carlisle-Settle train and then on to family in Leeds.

May 15th - Joe Foster's TV and DVD player found in T/DC's house, along with her car in garage.

May 17th - Checked with T/DC family in Leeds. Yes, she was expected but No, she never showed. Very concerned as not typical. Knew of her work ethic and commitment but she always communicated her plans, revised or not.

May 20th - Mr Murray (father) remembered contact of friend in Carlisle where T/DC would leave car for such journeys. The friend, Sarah Shaw confirmed that it was an open invitation and she too had been expecting T/DC on that Sunday.

Supplementary notes:

T/DC Murray had a soft spot for her boss, DI Barnham, which was a known fact in the office. Jessica Lambert, the profiler co-opted to the case had upset that equilibrium. Joe Foster, whose house

203

the T/DC had visited was a colleague of JS and the mobile texts/messages related to an evening meal that they were meant to have organised - possibly on the night he was murdered. Joe intimated that he had found a connection between the murders. Shame we don't know what the conversation was between DI, T/DC and JL, as I cannot locate JL anywhere either; presume she is not in the country. (See note below under DI Barnham, for context of conversation.)

Why does T/DC drive to Carlisle and not catch train in Edinburgh? Sarah Shaw says that, 'She parked on my drive many a time. It's free and secure. She has always done it. I've known her for years, since college days in fact. Always been very reliable and punctual, what with the train always leaving on time. Said she enjoys the scenic panorama of the Lakes and Dales, particularly crossing the Ribblehead Viaduct with all three Yorkshire Peaks in view. Stops off at Settle to buy local produce in the Market Square, has a coffee and then continues on to Leeds.'

So, the questions are: What has happened to change this person's habits so drastically? How did she get to Carlisle if her car's in the garage? What did the DI say to her on the Friday evening before she left work? What's she doing with Joe Foster's TV and DVD player?

DI Barnham

Sunday 28th April - DI landline telephone records indicate that last call received at Barnham's flat was from T/DC. Call out to same number at later time, same day.

Monday 29th April - Bank Holiday, therefore short staffed at the station. Jessica Lambert (JL) absent; phoned in ill.

Tuesday-Wednesday 30th April/1st May - JL returns on Tuesday. DI showed surprise when JL advised him that T/DC had not made agreed appointment on the Sunday. What were they doing, anyway?

Investigation continues. WPC Whitely mentions begrudgingly that DI was having a fling with a witness – Emma Flynn, and that T/DC was not happy.

Wednesday 1st May – Last day anyone saw DI. He booked a room under his own name at Bank Hotel, High Street, just off The Royal Mile. Spoke to manager, Mr Peter Phelps. He said that, 'He had been seen dining with young lady and afterwards they left the hotel together. Never returned at night; never paid. No reply from mobile. Sent invoice to address given on booking form but no payment received. Too late for any CCTV to verify whom the lady was, but description being checked out, possibly Emma Flynn.

Thursday 16th May – Freddie Brown rang asking to speak to the DI 'Wondered where his keys to Greyfriars Kirkyard were, as he can't now lock the gate?'

Supplementary notes:

Still don't know why the T/DC rang Barnham's house on Sunday morning but it transpires that both the T/DC and JL were undertaking a covert operation at JL's usual place of work, The Borders Agency – in order to retrieve a file, which Joe Foster thought could be helpful with the case. T/DC never turned up, so JL sorted on her own. But where is the file? According to JL, there wasn't one of any value, to be found.

Far be it from me to say that the DI didn't have his eye on the ball but he did seem to like his socialising and therefore probably didn't.

My guess is that the hotel assignation was with Emma Flynn but now I cannot find her to verify that either. Why do all these witnesses seem to go missing? Are they dead too? And what happened for the DI and his companion not to return to the Hotel?

And what does it have to do with Greyfriars Kirkyard? If the gate has been left unlocked, someone must have used those keys?

'So, there it is. As clear as mud,' he thought, 'and I've not trodden all over the other part of the investigation either, well not much, anyway. Perhaps I'll trawl through the press cuttings and see what JL has to say for herself and I could do with talking to her boss, what's her name ….,? Ah yes, Tess Danvers, she might be able to shed some light on her colleague's actions.'

CHAPTER TWELVE

The plan was a simple one; the two girls needed to get from Italy to Switzerland; and be accompanied for their safety, but by whom? Pietro and Eduardo were the likely candidates but would it add a little camouflage to take the padre too? There was no doubt in their minds that the opposing cell would now know of the girls' presence but hopefully not their disguise. However, there was no getting away from the fact that shadows would be stalking shadows for the foreseeable future. Their only true advantage, albeit a significant one, was that they knew exactly where they were going and how they were going to get there. So with all their new unknown support subliminally blending into the background the charade began.

Emma and Jessica; dressed in their unbecoming 'old ladies' outfits set off again, to all intents and purposes on another sightseeing tour. They took a taxi to the railway station in Naples and then the local train to Sorrento, where they alighted and sauntered the two hundred metres along the Corsa Italia to the centre of town. Emma, window-shopping along the way, admiring all the youthful bright summer fashions, before she caught a reflection of herself and remembered what age she was meant to be. At the Piazza Tasso they took a right, which led them toward the Marina Piccola, passing The Foreigners' Club and then unsteadily stumbling down the steeply cobbled road, whilst at the same time clinging on to the wall side, more for effect than necessity. The bottom opened out into a small port with a large number of people milling around the semicircular ticket office and queuing onto the quays. The two old ladies joined the longest line, as only the English do and bought tickets for the first available sailing to Capri. Once on board, they found seats on deck and remained quiet yet observant as they took in the scenery of the Amalfi coastline to their left. The breeze proved a godsend and replaced the need for Emma to improvise with a makeshift fan, leaving her only problem to be that of possible sunburn; so pulling the brim of her straw-hat forward instantly resolved that dilemma, before it became a major issue.

Within fifteen minutes of departure, Capri's outline began to take physical detailed shape, as it etched itself on to the horizon; small white sails dotted the coastline as they navigated their way around the island, which although small in itself, stands tall as a rugged landmass with Mount Solaro as its highest point. On disembarking at Marina Grande, the old ladies headed for the funicular cableway, which ascended at a stately pace and unhurriedly dropped them off in the town centre's Piazzetta. As on the ride up, here too the views were breathtaking and the fashionable bars were exceedingly inviting but not available as no sooner had the two alighted from the terminal than Pietro beckoned them to an awaiting taxi. They left Anacapri to Emma's dismay, leaving behind its winding alleys that epitomised the elitism of world famous brands, and headed down the narrow winding road to the Bay of Marina Piccola, overlooked by the former old fort, Canzone del Mare. Made famous by the 1940's British sweetheart, Gracie Fields and now a thriving exclusive restaurant.

Emma was even more disappointed on being escorted to the small Marina itself, where she caught sight of the padre standing adjacent to a small dinghy. He saw her consternation and pointed over his shoulder with his thumb, in the direction of Faraglioni rocks. There, at anchor and standing majestically proud in the water whilst bobbing ever so gently was a 70ft teak decked, sleek white sports cruiser with a flying bridge, no less; just waiting for their arrival.

"Fuck me," exclaimed Emma, "is that for us?"

"Excuse me, Senora. But this is not the language of an elderly English lady," responded the sacerdote, "Sorry, we couldn't moor it on the beach for you."

"Yeah, well. Sorry about the blaspheming, Rev.," she replied sheepishly, but still with amazement lighting up her face and a laugh in her voice as she gauged the gap from the beach to the cruiser, "I reckon I can slum it for that short distance. I'll even swim if needs be!"

The four of them took the diminutive journey across the bay to the motor cruiser and stepped out of the dinghy from one mode of boating in to an altogether different one; the VIP luxury lifestyle with the one million plus, euro price tag. Pietro ushered them quickly below deck where they met up with Eduardo who introduced them to the skipper, Alonzo Berti and pointed over to the galley at his deckhand, Damiano Castantini, or 'Cas' for short, who was busily preparing vegetables for lunch. Introductions complete, the skipper moved on to the bridge and shouted, "Weight anchor" whilst checking the controls and starting up the engine for their journey northwards; his intention being to hug the coastline all the way. The five passengers now sat in comfort and containing their excitement; were rewarded by Cas with chilled spritzers and an assortment of canapés. Once he was out of earshot Eduardo began to explain the next part of the plan.

"Ladies, we are obviously leaving here for a boat journey, which should take around ten hours, as we are plotting a course north for Fiumicino Airport." Here, he paused for any recognition of the name; as there was none, he continued, "We could travel faster but that might attract attention and would not benefit us in reaching our destination. Fiumicino Airport services Rome, our great capital and the Holy See of the Roman Catholic Church," this time he gave a nod of recognition to the sacerdote. "The plan from there is that you will fly to Zurich, to all intents and purposes giving the allusion that you are travelling by yourselves. And even though we wish you to retain control of the operation, there will be the three of us in the background, along with many others, unseen I might add. I'm sure you'll both be pleased to know that, after leaving the marina and hitting open water, you'll have a chance to change into clothing more suitable for a voyage of this nature. The aft desk is at your disposal and with the sacrifices you've already made in this heat, it's probably not before time that you should be able to relax and cover up or not, to whatever degree you wish. The only request I would make is that you dress appropriately when moving about the remainder of the boat and should another craft be sighted, it may be necessary to descend below deck until it has passed by."

Jessica acknowledged this with thanks, at the freedom that they were being given and agreed that the requests made were sensible and thereby equally as acceptable, too. They then finished their drinks and walked quickly, ran actually, to their stateroom to rip off the stiflingly cumbersome clothes and wigs, which had made up their charade for some days now. Emma, always being at one with her body, dressed in the skimpiest T-shirt that she could find along with an equally micro skirt; Jessica settled for a short cotton summer dress, so enabling air to circulate where none had been for several days.

On their short journey to the aft deck, they bumped into Cas going about his duties. Emma reciprocated the once-over examination she was being given with one of her own and liked what she saw, liked it a lot. Cas just thought, 'This little boat trip has got a whole lot more interesting now!'

Once on the aft deck, all the creature comforts were available there to enable the girls to relax, probably for the first time since stepping on to Italian soil or to be more accurate, floating in Italian waters. They could sleep, read, laze about, drink and eat; with all amenities provided courtesy of question mark? 'Who is providing all this? Surely not the poor people of Secondigliano, or the sacerdote's parishioners; who were probably one and the same, anyway.' Jessica's mind had too much time on its hands, or brain if you prefer. Thinking was not one of the relaxations in which she should be partaking, but she acknowledged that she could not switch off totally. Checking her reflection in the window before descending into the saloon area, she knew her face would betray her; but she had to do it anyway.

Pietro was the only one sat there, drinking an espresso and refreshing himself of various statistics from reams of data, spread across the table. Hearing footsteps, he looked up and welcomed Jessica; and admiring her dress, he said, "That looks more like it. I hope you don't mind me saying but I can see in you a resemblance to Luigi; but then again, that maybe just your subtle tan as your looks definitely comes from Laura. She was a beautiful woman. But I thought you would be on deck enjoying the sea air and snoozing, by now."

"That was the intention but unfortunately, I got to thinking and sometimes that does you no good. So, I've a question for you? The boat and all these trimmings," she said whilst moving her eyes in complete 360-degree circles, by way of emphasis. "Who is paying for it all?"

"Well, a bright girl like you, who is after all my brother's daughter, what do you think?"

"I think the Mafia."

"And you would be right. As you know, Eduardo and I have worked for them, well for most of your life and we have an understanding. They appreciate that home is home and, over time, have repaid our loyalty by helping the Di Larno cell wherever possible. Don't be naive in thinking that they don't know what's going on or where we are at any particular time. If we are all convinced that Pugliese's cell are tracking us then we need the Mob's power base, whether you like it or not. All you see is what you are meant to see; everything else is just played out in the tenebrious shades. But I guarantee on my life that neither your sister nor you will be harmed in any way whilst under the Mob's protection."

"It wasn't really my safety that I was worried about, it was more the gold and diamonds and whatever else we find. I thought it was going to be distributed amongst the poor of Secondigliano and not filling the coffers of the Mafia!"

"It will go to the poor, mark my words. However, have no doubts that my bosses will take a cut, usually ten percent; but ten percent of millions will still leave plenty to make a lot of poor people rich."

"OK. I believe you and have faith in you, for my Dad's sake. I just hope you have that same belief and trust in your bosses?" With that Jessica left the saloon and headed to the en-suite bathroom of the stateroom that she was sharing with Emma. There, as she washed her hands and threw water over her face, she looked into the mirror and washed her mind too. 'Still eight hours left on this boat and I'm going to make the most of it. It's impossible for me alone to keep this whole juggernaut of a quest on track, so why do I punish myself so?' And with that, and still with a wet face, she went back into the saloon and made another spritzer; 'Two alcoholic drinks in one day, what's the world coming to?' she thought as she made one for Emma too but on returning to the deck she found her gone. Taking to heart her new resolution she laid on a lounger, read a magazine, sipped her drink and allowed the world to literally sail by; knowing Emma was, wherever Emma was.

An hour passed before she found where Emma was. Shouting broke out below deck in the vicinity of the Captain's cabin as a red-faced Emma; far too red-faced to have just been catching the sun's rays, struggled womanfully to contain her modesty in not much more than a hand towel. She ducked and dived through the corridor as if trying to avoid all the Italian rhetoric spilling out in all directions and bouncing off the walls themselves. Cas was next to appear sporting, well sporting nothing; his hands covered the essentials whilst his exquisitely defined torso glistened from intense exercise. The author of the shouting was last to appear with thunder in his face and a 'modello CUD' in his eyes, the Italian equivalent of a P45. This time Cas had taken his deckhand responsibilities too far and besmirched the integrity of the Italian cruising fraternity, not to mention dishonouring one of the boat's guests.

The dishonoured guest found her way back to the aft deck, via her cabin; and was clad to an acceptable degree when she approached Jessica with a wolfish grin and shrugged, "Well, it would have been rude not to, wouldn't it?"

"Yes, I suppose it would, but surely you must know that, 'shitting on your own doorstep!' or in this case poop deck, only leads to trouble. Aren't there enough men in the whole of Italy for you to hit on, without seducing one who should be working? And, did he pay you? I'll bet not. Where's your principles gone? You know, 'the no free lunch' idiom?"

"It takes two!" retorted Emma before snubbing her sister by grabbing and drinking the spritzer that had been previously placed by her lounger. This gave her time to formulate a more complete answer, "No, he didn't pay. I make it a point of only charging on land, never at a 'mile high', nor on water! And I haven't decided yet what I'd do if I go underground?" she joked, by way of acceptance of the rebuke and to put an end to the bickering.

Time dragged after all the excitement and the early evening meal proved to be a good focal point for analysing and rerunning the action. Emma retained her 'Fifth Amendment' right, even though she was not American, and did not know what the Fifth Amendment was anyway. So it was left to Cas to be ribbed incessantly over his apt eponymous Casanova nickname with antics to match, as he, reverting back to deckhand, served up 'seafood and shellfish stew with squid ink pasta'. No matter whether Emma admitted or not that Cas was an expert in the bedroom department, there was no getting away from the success of his culinary skills in the compact galley kitchen. The stew: consisting of a generous amount of monkfish, clams, sole and crab amongst other seafoods was a hit and the chilled Soave Classico complemented the meal, to perfection. Within the hour, both girls had performed their own version of the classic vanishing trick; only they did not disappear but just reverted back to their two old ladies' personas; and they were glad of it. The outside temperature had dropped significantly as the sun chased the western horizon, so both were now feeling quite comfortably dressed, for a change. They remained on deck with the full orb of a slightly diffused moon hanging in the last remnants of a navy sky, neither yet quite black nor yet displaying its myriad clusters of clear-cut stars.

The sudden drop in warmth and the coolness of the westerly Libeccio breeze meant that the final three hours of their journey northwards were taken up by the watching of a film with stunning surround sound, accompanied by a snooze, both during and after it. They were awoken to the multitude of nondescript external noises associated with a marina full of yachts: the flapping of flags; rigging knocking on the mast poles and ropes creaking under tension; water slapping on the hulls' sides; throbbing engines; pumping of bilge wells and propeller screws churning, unseen to the naked eye.

This was the Cantiere Nautico Albula Marina, literally two miles distant from Fiumicioni Airport. The cruiser had made good time on its 122 nautical miles journey at a steady 12 knots, as much to not attract uncalled-for attention, as due to the flight not being until 6.50am. Both girls were now either too tense or too excited to sleep and Emma had to be content with taking two of her remaining codeine to help with her concentration, whilst all five ran through their plan one final time. In light of Emma's dalliance, she was to be assisted by the padre more so in a chaperone capacity, whilst Jessica and Pietro would be paired up; so ensuring that the two old ladies would not become noticeable as a single item and nothing would be lost in translation, should difficulties arise. Eduardo was left to travel solo and keep an eye on both the odd-couples. And, before they knew it, they were packing and checking their bags for disembarking and the short drive to the airport terminal.

In essence, the plan proved in vain from the outset, with it being foiled even before its earliest inception. Cas, after having been unceremoniously dumped on the quayside of the docks, wasted no time in revealing his true colours as he phoned Pugliese's cell immediately. He had already found his time with Emma, both satisfying and profitable and he could still remember his rewards, both physically and when including her small talk, with total satisfaction; which proved far more fruitful than Emma had ever intended. His own reward was that now, he would be remunerated handsomely, by the Boss; for his loyalty and commitment; his only worry being that he had to stay alive to collect.

But even though he had shown his positive qualities, he too had been trumped; *SpiyWeB* already knew of the cruiser's docking and of its passengers' intentions; and again thanks to Cas. A command had originally been transmitted requesting for any news of the whereabouts of two old English lady interlopers. The retrievers had intercepted Cas' original text which stated that two old English ladies had indeed boarded his boat, when it was anchored in the small marina on the south of Capri and this after they had traversed across the island. And so, from the moment he relayed Emma's unsolicited pillow conversation; the boat's every move had been plotted via GPS, tracking his mobile. With the consequence being, that Pugliese's cell had been made fully aware of its progress and men were in position even before the cruiser entered the canal, on its way to the marina.

The machine gun fire rudely awoke the quiet of the early dawn, disrupting the natural calm of the morning as the staccato echo bounced between the warehouse buildings and multiplied in quantity as it amplified in sound. Its intended targets were the previously unaware travellers, who were in the process of accessing a minibus for the short journey to the airport terminal. The lackadaisical direction of the gunfire was accurate enough to nick Eduardo's shoulder as he safeguarded Jessica with his body but that, along with the peppered bodywork of their mode of transport, were the only collateral damage. The targets remained shielded behind the riddled vehicle until silence returned, punctuated only by the clatter of two bodies crumpling and falling to the ground, precipitated by the sound of two handclaps signifying handguns with silencers

"Wow, that was close. Are you OK, Eduardo?" asked Jessica raising a hand to his injured shoulder as she helped him to unbutton his blood soaked shirt. "What's the point of killing us now? If they think we've got some sort of magic key, how will they benefit if we're dead?" She asked this more to herself, but Pietro answered it anyway as he pressed a clean handkerchief firmly on to Eduardo's wound.

"They were not trying to kill you. It was us that they wished to neutralise. Then they would have taken you and yes, you would have talked. You would have told them everything, because they are those sorts of people. They want the knowledge that you have and, in turn, the riches that it will bring and preferably without any outside influence or interference. So, after this little episode, we now know that they will stop at nothing." Jessica knew this to be true as she thought of the fate of Jeremy, their newfound friend, who was no more.

"But why must you all fight and kill each other? And how did they know to ambush us here?" asked Jessica again. Seemingly the fright of all the shooting, Eduardo being shot and the two dead 'would-be' assassins had switched her brain in to lucid mode, which now could not stop her from asking questions.

With Pietro concentrating on stemming the flow from Eduardo's wound, the sacerdote responded, "It is a fight that has been ruminating for some years now, in fact since your father's time and the reason for your presence has now brought it back to the boil. The whole of Naples will be aware of your quest, if not all of Southern Italy. As for the ambush, it is easy to see that someone has been playing both ways, possibly the skipper of the cruiser, but more than likely his deckhand, Cas. If I'm right and it is the latter, then I pray for his soul as he will surely need it."

Eduardo winced as the strapping was tightened but looked happy that the blood had been staunched and that the bullet had only winged his shoulder, rather than remained there, embedded. He now joined in the conversation, "Why does anyone fight and kill? To gain: power, riches or sometimes, geographical expansion or perhaps more often than not a mix of all three. And in this case it is our ideology too, our people have waited thirty years for this justice and justice they shall have."

Jessica not quite done with the debate continued, "But you are all the same people. Cannot the two sides become one and share in the good fortune and so ...," then she stumbled to follow her rhetorical path, "...and so you wouldn't leave your Sacerdote, here, 'playing Padre in the middle,'" she finished lamely.

All three men chuckled and Emma whooped for more, hoping that Jessica would remain on her soapbox. But time was pressing, they were safe now for the present with a back up vehicle being made available for the short trip to the airport. Eduardo's injury looked more promising now with no blood-show through his clean shirt, but just to be on the safe side he wore a dark jacket too.

Cas' life, on the other hand, was not looking promising at all. In reality, he had already relinquished his claim to fourth generation Castantini, as he lay in the gutter with a bullet hole through his forehead, and a disappointment on his face. A disappointment of a life lost through making a wrong decision and the backing of a 'lame horse' that had no right to win anyway.

They boarded the aircraft for Zurich as planned, although all now with the realisation that their seating arrangements were compromised but they still kept up the pretence all the same. Emma in particular wished it to be otherwise, as the charade of playing an old dear with switching clothes for the passport control and then switching back again was making her hot and flustered and the tightness of the dress, particularly across her bosom, was again making it difficult for her to breathe easily. Jessica had sympathy there, as she too was concerned about putting on the odd pound with not having much opportunity to run as often as she would have wished. But for the moment, she sat back and relaxed, having no desire to communicate until her sister made her only significant contribution of note to the conversations that had preceded, as she walked past Jessica whilst making one of several trips up the aisle to the toilet. She leaned in and whispered, "This whole journey's a bit like a topsy-turvy 'Midas Touch' fairy tale, don't you think? What with dead bodies strewn about in our wake before we even get to touch the gold, ourselves."

"Well, it's Greek mythology actually, not a fairy tale but I won't split hairs about that, although I do get your drift. It does all seem to be happening in reverse." Jessica replied poignantly, hoping that their final arrival at the bank would see no further bloodshed.

*

As it was now 11pm, Babyface and Lydia were given the opportunity of a late supper and then transported direct to the Charming International Hotel, which for convenience sake, was within two kilometres of the Naples airport terminal. They were left to book-in with the understanding that they would be collected the following morning at 8.30am and taken to the prearranged review meeting with the agents' overseers. This was to take place at a hotel in Naples city centre; a city that Babyface had not visited for over ten years.

Decumani Hotel de Charme in the heart of Centro Antico, just off Corso Umberto, was the venue. A totally refurbished Palazzio, very much in the Renaissance style; featuring high vaulted ceilings, faded grand décor, elegant tasteful antiques and a grand staircase, leading to the opulent gilded reception room, which catered for discreet meetings, amongst other things.

The two travellers were ushered into the magnificent room and greeted by three colleagues, one being from the higher echelons of the Camorra, already seated in position. The more senior of the three stood and approached them. "Welcome to Naples, I hope you've had a pleasant journey, although I'm sorry to say that I think it has been a somewhat wasted one and that your travelling is not over, yet," he said as he shook hands with both, in turn. "My code is C/IT/165 and my two colleagues are C/IT/667 and C/IT/891."

The two new operatives also shook hands with Babyface and Lydia as C/IT/165 continued. "As our two targets are proving to be somewhat elusive, both of my colleagues here are now assigned to the mission and will be accountable on the same levels as your own designations. At present, names are not important but as rules dictate they are at liberty to divulge them to you during the operation, should they so wish. I'll let C/IT/667 supply an update of the latest intel that we have received from the retrievers."

"Thank you, C/IT/165. We know that the two girls landed at Naples International and visited the ladies toilets after having recovered their cases from the baggage carousel. They were then lost from sight and so eventually it was presumed that they must have come back out in disguise. Little was seen or heard in the area until late yesterday afternoon; when two elderly ladies, whom we had taken no particular interest in previously, returned to a church in Secondigliano via a Pugliese sympathiser taxi driver. His suspicion was aroused when one of the ladies began talking profusely and in a far too youthful voice and tone, which he judged to be at least half of the age of the person she allegedly portrayed. Once we were in possession of this information, the search was redefined with a rebrief to *SpiyWeB*. Needless to say, the London hub is disappointed and somewhat shocked at your lack of success so far, and the expense it continues to incur in chasing the girls across Europe. Hence the additional assistance, in the hope of a speedy conclusion; and note clearly, they are not an option but an order. It is imperative that we unearth the girls' final location and so are placed in position to retrieve the monies that were taken so many years ago and which we feel are still rightly ours. Therefore, you'll return to your hotel, relax and await further instructions; nothing can be achieved by running around aimlessly until we have sight of either two young English women or two old English ladies, whomever are seen the sooner."

Smarting from the reprimand, Babyface acknowledged in the affirmative his acceptance of the two additional operatives and stood waiting for the senior operative to dismiss them from the room. Inwardly, he knew that this slight on his ability would have repercussions on his career progress and so was already mentally assessing what other future options were available to him.

At least the wait was not long in ending, but long enough for any personal phone calls or text messages to be sent, should the worst become a reality. Three hours later, saw Babyface pacing the room, anything but relaxed as the senior Camorrati rang to advise him and his now, team of three, that the quarry had boarded a cruiser on the southern side of Capri island. As they were in Naples, Babyface was tempted to pursue the cruiser but patience and his recent rebuke, held his hand. Instead, he continued to brief the two new recruits and run through various scenarios, should the opportunity arise of capturing the, by now, two annoyances. Finishing the role play in the early afternoon, led the team to set off in search of an even later lunch; a lunch which was curtailed by notification that all four were booked on a flight to Zurich, leaving Naples Capodichino Airport at 7.05 that evening. By now, they were just as familiar with the retrievers' directives in not knowing via which airline, as they were, never knowing whether they would eat lunch. Babyface with a shrug of the shoulders, had long since accepted to leave be what could not be changed.

It had been an educated guess that the cruiser was plotting a course northwards, taking the option of flying out of Rome Airport. This was confirmed by the initial text from Cas as he verified that the troublesome passengers might be on board. So, the retrieving agent covering all eventualities had estimated its arrival at the marina and then judiciously checked for passengers departing on flights the following morning.

Both girls' names had been identified but they had not managed to obtain seats next to each other. The agent's guesswork had not taken it that stage further to consider that the two girls may be flying with other companions. However, for the first time in the cat and mouse chase across Europe it now seemed possible that Babyface and his team would actually be ahead of, rather than behind the curve. In fact, if everything went according to plan, they might actually be over twelve hours ahead.

Lydia claimed the best laugh of the day as after having collected, and then handing over their tickets to the flight attendant she was immediately recognised by him; he had registered her beauty from the Geneva inbound flight along with Babyface on the previous night. He could only consider Babyface, although he did not know him as such, a lucky bastard for being in her company. This prompted him to say, by way of conversation and in the hope of Lydia taking notice, "Mr Nelson, a short trip? Further pressing matters back in Switzerland?"

To which Babyface, himself taking umbrage at being the butt of an impertinent question about his movements by an impertinent airport employee, replied sarcastically, "It's the chocolate. I just can't stay away from it."

Lydia's laugh was the attendant's ruin, there was no regaining faith from that put down and so the four travellers moved on, boarded the flight and landed at 9.00pm prompt, where they proceeded to yet another hotel, went in search of yet another meal, slept as many hours as their consciences would allow and awoke in anticipation of a retriever's call, informing them of the latest development.

CHAPTER THIRTEEN

And what a development. It turned out to be a call from a senior member of the Camorra, actually based in Italy, itself. He contacted Babyface at 7.00am: firstly, to question whether all had gone well with their arrival in Zurich and secondly to ensure that the now, four agents were all still in robust health. He had then continued, "The reason I ask this, is due to our loss of three agents earlier this morning: two in a shoot out with our intended targets and the third, who had acted more as an informant, shot dead close to the scene and then unceremoniously dumped next to the two operatives."

"That is disappointing news, Boss. But, yes we are all OK and waiting further orders. Presumably, the two females are still going to be on route to Zurich, anytime soon?"

"Yes, that was the main reason for the call. They will be arriving in Zurich on the 6.50am from Rome; its expected arrival is 8.20am. Be there, but 'Don't meet and greet.' Discretion is the word as I suspect that they will have more supportive protection lurking in the shadows than even they know about. And now, after our failure in the marina near Rome we don't really need any further disastrous PR, culminating in a shoot out in an international airport."

"Just one question, Boss? With the call, are we now taking direct orders or still being informed through the retrievers' agents?"

"Stick with the retrievers for the present, but take it as read that now *SpiyWeB* will be more than likely working for the opposition too, as proved by the double ambush we just encountered. They won't actively do anything to jeopardise either side but they won't go out of their way to prevent a confrontation either, if that's where their Intel leads them. But I just wanted to check, personally, that you were in position, as we suspect this could turn out to be the last port of call, so to speak. It is no surprise really as we always suspected that Zurich would be the ultimate destination, where the final action takes place. But we still don't know the actual bank yet! And finally, be aware, just as they have shadowers playing at guardian angels, so do you too. Learn to recognise them."

"OK. We'll discuss that possibility en route to the airport and once there, await further instructions," concluded Babyface.

Arriving in good time still did not relieve the tautness of the tension, Babyface and his team, felt. The four split into two teams with Babyface and Lydia each taking their respective paired operative. It was then a matter of milling around within the arrivals' terminal as if waiting for the return of long gone loved ones, relatives or just friends. For whatever reason, Babyface was expecting to see two strangely disguised, old ladies coming through the customs exit, when in fact the opposite was the case. Two attractive young women caught his eye but each one was attached to an older gentleman, whom he was sure were of Italian origin. Confused, he met up with Lydia and her counterpart, and she was able to, at least, allay part of his mystification; as she said, "Clever, they've ditched the old lady look. Obviously, needed to go through customs matching their passports and must have presumed we were on to them and so felt it wasn't worth changing back, especially after the shoot out at the marina. And they even give off the illusion that one was accompanied by her sugar-daddy and the other, a padre."

"Yes, obviously," said Babyface, thinking that he was losing the plot as that fact had not dawned on him at all. The targets were on the move and could not be lost again, so the four protagonists kept their distance and soon learnt that these two males were indeed escorting Jessica and Emma, and that a third man had met up with them once through customs.

They followed at a safe distance, as the five unsuspecting travellers left the terminal perimeter by way of a Mercedes-Benz SUV Crossover. Jessica and Emma's chaperones were quite relaxed at this point knowing that the airport and its immediate surroundings were too visible and too highly populated for an open attack and they were confident anyway that their backs were being covered and protected. Emma, in particular could see no danger, and so continued her enjoyment of being chauffeured around in far more style than she had previously been accustomed to, in her whole life.

Once on the move, Pietro leaned over from the front of the vehicle and said, "Jessica, it's over to you; you're the boss now."

She looked back at him but spoke to the driver, "Do you know where the Credit Suisse Bank is situated?"

"No problem, lady. It's in District 8, so we head due south on the E41 and it's just past the Zurich Hauptbahnhof. Ten kilometres tops, it should take us about 20 minutes, in this traffic."

She then redirected the conversation to Pietro, "Supposing that Emma and I can do what we are all thinking we can do, what method have you come up with for moving it out of the safe deposit box? It's more than likely safer where it is than the five of us running around Zurich in a reinforced truck."

"Yes, Jessica. We are aware that it could prove a logistical nightmare but let's say for now we just take a look and then work out the practicalities after that. Based on what we know I feel that Pugliese's cell will also know where we've been looking and maybe what we've found too, so removing it from the premises isn't going to be our only problem. But don't forget, not only have we the full backing of Di Larno's faction, we also have the might of the Sicilian Mafia. And as you can see from Emma's relaxed demeanour, the quicker you get used to that idea the more confident you will be."

"OK. We'll presume that we have this one opportunity to case the Bank and do a rehearsal of the real thing. If the cupboard is bare, then we all walk away empty handed but still breathing?" asked Emma.

"I thought we were going in to a vault, not a cupboard?" replied Eduardo.

The sacerdote, who had been quiet up to this point interjected, "English saying, Eduardo. We are still really talking about a safe deposit box in a vault."

"Right. As for still breathing, we are all hopeful of that."

The SUV pulled up on Talstrasse, allowing the two girls and the sacerdote to alight, it having been decided that a padre would provide the best cover with his peaceful profession and his ability to act as their interpreter, if required. They walked the short distance on to Paradeplatz: a wide open square expanse with criss-crossing funicular lines, bordered by attractive looking buildings that oozed opulence and featured expensive boutiques and shops at ground floor level; this was indeed the banking district.

On locating the Credit Suisse premises, they entered the front door of yet another imposing building and were immediately faced with a cavernous marbled reception lobby with a central hexagon shaped desk; at first glance not dissimilar to the Tardis' central control unit. The vast room had no walls as such and therefore no doors either, it was basically an illusion made possible by huge green marbled columns spaced evenly around the edge of the open area. These were the supports to hold suspended an even more elaborate marble cornice and vertical structure containing three semi circular windows running horizontally along each aspect. Through the mighty columns could be seen totally glass fronted illuminated offices with built-in doors leading down corridors, also made of glass. The whole structure was seated on a sea of vast white veined marble flooring with black geometrical lines running from north to south and east to west beneath their feet. With bright light emanating from the equally imposing glass ceiling above their heads, from what appeared to be a myriad of pendulous shaped window tiles. Jessica stood in awe at its magnificence, until Emma nudged her out of her wonderment by saying, "Go on, be quick. Ask them where the nearest loo is, I'm busting!"

The question was embarrassingly asked and both Jessica and the padre made use of the intervening time by introducing themselves and requesting that they be shown to the vaults, once their remaining party member had returned. Emma came back with a bounce in her step and a smile on her face and whispered, "If you think this looks impressive, you should see the toilets."

Both Jessica and the padre ignored the invitation and all three were quickly ushered into an awaiting lift, which descended the three floors to the underground vault area. Here, they were met by a conservatively dressed young lady; even younger than the two clients, whose identity tag informed them she was called Larissa Friedli. She smiled pleasantly and asked for the number of their safe deposit box, by way of confirming that they had a legal right to enter the vault area. Jessica produced the juvenile key ring, which she had cherished through her childhood and which the young lady now looked at both inquisitively and perhaps somewhat sceptically too.

However, the key itself was certainly the correct shape and size and the number engraved on its bow, 'V3/293' corresponded to one of their vaults and to one of their boxes. That being the case, she steered them to the correct vault, with its huge circular safe door already open for the day's trading. Here, she asked for their patience whilst she checked the exact location of the particular box. Several minutes later she returned to the barred gate, which had denied them access through the opening of the circular safe door, apologised for the delay, unlocked the gate and beckoned them through. All four stepped across the threshold to be met by row upon row of compartments and drawers of differing sizes but all featuring the same symmetrically engineered and accurate precision craftsmanship. Each receptacle fitted perfectly flush into the pristine walls, emulating a geometrically wallpapered salon rather than a strong room containing unimaginable wealth. The young executive indicated the direction of the section they required and left, so that they could complete their transaction in peace and privacy; whether it be: adding to, subtracting from or just counting, it was all immaterial to her.

Left alone in the eerie quietness, the two girls looked at each other and then at the sacerdote, hoping that he could call down divine intervention to ensure that their assumptions and guesswork had been correct, all along. Arriving at their corresponding numbered box, all three were surprised at how big it looked. Jessica, now slightly daunted that the moment had finally arrived, took a deep breath, located the keyhole and let the blade of the key run smoothly up to the hilt. At that point she turned it clockwise, to forty-five degrees before reaching a pressure point preventing any further movement. Emma broke the silence with, "Do we need the combination number now?"

Jessica, wiped her brow before hugging her sister, "M, I'd forgotten all about the combination. I was so wrapped up in the moment and was convinced it wasn't going to work; but it's because we need to input the combination. You do it; you worked it out so it's only fair that you input it. Just think, it's probably the first time in over thirty years, since Dad's fingers touched the keypad."

"Stop it Jess. You're making me shaky. OK, here goes nothing. 2-3-4-4." Emma stood shocked that the box front had not sprung open. She looked across at Jessica pleading for help. Jessica, having by now regained her confidence and composure, and on hearing the tumblers click into position coaxed Emma with, "It's OK, M. Just turn the key further to the right, it will turn now."

Emma turned it gingerly and sure enough a satisfying snap was heard as the final barrier to the unknown was relinquished. Cautiously and effortlessly, she pulled out the drawer, warily raised the lid as if in anticipation of finding a dead mouse or some such atrocity. The image that greeted her could not have been more different. All three leaned over and were met by various white envelopes plus an accounts book dated 1978 – 1983. The envelopes were inscribed with various messages: those referencing other safe deposit boxes within the vaults contained a relevant key and a further code but one envelope was written in a now recognisable script style with the inscription:

To our Darling Daughters with much Love.
We are so proud. Mum & Dad xxx

The academic in Jessica forced her to pick up the accounts book; whilst the sentimentality in Emma saw her hugging her Mum and Dad's envelope; leaving the padre to exclaim, "Holy Mother of Christ," as he burrowed into the depths of the deposit box, after the removal of the top layers had made the way clear.

"That will be two 'Our Fathers', Padre," joked Emma before she too realised what had caused his blasphemy. Looking in to the box she was met with a raft of small gold ingots, innumerable rolls of gold coins plus wads of banded notes and black, ribbon tied, velvet bags. Being a girl she immediately went for one of these and opened the drawstring; inside, catching the light from above was a cluster of blue and pink diamonds. "Bloody hell," she exclaimed, "I bet there's more diamonds here than in Hatton Garden! It's like …., it's like we've found the cross on a treasure map."

"Now, now. Don't exaggerate," berated Jessica as she shook herself out of her nostalgia at seeing how closely the handwriting in the accounts ledger represented her own; she could only imagine that it was Mum's but now she too was taken with the handful of sparklers Emma was holding out.

"Although, I see what you mean. You're no doubt cradling a handful of your new best friends! But make sure you don't drop any, we don't want the cleaners benefiting at our expense."

Emma gently and safely tipped them off her hand and returned them to the velvet bag. The sacerdote, who at this point had just completed his two 'Our Fathers', remarked, "Looking at all this wealth, it is going to do the power of good to the people of Secondigliano, if only we can move it out securely. What do the other envelopes say?"

Jessica informed him that even though they had just uncovered an untold fortune, she thought that the additional envelopes were yet more keys and codes for other boxes; boxes necessary due to the volume that had been bought from Lira currency and subsequently stored here. "I suggest we put it all back now before we get too excited. I don't think it's necessary, at this stage, to check the other boxes, as according to the accounts book it definitely looks like it's more of the same. And you Queen Midas, you can put that gold bar back. Isn't it enough that you can look and touch without the need to keep it as well? I'll let you stick that envelope from Mum and Dad in your bag but otherwise we leave empty handed. In a funny sort of way I think our lives depend on that."

Emma concurred and all three, checked and double checked that everything had been replaced with no spillage and that the box was fastidiously locked and repositioned correctly in its housing. The three customers, replaced their happy yet shocked faces with ones of slight boredom, met up with the bank employee, left through the metal barred gate, ascended in the lift to ground level, and walked out through the fabulous lobby, which once again left Jessica in awe.

Pietro and Eduardo came out of nowhere to meet them and became dejected at their demeanours. The padre said, "It's not as bad as it looks but with a strong likelihood that we are being watched, Jessica quite rightly, felt that we should wear composed faces, so as not to give anything away. But she's right about one thing, we need to jump back in the car and check on the nearest safe house."

The word safe house relieved the two men, as it meant that there was most probably something that needed keeping safe; although it brought its own conundrum too as to whether it would be used just to keep people safe, or looking optimistically, perhaps both people and extremely valuable collateral. Once asked the question, the driver phoned 'support' and was directed north-west to a property close to the Männerbad Schanzengraben, which was located behind the Old Botanical Gardens. Emma and Jessica were advised to remain in the house and stay clear of the 'Männerbad' itself, for the present anyway, as it was an open-air pool available to men only during the day. But 'equality rules OK' at night when women are allowed to eat, drink and fraternise in the adjacent bar; 'Oh, the power of women's lib,' thought Jessica, whilst Emma took it in her stride and was happy not to be socialising in too much male company as she needed time off from her regular job.

The surrounding area itself was pleasant enough and unobtrusive with imposing art deco architecture; and the safe house fronting on to the Schanzengraben canal had somewhat of a theatrical makeover at night when the light reflections from the rippling canal strobed across the windows. The excitement at the find was hard to contain and concrete plans needed to be devised to implement the secret removal of the thirty years plus stash of bullion, currency and jewels. Pietro and Eduardo took on this mantle and before the night was much colder in contrast to their mobiles being red hot, a strategy had been devised, developed and refashioned with a contingency of the Sicilian Mafia being drafted in to assist with its execution. But not to be outdone, the Di Larno cell of the Camorra was co-opted too, and accorded a major role in the frontline action.

*

Larissa Friedli almost had sympathy for the clients who presumed that they had just struck it rich knowing that on their return tomorrow their find would be gone; vanished without trace. But the sympathy was just that, an 'almost', and would soon be dismissed in order to clear her mind for far more important work. The requirement of her 100% concentration on, and completion of, a task before the night was done; before her thoughts could possibly consider the luxury of sleeping, dreaming or maybe even sympathising. Larissa felt privileged to have been trained and manoeuvred into this fortuitous position by Alberto Pugliese's supporters. Her talents belied her years and so far the tasks she had undertaken had worked to perfection.

Having once been notified earlier in the day of the likelihood of two young women visiting the vaults she had followed the prearranged procedure flawlessly. As under the pretext of checking out the deposit box's physical location, Larissa had bought herself enough time to apply a fine gossamer film of heat sensitive latex to the numerical keypad; latex bonded with a blend of polymer. And just prior to the point of contact the fine film was sprayed with a coagulating sensitizing agent to assist in identifying which keys had been pressed via the heat given off by touch of the client's finger. But not only that, it also had a built-in time delay property, allowing for the transference of the touch of one layer on to another in an accumulative fashion thus enabling the instigator to accurately identify in which order the keys had been pressed too. This information was then scanned via a ProScope HR2 hand-held microscope at 400 times magnification and the data transferred via USB attachment to an iPhone with the app software to play back the whole sequence. Larissa's youth ensured that neither the pressure of the subterfuge nor the technology fazed her.

So, on accompanying her clients back to the lift, she was confident that she had at least a seven-hour window to acquire the access code for that particular box. This being a maximum guaranteed time period based on past experience when the materials had been tested in a controlled stable environment. However, with Larissa being both young and impetuous, she felt that the sooner the job was undertaken the less chance of fate taking a hand. She, therefore, set too straightaway and completed the task within a ten-minute period; not even long enough for her absence to be noted as anything more than a coffee break. A slight confusion arose when the sequence highlighted that only three keys had been touched; but it took only moments for her to identify that the last key to be pressed, was in fact, done so twice. And now totally confident that with the duplicate key from the master key safe, there would be no problem in illegally opening the safe deposit box that had been opened legally only thirty minutes earlier.

This part of the sting concluded, it permitted her the freedom to concentrate on other aspects of the elaborately prepared plan. A plan which had been in the making for thirty years and which had been refined and finessed as new technologies became available; a plan that involved the continual recruitment and replacement of a sleeper in each of the three banks in Zurich and all for this one eventuality, for the arrival of the mark. Larissa knew that her time was now; she was the chosen one and those above her had total faith in her abilities and hence in the successful outcome, even for one so young.

*

In the rarified atmosphere of 30000 feet, statistics show that the brain still functions to the same degree as at ground level, or so air travellers would have you believe. The only difference, if any, is that people may tend to drink more alcohol at this height and perform more sexual acts in the cramped toilets, given half the chance. Jenny Johnson had other things on her mind, than either of these activities, courtesy of the buff coloured envelope in front of her. Whilst waiting for the flight back to London, she had logged into Metropolitan Police and Police Scotland records requesting any available information on Emma Flynn or Jonnie Raey. The latter drew a blank but the former had form. Emma Flynn had a history of minor misdemeanours: mostly relating to drug or sexual activity right up to suspected murder; her convictions showed Jenny the way. The buying or pushing of drugs; prostitution itself, which was suggested as being her chosen method of finance; but these did not interest Jenny, whereas a suspected murder charge was something else altogether.

On reading, she found that the charge had been dropped, as Emma herself transformed into a witness from a suspected perpetrator. This led Jenny to surf the Internet for national and local news on the subject. Kicking herself, she should have realised that Emma Flynn was the name linked to the serial killings around the Scottish Borders, but 'better late, than never,' she thought. Thinking that the expectant call for the flight back to London would be announced at any moment, Jenny called at the on-site Police suite, showed her warrant card and made her request. Five minutes later, she was on her way to the departure lounge with an envelope containing all of the reading material that she could wish for on her flight south.

The envelope contained several mug shots of Emma, taken over a period of time and showing how well life had or had not treated her. There was a report on the relevant murder inquiry, which named the deceased as Peter Faulk. Apparently, Emma had been found entwined with the body of the victim; either part on top or part underneath, the report was a little confusing in that respect. Both bodies had been found in a builder's skip on a secluded crescent in a salubrious area of Edinburgh, not far from the city centre. He was killed via a highly toxic drug fuelled drip leading into his arm and she nearly died from an overdose of heroin. For a short time she became suspect and then a leading witness, as the detective in charge had a gut feeling that she might have caught sight of the killer; but it came to nothing and the detective himself vanished not long after. Jenny now had her own gut feeling that all was not as it should be and made a mental note to find out the present investigation officer's name and the present status of the case.

She then changed tack and began reading the printed copies of the media editorials, which covered the murder of Peter Faulk and the other murders associated with the serial killer. One thing that struck her was the hype given to the introduction of a profiler to the cases. A Jessica Lambert was shoe-horned in to the inquiry after Peter Faulk's body had been discovered and several papers showed photos of her, standing on steps outside a building, along with several other colleagues: one being a DI Barnham, the officer in charge of the case and another the Police PR executive, Laura Davis. Jenny studied the photograph with the strange sensation of déjà vu. She thought of making another mental note to get hold of a better quality photograph from one of the newspapers, but then realised that now having two mental notes and being at 30000 feet, her chances of forgetting to do either or both were high as statistics might prove; so she input them on her 'things to do' list on her iPhone, and then took the first sip of her well deserved gin & tonic, relaxed and let her stream of consciousness wash over more fanciful notions.

CHAPTER FOURTEEN

Tess Danvers had been disappointed that the impetus had dissipated on the Scottish Borders murders, particularly in the light of one of her colleagues having been killed and another having been seconded to the investigation in her profiler capacity. So her hopes were high when a DC Blister contacted her regarding a meeting to review the case. He called at her place of work in Dalkeith and upon sight, proved a further disappointment to her as he was nothing compared to the missing DI Barnham. She still held a flame for the DI, although she was now beginning to think of it as more a metaphorical vigil, rather than a romantic torch. Ms Danvers, he was too young to be allowed to call her Tess, did not think that she could add anything new to the statement that she had previously given. However, the young officer persisted with, "Is there nothing new that your colleague, Joe Foster, was working on, which could have relevance?"

"No, nothing more than I told T/DC Murray. There was a file that she wanted to see but what with Data Protection, I refused permission unless the T/DC could supply a written authorisation. It is a few weeks ago now and I can't even remember the file's number, let alone not let you see it!"

"Can I change the subject then, and ask how Miss Lambert is doing? I presume she is back at work now that that the original inquiry team has been disbanded?"

"Well, she was back but is now off again on compassionate leave. Reception has tried to contact her on several occasions but I've been informed that her house phone rings out constantly and her mobile is dead. Mm, sorry, a bad choice of adjective. The view doing the rounds here is that she maybe travelling the world to forget about the murders, but as I keep advising my staff, I have not authorised her to take a gap year, so it's highly unlikely she's on a cruise or snorkelling on the Great Barrier Reef."

"Can I take you back to late Friday, April 26th. Do you recall that being the date when you discussed the particular file in question?"

"It possibly is, but I've no records to prove it: there's nothing in my diary and I've no written notes to support the meeting. But I do remember that it was Good Friday."

"So, if I was to suggest that the T/DC and Miss Lambert may have devised a plan to enter these premises over that weekend, what would be your thoughts on that?"

"Couldn't say, and as neither of the two ladies are here to defend such an implausible statement for an unauthorised action, I will take your suggestion with a pinch of salt. We are a Government organisation and as such have full data protection on all our information under present UK Law. I am truly sorry for the death of my colleague in this series of murders and for the other victims too, but it will probably take you just as long to make a mountain out of this molehill as it will for you to find the actual killer whilst making a nuisance of yourself, all at the same time!"

The DC took this as a reference to his annoying presence and therefore also as a conclusion to their conversation, and so stood saying, "Thank you for your time and I hope I haven't brought back too many painful memories?"

DC Blister still felt the need to talk to someone; but of the five names on his list sadly Tess Danvers had been the only available one. DI Barnham, T/DC Murray, Emma Flynn, Jessica Lambert – were all unaccounted for. So, when the call came from a colleague in London, he was more than happy to converse. Jenny had kept herself busy wheedling out the minutest of leads on the Dennis Stanning murder whilst waiting for The Scotsman to forward a hard copy of the photograph from their paper, so that she could then meet up with her new found friend, Roger Duffy; the engineer with the video editing magic skills. She hoped he was as good with still photographs as with moving pictures, but that was yet to be demonstrated.

The results were stunning, not only had he been able to sharpen and contrast the original, he had also cropped in to Jessica Lambert's face and supplied a 10"x 8" print, so that she appeared similar in size to the mug shot of Emma Flynn. The whole process had proved very worthwhile and very interesting too. DI Johnson was now looking at two faces, both confusing to the eye, as they ostensibly appeared to be the same person, in disguise. She had no doubt that they were different people: had physically worn and aged differently and styled their hair in different fashions; but she also had no doubt that they were related: sisters at worst and twins at best.

So now her phone call to DC Blister was one of fact finding and hopefully joining up a few dots. Not only was the DC happy to talk, but also happy that someone else was taking such an interest in the work he was undertaking. He reiterated to the DI the information he had pieced together and confirmed he had a missing link too; with the alleged mysterious visit of Jessica Lambert on the Sunday to the offices of her place of work; this being at a time when she was seconded to the murder cases. Also, that Jessica's boss, who ran the department was a stickler for paperwork and therefore could not, or would not, shed any light on whether or not her organisation had any involvement. Unfortunately, for the DC, Jenny also left him wanting more. She had taken what she needed to assist her investigation but had not given back to him the vital piece of her evidence she had just found and now held in her arsenal. 'Perhaps later, when I'm a little further down the road. I don't want too many waves crashing about, just yet,' she thought selfishly.

She immediately put feelers out at ports and airports and cross-referenced both girls' names with passenger lists on all forms of travel leaving from any location within the UK. Her result was definite but unrewarding, as it showed they had purchased tickets for Paris on an early morning Eurostar; but after that, she knew the scent would go cold. She could alert Interpol but as yet the girls in question were not suspected of any criminal offence and so time and expense would no doubt be wasted unnecessarily. The only choice remaining was to keep alert and monitor activity on mainland Europe, with the slim possibility that the two sisters could become newsworthy.

*

Weeks would soon be turning in to months, and still in Joe Doe's mind John Dear was the only person that he had ever known. Of course, he remembered certain things, such as how to read and tie his shoelaces and use a knife and fork and make a cup of coffee. No, wait a moment; he did not know how to make a cup of coffee, because it had always been made for him; now why was that? And that's where the loop ended and began all over again.

He enjoyed the early morning walks with John along the cliff tops but never too close to the edge, not now. Here, above the windswept beach they would sit and watch the sun rise and then see it peep through the scudding clouds, its weak beam occasionally hitting the sea as a pale illuminated searchlight; giving the illusion of a lone surfer riding the waves towards shore. Simple things for a simple mind; but Joe could not help feeling that there was more to life, plenty more and at some point he was going to have to rediscover what that 'more' was.

Eventually, solitude began not to suit him, especially as conversation with a recluse proved anything but satisfactory. He was grateful for all the care John had given him during his convalescence and for his help in keeping him fed and watered but he could not see himself continuing on this remote North East Coast, leading a life in limbo, just like his location. An area that was only just inside the Scottish Border and so neither totally Scottish nor yet English. He chose his moment well and broached the subject as they both watched the waves break yet again on the isolated coastline. Far from being disappointed, John was ecstatic; he too had been thinking it time that Joe moved on; but to where?

The answer came as John re-entered the real world to buy essentials that he could not grow, bake, catch or kill. He bemusedly browsed over a newspaper headline whilst at the checkout in the grocery store, which although not his usual habit, turned out to be very beneficial to his cause. Staring back at him was the image of Joe Doe; but to be honest, wearing a slightly fatter face and sporting a slightly grey pallor. 'That's something Joe Doe can't be accused of now,' he thought. Realising he had enough change left over, he bought a copy, perhaps as a parting gift to his, now returned to ruddy health, lodger.

Joe was equally as shocked at seeing the face mirroring himself, and from a newspaper, of all things. However, he had to admit, that he did not feel the photograph did him justice, if anything he looked ill. Greedily reading the editorial, which took considerably longer than it should have, due to his present memory decline, he began to conjure up a life that possibly someone he might have known, had led. A life, as a police officer looking for criminals, cut short, by his own vanishing act. Names that were vaguely familiar: Chief Inspector Brogan; Jamie Scott; T/DC Murray; Emma Flynn; Jessica Lambert; all seemed to ring a distant bell or were they perhaps just names that he was learning to know again as he read them? More confusion.

But with John's encouragement, he made the decision to hand himself in at the local police station, after first asking John for directions. There, he owned up to the thought that he might be Terence Barnham, the lost DI and not Joe Doe as he had recently been led to believe. This simple action brought a excitable tsunami from the media world heading directly for Police Scotland. Before the day was out, the whole of the UK and beyond knew of the DI's safe return; even though nobody yet knew from where, but again the question on everyone's lips became, 'Are we now going to know who is the Scottish Borders serial killer?' and everyone presumed he would reveal this, just by brandishing a proverbial magic wand. The theory was simple but the practicality was not so; the DI became dazzled by the TV lights; confused by the mass attention; and was in no mental state to formulate coherent dialogue appertaining to his previous life, let alone the investigations he supposedly had led. The Super realising that a huge PR own goal had just been enacted, curtailed the circus and arranged for the DI to receive immediate medical attention at Edinburgh Royal Infirmary.

*

As late afternoon arrived so too did a female customer and her boyfriend to Credit Suisse. On entering, the girl was desperately in need of a sit-down as she appeared disorientated and faint. Larissa, not likely to be chaperoning any more clients down to the bowels of the bank at this time of day, volunteered herself as a likely nursemaid to care for the stricken customer. But instead of taking her to the sickbay, she and the girl's boyfriend helped the now sprightly pseudo invalid to her own office, which was devoid of other staff due to the new flexi-time regime. Once inside, the girl immediately stripped off her outer clothing, as did Larissa; the two girls then swapped clothes and headed for the exit, keeping to the edges of the lobby so as not to be too closely scrutinized. Once, near the front door, the infiltrator now dressed in bank uniform, half turned back to the central desk and mouthed, "All sorted. The couple has been escorted off the premises and I'm going on flexi now too, so I've locked up the office. See you tomorrow," but in reality, it was Larissa who said this as she hid behind one of the vast marble columns.

The deception fooled reception in to believing that the off-colour customer and her partner had left along with Larissa and that would be the message forwarded to their security company at close of play, as confirmation that she had indeed vacated the building for the day. She gingerly retraced her steps along the outer edge of the lobby and re-entered her now empty office; empty, excepting for the previously mentioned boyfriend already ensconced there. She relocked the door in the knowledge that they would be there for some time. They both sat under her desk eating chocolate and drinking cola; she listening to her iPod until 9.00pm came round, whilst the fake boyfriend continually studied and memorised an A1 poster, containing all the electronic wiring from throughout the whole building.

The Italian Boss informed Babyface, Lydia and their two new colleagues that the game was back in play, as the two girls and their new accomplices had surfaced and located the lost millions. Now positive steps were being taken to lift the spoils from under their very noses. And as they had been chosen to be instrumental in carrying out those steps, they were advised to await instructions but to be prepared for action by 22.00, at the latest.

At 9.00pm prompt, Larissa accompanied the boyfriend, who went by the reference C/SU/779, to the IT unit; this was done circuitously to avoid being picked up on the active CCTV cameras. Once there, C/SU/779 came in to his own by exploding into a flurry of activity: exposing and stripping wires, connecting several loose ends to his own gizmos and rerouting others back the way they had come. The thirty minutes' flurry of activity was enough to: ensure the unlocking of and access to the outer door of the underground loading bay and without CCTV monitoring their every subsequent move; enable all other CCTV's time codes to continue running whilst constantly displaying a frozen picture; open the outer circular safe door by tricking the dedicated timer into thinking that its twelve hour cycle of shutdown had been completed; and releasing the digital lock on the master safe key box, by use of a Neodymium magnet.

Larissa being somewhat bamboozled by his manic movements in opening the key box with such apparent ease had foolishly asked the techie how he could possibly do that, so he told her. "Basically, it's just a matter of optimizing the BDHd; that's the maximum magnetic energy that can be supplied to the external circuit. See, this gauge here measures it in 'megagauss-oesteds'. At this time, I'm looking for the release point on the demagnetisation curve." Larissa looked blankly back as the enthusiasm of her colleague washed over her, very much like her morning shower, literally, to the extent that it was going over her head.

"OK, you're good to go." And she was; she was able to take the correct duplicate key, along with the master gate key and enter vault three through the robust, circular safe door, which was now securely unlocked in its daytime position. She carried out the routine that she had seen hundreds of customers do in the past and sure enough the box slid out smoothly and the lid opened revealing all its delights. Not being party to the original clients' excitement at the sight of the wonders, she had not appreciated that there would be additional envelopes for further boxes, either. The majority of her job complete, it was just a matter of her making her way to the loading bay to await the transport, which duly turned up at 21.15, and was closely followed by Babyface and his team, armed with canvas bags but without the 'SWAG' stencilling. Larissa introduced herself as C/SU/884 and led them through the underground labyrinth to vault three. Here, they met up with the techie and the whole group collectively exclaimed their surprise at the sight of the treasure their eyes feasted upon. At the same time, Larissa drew to their attention the fact that there were three other boxes still to be checked, with one being twice the depth of the other two, in addition to the one they were already drooling over!

Babyface soon had a conveyor belt system in operation with Lydia and Larissa at the head; both scooping everything in front of them into each bag until it was brimming, regardless of weight. C/SU/779 then manhandled it to the safe door, where it was dumped unceremoniously on to one of two carts with the three remaining adversaries taking it in turns to wheel it to the loading bay. By the time most of the four boxes had been emptied, there were eight sacks completed, with one remaining, which Larissa had started to fill. Lydia, being stronger at handling the bulky weights, was manfully struggling to hand ball the eighth sack through the door. As it passed through, a red revolving light began flashing erratically. "Quick, jump through the gate, Lydia," shouted Larissa knowing that she herself had not enough time to bridge the distance before the robust gate barred her exit. Fifteen seconds later, the circular safe door was also half way to closing as Lydia, caught sight of Larissa for the last time, holding her head in her hands and openly weeping; knowing she was on the wrong side of freedom whilst the door, oblivious to the drama being played out, completed its own task by systematically throwing out all five of its bolts by pneumatic power.

Babyface, having just arrived back with the cart also witnessed the closure and asked, "Was she on the last bag?"

Lydia, replied in the affirmative, "Yes, but I think most of it really looked like 'treasure'. You know gold cups, plates, crosses and chalices. Mostly, church icon things."

"Well, we had better move, we're not going to get it or her now, unless the techie guy can do anything?"

He shugged and said, "I doubt it. Looks like the system has been overridden."

Babyface's face blanched as he realised the implications of that statement. "The truck," he shouted, running back towards the loading bay.

The techie thought, 'The truck. Oh shit, the truck, he's going to be too late!'

Sure enough on arriving at the loading bay, the two operatives and the truck driver were shell-shocked at the fact that the outer door had closed remotely, without any of them touching a single thing. The techie turned up with the eighth, and now their final bag and Babyface immediately turned on him. "Get it open now. I don't care what you've got to do but get that bloody door open." The techie pulled out his relays network poster and unfolded it to its full size; tracing the wiring from the vaults and loading bay door through to the master hub, which governed the applications and managed their load and efficiency. The hub was situated along the corridor from Larissa's office, in the IT unit and backed onto the now redundant security office. Redundant, as the total responsibility for the physical protection of the Bank: its assets, staff and customers, had been given over purely to technology and the future, with 'remote' security seen as the most cost effective, safe and efficient option.

The majority of the team retired to Larissa's office with their one bag of bullion, leaving the techie to investigate the master hub in all its glory, and the driver of the truck sitting, in isolation, on what they held so far. The techie clipped his gauge on to the fibre-optic feed leading into the master hub; and in answer to the assessment of his findings, he slapped his forehead with his hand as he muttered, "Shit. The management system is an information silo and so it's incapable of reciprocal operation with other, related information systems." As he was on his own he had to walk back up the corridor to the office and repeat to the room in general the sentence that would confirm he had been beaten, "The management system is an information silo and so it's incapable of reciprocal operation with other, related information systems."

Confused faces looked at him and Babyface answered blankly, "I don't do 'techese'. Could you translate it in to a language we can all understand?"

"Yes, sorry there, got carried away. I implanted an alternative information system, which it took on board but has now ejected. A bit like a human transplant rejection."

"Is it reversible?"

"No, not when the patient's dead, it isn't!"

"Don't be flippant. There must be millions in those sacks and we've got to move them and quick."

"I'll give it a go but my guess is that someone higher up the chain will have to reboot the whole system to get things moving. And that most likely is not going to happen until the morning so unfortunately my most optimistic opinion is that we'll probably be here for the rest of the night. I suggest we hunker down, before the system reports the malfunction back to security and they come looking for the fault. But, on the bright side, at least Larissa's left snacks and drinks here."

"Who's giving the orders around here? You'll have plenty of time for your snacks and drinks when you get thrown in jail. Now study that network and do what you're paid to do."

No matter what option came to the techie's mind, neither the safe nor the loading bay doors budged. And at 11.00pm, after exhausting all possibilities, he threw in the towel with, "It isn't going to happen. My guess is that the override has been configured to initiate complete shutdown on all external doors plus the vaults' doors, should a sudden surge of energy be detected; even bona fide encrypted cards will be inoperable in the card readers under this 'threat' application. In a nutshell, I sent in the Trojan horse to do the dirty work and it got found out, whilst going about its business. And now when the bank opens, someone else will have to clean up its mess!"

"Well, Trojan horse or no Trojan horse. I'm not sitting inside it waiting to be meekly led out in handcuffs at 9.30am or whenever this higher up person decides to grace the bank with his presence. At 7.00am, if we haven't been found sooner, we'll try and make our way back to the truck, sit tight and attempt to ram our way out as the door rises," said Babyface, feeling that the responsibility was his to lead the charge for freedom.

"I don't even think that will be possible as I've a sneaking suspicion that the internal doors leading to the loading bay will remain locked too," said the techie in a whisper. "Are you in communication with the driver to suggest that idea anyway?"

"And what about Larissa?" asked Lydia.

Two questions at once threw Babyface off balance and the techie silently thanked Lydia for his rescue from the constant wrath, as Babyface said, "No, I never expected this debacle, so I didn't think I needed a communication satellite. I mean, how was I to know all the doors would be on an automatic security device? And yes, our Helen of Troy is safely in lockdown," he smirked. "She knew the risks, just like the rest of us. In fact, she's no worse off really, as we have not in effect found an escape route either, so we all still remain imprisoned too."

This left the only remaining problem being that of time and its slowness; the seconds became minutes and the minutes became hours and for all the brainpower that had been put to use in devising the original plan, there was now nothing in their collective power to prevent each individual's mind from dwelling on their predicament and pondering what else could go wrong between now and 9.30am; until the expected opening of the bank and its vaults. So, innumerable coffees were made and drunk; various snacks were opened and eaten; plans were discussed and refined but still time lingered the wrong side of midnight and even exhaustion could not encourage anyone to sleep; nor did anyone want to, as to sleep and dream of untold treasure would only turn to dust on their awakening.

Just as one faction of the Camorra was locked in the bank, the other faction was locked out of it. But those outside, having already been given the excellent news of the girls' success earlier in the day, had the upper hand and were not about to let the newfound treasure slip from their metaphorical sight or grasp. After being given Pietro and Eduardo's report, a discreet, continuous, monitoring activity had been placed on the bank, front and back. A 'plan A' had already been devised plus backup 'plan B' to cover all other eventualities. Eduardo had recently received information that prompted the latter as Babyface's team had triggered the bank to go into lockdown mode due to their impetuosity in reaching the bullion. So at

11.30pm, a second armoured truck pulled up outside the rear of the bank adding back up to back up 'plan B'! A team of professionals alighted along with their tools, indicating that they meant business.

Their drilling through the two feet thick wall would have been cause for disquiet if not for the bafflers fitted to the industrial hammer drill, which kept the noise level registering below 40 dB, apparently a level of no concern at all to any of the few near neighbours. The irony of the industrial diamond core bits was not lost on the drillers either as they were using only several of these to retrieve possibly hundreds of gem-grade diamonds! Once through the wall, an industrial video endoscope was threaded through the 58mm gap, which enabled a 360-degree view of the immediate interior. It showed empty loading bays, apart from a sole vehicle parked in front of bay two. One person, presumably the driver was anxiously looking constantly from the back entrance door leading into the bank proper, to the underground exit door, and back. Both were shut and as neither responded to any of the driver's verbal commands or physical abuse, he just sat tight and resigned himself to an uncomfortable night in the cab. The surveillance team sat tight too, now patiently waiting for the next piece of the jigsaw to be turned and turned again until it fit snugly into position.

CHAPTER FIFTEEN

So far, life had been good for Jonas Gohl and he was constantly grateful to his young, attractive wife Helene, for initially accepting his marriage proposal and then for producing their '2.4' children. The '2' were real live children: one boy and one girl, five and three respectively and the '.4' equated to his wife's three and half months pregnancy of their third child. Their stunning house in the Hirslanden neighbourhood, being part of the Kreis 7 district, exuded affluence and success as it sat proudly on Klusweg, in tune with many other equally impressive executive properties. His rise in status replicated the rise in his career as he had reached Deputy CEO, at the young age of 38 years. And similar to the present CEO, he too was able to delegate, due to his excellent choice of subordinate who would, no doubt climb into his shoes the moment he relinquished them. That climb and relinquish were anticipated to be in two years time at the maximum when the present CEO stepped down and took up the surefire position of Non Executive Director. And with all three transitions being guaranteed so, they would cement each other's living standards as long as nothing untoward happened to create a lack of confidence in the bank or bad PR in the media.

Such an example of both unlikelihoods' happening would be the theft of unaccountable wealth from one or more of the bank's safe deposit boxes; that would certainly be frowned upon. Or, the immediate disappearance of the wife of a senior executive at the bank; that would set a worrying precedent as to how such leverage could be used by an opportunist kidnapper. With hindsight, procedures should have been in place to counteract and remedy such possible scenarios but that necessity was still in the future, as this was the first example of such an event. For the present, Helene Engman-Gohl was not part of the procedure nor was her '.4' child.

The whole family had enjoyed a pleasant evening, with the children being put to bed at their usual hour and with the usual loving equanimity. Jonas then spent time reading and annotating a report due to be presented to the Board in two days' time before savouring a glass of red Gaja Barbaresco, one of his favourite Italian wines, as he watched Sky News through half closed eyes. So enjoying his relaxation time whilst allowing the wine's fragrant raspberry notes to play on his tongue, at one and the same time. Helene was satisfied with a glass of cool milk and embraced the brilliance of the night sky's magnificence and the welcome solitude of her own company as she meditated in the darkness of the garden room. Their perfect life came to a close for another day and on their way to bed they both thanked God for all the luck and good fortune which had been bestowed upon them, their children and their home.

At 2.45am their thanks went unanswered as their luck ran out. Masked men crept into their bedroom and awoke them, simultaneously. Helene was not allowed time to scream and Jonas was not allowed time to be disgruntled or shocked, but neither could be prevented from being frightened for either of their two young children or themselves. One of the masks said sternly, "Do exactly as we say and neither you nor your children will be hurt." The two masked men then offered the nearby dressing gowns and the one who had just spoken continued, "We're all going downstairs now, as quietly as possible and once there we'll let you know why we're here."

In the kitchen, nonchalantly looking through cupboards for coffee and cups et cetera, was a middle aged lady dressed in a nurse's type of uniform. The Gohls' were advised that she was a professional nursery nurse who would be looking after the two children whilst their parents helped the masked men. Helene threw her hands up to her now gagged mouth and managed a muffled sound where there should have been a scream. The couple was ushered around the breakfast bar opposite to the previously masked men, who were now unmasked; and were calmly being served their own coffee at three o'clock in the morning by a lady dressed in a nurse's outfit!

The two men were Pietro and Eduardo, but the homeowners obviously did not know that, and it was Pietro who continued to speak, "Sorry for the theatrics, but I needed to make sure I had your full attention. We need your assistance in entering the Credit Suisse Bank, of which I understand you are deputy CEO?" He did not wait for any acknowledgment or confirmation but just continued, "Surprisingly, we do not wish to steal anything, only take what is rightfully ours and I don't mean that in either a communistic or an anarchistic way. We know for a fact that, at present there is a group of people locked in your bank who have spent most of the night emptying certain safe deposit boxes, which they have no right to empty. We want to rectify this miscarriage and take back what is rightfully ours and what has been unavailable to us for over thirty years. Raise your finger if you wish to speak."

Jonas raised his finger and his gag was removed. He replied, "There is no way I can help; my loyalty is to the Bank and not a bunch of thieves. The Bank's and my reputation will be in ruins and all this," he swept his hands around the room as Eduardo leapt up at his sudden action, "I can not sacrifice all this for some fairy tale about money owing for thirty years. It's impossible."

Pietro replied, "I'll tell you what's impossible. Coming home tonight to find that your pregnant wife is not here and that your two delightful children have vanished too. Herr Gohl, we are not crooks, that money was banked in good faith well over thirty years ago by members of our families and we

251

need you to prevent a serious injustice. And anyway, the incident you wish to avoid has already happened. Even now, goodness knows how many are trapped in your precious bank? How are you going to explain that away to your shareholders? Your customers? The media? The general public? The damage is already done. It's now your decision as to how you contain it!"

Without all the added questions, Jonas would have capitulated anyway; the thought of his wife and children being punished in any way due to his own career advancement and selfishness did not bear thinking about. He leant forward, placed his elbows on the breakfast bar top, his head in his hands and said resignedly, "What do you want me to do?"

Pietro replied, "This is how it will work. We are going to take you to the bank and you will override the electronic shutdown that we think has already been initiated. At the same time, your wife will be taken to a safe house where she will remain safe, as long as you don't try to be clever. Your children will remain here, in the care of this nurse. By 8.00am, everything should be back to normal and you can then think of how to contain the PR disaster."

At this point he addressed the nurse by saying, "Can you take Frau Gohl up to the bedroom to get dressed and ensure that she doesn't try and contact anybody, and so raise the alarm." The same courtesy was offered to Herr Gohl and he was overseen by Eduardo's watchful eye. On leaving Pietro said, "Don't forget we'll send you a text, hopefully around 7.00am to let you know that you can arrange the switchover with the new nurse." By 4.00am, Frau Gohl had been deposited at the safe house and into the protective hands of the sacerdote, which had a soothing effect on her. The remaining members of the vehicle travelled the short journey west to meet up at the rear of the bank building with the surveillance arm of their cell already at work.

Once there, Pietro was informed that all was quiet inside and that the only person in the loading bay proper was the truck driver, who seemed to be now asleep in the cab. To prevent any further quizzical looks, Jonas Gohl was introduced to the team and it was enquired of the leader of the surveillance team, Gino Fontana, as to what use should be first made of him. He replied, "Looking through the endoscope, it appears that the door leading from the bank itself through to the loading bay area is closed. Is that part of the security measure or has it just been shut after the other accomplices left the area?"

The deputy CEO replied positively and without encouragement as it helped keep his mind off the other misfortunes beyond his control, "An immediate shutdown means that all outer doors are double locked the instant that the information is relayed and all secondary doors leading to the outside have a fifteen minutes time delay before they too initiate lockdown procedure. This is to allow staff to shepherd customers and themselves to one of the three marshalling areas; one per floor."

"How do we get round it?"

"There are only two ways. One is by using the master card key and inserting the override code and two is by creating a fire. A fire will trigger the sprinklers, which immediately instigates an evacuation procedure and ensures all doors are permanently unlocked for those trapped inside to escape and for firefighters to get in. They and the police will be automatically informed of the fire and arrive within minutes of the emergency transmission."

"Well, fortunately for you I don't see any smoke, nor do I hear any sirens. Is this not something your staff are made aware of?"

"Oh yes, some staff. We do regular fire drills, but only very senior personnel know of the intricacies of the security protocol. We're talking about unimaginable assets locked away in this bank and it is our equal priority to protect those assets as well as its owners' future prosperity. So, the majority of staff expects that someone more senior will have carried out their own job to protect the lives of those accessing the bank and its facilities."

"OK. So, back to 'no fire'! Can we single out a door to access without unlocking the whole building?"

"There is a fire exit door on the side of the building; the side which is not really part of the bank but which has a corridor leading into the centre of the loading area. That will open independently."

"Is there a door at the loading area end of the corridor? If so, can that be opened singly?"

"Yes. I have a master key card and a code for requiring single doors to be opened and another code for all doors."

"Great. I'm sure that you and your family will be happily reunited before too long." Although, this was what Jonas Gohl wanted to hear, he also did not want to think about it too deeply as it reminded him of the precarious position his wife and children were in and how it was the interpretation of his actions, which would bring them safely back to him.

As he swiped his card and punched in the override code he asked inquisitively, "Why are we doing it door by door, why not all at once, it would be far quicker?"

"Well, as far as our information tells us there are already at least five people on your premises. We don't really want to allow whoever's in there to move about freely, when we're trying our best to contain and surprise them?" Pietro waited for a reaction. It came but it was only one of puzzlement. "Is that five people too many for you?" he asked.

"How many different sets of people are trying to rob my bank tonight? And why tonight, what's so special about tonight?" demanded Herr Gohl in puzzlement.

"Let's just call it coincidence. Look on the bright side; you're getting it all over and done with in one fell swoop. Sorry, that little colloquialism is courtesy of my brother Luigi; by the look on your faces it seems like it past you all by! Let's just say, open the doors I tell you to open." By now they were through the corridor and about to open the door leading to the loading bay. Pietro made various signs indicating that everyone should remain quiet. Eduardo and a companion were earmarked to sneak up each side of the truck, wrench the doors open and drag out the driver. Both wore masks, purely for the intimidation factor rather than for disguise. The door, by way of acknowledgment to Pietro's authority, opened equally as quietly and the execution of the plan went without a hitch. The driver was taken totally unawares and within seconds his hands were behind his back and cable-tied securely.

As professionalism goes, the former driver was slack to say the least. The keys were still in the ignition; so the vehicle was started up and just waiting for Herr Gohl to wave his magic card and press the right numbers. As he did so Eduardo and his accomplice checked the sacks stowed in the back and verified that each one contained large quantities of gold coins, ingots, bank notes and small bags of precious stones. Thereafter, the truck was gone in 60 seconds! The door had opened and the two nominated drove off in the direction of Waaggrasse, then continued on towards Storchengrasse and a landing ferry stop called Zurich Storchen, which was situated by the side of the River Limmat. Here a boat was waiting to load up and head south on to Lake Zurich itself. And all this done in order to protect the cargo, on the assumption that the Alberto Pugliese cell would be observing proceedings from a distance. Even if they assumed that their own colleagues were transporting the bullion; back-up support would be automatically provided in order to assist or prevent a double-cross; so, gaining a few vital minutes was all-important in aiding the escape.

Another decision that Jonas Gohl needed to take was regarding the people already trapped in the building. No one had any idea where they were or whether they were armed. And should the police become involved, how could he explain away the fact that various safe deposit boxes have already been pilfered and a reinforced truck had departed with the spoils? The deputy CEO's action confirmed his decision as he headed towards yet another closed door and turned, saying, "Coming?"

The remaining cell members heeded his command and followed him through the door. The two leading operatives were now both carrying MP38 submachine guns, and constantly sweeping left and right as they advanced along the silent corridors. The escort passed through the building like a ghost, continuing in the same formation until meeting a locked door. Here, Herr Gohl would step forward surrounded by the weapon protection, unlock the door and step back to re-blend into the group, thus allowing the firepower to retake the initiative. Inevitably, they arrived at the IT unit and immediately realised why the building had shut itself down.

Wires were spilling out of various control panels mimicking a spaghetti dish gone wrong; but as to human life there was none. The stalkers moved forward and entered the designated office area of the building, where the bulk of the staff were accommodated; all locked doors were unlocked and already unlocked doors were treated with respect. One such door faced them where the handle gave freely; the team outside crouched in silence whilst the trapped inside remained hidden under the three desks. Pietro indicated that the video endoscope should be brought forward; he then directed the end of it under the door and sent it snaking across the pitch-black floor, searching out for possibly hidden humans.

The camera equipment being fitted with Infrared technology did not lie, as sure enough there were glowing bodies inside. Pietro addressed them collectively, with, "Listen up. We need you to reveal yourselves and stand in the centre of the room with your hands raised. I have to warn you that we are armed and will use force if threatened. To verify our status I will ask Jonas Gohl to say a few words; Herr Gohl is the deputy CEO of the Bank." Here he nodded to Jonas and left him in the lurch and on the spot!

"Yes. My name is Jonas Gohl and as has already been said, I am the deputy CEO of this Bank. As yet I am unable to count the total number of violations you have committed against Credit Suisse and its customers; but the protocol of the bank specifically dictates that anyone found breaking into the vaults or damaging bank property must be reported immediately to the Polizei. However, as my new friends here, on the outside of this door, claim to own the said items that you have already stolen; then there may be a way of mutually reaching a satisfactory conclusion, without bloodshed I hasten to add." He turned to Pietro pitifully and said, "Was that what you wanted? I hope I didn't go on, you know, what with the worry of it all?"

"That was just great,' replied Pietro as he turned to the door. "OK. You've been thrown a lifeline. Herr Gohl wants this all brushed under the carpet and he needs to get home for breakfast too. The bullion and gems you took from our safe deposit boxes belong to the people of Secondigliano; well our cell of the Camorra that are based there, anyway. A generation which has been born and grown up since that money was taken and invested; a generation who thought that it was never to be seen and enjoyed and all because of Alberto Pugliese's brutal, bullying and murderous policies which decimated our village and ended up leaving whole families living way below the poverty line. The bullion sacks you filled earlier are long gone under our protection and will now go some way to righting the wrongs done to our people."

Those inside listened and deliberated, waiting for a lead from Babyface, their nominated leader. He looked behind at Lydia and made a silent sign that she should take out her gun, as it was his intention that they would shoot their way out. Lydia nodded her comprehension, crept up to his side, watching and anticipating, as Babyface began the silent countdown. When his fingers indicated two seconds remaining, Lydia calmly placed her gun into the back of his right shoulder, causing him to make a sound when he was meant to be silent. "Drop the gun, big boy. The rest of you, drop yours too or you're all going to be dead within the next ten seconds." One of the two recently inducted operatives was happy to comply with the request; however, the other just smiled and had that smile reciprocated by Lydia. The techie did not smile, nor drop his gun, as he was not carrying one in the first place. Babyface took the opportunity of the slight distraction to pull back and release the slide mechanism of his semi automatic; just a fraction of a second, the same amount it took Lydia, who had previously racked hers, to gently squeeze the trigger. She kicked his gun away and then shouted, "OK, Pietro. It's all over. We're coming out," and turning to the others, said, "Make sure the rest of you have your arms held high; we don't want any more accidents, do we?"

As they were about to leave the room, Babyface managed to stretch out with his left hand and grab her arm, pleading through the pain, "But why, Lydia? I thought we were on the same wavelength?"

She turned slightly to face him and replied, "Forget the Lydia. My name is Pernille and just as I was instrumental in causing the death of your previous accomplice, Ollie, by framing him with planting forged expenses' sheets in the Finance Department, so I now have the power to complete that circle. You see, my real likeness to Lydia is that you'll never know which persona is the genuine me. But how you and the likes of you, could continue to live comfortably whilst the real people, those all around you, your old neighbours and ex friends have been left to grovel and starve at your expense, just disgusts me. And as this whole disgrace started with my father, Alberto Pugliese, so it must end with his daughter; the daughter that should never have been, but the one who kept those two flames, of anger and charity, alive knowing that justice would be given to my downtrodden uncomplaining friends."

Babyface interrupted with, "Such chemistry? I was going to send in such a good report, after this was all over."

"As far as I'm concerned this is the only report I want to hear."

Through the pain Babyface looked puzzled whilst picturing his now ruined career, but at least he was still alive; or so he thought until, he studied her face and then it dawned, 'the only report'. Pernille looked into his baby blue eyes and pulled the trigger again, leaving a hole between them. "That's so your friends know who they are dealing with." Jonas shuddered at the shock of the noise the two bullets made and the now prone man, laying dead in one of his business suites with two pools of blood collecting on the hardwood flooring. Holding on to the doorframe to prevent himself from falling over he recalled his original suggestion that it might all end without bloodshed, but now a hope in vain. "Perhaps, I can assist you all off the premises?"

"We'll just tidy up here, first. Don't want any difficult questions, do we?" said Pietro as he nodded to two of his colleagues. And pointing at the body he said to Jonas, "If anybody asks, he was never here and when we've finished, you won't even know we've been here either, apart from that mess that they left you in the IT unit."

"Oh and one other thing that you might find it difficult to explain away is the fact that Larissa Friedli is locked in vault three. If she's any sense, she'll have tidied up behind herself already," said Pernille, talking as if butter would not melt in her mouth as she held on to one sack of bullion in one hand and clutched her gun in the other.

Pietro concluded with, "Herr Gohl, I hope this doesn't sully what could otherwise be a blossoming relationship?"

"That depends on the outcome with my family? And the safe boxes that have been ransacked, those customers that have lost everything; how can I look them in the eye? What can I tell them?"

"Your family is quite safe. We returned your wife safely to her home and your children as soon as you began to co-operate and now they will be awaiting your safe return too. And don't worry about the customers, if we're happy, they're happy and vice versa."

"By the way, Herr Gohl. One of the boxes was not quite emptied; so can you ensure that everything is replaced back where it should be and when two young English ladies call, would you be kind enough to return the relevant keys and codes to them and afford them a little VIP courtesy as it is only their boxes which have been ransacked," suggested Pernille, before relinquishing their bargaining power totally.

Herr Gohl became silent as he mused over the little problem of Larissa Friedli but felt that the other part of the request would not be too problematic. "Well, we try to treat all our investors with equal deference anyway so in the scheme of things I don't suppose it stretches beyond the bounds of possibility. I feel I'm going to have to throw away the rulebook now anyway and create a new one just for you Italians? And I'll take a personal discreet look in the vault, release Fräulein Friedli whilst I'm at it and relieve her of any keys and codes that still may be in her possession."

He then escorted both factions back through the various doors and out of the rear exit by the loading bay, leaving the way clear for the clean-up operation to ensure that the unanticipated body, stains and detritus simply vanished. Outside, Pietro and his team attached cable ties to two of the remaining accomplices' wrists and lined them up beside the, already bound, driver of the other truck. Lydia vouched for the other would-be accomplice, as he had been the one who passed over Eduardo's mobile number, in their initial handshake back in Naples, which subsequently enabled her to be in inconspicuous communication. The three were then hustled into the now spare truck, more in order to contain them rather than transport them, as Pietro had no edict regarding the taking of captives. But he certainly didn't want any more killings; so they would be held hostage until such a time as a deal was struck.

Herr Gohl went about his business as best he could. The vaults would not be reopened until 9.00am and he was slightly concerned as to his personal appearance: casual clothes, unshaven, dark rings under his eyes and worry frowns; just for starters. But he reconciled it to the fact that it had been a strange night to say the least and the day could surely not be any worse, no matter what he wore or how he looked. Therefore to rid himself of any further unknowns, at the first opportunity he opened the circular vault door and unlocked the metal barred gate, to vault three. A sheepish Larissa Friedli stood before him, looking equally worn and stressed. She had had hours to prepare the argument as to why she was trapped in a safe vault overnight, but the argument melted away and left her dumbfounded at the sight of the deputy CEO as she listened to him speak.

"Larissa, Larissa, what am I going to do with you? I employed you when you were only seventeen, at the time as a favour to your father and ever since I have had your progress monitored. And, quite honestly you surprised me with your quick aptitude and ability to learn; to such an extent that I was prepared to fast track you into a management role. But now sadly, all that will come to naught. A suspicious break-in with an employee actually locked in the vault, how does one explain that away? I've already requested your line manager to join us and then you will be taken to the sickbay, where you will be strip searched by the on-duty nurse. You know that this is standard procedure for any staff member found in one of the bank vaults, within access of open safe deposit boxes. Once completed, you will then be shown off the premises and your position within the bank will be terminated. You will never be able to apply here for another position. Any monies owing, either: salary, holiday pay or bonus, will be forwarded to your bank account by close of play today. Do you understand?"

"Yes, perfectly, Sir. Sorry to have offended, Sir."

Larissa found the search intrusive, but she had expected that. She found her sacking even harsher, but she had expected that too. But neither could take the smile away from her face as she limped ever so slightly out of the bank for the last time. She was smiling knowing that the Camorra cell, which coached her in the undertaking of the crime, had agreed to pay 10000 euros to the actual bank clerk carrying out the deed. This to be deposited in another account, in another bank, in another country and then as added insurance, she had taken on an extra risk off her own bat. She had spent her incarceration productively and had chosen four diamonds: two blue and two pink ones; with all four looking just perfect to her. Two had been placed between the underneath of her middle toes of each foot and her ballet lessons of old had ensured that that was where they remained.

CHAPTER SIXTEEN

It took three minutes for four people to load seven sacks on to the boat, cast off and begin the five kilometres' journey heading in the direction of Lake Zurich's open water. A Bell 206 helicopter whirred overhead at their approach to the west side of the lake, where they were expecting to dock at a public port and pier named Wollishofen Port, which was immediately adjacent to Seestrasse. Due east was Turnhaus An der Egg, their destination, a 400-metre running track with an open flat grass surface at its centre. The boat docked and the waiting vehicle was loaded up for the short journey to the track, again in three minutes flat. It followed the circuitous route along Widmerstrasse and turned right on to Kilchbergstrasse.

As they arrived so too did the downdraught of the helicopter and with exact precision, it attempted to take off again three minutes later but this time with the inclusion of four additional passengers plus precious cargo. However, in order to prevent the manoeuvre twenty uniformed officers appeared as if from nowhere, and converged around the now stationary helicopter with a resultant Mexican standoff ensuing. Neither Eduardo, nor the rest of his team, nor the pilot wanted to lose the helicopter or their lives but most of all not their hard earned bullion.

The officers' threat moved closer as they closed in and encircled the helicopter, oblivious to their own safety. They lay prone on their stomachs evenly positioned, not dissimilar to a clock face, and with their weapons pointing directly in front. For the two teams of combatants time froze as six young, up and coming athletes, a mix of boys and girls and all dressed in white kit, ambled on to the track as they chatted amongst themselves and then began stretching and jogging in an anticlockwise direction. They continually glanced across at the tableau presented, of the helicopter being surrounded by uniformed men with guns, but just took it in their jogging stride as if it was an everyday occurrence transported from an action movie or lifelike computer game; their young ages not equating that such a situation should spell danger.

This distraction gave Eduardo an opportunity to break the deadlock. At first, he had thought that the armed men were polizei but then he rationalised that they would not have responded so quickly to the bank's alarm, even if one had been raised. Therefore, he opened the helicopter door, stood in its entrance and holding a makeshift white flag shouted, "Enough tears have already been shed over the last thirty years plus, without shedding tears of blood now. This is our people's time, the one cell that supported and believed in Franco di Larno, the people who mourned his death but continued to keep truthful to his just ways. These people have suffered for all this time whilst you and the likes of you have lived the high life under Alberto Pugliese's protection and generosity. If you retreat now without bloodshed I promise that this day will be remembered; you and yours will be rewarded accordingly for your common sense and who knows, it may be the beginning of the closure of the rift that has existed for some many years. And just so you know, we already hold three of your colleagues who were caught earlier today breaking into the Credit Suisse Bank. So, let these innocent Swiss children become the symbol of our truce today and our future tomorrow. Not to retreat now will end in carnage both here and in our homeland."

An eerie silence reined, except for the pitter-patter of six pairs of feet as they made their way around the synthetic track. The leader of the uniformed troops considered his options and, as if in answer to the rhetoric he had just heard he stood up and made a hand signal for his men to pull back and blend back into the bushes; leaving him as the only remaining combatant/ambassador.

"I hear your wise words and although the outcome is not what I was ordered to achieve, I can understand your concerns and bow to your wisdom. This fight has, indeed, been too long in its execution and it would not be right to continue it on foreign land, amongst innocent people, particularly children. I will tell my superiors that a meeting will take place, where the spoils will be divided in proportions, to be agreed." With that, he turned on his heels and he too was lost to the undergrowth.

*

The two English girls, who had been instrumental in setting this whole drama in train, now felt like spare parts. They were enjoying the rest and security of the safe house but had absolutely no idea what was happening on the outside. Their guesses and hopes ranged from very optimistic to very pessimistic and all within a very short time span. Their only saving grace was that Frau Gohl had a very outgoing personality, considering her circumstances and spoke very good English too; which proved of great benefit to them until she was whisked away at 4.30 in the morning. They had been told, on the one hand, to sit tight, and on the other, to be ready to leave for a journey back to the Airport. So, they spent the remainder of the night resting, a combination of dozing and drinking coffee, along with the sacerdote who carried out his dual role as bodyguard cum babysitter zealously. That was until Emma remembered that she had the envelope, the one Jessica had given her when they originally opened the safe deposit box, still less than twenty-four hours earlier.

Emma reached over for her bag and pulled out a slightly crumpled envelope, with the same message on the front that they had read earlier:

To our Darling Daughters with much Love.
We are so proud. Mum & Dad xxx'
And noticing for the first time, *'SWALK'* in fountain pen
across the sealed flap on the back; like some old fashioned text
speak. Both elements being written in their loving mother's
own hand, a hand that Jessica now easily recognised as being
very much her own hand too.

Emma's throwaway, "Bless," did nothing to lighten the
gloomy atmosphere that had suddenly descended on them, an
atmosphere of lost love and missing memories. Sitting crossed
legged on the bed she opened the envelope and allowed the
contents to spill into the gap she had made. They each looked
at the various items and chose one to pick up and examine.
Emma's was a key, exactly like the bank safe deposit box key
of earlier. Attached to it was a tag with a four-digit code and
Dad's scribble saying,

Darlings, this is your inheritance.
With all our Love, M & D xx.

"Not another safe box key? This one's numbered
'V3/298'. Hasn't one of these caused enough problems
already?" said Emma, thinking about Jeremy's murder and
now Frau Gohl's kidnapping and all that both entailed.

Jessica only half heard her comment as she studied the
Polaroid snap that she held showing their youthful parents;
looking even younger than Emma and she were now. Her
father's arm draped lovingly around her mother's shoulders
with her looking in to his eyes as his were directed at the
camera lens, and all set in a backdrop of glorious colour: with
the blooming flowers, sun kissed, white walled buildings,
azure sea and clear blue sky all fighting to grab her attention.
She nonchalantly flipped it over and read, 'Positano 19/08/77'.

Holding back the tears that pricked her eyes she let
Emma's babbling divert her attention. "Jess, it's another letter.
There's another letter! Shall I read it? Oh, I don't know if I
should, it might make us wish to be back there, for the life we

never had?"

"Give it here, M. I'm sure it will but we're already way past that point. It's not wrong to want your parents and to want them to love and nourish you, never think that. But our lives were not meant to work out that way." Her strength of character shook off the morose mood she had just experienced and led her to continue, "Shall we make another coffee to relax ourselves whilst we read it; maybe even get a box of tissues handy, what do you think?" Emma nodded and headed off towards the kitchen hearing Jessica say, "I can't believe all that has happened in less than twelve hours and we're still getting surprises. It's like all our birthdays and Christmases have been rolled up together."

"Well, I suppose it is," shouted Emma from the kitchen. "But I didn't realise how much hard work went into the gathering and unwrapping of the presents!"

So at six o'clock on the morning after Jessica and Emma had finally seen what their mother and father had to show for the lives they had led, the two girls sat down with their coffees hoping to gain more insight into where they actually fit into this crazy scheme of things. Jessica took on the mantle of reading aloud.

Dearest Darling Girls (or should that be grown women now?)

How clever you are to be reading this, our last communication. Promise. You've obviously worked out your mother's cryptic crossword and my clue for the code as here you are at the final conclusion.

We didn't feel it fair that we should leave a letter of this nature with our good friend Jeremy, in fact our only true friend in the whole of the UK, apart from family. He had kindly offered to safeguard the other one along with the clues etc, until such a time, as you were adult enough to deal with them. So, now you've obviously met him we hope you feel the same way about him too. In fact, say, 'Ciao, amico mio!' from me.'

As Jessica finished that sentence, both girls felt that a few seconds silence was required, not only for the sacrifice that Jeremy must have made on their behalf but also for the fact that he literally kept a lifelong promise to his best friends and did indeed carry it out.

She continued,

You do know that all the bullion you have found belongs to the people of Secondigliano and not you? I'm sure that if you are your mother's daughters, then it will not be a problem to relinquish it, all of it. However, as a sweetener and because I would have really loved to see your beautiful faces, not only at the age you are now but throughout all your lives up to this point; we have been saving for your futures too. That's what the other key and code are for, I'm sure you'll know what to do with them, now.

Because of our vanishing act and the fact that we never wanted you traced by the Alberto Pugliese Camorra faction, there are not many photographs in existence of either Mum or me. Not that your Mum took a bad one, if anything it was exactly the opposite, but I must admit even without our circumstances, you would not have found many of me. Anyway I digress; the photo was taken on a romantic day out, actually one of the few days when Laura managed to drag me away from family meetings and we did the sights. I remember it as glorious weather, as it always was, and no doubt still is; and she looked beautiful, radiant and happy as only an Italian could make her.

At this point Jessica looked up and said, "I told you that Mum and Dad will have done the same sightseeing we did. Just think, nearly thirty-seven years ago they could have been stood at the very spot where you were complaining of being hot!"

"Yeah, OK. But it was bloody hot in that country. Anyway, get on with it," replied Emma.

So Jessica continued again,

We had been very close since first meeting at Aberdeen University and our marriage and your subsequent births certainly made it the icing on the cake. Unfortunately, only Mama had the pleasure of meeting you as Uncle Pietro had already left for Sicily where he was hoping to make a name for himself with the Mafia; and those two are the only immediate family I have left. I hope you have a chance to meet up with them. I'll now hand over to Mum.

Hello my little precious Darlings - or as Dad says big grown up girls

How has life treated you? To read this you must be at least twenty-one as that is the age at which Jeremy can hand over the package. Sorry to be so clandestine but things are not good with the Camorra and since Franco's death we have had to quickly rethink a few of our plans. We hope you were not too confused with our deaths and that you don't hold it against us as we did it for all the right reasons, with the protection of you two our main priority, above all else. And, with me writing this, you must never believe that any of the happenings were your faults; how could it be as you were barely three years old. As the plan began to unfold I became concerned for my sister Cathy too, who so kindly offered to take you on Emma, and raise you as her own. I hope it worked out, although I knew at the time that our request posed serious risks with her job as a midwife; nobody in their right mind would be constantly on the look out for two recently deceased girls of around three years of age. And her ability to supply them at such short notice, that was truly amazing. So please look on her kindly when you have made good use of the key and code.

Emma burst in with, "So, that's what happened. Do you know in the twenty years I knew her, she never once mentioned it. Never moaned about what might have been and never really told me anything about Mum and Dad at all. But that must be the reason she went downhill, she must have got found out and sacked, possibly even prosecuted. I'll have to go back on that ... what do you call it? That microbe fish thingy."

"Microfiche?"

"Yes, that's it 'microbe fish'. I'll see if I can find anything about it in the papers."

"OK, do that. Now, back to the letter."

And Jessica, I hope Gran, Gramps and you had a happy life? It was a toss up who went where, but in my heart I felt you would be more suited to Gran, what with your temperament and Emma seemed to have an affinity with my sister, Cathy. Hopefully both your grandparents stayed healthy or are still healthy, should I say? Blow them a kiss from me.

What are you both doing for your livings? Do we have a solicitor, accountant, teacher or hairdresser in the family?

"I know she's my Mum and I know she's dead too but why would she think I'd be a hairdresser?" complained Emma.

"What's up with hairdressers? It's a far more worthwhile career than the one you chose and, anyway how do you know she wasn't referring to me?" replied Jessica defensively.

"Because of Jessica's temperament. It's in the letter. You're not going to be a hairdresser with that 'temperament', now are you?"

"OK, moving on."

Or are you both now mothers yourselves? I hope all these questions aren't causing friction between you, as it's the last thing I'd have wanted, especially if you are good friends as well as twin sisters? But the reason we had to split you up was to keep you safe from prying eyes and to ensure that neither you nor the bullion and whatever other treasure (can't remember it all), fell into the wrong hands.

As you have now found it I pray to God that it is put to beneficial use without bloodshed, and I hope that the good people of Secondigliano, that Luigi knew and loved and that I came to love, have not had to wait too long for its arrival. I would give anything to see their faces when it is handed back to them. But don't you two be thinking that you are missing out; we have been well rewarded over the years for our husbandry of the Camorra cell's monies and as an accountant I'm convinced that all the right decisions were made to at least keep ahead of inflation.

I have to leave you now as your father is setting off for Italy in the morning and then making, what we think will be the last trip over to Switzerland. Alberto Pugliese, not the sort of man you would want to meet, is the other faction's leader. He has instigated and carried out the murder of Dad's dear friend, Franco di Larno and we always felt that this would be the tipping point and our turns would not be far behind. But they'll either have to catch us first or our own plan will beat them to it.

And so, just as part of the secret of the cell's treasure died with our leader, so the other part dies with us; until you clever girls reawaken the dream and bring alive the hopes and aspirations of the downtrodden people of Secondigliano; to enjoy a new life in goodness knows what kind of environment.

Truly all our love goes out to you and we wish it could have been any other way than this. But by you

*reading this letter it vindicates us and means that
many others and their future generations can live on.
Love, Love, Love xxx
Mum and Dad*

Jessica was stunned into silence and Emma was just
stunned. Tears were streaming down their cheeks as they
realised the magnitude of what Jessica had just read and the
sacrifice that had been made, in the main, for all of the people
that they would never personally know. They reached for more
tissues and the untouched cold mugs of coffee; even with
Emma's craving for all things addictive, she had not felt the
call of the caffeine. Never remembering their parents, this
communication was the closest that they would ever come to
connecting with them and it made them both feel slightly
uneasy at what their perceptions of Auntie Cathy or Grannie
had been, as second-best carers.

But that was all in the past, everyone has decisions to
make on their paths through life and now it was the turn of the
two girls to look forward. For whatever reason they had been
given a second chance, after the murdering spree of the
Scottish Borders, and they were each desperate to grab it with
both hands. Emma turned the safe deposit box key over and
over in her hands saying, "This key could lead us to a fortune
but I'd gladly give it all up just to be three years old again and
living a normal life with normal parents."

"Me too, M. But it's not going to happen. Everybody's
'made their beds and laid in them'; what's done is done. We
can either, give up now and spend the rest of our days pining
over what's gone before or we can build a future. Perhaps
even have kids to carry on where we leave off."

"Kids, me! What do I know about kids? All I know is how
to prevent them."

"No you don't, silly. You'd make a great mother. You're
far more caring than I am and you're generous too, of both
your time and love. Those are the most important qualities.
Nobody has any idea how it works until a child arrives. Unless

you're upper class that is, and then you get all the nannies and helpers to bring the child up, in fact you'll be able to have lots of children, what with all this money. That reminds me, what time is it? We'd better get the sacerdote to make some arrangements, so we can be waiting at the bank door at 9.00am; does it open then?"

"Yes, we'll start with the money and then go from there; at least it will give us a head's start with our future prospects."

"Padre? Why can you never find a priest when you need one?" questioned Jessica.

CHAPTER SEVENTEEN

"Well, all I can really say is, 'That the wheels are slowly turning but the cogs are not quite engaging'. He's well enough in himself and certain cognitive responses are fine but his long- and short-term memory loss is, well, something of a mystery. The blow to the head most probably led to mild concussion, causing a temporary disturbance in brain function but it is his temporal lobes, which govern his memory and hearing that I fear may be damaged. Either that, or he has some inbuilt mechanism which is making him consciously suppress his memory; but then you're talking psychology." So deliberated the neurologist and it had been over a week ago that the comments had been made. Since that time Terence Barnham had been studied as he underwent occupational therapy tests; simple everyday tasks that you and I would pass easily but that the DI needed full concentration, in order to achieve anything like full marks. Simple processes that involved more than three actions posed the most degree of difficulty, as his brain could not retain the steps required or the order in which to undertake them. But that was starting from nothing, and now he was more familiar and confident about the exercises his execution time had reduced dramatically. However, he was still struggling to recall events of the past and DC Blister's daily visit was proving a chore.

"Hello, Sir. How are you today? I just want to ask you a few questions about events that occurred in your recent past, do you feel up to it?" Barnham did feel that he was getting better as the DC used the same terminology everyday, and at least he was beginning to remember that, by heart.

"You go for it, son. If it's in there, I'm sure it will come out at some point. Only problem is, it feels like someone's erased it all by sending it to the rubbish bin." The DC smiled, but thought that a breakthrough had been made of sorts, as the DI's association between erasing and rubbish was possibly a new computer analogy link. However, that was the only result of the day and the cogs did indeed remain disengaged.

*

The bank didn't in fact open until 9.30am, which was beneficial to the girls as it gave Pietro, who had now relieved the sacerdote of his babysitting responsibilities, additional time to relay all the excitement of the night before, but first he introduced his companion, Pernille; a tall slim youngish woman with cropped blond hair. Emma and Jessica welcomed her and showed their surprise when they were informed that she was one of Alberto Pugliese's daughters, but that she had never had an affinity to his faction, nor to his philosophy, nor to his family, nor to him being her father, for that matter. Both girls had some empathy with Pernille, as they too had felt alienated to a degree in their early formative years. On arrival, the sacerdote had embraced her as he had done since she was a young girl.

Pietro now elucidated on the activity of the previous night and both girls expressed concern; then relief and then concern again as they heard about all the dealing and double-dealing that had transpired. And Pietro admitted that the mission could still have been in jeopardy until the bullion had been loaded on to their helicopter and safely in the air.

"Well, we better hold on to this then. It looks like there may be a need for our little fortune after all," jested Emma, waving the tagged key in the air.

Pietro and Pernille looked on confusedly, so Jessica took the opportunity of updating them both as to what had been found in the envelope, then turned to Emma and jokingly replied, "Come on then. We better get it over with, there will be no shutting you up until you've opened that box. Anybody would expect you to be used to it by now."

The two girls were escorted to the bank by their uncle and his new companion and upon arrival, for whatever reason, were not allowed in until 10.00am. Pietro and Pernille remained in the lobby watching the entrance door as a young man came and ushered the two sisters to the lift, which again descended the three floors into the bowels of the bank. Here, he asked to see the key and began to say which direction they should take, but familiarity taking over anyway the girls immediately set off for vault three and waited patiently whilst he opened the barred gate. Again, they set off in the same direction as previous and just as they were about to open their safe deposit box a conspiratorial sounding voice said, "Fräulein, I am glad to have caught up with you," this from a still rather unkempt Herr Gohl. "I just want to thank you for your hospitality towards my wife in the early hours of this morning, especially under the circumstances." The last word said somewhat tongue in cheek. "And as agreed with your fellow associates, I am returning all the keys and codes which were found on my former member of staff and these particular ones, I do believe, will open the remaining box, which had not been completely emptied last time; eh, before the vault …"

"No need to elaborate, our Uncle Pietro has told us of the circumstances," this time Jessica exaggerated the last word, just for fun. He then departed and left them to the task in hand. Neither had prepared for it but fortunately Pietro knowing that there was still one box to empty which belonged to the people of Secondigliano, had. He had the foresight to bring along and pass over a couple of sturdy bags, so that they didn't end up leaving the bank with gold, bank notes and other priceless treasures bulging out of their pockets. First off, they opened the box with the key and code they had just been given by the deputy CEO and emptied it of all the gold plated candlesticks, chalices, crucifixes and other religious artefacts. These alone took up the whole of the two bags, so the girls approached their own box with trepidation, knowing that their two handbags were the only remaining carrying devices

They found the box; 298 and followed the previous box opening procedure; once released from its locking mechanism they pulled it towards them, still marvelling at the precision of the craftsmanship and the smoothness of the glide and the snugness of the fit as it exited its housing. But when they lifted the lid, well that was a totally different marvel, altogether. Nestling in the cramped, compact space were: ten gold ingots; three rolls of gold one ounce krugerrands; a large quantity of American dollars, in one hundred dollar bills; and two black bags, which they presumed contained diamonds and other exotic gemstones. Both were flabbergasted at the sight and agreed to only take a quantity of the American dollars at this time. "We can always have another trip back when things have quietened down," surmised Jessica.

"Yes, good idea. And thank goodness, we have Pietro and Pernille to protect us," replied Emma as she squeezed bundles of notes in to the pockets of her already tight jacket. Once, back in the lobby the four met up and the girls handed over the two bags that had been filled with the religious artefacts. Then all four were chauffeur driven back to the safe house to collect the sacerdote, their bags and repack their new currency. Afterwards, the driver took Seebahnstrasse and proceeded north-west, picking up the E60 to Basel, a journey of no more that 50 miles, with their destination being EuroAirport. During the journey a call was received from *SpiyWeB* retrievers stating that the helicopter had already adhered to its flight schedule and that parties should rendezvous at the south-west aspect of the airport. The beauty of the airport being that it was operated by three countries: France, Germany and Switzerland; and even though the airport itself was on French soil, its coup de grâce was that there were no customs or other border restrictions, in operation.

Both forms of transport rendezvoused on time and in the correct location; the helicopter having touched down some hours before. The pilot of the Citation XL, welcomed both, the prospective passengers and their valuable luggage on board the private jet and encouraged them to relax and refresh themselves as he watched the clock tick down to their allotted take-off time. It arrived and they departed, immediately leaving French air space, to head south-east and make their way home to Naples, Italy enjoying blue sky all the way; whilst the helicopter itself, had one more pick up and drop off in the Mediterranean, literally. A drop, anticipated as finite but which Babyface and the underlying currents had other ideas about.

Their welcome home to Naples International proved a bit of a damp squib as they were greeted by a freak thunderstorm, but that in no way made them downhearted. And as they were driven the remaining short journey northwards in to the underbelly of what Naples' surrounding districts had become, no one could help but feel exhilarated that they had pulled off the 'sting' of a lifetime. They were coming home the heroes and the saviours of what would very likely have disintegrated into a more neglected and downtrodden neighbourhood than it already was at present.

Arriving in Secondigliano was a cavalcade of three vehicles with the main players being contained in the middle and flanked by a front and rear guard of gun-toting Mafia and Camorra clansmen respectively. The original team who had now become friends was welcomed with open arms into, Francescane Missionarie Del Cuore Immacolato Di Maria, the church where it had all begun. The Sacerdote, Cristiano Abatangelo, led the whole of Franco di Larno's supporters in a prayer of thanks for both their safe return, and that of the neighbourhood's future fortunes. And both Jessica and Emma were called up to the altar steps to be gazed upon as the people's saviours, in everything but spirit. Emma now fidgeted with her own tight fitting clothes, as both old and young recalled her mother, Laura, and compared how alike the two girls were to her. Jessica stood there unbelieving; unbelieving that at last it was over, whilst at the same time, having her darker Mediterranean looks and skin colouring discussed, picked over and compared to her father, the great Luigi. His claim to fame now being that, through their children, both Laura and he, had fulfilled their promise of over thirty years ago. Having delivered back to the villagers what belonged there and was rightfully theirs before Alberto Pugliese and his thugs had brutally intervened. But today was a day to celebrate, a day to forget the past if just for one day.

Pietro looked across at these two English girls and catching their eye, he beckoned them to follow, whilst he led Pernille by the hand. Soon, a small train of a half dozen or so people were weaving through the crowded church to the side door. Once there, the same half dozen or so made their way to the little bar that the girls had first visited, not so long ago. And there they met Mama, sat serenely at an empty table; in fact the whole place was empty, as all its prospective customers had not yet left the church. Mama welcomed the girls with, "How clever you both are. Do you realise what you have done? Not only for the village but also for the whole God forsaken community, whose people had started with nothing until Franco fought for their rights? And even when he died with his promises unfulfilled those same people still had nothing but managed to retain their dignity, integrity and decency and now here you are, to free us all." Both girls kissed their Mama and hugged her, as she said, "Not too tight. It makes me breathless; that's why I can't stand the large crowds."

"I know what you mean, Mama. I'm finding it just the same," replied Emma trying to loosen clothing that had nowhere to go.

"OK, everybody. Please be seated. I think we all deserve a glass of wine by way of celebration." Seven glasses were filled and seven toasts were raised. "To the people of Secondigliano. Salute." Six 'Salutes' rang out in reply. "Now, you have all played important parts in our mission and helped in bringing it to a successful and thankfully, almost bloodless conclusion. However, we have decisions to make and just as both Franco and Luigi would have wanted, we have to do it democratically with those decisions ideally being unanimous." Sitting around the table were: Emma, Jessica, Pietro, Pernille, Eduardo, the sacerdote and of course, Mama; and all were looking at Pietro to continue, all except Eduardo. As Eduardo was the next male in blood related terms to Franco, their former leader, Pietro and he had already agreed that he would chair the meeting.

"Thank you Pietro. I speak here on behalf of our former leader, Franco, my uncle. I also acknowledge the presence of Pernille, who as one of Alberto's daughters; she must find herself in a very difficult position but we all respect and support her stance in our argument, take strength from it and welcome her to this table. And to the two lovely sisters, without whom, none of this dream would ever have reached reality, let alone fruition. Thank you for truly being your parents' daughters. Salute!"

The word rang out around the table as each participant drank from their glass and immediately started chattering. Eduardo allowed a few moments for the celebrating, brought on by his eulogising to abate and then continued, "As Pietro has mentioned, decisions need to be made and in the main these are to do with money; always a difficult subject but in this case it should be a very happy one too. As Pietro and I wear two hats, the larger one being owned by the Mafia, we already know that for their input in this project they expect their remuneration to be 10% plus expenses. The expenses will be to cover: additional manpower support; and the hire of cars, helicopter, boat and airplane plus fuel for those items. A figure for this will be calculated and given within the next 24 hours, which will then ensure that their total cost is clearly transparent. Next, if it is not too embarrassing for these two ladies, we need to offer our thanks by discussing their value in our struggle; and please remember, without them, we would not now be sat around this table."

Jessica interrupted with, "Thank you Eduardo. But we do not wish for you to spend time, considering our contribution. We came to Italy, frightened, lonely and confused but we leave with a new family and a love for the area that we know made our parents so happy. With foresight, they had already made financial provision for us, so we accept your thanks with gratitude and that is payment enough. Our gift to you and your people is the same as Dad and Mum wanted for you all those years ago: one of health, wealth, prosperity and happiness for today and the future."

"Well thank you both for your generosity, it will certainly contribute in ensuring the financial security of our community. That moves us on to the problem of what to do about Alberto's supporters. I know the majority of them have not been sympathetic of our people's woes, but if I am to take control of this cell and reunite both factions into one, then the offering of an olive branch may be the only solution. In fact, when we had our Mexican standoff at the running track in Switzerland I did intimate that there was a deal to be had if bloodshed could be avoided. So I throw it open to the rest of you to make suggestions as to how we can secure a truce and maintain a peace, one that will last at least as long as our ignominious split and with a minimum amount of fuss, too. I could make our life easier by inviting the Sicilian Mafia to deal with the negotiations, but that would only put them and the Napoli Camorra at loggerheads, so ensuring our peace would be short lived."

At this natural break in the rhetoric, the sacerdote said, "I think now is an opportune moment to refill our glasses, perhaps the wine will enable us to think more clearly."

"More like cloud your judgment, Cristiano. But I am not going to refuse the offer," replied Mama holding her glass out expectantly. As glasses were filled, the adverse could be said for the lack of forthcoming ideas; over thirty years of anger was stored up in several people's minds and it was doing its best to confuse and cloud the issue. Exasperation and raised voices continued to be the hallmark of the meeting's progression with no forward progress being made at all.

That is, until Emma slammed her hands down on the table as she rose from her seat, "Right, now, I've got your attention. I don't do speeches, in fact I'm not one for talking much at all, but can I just remind you that this is meant to be the best day of your lives, in how many years? You can already hear the jubilation out in the streets and yet here we are cooped up arguing about the other side and wrangling over money; money that you've had for less than 24 hours, for heaven's sake. Sorry, Padre. Eduardo's already said that there has to be some sort of deal or the feuding will never end. Alberto what's his name – you know, Pernille's dad, well his people have had all the good times so far but if you want to live in harmony and with some kind of equanimity then you do have to compromise. You might not like it now but you will if it brings you peace and friendship with neighbours who either you have shunned or have shunned you; or do you all want to up sticks and build new homes elsewhere? No, I thought not. So this is what you do. Whatever is left after the Mafia has taken their slice; the remainder is counted up and 25% is given graciously to the other side and you and your people keep 75%."

Here there were murmurs but Emma ignored them, "But this offer is only on the understanding that you hold the majority in the village council and that everybody begins to pay a fixed amount into a fund for tidying up all of the neighbourhood and it isn't just left to those who have newly acquired wealth and may feel committed to take it on as their responsibility. And finally, there is no longer to be two factions, you are one Camorra clan and can only have one leader; and my nomination would be Eduardo. Sorry Uncle," she said sheepishly looking at Pietro. Silence fell, except for the sacerdote; he leapt up and kissed Emma on the lips. Emma gasped and laughed at the same time; her proximity to men had never been a problem, whether they were men of the cloth or not.

"Pardon me, Emma. It was a rush of blood to the head. It's my turn to say sorry now. But I think your little speech is wonderful. If only the Pope would allow female clergy …"

Here the padre trailed off and Emma picked up, "Yes, if only. In another life, perhaps! That would really spice things up."

Eduardo asked, "Joking apart. Does Emma's proposal meet with all our approvals?" Everyone raised their hands, including Emma. "OK. Unanimous: just as Franco would have wanted. Quickly, we need pen and paper so we don't forget the points she made. In the meantime, Emma, 'Salute'." And all raised their glasses, as did Emma.

Once notes had been taken with Pietro and Eduardo quietly conferring, and then waiting whilst Emma's further plaudits had died down, the two brought the meeting to a close but not before one further position had been filled. Pietro called everyone to order with, "Attention, please. This is going to be the final word, unless anybody else wishes to speak, that is. Eduardo, having accepted the new post as leader of the clan wishes to appoint his second in command and he wants the honour to be given to Pernille. May she be forever the glue that binds the two factions together? What say you, Pernille?"

Pernille sat there as colour charged across her face, took a deep breath and said, "I would be delighted to help in any way I can to bring back the prosperity and happiness, stolen from these good people by my father. These people have made a life of sorts over the years but now with the help of this new found wealth we can all really live." As everybody rose and offered up another, 'Salute', Emma quietly remarked to Jessica that she was not feeling too good and wanted to go lie down. So, they both excused themselves just as the celebrations were getting into full swing. Mama fussed over Emma and invited them both back to her humble home, being as her partying was over too.

There, the girls remained for another seven days, until the heat got too unbearable for them and their other home and cooler climate began to beckon.

CHAPTER EIGHTEEN

"It was the bald head that did it. And from that moment, I just had to look at every man with a bald head. It's not that I have an aversion to hair: whether on top or facial; it became more than that, more like a crusade, there was just one man on mainland Europe who I had to find. And, here he is; looking slightly worse for wear with a bullet through his skull. Now if that isn't telling us something? And Babyface Nelson, what sort of name's that?" So extolled DI Jenny Johnson, to no one in particular but when she realised it was her superior who stood patiently waiting for her to finish, she wrapped it up instantly. "Sorry Sir. Got carried away."

"Quite all right, Johnson. It isn't everyday that a DI's wish comes true. And good work, tracking him down in the first place. All Interpol did was supply the final mug shot and name, once they'd fished him out of the Med. His name, by the way, was the pseudonym for a gangster in the US in the 1930's, just to add it to the evidence if you've not already done so. You've killed two birds with one stone: solved our DS Stanning murder and the one in Aberdeen too."

"Yes, thank you, Sir. I'm thinking of sending the mug shot along to Edinburgh; they have a couple of links between the solicitor who was murdered in Aberdeen, a Mr Jeremy Longthorne, and at least one if not two girls that his mobile records show he contacted, just before he ended up being killed."

"Do you need me to put you in touch with a name up there?

"No, Sir. I already have a contact: DC Blister. A young lad, bit like a bull in a china shop but he knows what he's after and keeps worrying it until it shows itself."

"Mm. I think the force could do with a few more bulls in china shops, don't you?"

"Well. Being biased, I'd actually say cows, Sir."

"Touché. Keep up the good work Johnson."

And with that her audience was gone and the DI heaved a sigh of relief and gave her mouth a good telling off for running away with itself. She picked up the phone and dialed DC Blister in Edinburgh.

"Good Morning, DC Blister. This is DI Johnson at New Scotland Yard. I've got some good news."

"Good Morning, Sir, I mean Ma'am. What good news would that be?"

'Good for you Blister, straight to the point,' thought the DI. "We've tracked down the murderer of Jeremy Longthorne, the solicitor in Aberdeen. Turns out he was a member of the Camorra in Naples and both the solicitor, and DS Stanning's murder in London somehow have a direct link back to his clan. He was fished out of the Med, just south of Genova. Have you got any further with the girl you mentioned, or was it two girls?"

"No and yes. No further and yes it still is two girls. They have different names but I think that they are sisters and goodness knows where they are, at the moment. After researching the various methods of leaving the UK I've got concrete proof that they left on the Eurostar; over a couple of weeks ago but nothing's been seen or heard of them since."

"That's another reason for my call. I'm of the opinion that they are sisters too, possibly even twins. Perhaps they are just on holiday?"

"Somehow, I don't think they are the type to take normal holidays, although the boss of one of the girls, a Tess Danvers did say she had given Jessica Lambert, that's one of the girl's names, compassionate leave. I've got the UK Border Agency keeping a check for any return."

"Right, well I'll leave it with you. I'm going to speak to Aberdeen now and tell them the good news."

DC Blister replayed the conversation in his head but still could not take any advantage from it. Well, maybe just one; he thought that on his next visit to DI Barnham, he would mention again, a few names from the DI's past and see what response or reaction they might bring now.

*

The girls spent another week in Naples, primarily doing the sightseeing that had been cut short at the beginning of their visit; but they also managed to spend a lot of time with Mama and Uncle Pietro, who had been given extended leave from his duties in Sicily. It had been agreed that Eduardo would not be returning and the Mafia were happy with that, considering the amount they had just earned; and not to mention the fact that they now had a firm supporter ensconced in the Camorra heartland. And if the twins had not had enough excitement and surprises to last a lifetime let alone several weeks, there was one last one just arriving by taxi. An attractive middle-aged woman, looking decidedly cool in her Theyskens' Theory white blouse, Etoile by Isabel Marant grey slacks and Michael Kors boots, alighted. She immediately approached Mama and hugged her until she squeaked. "Gabriella, do you want to make this my last day on earth?" Mama gasped breathlessly. "How lovely it is to see you, but is it purely coincidence that you are here or had you been invited to the festivities?"

"What do you think, Mama? Nothing happens here without reaching the outside world. Pietro let me know that we had come into some good fortune due to unexpected visitors and I couldn't miss the opportunity of meeting up with them, so I jumped on the first available flight from Dulles International Airport. But, how rude, we're forgetting your guests."

At this point Mama introduced Emma and Jessica to Gabriella, one of her nieces and a cousin of their father; she had only been a young schoolgirl, during the time of their mother's courting days. She too had had ambitions and was now working in a senior managerial capacity at the Smithsonian in Washington DC. Gabriella warmly took both girls' hands and retold of the occasion she had met Laura and of their day of sightseeing. She concluded with, "And it was because of Laura that I raised my own aspirations and through hard work, diligence and some good fortune, I have reached that goal and am now able to live the dream. So, you should be extra proud of all that your parents have achieved here, not only by themselves but through you too, and if you are ever in the US, please look me up and visit."

But as usual with all holidays, they fly by after the initial couple of days and so the twins were preparing to leave their newfound friends and family in totally different circumstances than they had found them. Everyone filled the village square to cheer them off as they stepped into the limousine, which had been ordered on the new Mayor of Secondigliano's authority. Both girls had been hugged and kissed innumerable times as only Italians can do and finally had sunk back into the luxurious leather seats with a sigh of exhaustion and a regret at leaving. Out of the window, Jessica shouted, "Thank you all so much for your love and hospitality."

Emma followed it up with; "We'll never forget you and we'll be back before you know it, see if we aren't."

With the TV cameras rolling, Pernille came up to the window, holding a copy of the Il Mattino, Naples' local paper. The two girls looked on in shock, as the front page featured a huge photograph of them both being celebrated by the people of Secondigliano, on their return the previous week. She said, "Now the whole community is being recorded for posterity, thanks to you. We will never forget what you have done and we will always be here to repay your kindness, should you ever have need of it." And with one final clumsy hug through the window for both of them, the car ignition silently turned the engine as their venture loudly ended; and they were heading for the airport, in style. Next stop, Edinburgh.

The girls sat back exhausted, as the airplane went to full thrust for the take off: exhausted from all the celebrating and 'salute'ing' over the previous hectic week. The full-bodied red Taurasi and dry white Fiano di Avellino, both local wines to the area and now becoming famous worldwide, were consumed in equally large volume. Jessica found a rest from the partying most welcome, as the past seven days had played havoc with her fitness regime, even taking into consideration the time off for sightseeing; but Emma was juxtaposed in her view as the merry making had dulled her urgent need to even think about drugs of any description, legal or otherwise, let alone consider taking them. Their flight passed by in the blink of an eye and Jessica awoke with a shock as the aircraft hit slight turbulence on its decent into Edinburgh Airport. Emma meanwhile continued with her REM sleep, even when Jessica began nudging her with embarrassment at the sound of her snoring and the sight of her gaping mouth.

The next person to study Emma's features was at passport control, where they were both being scrutinised by one of the officers as he compared their faces to their photographs. Jessica had already been ushered through the security scanner, when several men approached her, a uniformed policeman amongst them.

"Jessica Lambert?" asked one of the several. Her nod and confused face led him to continue, "My name is DC Blister. Could you come with me? I'd like to ask you a few questions."

Jessica, still disoriented, caught a glimpse at the man behind the questioner and thought she recognised him, not the one in uniform, the other one. Although, now he looked a shadow of his former self, thinner and even somewhat shorter in stature. 'Surely that's not DI Barnham?' she thought, bemusedly.

Emma confirmed Jessica's disbelief by unselfconsciously rushing through the electronic scanner, up to the man in question, not the questioner, and threw her arms around his neck. Then she proceeded to shower him with kisses, "Terry. You're alive? Am I glad to see you? Have you come to welcome me home?" she asked, totally misreading the situation.

Thank you for taking the time to read book two in 'The Gemini Borders Trilogy'.
I hope you enjoyed the chase. If yes, would you please be kind enough to visit Amazon and leave a review.
Book three, as yet unwritten and untitled, will be available at some point in 2015.

Regards

Toni Parks